The Very Best of
Fantasy & Science Fiction

VOLUME 2

"I'm so envious of those of you who might be reading some of these for the first time. I was repeatedly blown away by the impact such short pieces...still had on me. Half an hour's reading, and I spent the next day or so catching myself staring off into space muttering, 'Oh wow.'"
—*io9.com*

"...this is a rare treasure that compiles some of the best genre stories over the past six decades, and through it, we witness the field's history and growth."
—*Bibliophile Stalker*

"...I dropped everything to read it."
—*Black Gate*

"I cannot picture any fan of either fantasy or science fiction not liking this book. Perhaps the only reason to stay away is if you have all the stories in it already. But if, like me, several of them are missing from your collection, what are you waiting for? Buy it."
—*Visions of Paradise*

"...the contents are sheer pleasure, full of classics that feel as comfortable as an old sweater."
—*Bookgasm*

"...this is a high-quality anthology showcasing the diversity of *Fantasy & Science Fiction*'s stories over the past six decades. It shows that short genre fiction has always had the power to surprise and excite, and it proves that this remains just as true today as it has ever been."
—*SF Crowsnest*

"Every story is a priceless gem showcasing its author's superlative craftsmanship and ability to engage the emotions while captivating the imagination."
—*Booklist*

"There's something for everyone in this amazing anthology, and it will certainly provide hours of entertainment for anyone who reads it."
—*San Francisco Book Review*

The Best from Fantasy & Science Fiction: 20th Series (1973)
The Best from Fantasy & Science Fiction: 22nd Series (1977)
The Best from Fantasy & Science Fiction: 23rd Series (1980)
The Best from Fantasy & Science Fiction: A 30 Year Retrospective (1980)
The Best from Fantasy & Science Fiction: 24th Series (1982)
The Best Fantasy Stories from The Magazine of Fantasy & Science Fiction (1986)
The Best from Fantasy & Science Fiction: A 40th Anniversary Anthology (1989)
Oi, Robot: Competitions and Cartoons from The Magazine of Fantasy & Science Fiction (1995)

Edited by Edward L. Ferman and Robert P. Mills
Twenty Years of The Magazine of Fantasy & Science Fiction (1970)

Edited by Annette Peltz McComas
The Eureka Years: Boucher and McComas's Magazine of Fantasy & Science Fiction 1949–1954 (1982)

Edited by Edward L. Ferman and Anne Devereaux Jordan
The Best Horror Stories from The Magazine of Fantasy & Science Fiction (1988)

Edited by Edward L. Ferman and Kristine Kathryn Rusch
The Best from Fantasy & Science Fiction: A 45th Anniversary Anthology (1994)

Edited by Edward L. Ferman and Gordon Van Gelder
The Best from Fantasy & Science Fiction: The 50th Anniversary Anthology (1999)

Edited by Gordon Van Gelder
One Lamp: Alternate History Stories from Fantasy & Science Fiction (2003)
In Lands That Never Were: Swords & Sorcery Stories from Fantasy & Science Fiction (2004)
Fourth Planet from the Sun: Tales of Mars from Fantasy & Science Fiction (2005)
The Very Best of Fantasy & Science Fiction: Sixtieth Anniversary Anthology (2009)

THE VERY BEST OF
FANTASY & SCIENCE FICTION

VOLUME 2

Edited by Gordon Van Gelder

TACHYON

Tachyon Publications
1459 18th Street #139
San Francisco, CA 94107
www.tachyonpublications.com
tachyon@tachyonpublications.com

Series Editor: Jacob Weisman
Project Editor: Jill Roberts

ISBN 13: 978-1-61696-163-3

Printed in the United States by Worzalla
First Edition: 2014
9 8 7 6 5 4 3 2 1

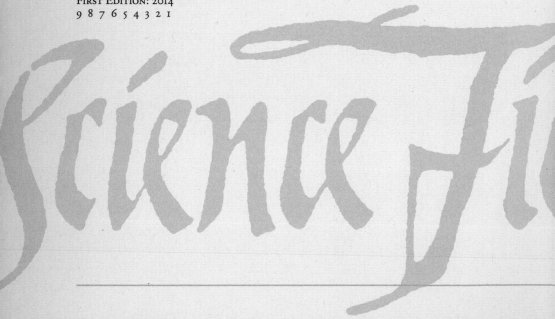

For Jacob, Rina, and Jill

ACKNOWLEDGMENT IS MADE FOR PERMISSION
TO PRINT THE FOLLOWING MATERIAL:

"The Third Level" by Jack Finney. Copyright
© 1950 by the Crowell Collier Publishing
Company, 1957, renewed 1985 by Jack Finney.
Reprinted by permission of Don Congdon
Associates, Inc.

"The Cosmic Expense Account" by C. M.
Kornbluth. Copyright © 1956 by C. M.
Kornbluth. First published in *The Magazine
of Fantasy & Science Fiction,* January 1956.
Reprinted by permission of the author's
agents, Curtis Brown Ltd.

"The Country of the Kind" by Damon
Knight. Copyright © 1956 by Damon
Knight. First published in *The Magazine of
Fantasy & Science Fiction,* February 1956.
Reprinted by permission of the author's
estate.

"The Anything Box" by Zenna Henderson.
Copyright © 1956 by Zenna Henderson.
First published in *The Magazine of Fantasy &
Science Fiction,* October. 1956. Reprinted by
permission of the author's agents, Virginia
Kidd Literary Agency.

"The Prize of Peril" by Robert Sheckley.
Copyright © 1958 by Robert Sheckley.
First published in *The Magazine of Fantasy
& Science Fiction,* May 1958. Reprinted by
permission of the author's agents, the Donald
Maass Literary Agency.

"'—All You Zombies—'" by Robert A.
Heinlein. Copyright © 1959 by Robert A.
Heinlein. First published in *The Magazine
of Fantasy & Science Fiction,* March 1959.
Reprinted by permission of the author's
agents, the Spectrum Literary Agency.

"A Kind of Artistry" by Brian W. Aldiss.
Copyright © 1962 by Mercury Press, renewed
1990. First published in *The Magazine of
Fantasy & Science Fiction,* October 1962.
Reprinted by permission of the author and
his agent, Robin Straus Agency, Inc.

"Green Magic" by Jack Vance. Copyright
© 1963 by Jack Vance. First published in
The Magazine of Fantasy & Science Fiction,
June 1963. Copyright renewed 2000 by
Jack Vance.Reprinted by permission of the
author's agents, the Lotts Agency.

THE MAGAZINE OF
Fantasy AND
Science Fiction

CONT

Foreword

Gordon Van Gelder

My nickname for this book is *"F&SF's* Greatest Hits, Volume 2," which has prompted several of the contributors to suggest getting Ed Ferman, Kris Rusch, and me to put on sweaters, sit by a fireplace, and read poorly scripted infomercial copy about how we love curling up with old favorites. Then the book's table of contents scrolls up the screen over moody clips of writers reading their own work while David Bowie's "Golden Years" plays. (Is there a rendition of that song on the theremin?)

But let us banish all thoughts of infomercials to the nether plane where they belong. What we have here is proof that *The Very Best of F&SF*, the anthology I assembled five years ago, barely lives up to its title. When you've got more than six decades' worth of material from which to choose, you're never going to fit all the finest works in one volume. (Or two, for that matter.)

But here in the second volume, I've tried to assemble a good representation of the magazine's whole history, from the "Eureka Years" when Tony, Mick, Phyllis, and Annette established the magazine's standards, on through the second decade of the twenty-first century, when I've done my best to maintain them.

The last five years have not been an era of big changes. We've switched from a monthly publishing schedule to bi-monthly and electronic publishing is a bigger part of our endeavor, but by and large, *F&SF* continues to do what it has done since 1949: publish the best works of speculative fiction that it can. And every once in a while, we collect the best of the best into a book.

Here's hoping you enjoy the nightmares, speculations, and flights of fancy assembled here.

Introduction

MICHAEL DIRDA

(THIS INTRODUCTION CONTAINS NO SPOILERS.)

NOT LONG AGO, I met a young man at a literary festival who told me he was an ardent science fiction fan. He even showed me the words "Use the Force" tattooed on his upper arm. Naturally, he'd read Kurt Vonnegut and Phil Dick and Neil Gaiman. I'm sure he must have seen *The Avengers* and *Iron Man*, watched *A Game of Thrones* and the latest *Star Trek* movie.

As we chatted, he casually asked me about my favorite science fiction novels. I reeled off a few titles, almost at random: *The Time Machine, Last and First Men, The Stars My Destination, More Than Human, Double Star, Pavane, The Left Hand of Darkness*...I paused. He was shaking his head, looking distraught. He hadn't read a single one.

Sigh.

So I told him the plot of *The Stars My Destination* and watched as he grew more and more excited. "I've got to read that. It sounds really amazing." I said it was all that and more. He made me repeat my little list of novels and carefully wrote them down on a bar napkin. "I'm going to look for these."

I hope he does.

Having taught occasionally at various colleges and universities, I've grown increasingly distressed over a widespread "presentism" among young people. English majors know the hot authors of the moment—whether Raymond Carver or Lorrie Moore, Cormac McCarthy or Gary Shteyngart—and well they should. But venture beyond the twenty or thirty most familiar names, or mention slightly unusual writers, such as Wilkie Collins or Stella Gibbons or Ford Madox Ford, and you will have entered what is for them *terra incognita*.

Yet how can you love English literature, let alone major in it, while ignoring *The Woman in White,* perhaps the greatest "sensation" novel of the nineteenth century, or the hilarious *Cold Comfort Farm,* one of the world's best comic novels, or *The Good Soldier,* with its famous opening sentence: "This is the saddest story I have ever heard"?

Stick with me for a moment longer. We are coming round to the superb anthology you now hold in your hands.

For a long time science fiction and fantasy fans were pretty much expected to know the classics and past masters of the field. And, if they didn't, at least they wanted to. But in recent years some writers and readers have announced that they see no need to be familiar with the works of, say, Robert A. Heinlein. One of those old pulp writers, wasn't he? Misogynistic and militaristic, too. Who needs him?

This is roughly like saying, "William Faulkner, didn't he write about hillbillies and Southern degenerates?"

The great works of literature—and by literature I mean science fiction and fantasy, as well as horror and children's books and crime novels and all the more canonical suspects—are not old or fusty or out of date or corny or irrelevant. We read the classics because they continue to deliver esthetic pleasure, because they illuminate our human experience, because they show us how varied and marvelous verbal artistry can be. Most of all, we read these stories because they are extraordinary and wonderful.

Which is also what this anthology is, i.e., extraordinary and wonderful.

Fantasy & Science Fiction has been publishing exceptional imaginative fiction for almost two-thirds of a century. While there have been other terrific magazines in the field, *F&SF* nonetheless possesses a special cachet, in part because it has showcased so many ground-breaking and influential works. Volume 1 of this two-part "Greatest Hits" collection features, to name just four examples, "Flowers for Algernon," "Harrison Bergeron," "The Deathbird," and "One Ordinary Day, with Peanuts." I would hope that there's no real need to name the authors. If you don't already know these stories and who wrote them, you have been missing out. Or, to put it another, more positive way, you are in for a treat.

The same goes for the contents of this new volume, which is just as good as its predecessor. Here, for instance, is the greatest time-paradox story ever written, "'—All You Zombies—'" by none other than Robert A. Heinlein. A young writer or would-be writer could learn a lot about plotting by analyzing these dazzling, dizzying, Escher-like few pages. In "The Country of the Kind"—a shocking and heartbreaking parable about loneliness and alienation—Damon Knight reveals the cruelty of a supposedly humane society, and how achingly pitiable a monster can be. Just as powerful, in its way, is Jane Yolen's "The Hundredth Dove," a fairy tale so perfect you'll think you've known it all your life.

And those are only three of the stories. There are a couple of dozen others.

Some, like R. A. Lafferty's "Narrow Valley," C. M. Kornbluth's "The Cosmic Expense Account," and George Alec Effinger's "The Aliens Who Knew, I Mean, *Everything*," are brilliantly funny, totally gonzo. Others, such as Zenna Henderson's "The Anything Box," Ken Liu's "The Paper Menagerie," Paolo Bacigalupi's "The People of Sand and Slag," and Stephen King's "*The New York Times* at Special Bargain Rates," are tender and beautiful and quite heartbreaking. Many are fast-paced and action-movie thrilling: try James Patrick Kelly's "Rat"—about drug-smuggling in a future New York where people can genetically alter their bodies—or Robert Sheckley's "The Prize of Peril," a prefiguration of Reality TV shows and *The Hunger Games*.

To be taxonomic, the chosen stories can be loosely divided into two sorts: The plain and the fancy. In the first, the emphasis is on transparent diction and the clear unfolding of a plot. The stories mentioned in the previous paragraph are examples of this (with the partial exception of "Rat"). In "The Lincoln Train," to take another example, Maureen F. McHugh simply describes a young Southern girl who is being relocated by the victorious Northern Armies to some western settlement. The language is direct and unadorned, the action crisply presented and—upsetting. What gives this alternate nineteenth-century history its power is how close it comes to real and all-too-familiar twentieth-century history. In "Have Not Have" Geoff Ryman's language is comparably plain, yet timelessly serene, perfectly cadenced. Almost nothing of consequence happens: a dressmaker in a small Asian village describes her life and the people she interacts with. We gradually recognize that technological "progress" will alter the age-old routines, and that there will be consequent cultural and personal losses. But this knowledge is only lightly touched on. Nevertheless, the delicate beauty, the tonal equipoise of this story, hold the reader enthralled.

In the fancy stories, by contrast, language draws attention to itself. The mode of narration, the style, the diction, the whole storytelling apparatus struts and frets and shouts or whimpers. In such works we value the razzle-dazzle on the page as much as the turns of the plot. Jack Vance's slightly world-weary elegance in "Green Magic," the psychedelic "trip" that is Robert Silverberg's "Sundance," the restless baroque inventiveness of Brian Aldiss's "A Kind of Artistry," the rat-a-tat Vietnam-memoir prose of Lucius Shepard's harrowing "Salvador"—these stories triumph through their verbal firepower. Their style is their substance. Almost.

As one reads through these sixty years of great short fiction, one occasionally detects loose patterns. The tension of past and present that haunts Harlan Ellison®'s "Jeffty Is Five" is taken up again in Ryman's "Have Not Have." Jack Finney's "The Third Level" focuses on a mysterious floor of Grand Central Station; in Stephen King's story the dead congregate in what looks to be Grand Central Station before exiting by one of its many doors. Even as Sheckley's "The Prize of Peril" sends up television's excesses, so Kit Reed's "The Attack of the Giant Baby" reworks the clichés of 1950s monster movies.

Some stories are masterfully composed yet tantalizingly oblique—Gene Wolfe's revenge tale "The Friendship Light," for example, or Elizabeth Hand's confession of desolation and desperate yearning, "Echo." Urban fantasist Charles de Lint is represented by his signature work, "The Bone Woman," while Robert Reed's "Winemaster"—a combination of sf thriller and metaphysical mystery, with a few touches from a famous *Outer Limits* episode—reminds us that he should be more widely acknowledged as one of the best short story writers in the field. Not least, the anthology includes masterly work from the multi-talented Bruce Sterling (the funny "Maneki Neko," which extrapolates a future based on Japan's traditional gift economy) and the contemporary English sf master, M. John Harrison, whose "Suicide Coast" probes what one might call the risky business of life.

Overall, though, one aspect of *The Very Best of Fantasy & Science Fiction* stands out: the continuity of excellence. While we shouldn't over-privilege the present or neglect the achievements of the past, neither should we undervalue the artistic mastery of contemporaries such as Liu, Hand, Ryman, or Bacigalupi. Such writers of today are by no means pygmies, even if they do stand on the shoulders of giants. Nonetheless, the fantastic in their stories, while present, may sometimes seem distinctly attenuated. As Gary Wolfe and other critics have pointed out, the traditional boundary lines of genre are breaking down even as the world we live in is growing increasingly science fictional.

Together, the two volumes of *The Very Best of Fantasy & Science Fiction* will, if nothing else, persuade you that great imaginative fiction was being written in the 1950s—just as it is still being written in the 2010s. This is due, at least partly, simply because of the existence of *F&SF*, a home for virtuoso storytelling ever since Anthony Boucher and J. Francis McComas founded it in 1949. That's still the case, magnificently so, under the editorship of Gordon Van Gelder. To this day, *Fantasy & Science Fiction* remains, like *The New Yorker*, *The Atlantic*, or *The Paris Review*, one of the great fiction magazines of modern American literature.

The Third Level (1952)

JACK FINNEY

The author of *The Woodrow Wilson Dime, Marion's Wall*, and *Assault on a Queen*, JACK FINNEY (1911–1995) is best known nowadays for two works: *The Body Snatchers*, which formed the basis for the movie *Invasion of the Body Snatchers*, and *Time and Again*, a classic novel of traveling back through time to New York City in 1982.

Originally from Milwaukee, Wisconsin, Jack Finney worked in advertising in New York before moving to California in the 1950s. His appreciation of Manhattan as a place of magic and mystery is obvious in this short yarn.

THE PRESIDENTS OF the New York Central and the New York, New Haven and Hartford railroads will swear on a stack of timetables that there are only two. But I say there are three, because I've *been* on the third level at Grand Central Station. Yes, I've taken the obvious step: I talked to a psychiatrist friend of mine, among others. I told him about the third level at Grand Central Station, and he said it was a waking-dream wish fulfillment. He said I was unhappy. That made my wife kind of mad, but he explained that he meant the modern world is full of insecurity, fear, war worry and all the rest of it, and that I just want to escape. Well, hell, who doesn't? Everybody I know wants to escape but they don't wander down into any third level at Grand Central Station.

But that's the reason, he said, and my friends all agreed. Everything points to it, they claimed. My stamp collecting, for example; that's a "temporary refuge from reality." Well, maybe, but my grandfather didn't need any refuge from reality; things were pretty nice and peaceful in his day, from all I hear, and he started my collection. It's a nice collection, too, blocks of four of practically every U.S. issue, first-day covers, and so on. President Roosevelt collected stamps, too, you know.

Anyway, here's what happened at Grand Central. One night last summer I worked late at the office. I was in a hurry to get uptown to my apartment so I decided to subway from Grand Central because it's faster than the bus.

Now, I don't know why this should have happened to me. I'm just an ordinary guy named Charley, thirty-one years old, and I was wearing a tan gabardine suit and a straw hat with fancy band; I passed a dozen men who looked just like me. And I wasn't trying to escape from anything; I just wanted to get home to Louisa, my wife.

I turned into Grand Central from Vanderbilt Avenue, and went down the steps to the first level, where you take trains like the Twentieth Century. Then I walked down another flight to the second level, where the suburban trains leave from, ducked into an arched doorway heading for the subway—and got lost. That's easy to do. I've been in and out of Grand Central hundreds of times, but I'm always bumping into new doorways and stairs and corridors. Once I got into a tunnel about a mile long and came out in the lobby of the Roosevelt Hotel. Another time I came up in an office building on Forty-sixth Street, three blocks away.

Sometimes I think Grand Central is growing like a tree, pushing out new corridors and staircases like roots. There's probably a long tunnel that nobody knows about feeling its way under the city right now, on its way to Times Square, and maybe another to Central Park. And maybe—because for so many people through the years Grand Central *has* been an exit, a way of escape—maybe that's how the tunnel I got into... But I never told my psychiatrist friend about that idea.

The corridor I was in began angling left and slanting downward and I thought that was wrong, but I kept on walking. All I could hear was the empty sound of my own footsteps and I didn't pass a soul. Then I heard that sort of hollow roar ahead that means open space and people talking. The tunnel turned sharp left; I went down a short flight of stairs and came out on the third level at Grand Central Station. For just a moment I thought I was back on the second level, but I saw the room was smaller, there were fewer ticket windows and train gates, and the information booth in the center was wood and old-looking. And the man in the booth wore a green eyeshade and long black sleeve protectors. The lights were dim and sort of flickering. Then I saw why; they were open-flame gaslights.

There were brass spittoons on the floor, and across the station a glint of light caught my eye: a man was pulling a gold watch from his vest pocket. He snapped open the cover, glanced at his watch, and frowned. He wore a dirty hat, a black four-button suit with tiny lapels, and he had a big, black, handle-bar mustache. Then I looked around and saw that everyone in the station was dressed like 1890 something; I never saw so many beards, sideburns and fancy mustaches in my life. A woman walked in through the train gate; she wore a dress with leg-of-mutton sleeves and skirts to the top of her high-buttoned shoes. Back of her, out on the tracks, I caught a glimpse of a locomotive, a very small Currier & Ives locomotive with a funnel-shaped stack. And then I knew.

To make sure, I walked over to a newsboy and glanced at the stack of papers at his feet. It was the *World*; and the *World* hasn't been published for years. The lead story said something about President Cleveland. I've found that front page since, in the Public Library files, and it was printed June 11, 1894.

I turned toward the ticket windows knowing that here—on the third level at Grand Central—I could buy tickets that would take Louisa and me anywhere in the United States we wanted to go. In the year 1894. And I wanted two tickets to Galesburg, Illinois.

Have you ever been there? It's a wonderful town still, with big old frame houses, huge lawns, and tremendous trees whose branches meet overhead and roof the streets. And in 1894, summer evenings were twice as long, and people sat out on their lawns, the men smoking cigars and talking quietly, the women waving palm-leaf fans, with the fireflies all around, in a peaceful world. To be back there with the First World War still twenty years off, and World War II over forty years in the future...I wanted two tickets for that.

The clerk figured the fare—he glanced at my fancy hatband, but he figured the fare—and I had enough for two coach tickets, one way. But when I counted out the money and looked up, the clerk was staring at me. He nodded at the bills. "That ain't money, mister," he said, "and if you're trying to skin me you won't get very far," and he glanced at the cash drawer beside him. Of course the money was old-style bills, half again as big as the money we use nowadays, and different looking. I turned away and got out fast. There's nothing nice about jail, even in 1894.

And that was that. I left the same way I came, I suppose. Next day, during lunch hour, I drew $300 out of the bank, nearly all we had, and bought old-style currency (that *really* worried my psychiatrist friend). You can buy old money at almost any coin dealer's, but you have to pay a premium. My $300 bought less than $200 in old-style bills, but I didn't care; eggs were thirteen cents a dozen in 1894.

But I've never again found the corridor that leads to the third level at Grand Central Station, although I've tried often enough.

Louisa was pretty worried when I told her all this, and didn't want me to look for the third level any more, and after a while I stopped; I went back to my stamps. But now we're *both* looking, every week end, because now we have proof that the third level is still there. My friend Sam Weiner disappeared! Nobody knew where, but I sort of suspected because Sam's a city boy, and I used to tell him about Galesburg—I went to school there—and he always said he liked the sound of the place. And that's where he is, all right. In 1894.

Because one night, fussing with my stamp collection, I found—Well, do you know what a first-day cover is? When a new stamp is issued, stamp collectors buy some and use them to mail envelopes to themselves on the very first day of sale; and the postmark proves the date. The envelope is called a first-day cover. They're never opened; you just put blank paper in the envelope.

That night, among my oldest first-day covers, I found one that shouldn't have been there. But there it was. It was there because someone had mailed it to my grandfather at his home in Galesburg; that's what the address on the envelope said. And it had been there since July 18, 1894—the postmark showed that—yet I didn't remember it at all. The stamp was a six-cent, dull brown, with a picture of President Garfield. Naturally, when the envelope came to Granddad in the mail, it went right into his collection and stayed there—till I took it out and opened it.

The paper inside wasn't blank. It read:

941 Willard Street
Galesburg, Illinois
July 18, 1894

CHARLEY:
I got to wishing that you were right. Then I got to *believing* you were right. And, Charley, it's true; I found the third level!

I've been here two weeks, and right now, down the street at the Dalys', someone is playing a piano, and they're all out on the front porch singing "Seeing Nellie Home." And I'm invited over for lemonade.

Come on back, Charley and Louisa. Keep looking till you find the third level! It's worth it, believe me!

The note is signed SAM.

At the stamp and coin store I go to, I found out that Sam bought $800 worth of old-style currency. That ought to set him up in a nice little hay, feed and grain business; he always said that's what he really wished he could do, and he certainly can't go back to his old business. Not in Galesburg, Illinois, in 1894. His old business? Why, Sam was my psychiatrist.

The Cosmic Expense Account (1956)

C. M. KORNBLUTH

CYRIL KORNBLUTH (1923–1958) was one of the young New York science-fiction fans who formed the group known as the Futurians in the 1930s. He began publishing fiction as a teen and ultimately wrote about a dozen novels (including collaborations with Frederik Pohl and Judith Merril) and six dozen short stories before he died at the age of thirty-four. His sharp and cynical view of the future is perhaps best displayed in such stories as "The Marching Morons" and such novels as *The Space Merchants*.

Kornbluth suffered from heart problems and was prescribed medication, but the medication made his head cloudy, so he stopped taking it. In 1958, after shoveling his driveway, he ran to catch a train, and his heart gave out on the train platform. One aspect of his tragic death that is often overlooked: The train was going to take him into New York, where he was scheduled to meet with Bob Mills about becoming editor of *F&SF*. Sadly, we can only imagine what Kornbluth's tenure as editor might have been like, but at least we have "The Cosmic Expense Account" to suggest what he might have done as an employee of Mercury Press.

THE LACKAWANNA WAS still running one cautious morning train a day into Scranton, though the city was said to be emptying fast. Professor Leuten and I had a coach to ourselves, except for a scared, jittery trainman who hung around and talked at us.

"The name's Pech," he said. "And let me tell you, the Peches have been around for a mighty long time in these parts. There's a town twenty-three miles north of Scranton named Pechville. Full of my cousins and aunts and uncles, and I used to visit there and we used to send picture post cards and get them, too. But my God, mister, what's happened to them?"

His question was rhetorical. He didn't realize that Professor Leuten and I happened to be the only two people outside the miscalled Plague Area who could probably answer it.

"Mr. Pech," I said, "if you don't mind we'd like to talk some business."

"Sorry," he said miserably, and went on to the next car.

When we were alone Professor Leuten remarked: "An interesting reaction." He was very smooth about it. Without the slightest warning he whipped a huge, writhing, hairy spider from his pocket and thrust it at my face.

I was fast on the draw too. In one violent fling I was standing on my left foot in the aisle, thumbing my nose, my tongue stuck out. Goose flesh rippled down my neck and shoulders.

"Very good," he said, and put the spider away. It was damnably realistic. Even knowing that it was a gadget of twisted springs and plush, I cringed at the thought of its nestling in his pocket. With me it was spiders. With the professor it was rats and asphyxiation. Toward the end of our mutual training program it took only one part per million of sulfur dioxide gas in his vicinity to send him whirling into the posture of defense, crane-like on one leg, tongue out and thumb to nose, the sweat of terror on his brow.

"I have something to tell you, Professor," I said. "So?" he asked tolerantly. And that did it. The tolerance. I had been prepared to make my point with a dignified recital and apology, but there were two ways to tell the story and I suddenly chose the second. "You're a phoney," I said with satisfaction. "What?" he gasped.

"A phoney. A fake. A hoaxer. A self-deluding crackpot. Your Functional Epistemology is a farce. Let's not go into this thing kidding ourselves."

His accent thickened a little. "Led me remind you, Mr. Norris, that you are addressing a Doctor of Philosophy of the University of Gottingen and a member of the faculty of the University of Basle."

"You mean a privatdozent who teaches freshman logic. And I seem to remember that Gottingen revoked your degree."

He said slowly: "I have known all along that you were a fool, Mr. Norris. Not until now did I realize that you are also an anti-Semite. It was the Nazis who went through an illegal ceremony of revocation."

"So that makes me an anti-Semite. From a teacher of logic that's very funny."

"You are correct," he said after a long pause. "I withdraw my remark. Now, would you be good enough to amplify yours?"

"Gladly, Professor. In the first place—"

I had been winding up the rubber rat in my pocket. I yanked it out and tossed it into his lap where it scrabbled and clawed. He yelled with terror, but the yell didn't cost him a split second. Almost before it started from his throat he was standing one-legged, thumb to nose, tongue stuck out.

He thanked me coldly, I congratulated him coldly, I pocketed the rat while he shuddered and we went on with the conversation.

I told him how, eighteen months ago, Mr. Hopedale called me into his office. Nice office, oak panels, signed pictures of Hopedale Press writers from our glorious past: Kipling, Barrie, Theodore Roosevelt and the rest of the backlog boys.

What about Eino Elekinen, Mr. Hopedale wanted to know. Eino was one of our novelists. His first, *Vinland the Good*, had been a critical success and a popular flop; *Cubs of the Viking Breed*, the sequel, made us all a little money. He was now a month past delivery date on the final volume of the trilogy and the end was not in sight.

"I think he's pulling a sit-down strike, Mr. Hopedale. He's way overdrawn now and I had to refuse him a thousand-dollar advance. He wanted to send his wife to the Virgin Islands for a divorce."

"Give him the money," Mr. Hopedale said impatiently. "How can you expect the man to write when he's beset by personal difficulties?"

"Mr. Hopedale," I said politely, "she could divorce him right here in New York State. He's given her grounds in all five boroughs and the western townships of Long Island. But that's not the point. He can't write. And even if he could, the last thing American literature needs right now is another trilogy about a Scandinavian immigrant family."

"I know," he said. "I know. He's not very good yet. But I think he's going to be, and do you want him to starve while he's getting the juvenilia out of his system?" His next remark had nothing to do with Elekinen. He looked at the signed photo of T. R.—"To a bully publisher—" and said: "Norris, we're broke."

I said: "Ah?"

"We owe everybody. Printer, papermill, warehouse. Everybody. It's the end of Hopedale Press. Unless—I don't want you to think people have been reporting on you, Norris, but I understand you came up with an interesting idea at lunch yesterday. Some Swiss professor."

I had to think hard. "You must mean Leuten, Mr. Hopedale. No, there's nothing in it for us, sir. I was joking. My brother—he teaches philosophy at Columbia—mentioned him to me. Leuten's a crackpot. Every year or two Weintraub Verlag in Basle brings out another volume of his watchamacallit and they sell about a thousand. Functional Epistemology—my brother says it's all nonsense, the kind of stuff vanity presses put out. It was just a gag about us turning him into a Schweitzer or a Toynbee and bringing out a one-volume condensation. People just buy his books—I suppose—because they got started and feel ashamed to stop."

Mr. Hopedale said: "Do it, Norris. Do it. We can scrape together enough cash for one big promotion and then—the end. I'm going to see Brewster of Commercial Factors in the morning. I believe he will advance us sixty-five per cent on our accounts receivable." He tried on a cynical smile. It didn't become him. "Norris, you are what is technically called a Publisher's Bright Young Man. We can get seven-fifty for a scholarly book. With luck and promotion we can sell in the hundred-thousands. Get on it." I nodded, feeling sick, and started out. Mr. Hopedale said in a tired voice: "And it might actually be work of some inspirational value."

Professor Leuten sat and listened, red-faced, breathing hard. "You—betrayer," he said at last. "You with the smiling face that came to Basle, that talked of lectures in America, that told me to sign your damnable contract. My face on the cover of the *Time* magazine that looks like a monkey, the idiotic interviews, the press releasements in my name that I never saw. America, I thought, and held my tongue. But—from the beginning—it was a lie!" He buried his face in his hands and muttered "Ach! You stink!"

That reminded me. I took a small stench-bomb from my pocket and crushed it.

He leaped up, balanced on one leg and thumbed his nose. His tongue was out four inches and he was panting with the terror of asphyxiation.

"Very good," I said.

"Thank you. I suggest we move to the other end of the car."

We and our luggage were settled before he began to breathe normally. I judged that the panic and most of his anger had passed. "Professor," I said cautiously, "I've been thinking of what we do when—and if—we find Miss Phoebe."

"We shall complete her re-education," he said. "We shall point out that her unleashed powers have been dysfunctionally applied."

"I can think of something better to do than completing her re-education. It's why I spoke a little harshly. Presumably Miss Phoebe considers you the greatest man in the world."

He smiled reminiscently and I knew what he was thinking.

La Plume, Pa. Wednesday Four A.M. (!)

Professor Konrad Leuten
c/o The Hopedale Press
New York City, New York

My Dear Professor,

Though you are a famous and busy man I do hope you will take time
to read a few words of grateful tribute from an old lady (eighty-four).
I have just finished your magnificent and inspirational book *How
to Live on the Cosmic Expense Account: An Introduction to Functional
Epistemology*.

 Professor, I believe. I know every splendid word in your book is true.
If there is one chapter finer than the others it is No. 9, "How to Be in
Utter Harmony with Your Environment." The Twelve Rules in that
chapter shall from this minute be my guiding light, and I shall practice
them faithfully forever.

 Your grateful friend, (Miss) Phoebe Bancroft

That flattering letter reached us on Friday, one day after the papers reported
with amusement or dismay the "blackout" of La Plume, Pennsylvania. The
term "Plague Area" came later.

"I suppose she might," said the professor.

"Well, think about it."

The train slowed for a turn. I noticed that the track was lined with men and
women. And some of them, by God, were leaping for the moving train! Brakes
went on with a squeal and jolt; my nose bashed against the seat in front of us.

"Aggression," the professor said, astonished. "But that is not in the pattern!"

We saw the trainman in the vestibule opening the door to yell at the
trackside people. He was trampled as they swarmed aboard, filling, jamming
the car in a twinkling.

"Got to Scranton," we heard them saying. "Zombies—"

"I get it," I shouted at the professor over their hubbub. "These are refugees from Scranton. They must have blocked the track. Right now they're probably bullying the engineer into backing up all the way to Wilkes-Barre. We've got to get off!"

"Ja," he said. We were in an end seat. By elbowing, crowding and a little slugging we got to the vestibule and dropped to the tracks. The professor lost all his luggage in the brief, fierce struggle. I saved only my briefcase. The powers of Hell itself were not going to separate me from that briefcase.

Hundreds of yelling, milling people were trying to climb aboard. Some made it to the roofs of the cars after it was physically impossible for one more body to be fitted inside. The locomotive uttered a despairing toot and the train began to back up.

"Well," I said, "we head north."

We found U. S. 6 after a short overland hike and trudged along the concrete. There was no traffic. Everybody with a car had left Scranton days ago, and nobody was going into Scranton. Except us.

We saw our first zombie where a signpost told us it was three miles to the city. She was a woman in a Mother Hubbard and sunbonnet. I couldn't tell whether she was young or old, beautiful or a hag. She gave us a sweet, empty smile and asked if we had any food. I said no. She said she wasn't complaining about her lot but she was hungry, and of course the vegetables and things were so much better now that they weren't poisoning the soil with those dreadful chemical fertilizers. Then she said maybe there might be something to eat down the road, wished us a pleasant good-day and went on.

"Dreadful chemical fertilizers?" I asked.

The professor said: "I believe that is a contribution by the Duchess of Carbondale to Miss Phoebe's reign. Several interviews mention it." We walked on. I could read his mind like a book. He hasn't even read the interviews. He is a foolish, an impossible young man. And yet he is here, he has undergone a rigorous course of training, he is after all risking a sort of death. Why? I let him go on wondering. The answer was in my briefcase.

"When do you think we'll be in range?" I asked.

"Heaven knows," he said testily. "Too many variables. Maybe it's different when she sleeps, maybe it grows at different rates varying as the number of people affected. I feel nothing yet."

"Neither do I."

And when we felt something—specifically, when we felt Miss Phoebe Bancroft practicing the Twelve Rules of "How to be in Utter Harmony with Your Environment"—we would do something completely idiotic, something that had got us thrown—literally thrown—out of the office of the Secretary of Defense.

He had thundered at us: "Are you two trying to make a fool of me? Are you proposing that soldiers of the United States Army undergo a three-month training course in sticking out their tongues and thumbing their noses?" He was quivering with elevated blood pressure. Two M.P. lieutenants collared us under his personal orders and tossed us down the Pentagon steps when we were unable to deny that he had stated our proposal more or less correctly.

And so squads, platoons, companies, battalions and regiments marched into the Plague Area and never marched out again.

Some soldiers stumbled out as zombies. After a few days spent at a sufficient distance from the Plague Area their minds cleared and they told their confused stories. Something came over them, they said. A mental fuzziness almost impossible to describe. They liked it where they were, for instance; they left the Plague Area only by accident. They were wrapped in a vague, silly contentment even when they were hungry, which was usually. What was life like in the Plague Area? Well, not much happened. You wandered around looking for food. A lot of people looked sick but seemed to be contented. Farmers in the area gave you food with the universal silly smile, but their crops were very poor. Animal pests got most of them. Nobody seemed to eat meat. Nobody quarreled or fought or ever said a harsh word in the Plague Area. And it was Hell on earth. Nothing conceivable could induce any of them to return.

The Duchess of Carbondale? Yes, sometimes she came driving by in her chariot wearing fluttery robes and a golden crown. Everybody bowed down to her. She was a big, fat middle-aged woman with rimless glasses and a pinched look of righteous triumph on her face.

The recovered zombies at first were quarantined and doctors made their wills before going to examine them. This proved to be unnecessary and the examinations proved to be fruitless. No bacteria, no rickettsia, no viruses. Nothing. Which didn't stop them from continuing in the assumption embodied in the official name of the affected counties.

Professor Leuten and I knew better, of course. For knowing better we were thrown out of offices, declined interviews and once almost locked up as lunatics. That was when we tried to get through to the President direct. The Secret Service, I am able to testify, guards our Chief Executive with a zeal that borders on ferocity.

"How goes the book?" Professor Leuten asked abruptly.

"Third hundred-thousand. Why? Want an advance?"

I don't understand German, but I can recognize deep, heartfelt profanity in any language. He spluttered and crackled for almost a full minute before he snarled in English: "Idiots! Dolts! Out of almost one-third of a million readers, exactly one has read the book!"

I wanted to defer comment on that. "There's a car," I said.

"Obviously it stalled and was abandoned by a refugee from Scranton."

"Let's have a look anyway." It was a battered old Ford sedan halfway off the pavement. The rear was full of canned goods and liquor. Somebody had been looting. I pushed the starter and cranked for a while; the motor didn't catch.

"Useless," said the professor. I ignored him, yanked the dashboard hood button and got out to inspect the guts. There was air showing on top of the gas in the sediment cup.

"We ride, Professor," I told him. "I know these babies and their fuel pumps. The car quit on the upgrade there and he let it roll back." I unscrewed the clamp of the carburetor air filter, twisted the filter off and heaved it into the roadside bushes. The professor, of course was a "mere-machinery" boy with the true European intellectual's contempt for greasy hands. He stood by haughtily while I poured a bottle of gin empty, found a wrench in the toolbox that fit the gas tank drain plug and refilled the gin bottle with gasoline. He condescended to sit behind the wheel and crank the motor from time to time while I sprinkled gas into the carburetor. Each time the motor coughed there was less air showing in the sediment cup; finally the motor caught for good. I moved him over, tucked my briefcase in beside me, U-turned on the broad, empty highway and we chugged north into Scranton.

It was only natural that he edged away from me, I suppose. I was grimy from working under the gas tank. This plus the discreditable ability I had shown in starting the stalled car reminded him that he was, after all, a Herr Doktor from a red university while I was, after all, a publisher's employee with nebulous qualifications from some place called Cornell. The atmosphere was wrong for it, but sooner or later he had to be told.

"Professor, we've got to have a talk and get something straight before we find Miss Phoebe."

He looked at the huge striped sign the city fathers of Scranton wisely erected to mark that awful downgrade into the city. WARNING! SEVEN-MILE DEATH TRAP AHEAD SHIFT INTO LOWER GEAR. $50 FINE. OBEY OR PAY!

"What is there to get straight?" he demanded. "She has partially mastered Functional Epistemology—even though Hopedale Press prefers to call it 'Living on the Cosmic Expense Account.' This has unleashed certain latent powers of hers. It is simply our task to complete her mastery of the ethical aspect of F.E. She will cease to dominate other minds as soon as she comprehends that her behavior is dysfunctional and in contravention of the Principle of Permissive Evolution." To him the matter was settled. He mused: "Really I should not have let you cut so drastically my exposition of Dyadic Imbalance; that must be the root of her difficulty. A brief inductive explanation—"

"Professor," I said. "I thought I told you in the train that you're a fake."

He corrected me loftily. "You told me that you think I'm a fake, Mr. Norris. Naturally I was angered by your duplicity, but your opinion of me proves nothing. I ask you to look around you. Is this fakery?"

We were well into the city. Bewildered dogs yelped at our car. Windows were broken and goods were scattered on the sidewalks; here and there a house was burning brightly. Smashed and overturned cars dotted the streets, and zombies walked slowly around them. When Miss Phoebe hit a city the effects were something like a thousand-bomber raid.

"It's not fakery," I said, steering around a smiling man in a straw hat and overalls. "It isn't Functional Epistemology either. It's faith in Functional Epistemology. It could have been faith in anything, but your book just happened to be what she settled on."

"Are you daring," he demanded, white to the lips, "to compare me with the faith healers?"

"Yes," I said wearily. "They get their cures. So do lots of people. Let's roll it up in a ball, Professor. I think the best thing to do when we meet Miss Phoebe is for you to tell her you're a fake. Destroy her faith in you and your system and I think she'll turn back into a normal old lady again. Wait a minute! Don't tell me you're not a fake. I can prove you are. You say she's partly mastered F.E. and gets her powers from that partial mastery. Well, presumably you've completely mastered F.E., since you invented it. So why can't you do everything she's done, and lots more? Why can't you end this mess by levitating to La Plume, instead of taking the Lackawanna and a 1941 Ford? And, by God, why couldn't you fix the Ford with a pass of the hands and F.E. instead of standing by while I worked?"

His voice was genuinely puzzled. "I thought I just explained, Norris. Though it never occurred to me before, I suppose I could do what you say, but I wouldn't dream of it. As I said, it would be dysfunctional and in complete contravention of The Principle or Permissive—"

I said something very rude and added: "In short, you can but you won't."

"Naturally not! The Principle of Permissive—" He looked at me with slow awareness dawning in his eyes. "Norris! My editor. My proofreader. My by-the-publisher-officially-assigned fidus Achates. Norris, haven't you read my book?"

"No," I said shortly. "I've been much too busy. You didn't get on the cover of *Time* magazine by blind chance, you know."

He was laughing helplessly. "How goes that song," he finally asked me, his eyes damp, "'God Bless America'?"

I stopped the car abruptly. "I think I feel something," I said. "Professor, I like you."

"I like you too, Norris," he told me. "Norris, my boy, what do you think of ladies?"

"Delicate creatures. Custodians of culture. Professor, what about meat-eating?"

"Shocking barbarous survival. This is it, Norris!"

We yanked open the doors and leaped out. We stood on one foot each, thumbed our noses and stuck out our tongues.

Allowing for the time on the train, this was the 1,962nd time I had done it in the past two months. One thousand, nine hundred and sixty-one times the professor had arranged for spiders to pop out at me from books, from the television screen, from under steaks, from desk drawers, from my pockets, from his. Black widows, tarantulas, harmless (hah!) big house spiders, real and imitation. One thousand, nine hundred and sixty-one times I had felt the arachnophobe's horrified revulsion; each time I felt I had thrown major voluntary muscular systems into play by drawing up one leg violently, violently swinging my hand to my nose, violently grimacing to stick out my tongue.

My body had learned at last. There was no spider this time; there was only Miss Phoebe: a vague, pleasant-feeling something like the first martini. But my posture of defense this 1,962nd time was accompanied by the old rejection and horror. It had no spider, so it turned on Miss Phoebe. The vague first-martini feeling vanished like morning mist burned away by the sun.

I relaxed cautiously. On the other side of the car so did Professor Leuten. "Professor," I said, "I don't like you any more."

"Thank you," he said coldly. "Nor do I like you."

"I guess we're back to normal," I said. "Climb in." He climbed in and we started off. I grudgingly said: "Congratulations."

"Because it worked? Don't be ridiculous. It was to be expected that a plan of campaign derived from the principles of Functional Epistemology would be successful. All that was required was that you be at least as smart as one of Professor Pavlov's dogs, and I admit I considered that hypothesis the weak link in my chain of reasoning...."

We stopped for a meal from the canned stuff in the back of the car about one o'clock and then chugged steadily north through the ruined countryside. The little towns were wrecked and abandoned. Presumably refugees from the expanding Plague Area did the first damage by looting; the subsequent destruction just—happened. It showed you what would just happen to any twentieth-century town or city in the course of a few weeks if the people who wage endless war against breakdown and dilapidation put aside their arms. It was anybody's guess whether fire or water had done more damage.

Between the towns the animals were incredibly bold. There was a veritable army of rabbits eating their way across a field of clover. A farmer-zombie flapped a patchwork quilt at them, saying affectionately: "Shoo, little bunnies! Go away, now! I mean it!"

But they knew he didn't, and continued to chew their way across his field.

I stopped the car and called to the farmer. He came right away, smiling. "The little dickenses!" he said, waving at the rabbits. "But I haven't the heart to really scare them."

"Are you happy?" I asked him.

"Oh, yes!" His eyes were sunken and bright; his cheekbones showed on his starved face. "People should be considerate," he said. "I always say that being considerate is what matters most."

"Don't you miss electricity and cars and tractors?"

"Goodness, no. I always say that things were better in the old days. Life was more gracious, I always say. Why, I don't miss gasoline or electricity one little bit. Everybody's so considerate and gracious that it makes up for everything."

"I wonder if you'd be so considerate and gracious as to lie down in the road so we can drive over you?"

He looked mildly surprised and started to get down, saying: "Well, if it would afford you gentlemen any pleasure—"

"No; don't bother after all. You can get back to your rabbits."

He touched his straw hat and went away, beaming. We drove on. I said to the professor: "Chapter Nine: 'How to be in Utter Harmony with Your Environment.' Only she didn't change herself, Professor Leuten; she changed the environment. Every man and woman in the Area is what Miss Phoebe thinks they ought to be: silly, sentimental, obliging and gracious to the point of idiocy. Nostalgic and all thumbs when it comes to this dreadful machinery."

"Norris," the professor said thoughtfully, "we've been associated for some time. I think you might drop the 'professor' and call me 'Leuten.' In a way we're friends—"

I jammed on the worn, mushy brakes. "Out!" I yelled, and we piled out. The silly glow was enveloping me fast. Again, thumb to nose and tongue out, I burned it away. When I looked at the professor and was quite sure he was a stubborn old fossil I knew I was all right again. When he glared at me and snapped: "Naturally I withdraw my last remark, Norris, and no gentleman would hold me to it," I knew he was normal. We got in and kept going north.

The devastation became noticeably worse after we passed a gutted, stinking shambles that had once been the town of Meshoppen, Pa. After Meshoppen there were more bodies on the road and the flies became a horror. No pyrethrum from Kenya. No DDT from Wilmington. We drove in the afternoon heat with the windows cranked up and the hood ventilator closed. It was at about Meshoppen's radius from La Plume that things had stabilized for a while and the Army Engineers actually began to throw up barbed wire. Who knew what happened then? Perhaps Miss Phoebe recovered from a slight cold, or perhaps she told herself firmly that her faith in Professor Leuten's wonderful book was weakening; that she must take hold of herself and really work hard at being in utter harmony with her environment. The next morning—no Army Engineers. Zombies in uniform were glimpsed wandering about and smiling. The next morning the radius of the Plague Area was growing at the old mile a day.

I wanted distraction from the sweat that streamed down my face. "Professor," I said, "do you remember the last word in Miss Phoebe's letter? It was 'forever.' Do you suppose...?"

"Immortality? Yes; I think that is well within the range of misapplied F.E. Of course complete mastery of F.E. ensures that no such selfish power would be invoked. The beauty of F.E. is its conservatism, in the kinetic sense. It is self-regulating. A world in which universal mastery of F.E. has been achieved—and I now perceive that the publication of my views by the Hopedale Press was if anything a step away from that ideal—would be in no outward wise different from the present world."

"Built-in escape clause," I snapped. "Like yoga. You ask 'em to prove they've achieved self-mastery, just a little demonstration like levitating or turning transparent but they're all ready for you. They tell you they've achieved so much self-mastery they've mastered the desire to levitate or turn transparent. I almost wish I'd read your book, Professor, instead of just editing it. Maybe you're smarter than I thought."

He turned brick-red and gritted out: "Your insults merely bore me, Norris."

The highway took a turn and we turned with it. I braked again and rubbed my eyes. "Do you see them?" I asked the professor.

"Yes," he said matter-of-factly. "This must be the retinue of the Duchess of Carbondale."

They were a dozen men shoulder to shoulder barricading the road. They were armed with miscellaneous sporting rifles and one bazooka. They wore kilt-like garments and what seemed to be bracelets from a five-and-ten. When we stopped they opened up the center of the line and the Duchess of Carbondale drove through in her chariot—only the chariot was a harness-racing sulky and she didn't drive it; the horse was led by a skinny teen-age girl got up as Charmian for a high-school production of *Antony and Cleopatra*. The Duchess herself wore ample white robes, a tiara and junk jewelry. She looked like your unfavorite aunt, the fat one, or a grade-school teacher you remember with loathing when you're forty, or one of those women who ring your doorbell and try to bully you into signing petitions against fluoridation or atheism in the public schools.

The bazooka man had his stovepipe trained on our hood. His finger was on the button and he was waiting for the Duchess to nod. "Get out," I told the professor, grabbing my briefcase. He looked at the bazooka and we got out.

"Hail, O mortals," said the Duchess.

I looked helplessly at the professor. Not even my extensive experience with lady novelists had equipped me to deal with the situation. He, however, was able to take the ball. He was a European and he had status and that's the starting point for them: establish status and then conduct yourself accordingly. He said: "Madame, my name is Konrad Leuten. I am a doctor of philosophy of the University of Gottingen and a member of the faculty of the University of Basle. Whom have I the honor to address?"

Her eyes narrowed appraisingly. "O mortal," she said, and her voice was less windily dramatic, "know ye that here in the New Lemuria worldly titles are as naught. And know ye not that the pure hearts of my subjects may not be sullied by base machinery?"

"I didn't know, madame," Leuten said politely. "I apologize. We intended, however, to go only as far as La Plume. May we have your permission to do so?"

At the mention of La Plume she went poker-faced. After a moment she waved at the bazooka man. "Destroy, O Phraxanartes, the base machine of the strangers," she said. Phraxanartes touched the button of his stovepipe. Leuten and I jumped for the ditch, my hand welded to the briefcase-handle, when the rocket whooshed into the poor old Ford's motor. We huddled there while the gas tank boomed and cans and bottles exploded. The noise subsided to a crackling roar and the whizzing fragments stopped coming our way after maybe a minute. I put my head up first. The Duchess and her retinue were gone, presumably melted into the roadside stand of trees.

Her windy contralto blasted out: "Arise, O strangers, and join us."

Leuten said from the ditch: "A perfectly reasonable request, Norris. Let us do so. After all, one must be obliging."

"And gracious," I added.

Good old Duchess! I thought. Good old Leuten! Wonderful old world, with hills and trees and bunnies and kitties and considerate people...

Leuten was standing on one foot, thumbing his nose, sticking out his tongue, screaming: "Norris! Norris! Defend yourself!" He was slapping my face with his free hand. Sluggishly I went into the posture of defense, thinking: Such nonsense. Defense against what? But I wouldn't hurt old Leuten's feelings for the world—

Adrenalin boiled through my veins, triggered by the posture. Spiders. Crawling hairy, horrid spiders with purple, venom-dripping fangs. They hid in your shoes and bit you and your feet swelled with the poison. Their sticky, loathsome webs brushed across your face when you walked in the dark and they came scuttling silently, champing their jaws, winking their evil gem-like eyes. Spiders!

The voice of the Duchess blared impatiently: "I said, join us, O strangers. Well, what are you waiting for?"

The professor and I relaxed and looked at each other. "She's mad," the professor said softly. "From an asylum."

"I doubt it. You don't know America very well. Maybe you lock them up when they get like that in Europe; over here we elect them chairlady of the Library Fund Drive. If we don't, we never hear the end of it."

The costumed girl was leading the Duchess's sulky onto the road again. Some of her retinue were beginning to follow; she waved them back and dismissed the girl curtly. We skirted the heat of the burning car and approached her. It was that or try to outrun a volley from the miscellaneous sporting rifles.

"O strangers," she said, "you mentioned La Plume. Do you happen to be acquainted with my dear friend Phoebe Bancroft?"

The professor nodded before I could stop him. But almost simultaneously with his nod I was dragging the Duchess from her improvised chariot. It was very unpleasant, but I put my hands around her throat and knelt on her. It meant letting go of the briefcase but it was worth it.

She guggled and floundered and managed to whoop: "Don't shoot! I take it back, don't shoot them. Pamphilius, don't shoot, you might hit me!"

"Send 'em away," I told her.

"Never!" she blared. "They are my loyal retainers."

"You try, Professor," I said.

I believe what he put on then was his classroom manner. He stiffened and swelled and rasped towards the shrubbery: "Come out at once. All of you."

They came out, shambling and puzzled. They realized that something was very wrong. There was the Duchess on the ground and she wasn't telling them what to do the way she'd been telling them for weeks now. They wanted to oblige her in any little way they could, like shooting strangers, or scrounging canned food for her, but how could they oblige her while she lay there slowly turning purple? It was very confusing. Luckily there was somebody else to oblige, the professor.

"Go away," he barked at them. "Go far away. We do not need you any more. And throw away your guns."

Well, that was something a body could understand. They smiled and threw away their guns and went away in their obliging and considerate fashion.

I eased up on the Duchess's throat. "What was that guff about the New Lemuria?" I asked her.

"You're a rude and ignorant young man," she snapped. From the corner of my eye I could see the professor involuntarily nodding agreement. "Every educated person knows that the lost wisdom of Lemuria was to be revived in the person of a beautiful priestess this year. According to the science of pyra-midology—"

Beautiful priestess? Oh.

The professor and I stood by while she spouted an amazing compost of lost-continentism, the Ten Tribes, anti-fluoridation, vegetarianism, homeopathic medicine, organic farming, astrology, flying saucers, and the prose-poems of Khalil Gibran.

The professor said dubiously at last: "I suppose one must call her a sort of Cultural Diffusionist...." He was happier when he had her classified. He went on: "I think you know Miss Phoebe Bancroft. We wish you to present us to her as soon as possible."

"Professor," I complained, "we have a roadmap and we can find La Plume. And once we've found La Plume I don't think it'll be very hard to find Miss Phoebe."

"I will be pleased to accompany you," said the Duchess. "Though normally I frown on mechanical devices, I keep an automobile nearby in case of—in case of—well! Of all the rude—!"

Believe it or not, she was speechless. Nothing in her rich store of gibberish and hate seemed to fit the situation. Anti-fluoridation, organic farming, even Khalil Gibran were irrelevant in the face of us two each standing on one leg, thumbing our noses and sticking out our tongues.

Undeniably the posture of defense was losing efficiency. It took longer to burn away the foolish glow....

"Professor," I asked after we warily relaxed, "how many more of those can we take?"

He shrugged. "That is why a guide will be useful," he said. "Madame, I believe you mentioned an automobile."

"I know!" she said brightly. "It was asana yoga, wasn't it? Postures, I mean?"

The professor sucked an invisible lemon. "No, madame," he said cadaverously, "it was neither siddhasana nor padmasana. Yoga has been subsumed under Functional Epistemology, as has every other working philosophical system, Eastern and Western—but we waste time. The automobile?"

"You have to do that every so often, is that it?"

"We will leave it at that, madame. The automobile, please."

"Come right along," she said gaily. I didn't like the look on her face. Madam Chairlady was about to spring a parliamentary coup. But I got my briefcase and followed.

The car was in a nearby barn. It was a handsome new Lincoln, and I was reasonably certain that our fair cicerone had stolen it. But then, we had stolen the Ford.

I loaded the briefcase in and took the wheel over her objections and we headed for La Plume, a dozen miles away. On the road she yelped: "Oh, Functional Epistemology—and you're Professor Leuten!"

"Yes, madame," he wearily agreed.

"I've read your book, of course. So has Miss Bancroft; she'll be so pleased to see you."

"Then why, madame, did you order your subjects to murder us?"

"Well, Professor, of course I didn't know who you were then, and it was rather shocking, seeing somebody in a car. I, ah, had the feeling that you were up to no good, especially when you mentioned dear Miss Bancroft. She, you know, is really responsible for the re-emergence of the New Lemuria."

"Indeed?" said the professor. "You understand, then, about Leveled Personality Interflow?" He was beaming.

"I beg your pardon?"

"Leveled Personality Interflow!" he barked. "Chapter Nine!"

"Oh. In your book, of course. Well, as a matter of fact I skipped—"

"Another one," muttered the professor, leaning back.

The Duchess chattered on: "Dear Miss Bancroft, of course, swears by your book. But you were asking—no, it wasn't what you said. I cast her horoscope and it turned out that she is the Twenty-Seventh Pendragon!"

"*Scheissdreck*," the professor mumbled, too discouraged to translate.

"So naturally, Professor, she incarnates Taliesin spiritually and"—a modest giggle—"you know who incarnates it materially. Which is only sensible, since I'm descended from the high priestesses of Mu. Little did I think when I was running the Wee Occult Book Shoppe in Carbondale!"

"*Ja*," said the professor. He made an effort. "Madame, tell me something. Do you never feel a certain thing, a sense of friendliness and intoxication and goodwill enveloping you quite suddenly?"

"Oh, that," she said scornfully. "Yes; every now and then. It doesn't bother me. I just think of all the work I have to do. How I must stamp out the dreadful, soul-destroying advocates of meat-eating, and chemical fertilizer, and fluoridation. How I must wage the good fight for occult science and crush the materialistic philosophers. How I must tear down our corrupt and self-seeking ministers and priests, our rotten laws and customs—"

"*Lieber Gott*," the professor marveled as she went on. "With Norris it is spiders. With me it is rats and asphyxiation. But with this woman it is apparently everything in the Kosmos except her own revolting self!" She didn't hear him; she was demanding that the voting age for women be lowered to sixteen and for men raised to thirty-five.

We plowed through flies and mosquitoes like smoke. The flies bred happily on dead cows and in sheep which unfortunately were still alive. There wasn't oil cake for the cows in the New Lemuria. There wasn't sheep-dip for the sheep. There weren't state and county and township and village road crews constantly patrolling, unplugging sluices, clearing gutters, replacing rusted culverts, and so quite naturally the countryside was reverting to swampland. The mosquitoes loved it.

"La Plume," the Duchess announced gaily. "And that's Miss Phoebe Bancroft's little house right there. Just why did you wish to see her, Professor, by the way?"

"To complete her re-education..." the professor said in a tired voice.

Miss Phoebe's house and the few near it were the only places we had seen in the Area which weren't blighted by neglect. Miss Phoebe, of course, was able to tell the shambling zombies what to do in the way of truck-gardening, lawn-mowing and maintenance. The bugs weren't too bad there.

"She's probably resting, poor dear," said the Duchess. I stopped the car and we got out. The Duchess said something about Kleenex and got in again and rummaged through the glove compartment.

"Please, Professor," I said, clutching my briefcase. "Play it the smart way. The way I told you."

"Norris," he said, "I realize that you have my best interests at heart. You're a good boy, Norris and I like you—"

"Watch it!" I yelled, and swung into the posture of defense. So did he.

Spiders. It wasn't a good old world, not while there were loathsome spiders in it. Spiders—

And a pistol shot past my ear. The professor fell. I turned and saw the Duchess looking smug, about to shoot me too. I sidestepped and she missed; as I slapped the automatic out of her hand I thought confusedly that it was a near-miracle, her hitting the professor at five paces even if he was a standing target. People don't realize how hard it is to hit anything with a hand-gun.

I suppose I was going to kill her or at least damage her badly when a new element intruded. A little old white-haired lady tottering down the neat gravel path from the house. She wore a nice pastel dress which surprised me; somehow I had always thought of her in black.

"Bertha!" Miss Phoebe rapped out. "What have you done?"

The Duchess simpered. "That man there was going to harm you, Phoebe, dear. And this fellow is just as bad—"

Miss Phoebe said: "Nonsense. Nobody can harm me. Chapter Nine, Rule Seven. Bertha, I saw you shoot that gentleman. I'm very angry with you, Bertha. Very angry."

The Duchess turned up her eyes and crumpled. I didn't have to check; I was sure she was dead. Miss Phoebe was once again In Utter Harmony with Her Environment.

I went over and knelt beside the professor. He had a hole in his stomach and was still breathing. There wasn't much blood. I sat down and cried. For the professor. For the poor damned human race which at a mile per day would be gobbled up into apathy and idiocy. Goodby, Newton and Einstein, goodby steak dinners and Michelangelo and Tenzing Norgay; goodby Moses, Rodin, Kwan Yin, transistors, Boole and Steichen....

A redheaded man with an Adam's apple was saying gently to Miss Phoebe: "It's this rabbit, ma'am." And indeed an enormous rabbit was loping up to him. "Every time I find a turnip or something he takes it away from me and he kicks and bites when I try to reason with him—" And indeed he took a piece of turnip from his pocket and the rabbit insolently pawed it from his hand and nibbled it triumphantly with one wise-guy eye cocked up at his victim. "He does that every time, Miss Phoebe," the man said unhappily.

The little old lady said: "I'll think of something, Henry. But let me take care of these people first."

"Yes, ma'am," Henry said. He reached out cautiously for his piece of turnip and the rabbit bit him and then went back to its nibbling.

"Young man," Miss Phoebe said to me, "what's wrong? You're giving in to despair. You mustn't do that. Chapter Nine, Rule Three."

I pulled myself together enough to say: "This is Professor Leuten. He's dying."

Her eyes widened. "The Professor Leuten?" I nodded. "How to Live on the Cosmic Expense Account?" I nodded.

"Oh, dear! If only there were something I could do!"

Heal the dying? Apparently not. She didn't think she could, so she couldn't. "Professor," I said. "Professor."

He opened his eyes and said something in German, then, hazily: "Woman shot me. Spoil her—racket, you call it? Who is this?" He grimaced with pain.

"I'm Miss Phoebe Bancroft, Professor Leuten," she breathed, leaning over him. "I'm so dreadfully sorry; I admire your wonderful book so much."

His weary eyes turned to me. "So, Norris," he said. "No time to do it right. We do it your way. Help me up."

I helped him to his feet, suffering, I think, almost as much as he did. The wound started to bleed more copiously.

"No!" Miss Phoebe exclaimed. "You should lie down."

The professor leered. "Good idea, baby. You want to keep me company?"

"What's that?" she snapped.

"You heard me, baby. Say, you got any liquor in your place?"

"Certainly not! Alcohol is inimical to the development of the higher functions of the mind. Chapter Nine—"

"Pfui on Chapter Nine, baby. I chust wrote that stuff for money."

If Miss Phoebe hadn't been in a state resembling surgical shock after hearing that, she would have seen the pain convulsing his face. "You mean…?" she quavered, beginning to look her age for the first time.

"Sure. Lotta garbage. Sling fancy words and make money. What I go for is liquor and women. Women like you, baby."

The goose did it.

Weeping, frightened, insulted and lost she tottered blindly up the neat path to her house. I eased the professor to the ground. He was biting almost through his lower lip.

I heard a new noise behind me. It was Henry, the redhead with the Adam's apple. He was chewing his piece of turnip and had hold of the big rabbit by the hind legs. He was flailing it against a tree. Henry looked ferocious, savage, carnivorous and very, very dangerous to meddle with. In a word, human.

"Professor," I breathed at his waxen face, "you've done it. It's broken. Over. No more Plague Area."

He muttered, his eyes closed: "I regret not doing it properly…but tell the people how I died, Norris. With dignity, without fear. Because of Functional Epistemology."

I said through tears: "I'll do more than tell them, Professor. The world will know about your heroism.

"The world must know. We've got to make a book of this—your authentic, authorized, fictional biography—and Hopedale's West Coast agent'll see to the film sale—"

"Film?" he said drowsily. "Book…?"

"Yes. Your years of struggle, the little girl at home who kept faith in you when everybody scoffed, your burning mission to transform the world, and the climax—here, now!—as you give up your life for your philosophy."

"What girl?" he asked weakly.

"There must have been someone, Professor. We'll find someone."

"You would," he asked feebly, "document my expulsion from Germany by the Nazis?"

"Well, I don't think so, Professor. The export market's important, especially when it comes to selling film rights, and you don't want to go offending people by raking up old memories. But don't worry, Professor. The big thing is, the world will never forget you and what you've done."

He opened his eyes and breathed: "You mean your version of what I've done. Ach, Norris, Norris! Never did I think there was a power on Earth which could force me to contravene The Principle of Permissive Evolution." His voice became stronger. "But you, Norris, are that power." He got to his feet, grunting. "Norris," he said, "I hereby give you formal warning that any attempt to make a fictional biography or cinema film of my life will result in an immediate injunction being—you say slapped?—upon you, as well as suits for damages from libel, copyright infringement and invasion of privacy. I have had enough."

"Professor," I gasped. "You're well!"

He grimaced. "I'm sick. Profoundly sick to my stomach at my contravention of the Principle of Permissive—"

His voice grew fainter. This was because he was rising slowly into the air. He leveled off at a hundred feet and called: "Send the royalty statements to my old address in Basle. And remember, Norris, I warned you—"

He zoomed eastward then at perhaps one hundred miles per hour. I think he was picking up speed when he vanished from sight.

I stood there for ten minutes or so and sighed and rubbed my eyes and wondered whether anything was worthwhile. I decided I'd read the professor's book tomorrow without fail, unless something came up.

Then I took my briefcase and went up the walk and into Miss Phoebe's house. (Henry had made a twig fire on the lawn and was roasting his rabbit; he glared at me most disobligingly and I skirted him with care.)

This was, after all, the payoff; this was, after all, the reason why I had risked my life and sanity.

"Miss Phoebe," I said to her, taking it out of the briefcase, "I represent the Hopedale Press; this is one of our standard contracts. We're very much interested in publishing the story of your life, with special emphasis on the events of the past few weeks. Naturally you'd have an experienced collaborator. I believe sales in the hundred-thousands wouldn't be too much to expect. I would suggest as a title—that's right, you sign on that line there—*How to be Supreme Ruler of Everybody....*"

The Country of the Kind (1956)

DAMON KNIGHT

DAMON KNIGHT (1922–2002) was one of the preeminent writers in the science-fiction field. He was also one of its preeminent editors, critics, anthologists, historians, translators, and teachers. His many books include *Why Do Birds*; *Humpty Dumpty: An Oval*; *In Search of Wonder*; *Creating Short Fiction*; and *The Futurians*. Among the many works of short fiction he published are several classic short-short tales, such as "The Handler," "Not with a Bang," and "To Serve Man." Another story with a strong idea at its core, "The Country of the Kind," remains a bracing tonic.

THE ATTENDANT AT the car lot was daydreaming when I pulled up—a big, lazy-looking man in black satin chequered down the front. I was wearing scarlet, myself; it suited my mood. I got out, almost on his toes.

"Park or storage?" he asked automatically, turning around. Then he realized who I was, and ducked his head away.

"Neither," I told him.

There was a hand torch on a shelf in the repair shed right behind him. I got it and came back. I kneeled down to where I could reach behind the front wheel, and ignited the torch. I turned it on the axle and suspension. They glowed cherry red, then white, and fused together. Then I got up and turned the flame on both tires until the rubberoid stank and sizzled and melted down to the pavement. The attendant didn't say anything.

I left him there, looking at the mess on his nice clean concrete.

It had been a nice car, too; but I could get another any time. And I felt like walking. I went down the winding road, sleepy in the afternoon sunlight, dappled with shade and smelling of cool leaves. You couldn't see the houses; they were all sunken or hidden by shrubbery, or a little of both. That was the fad I'd heard about; it was what I'd come here to see. Not that anything the dulls did would be worth looking at.

I turned off at random and crossed a rolling lawn, went through a second hedge of hawthorn in blossom, and came out next to a big sunken games court.

The tennis net was up, and two couples were going at it, just working up a little sweat—young, about half my age, all four of them. Three dark-haired, one blonde. They were evenly matched, and both couples played well together; they were enjoying themselves.

I watched for a minute. But by then the nearest two were beginning to sense I was there, anyhow. I walked down onto the court, just as the blonde was about to serve. She looked at me frozen across the net, poised on tiptoe. The others stood.

"Off," I told them. "Game's over."

I watched the blonde. She was not especially pretty, as they go, but compactly and gracefully put together. She came down slowly flat-footed without awkwardness, and tucked the racket under her arm; then the surprise was over and she was trotting off the court after the other three.

I followed their voices around the curve of the path, between towering masses of lilacs, inhaling the sweetness, until I came to what looked like a little sunning spot. There was a sundial, and a birdbath, and towels lying around on the grass. One couple, the dark-haired pair, was still in sight farther down the path, heads bobbing along. The other couple had disappeared.

I found the handle in the grass without any trouble. The mechanism responded, and an oblong section of turf rose up. It was the stair I had, not the elevator, but that was all right. I ran down the steps and into the first door I saw, and was in the top-floor lounge, an oval room lit with diffused simulated sunlight from above. The furniture was all comfortably bloated, sprawling and ugly; the carpet was deep, and there was a fresh flower scent in the air.

The blonde was over at the near end with her back to me, studying the autochef keyboard. She was half out of her playsuit. She pushed it the rest of the way down and stepped out of it, then turned and saw me.

She was surprised again; she hadn't thought I might follow her down.

I got up close before it occurred to her to move; then it was too late. She knew she couldn't get away from me; she closed her eyes and leaned back against the paneling, turning a little pale. Her lips and her golden brows went up in the middle.

I looked her over and told her a few uncomplimentary things about herself. She trembled, but didn't answer. On an impulse, I leaned over and dialed the autochef to hot cheese sauce. I cut the safety out of circuit and put the quantity dial all the way up. I dialed *soup tureen* and then *punch bowl*.

The stuff began to come out in about a minute, steaming hot. I took the tureens and splashed them up and down the wall on either side of her. Then when the first punch bowl came out I used the empty bowls as scoops. I clotted the carpet with the stuff; I made streamers of it all along the walls, and dumped puddles into what furniture I could reach. Where it cooled it would harden, and where it hardened it would cling.

I wanted to splash it across her body, but it would've hurt, and we couldn't have that. The punch bowls of hot sauce were still coming out of the autochef, crowding each other around the vent. I punched *cancel*, and then *sauterne (swt., Calif.)*.

It came out well chilled in open bottles. I took the first one and had my arm back just about to throw a nice line of the stuff right across her midriff, when a voice said behind me:

"Watch out for cold wine."

My arm twitched and a little stream of the wine splashed across her thighs. She was ready for it; her eyes had opened at the voice, and she barely jumped.

I whirled around, fighting mad. The man was standing there where he had come out of the stairwell. He was thinner in the face than most, bronzed, wide-chested, with alert blue eyes. If it hadn't been for him, I knew it would have worked—the blonde would have mistaken the chill splash for a scalding one.

I could hear the scream in my mind, and I wanted it.

I took a step toward him, and my foot slipped. I went down clumsily, wrenching one knee. I got up shaking and tight all over. I wasn't in control of myself. I screamed, "You—you—" I turned and got one of the punch bowls and lifted it in both hands, heedless of how the hot sauce was slopping over onto my wrists, and I had it almost in the air toward him when the sickness took me—that damned buzzing in my head, louder, louder, drowning everything out.

When I came to, they were both gone. I got up off the floor, weak as death, and staggered over to the nearest chair. My clothes were slimed and sticky. I wanted to die. I wanted to drop into that dark furry hole that was yawning for me and never come up; but I made myself stay awake and get out of the chair.

Going down in the elevator, I almost blacked out again. The blonde and the thin man weren't in any of the second-floor bedrooms. I made sure of that, and then I emptied the closets and bureau drawers onto the floor, dragged the whole mess into one of the bathrooms and stuffed the tub with it, then turned on the water.

I tried the third floor: maintenance and storage. It was empty. I turned the furnace on and set the thermostat up as high as it would go. I disconnected all the safety circuits and alarms. I opened the freezer doors and dialed them to defrost. I propped the stairwell door open and went back up in the elevator.

On the second floor I stopped long enough to open the stairway door there—the water was halfway toward it, creeping across the floor—and then searched the top floor. No one was there. I opened book reels and threw them unwinding across the room; I would have done more, but I could hardly stand. I got up to the surface and collapsed on the lawn: that furry pit swallowed me up, dead and drowned.

While I slept, water poured down the open stairwell and filled the third level. Thawing food packages floated out into the rooms. Water seeped into wall panels and machine housings; circuits shorted and fuses blew. The air conditioning stopped, but the pile kept heating. The water rose.

Spoiled food, floating supplies, grimy water surged up the stairwell. The second and first levels were bigger and would take longer to fill, but they'd fill. Rugs, furnishings, clothing, all the things in the house would be waterlogged and ruined. Probably the weight of so much water would shift the house, rupture water pipes and other fluid intakes. It would take a repair crew more than a day just to clean up the mess. The house itself was done for, not repairable. The blonde and the thin man would never live in it again.

Serve them right.

The dulls could build another house; they built like beavers. There was only one of me in the world.

The earliest memory I have is of some woman, probably the cresh-mother, staring at me with an expression of shock and horror. Just that. I've tried to remember what happened directly before or after, but I can't. Before, there's nothing but the dark formless shaft of no-memory that runs back to birth. Afterward, the big calm.

From my fifth year, it must have been, to my fifteenth, everything I can remember floats in a pleasant dim sea. Nothing was terribly important. I was languid and soft; I drifted. Waking merged into sleep.

In my fifteenth year it was the fashion in love-play for the young people to pair off for months or longer. "Loving steady," we called it. I remember how the older people protested that it was unhealthy; but we were all normal juniors, and nearly as free as adults under the law.

All but me.

The first steady girl I had was named Elen. She had blonde hair, almost white, worn long; her lashes were dark and her eyes pale green. Startling eyes: they didn't look as if they were looking at you. They looked blind.

Several times she gave me strange startled glances, something between fright and anger. Once it was because I held her too tightly, and hurt her; other times, it seemed to be for nothing at all.

In our group, a pairing that broke up sooner than four weeks was a little suspect—there must be something wrong with one partner or both, or the pairing would have lasted longer.

Four weeks and a day after Elen and I made our pairing, she told me she was breaking it.

I'd thought I was ready. But I felt the room spin half around me till the wall came against my palm and stopped.

The room had been in use as a hobby chamber; there was a rack of plasticraft knives under my hand. I took one without thinking, and when I saw it I thought, *I'll frighten her.*

And I saw the startled, half-angry look in her pale eyes as I went toward her; but this is curious: she wasn't looking at the knife. She was looking at my face.

The elders found me later with the blood on me, and put me into a locked room. Then it was my turn to be frightened, because I realized for the first time that it was possible for a human being to do what I had done.

And if I could do it to Elen, I thought, surely they could do it to me.

But they couldn't. They set me free: they had to.

And it was then I understood that I was the king of the world....

The sky was turning clear violet when I woke up, and shadow was spilling out from the hedges. I went down the hill until I saw the ghostly blue of photon tubes glowing in a big oblong, just outside the commerce area. I went that way, by habit.

Other people were lining up at the entrance to show their books and be admitted. I brushed by them, seeing the shocked faces and feeling their bodies flinch away, and went on into the robing chamber.

Straps, aqualungs, masks and flippers were all for the taking. I stripped, dropping the clothes where I stood, and put the underwater equipment on. I strode out to the poolside, monstrous, like a being from another world. I adjusted the lung and the flippers, and slipped into the water.

Underneath, it was all crystal blue, with the forms of swimmers sliding through it like pale angels. Schools of small fish scattered as I went down. My heart was beating with a painful joy.

Down, far down, I saw a girl slowly undulating through the motions of sinuous underwater dance, writhing around and around a ribbed column of imitation coral. She had a suction-tipped fish lance in her hand, but she was not using it; she was only dancing, all by herself, down at the bottom of the water.

I swam after her. She was young and delicately made, and when she saw the deliberately clumsy motions I made in imitation of hers, her eyes glinted with amusement behind her mask. She bowed to me in mockery, and slowly glided off with simple, exaggerated movements, like a child's ballet.

I followed. Around her and around I swam, stiff-legged; first more childlike and awkward than she, then subtly parodying her motions; then improvising on them until I was dancing an intricate, mocking dance around her.

I saw her eyes widen. She matched her rhythm to mine, then, and together, apart, together again we coiled the wake of our dancing. At last, exhausted, we clung together where a bridge of plastic coral arched over us. Her cool body was in the bend of my arm; behind two thicknesses of vitrin—a world away!—her eyes were friendly and kind.

There was a moment when, two strangers yet one flesh, we felt our souls speak to one another across that abyss of matter. It was a truncated embrace— we could not kiss, we could not speak—but her hands lay confidingly on my shoulders, and her eyes looked into mine.

That moment had to end. She gestured toward the surface, and left me. I followed her up. I was feeling drowsy and almost at peace, after my sickness. I thought…I don't know what I thought.

We rose together at the side of the pool. She turned to me, removing her mask: and her smile stopped, and melted away. She stared at me with a horrified disgust, wrinkling her nose.

"Pyah!" she said, and turned, awkward in her flippers. Watching her, I saw her fall into the arms of a white-haired man, and heard her hysterical voice tumbling over itself.

"But don't you remember?" the man's voice rumbled. "You should know it by heart." He turned. "Hal, is there a copy of it in the clubhouse?"

A murmur answered him, and in a few moments a young man came out holding a slender brown pamphlet.

I knew that pamphlet. I could even have told you what page the white-haired man opened it to; what sentences the girl was reading as I watched.

I waited. I don't know why.

I heard her voice rising: "To think that I let him *touch* me!" And the white-haired man reassured her, the words rumbling, too low to hear. I saw her back straighten. She looked across at me…only a few yards in that scented, blue-lit air; a world away…and folded up the pamphlet into a hard wad, threw it, and turned on her heel.

The pamphlet landed almost at my feet. I touched it with my toe, and it opened to the page I had been thinking of:

…sedation until his 15th year, when for sexual reasons it became no longer practicable. While the advisors and medical staff hesitated, he killed a girl of the group by violence.

And farther down:

The solution finally adopted was three-fold.

1. *A sanction*—the only sanction possible to our humane, permissive society. Excommunication: not to speak to him, touch him willingly, or acknowledge his existence.

2. *A precaution*. Taking advantage of a mild predisposition to epilepsy, a variant of the so-called Kusko analog technique was employed, to prevent by an epileptic seizure any future act of violence.

3. *A warning*. A careful alteration of his body chemistry was effected to make his exhaled and exuded wastes emit a strongly pungent and offensive odor. In mercy, he himself was rendered unable to detect this smell.

Fortunately, the genetic and environmental accidents which combined to produce this atavism have been fully explained and can never again…

The words stopped meaning anything, as they always did at that point. I didn't want to read any farther; it was all nonsense, anyway. I was the king of the world.

I got up and went away, out into the night, blind to the dulls who thronged the rooms I passed.

Two squares away was the commerce area. I found a clothing outlet and went in. All the free clothes in the display cases were drab: those were for worthless floaters, not for me. I went past them to the specials, and found a combination I could stand—silver and blue, with a severe black piping down the tunic. A dull would have said it was "nice." I punched for it. The automatic looked me over with its dull glassy eye, and croaked, "Your contribution book, please."

I could have had a contribution book, for the trouble of stepping out into the street and taking it away from the first passer-by; but I didn't have the patience. I picked up the one-legged table from the refreshment nook, hefted it, and swung it at the cabinet door. The metal shrieked and dented, opposite the catch. I swung once more to the same place, and the door sprang open. I pulled out clothing in handfuls till I got a set that would fit me.

I bathed and changed, and then went prowling in the big multi-outlet down the avenue. All those places are arranged pretty much alike, no matter what the local managers do to them. I went straight to the knives, and picked out three in graduated sizes, down to the size of my fingernail. Then I had to take my chances. I tried the furniture department, where I had had good luck once in a while, but this year all they were using was metal. I had to have seasoned wood.

I knew where there was a big cache of cherry wood, in good-sized blocks, in a forgotten warehouse up north at a place called Kootenay. I could have carried some around, with me—enough for years—but what for, when the world belonged to me?

It didn't take me long. Down in the workshop section, of all places, I found some antiques—tables and benches, all with wooden tops. While the dulls collected down at the other end of the room, pretending not to notice, I sawed off a good oblong chunk of the smallest bench, and made a base for it out of another.

As long as I was there, it was a good place to work, and I could eat and sleep upstairs, so I stayed.

I knew what I wanted to do. It was going to be a man, sitting, with his legs crossed and his forearms resting down along his calves. His head was going to be tilted back, and his eyes closed, as if he were turning his face up to the sun.

In three days it was finished. The trunk and limbs had a shape that was not man and not wood, but something in between: something that hadn't existed before I made it.

Beauty. That was the old word.

I had carved one of the figure's hands hanging loosely, and the other one curled shut. There had to be a time to stop and say it was finished. I took the smallest knife, the one I had been using to scrape the wood smooth, and cut away the handle and ground down what was left of the shaft to a thin spike. Then I drilled a hole into the wood of the figurine's hand, in the hollow between thumb and curled finger. I fitted the knife blade in there; in the small hand it was a sword.

I cemented it in place. Then I took the sharp blade and stabbed my thumb, and smeared the blade.

I hunted most of that day, and finally found the right place—a niche in an outcropping of striated brown rock, in a little triangular half-wild patch that had been left where two roads forked. Nothing was permanent, of course, in a community like this one that might change its houses every five years or so, to follow the fashion; but this spot had been left to itself for a long time. It was the best I could do.

I had the paper ready: it was one of a batch I had printed up a year ago. The paper was treated, and I knew it would stay legible a long time. I hid a little photo capsule in the back of the niche, and ran the control wire to a staple in the base of the figurine. I put the figurine down on top of the paper, and anchored it lightly to the rock with two spots of all-cement. I had done it so often that it came naturally; I knew just how much cement would hold the figurine steady against a casual hand, but yield to one that really wanted to pull it down.

Then I stepped back to look: and the power and the pity of it made my breath come short, and tears start to my eyes.

Reflected light gleamed fitfully on the dark-stained blade that hung from his hand. He was sitting alone in that niche that closed him in like a coffin. His eyes were shut, and his head tilted back, as if he were turning his face up to the sun.

But only rock was over his head. There was no sun for him.

Hunched on the cool bare ground under a pepper tree, I was looking down across the road at the shadowed niche where my figurine sat.

I was all finished here. There was nothing more to keep me, and yet I couldn't leave.

People walked past now and then—not often. The community seemed half deserted, as if most of the people had flocked off to a surf party somewhere, or a contribution meeting, or to watch a new house being dug to replace the one I had wrecked.... There was a little wind blowing toward me, cool and lonesome in the leaves.

Up the other side of the hollow there was a terrace, and on that terrace, half an hour ago, I had seen a brief flash of color—a boy's head, with a red cap on it, moving past and out of sight.

That was why I had to stay. I was thinking how that boy might come down from his terrace and into my road, and passing the little wild triangle of land, see my figurine. I was thinking he might not pass by indifferently, but stop: and go closer to look: and pick up the wooden man: and read what was written on the paper underneath.

I believed that sometime it had to happen. I wanted it so hard that I ached.

My carvings were all over the world, wherever I had wandered. There was one in Congo City, carved of ebony, dusty-black; one on Cyprus, of bone; one in New Bombay, of shell; one in Chang-teh, of jade.

They were like signs printed in red and green, in a color-blind world. Only the one I was looking for would ever pick one of them up, and read the message I knew by heart.

TO YOU WHO CAN SEE, the first sentence said, I OFFER YOU A WORLD....

There was a flash of color up on the terrace. I stiffened. A minute later, here it came again, from a different direction: it was the boy, clambering down the slope, brilliant against the green, with his red sharp-billed cap like a woodpecker's head.

I held my breath.

He came toward me through the fluttering leaves, ticked off by pencils of sunlight as he passed. He was a brown boy, I could see at this distance, with a serious thin face. His ears stuck out, flickering pink with the sun behind them, and his elbow and knee pads made him look knobby.

He reached the fork in the road, and chose the path on my side. I huddled into myself as he came nearer. *Let him see it, let him not see me,* I thought fiercely.

My fingers closed around a stone.

He was nearer, walking jerkily with his hands in his pockets, watching his feet mostly.

When he was almost opposite me, I threw the stone.

It rustled through the leaves below the niche in the rock. The boy's head turned. He stopped, staring. I think he saw the figurine then. I'm sure he saw it.

He took one step.

"Risha!" came floating down from the terrace.

And he looked up. "Here," he piped.

I saw the woman's head, tiny at the top of the terrace. She called something I didn't hear; I was standing up, tight with anger.

Then the wind shifted. It blew from me to the boy. He whirled around, his eyes big, and clapped a hand to his nose.

"Oh, what a stench!" he said.

He turned to shout, "Coming!" and then he was gone, hurrying back up the road, into the unstable blur of green.

My one chance, ruined. He would have seen the image, I knew, if it hadn't been for that damned woman, and the wind shifting.... They were all against me, people, wind and all.

And the figurine still sat, blind eyes turned up to the rocky sky.

There was something inside me that told me to take my disappointment and go away from there, and not come back.

I knew I would be sorry. I did it anyway: took the image out of the niche, and the paper with it, and climbed the slope. At the top I heard his clear voice laughing.

There was a thing that might have been an ornamental mound, or the camouflaged top of a buried house. I went around it, tripping over my own feet, and came upon the boy kneeling on the turf. He was playing with a brown and white puppy.

He looked up with the laughter going out of his face. There was no wind, and he could smell me. I knew it was bad. No wind, and the puppy to distract him—everything about it was wrong. But I went to him blindly anyhow, and fell on one knee, and shoved the figurine at his face.

"Look—" I said.

He went over backwards in his hurry: he couldn't even have seen the image, except as a brown blur coming at him. He scrambled up, with the puppy whining and yapping around his heels, and ran for the mound.

I was up after him, clawing up moist earth and grass as I rose. In the other hand I still had the image clutched, and the paper with it.

A door popped open and swallowed him and popped shut again in my face. With the flat of my hand I beat the vines around it until I hit the doorplate by accident and the door opened. I dived in, shouting, "Wait," and was in a spiral passage, lit pearl-gray, winding downward. Down I went headlong, and came out at the wrong door—an underground conservatory, humid and hot under the yellow lights, with dripping rank leaves in long rows. I went down the aisle raging, overturning the tanks, until I came to a vestibule and an elevator.

Down I went again to the third level and a labyrinth of guest rooms, all echoing, all empty. At last I found a ramp leading upward, past the conservatory, and at the end of it voices.

The door was clear vitrin, and I paused on the near side of it looking and listening. There was the boy, and a woman old enough to be his mother, just— sister or cousin, more likely—and an elderly woman in a hard chair holding the puppy. The room was comfortable and tasteless, like other rooms.

I saw the shock grow on their faces as I burst in: it was always the same, they knew I would like to kill them, but they never expected that I would come uninvited into a house. It was not done.

There was that boy, so close I could touch him, but the shock of all of them was quivering in the air, smothering, like a blanket that would deaden my voice. I felt I had to shout.

"Everything they tell you is lies!" I said. "See here—here, this is the truth!" I had the figurine in front of his eyes, but he didn't see.

"Risha, go below," said the young woman quietly. He turned to obey, quick as a ferret. I got in front of him again. "Stay," I said, breathing hard. "Look—"

"Remember, Risha, don't speak," said the woman.

I couldn't stand any more. Where the boy went I don't know; I ceased to see him. With the image in one hand and the paper with it, I leaped at the woman. I was almost quick enough; I almost reached her; but the buzzing took me in the middle of a step, louder, louder, like the end of the world.

It was the second time that week. When I came to, I was sick and too faint to move for a long time.

The house was silent. They had gone, of course…the house had been defiled, having me in it. They wouldn't live here again, but would build elsewhere.

My eyes blurred. After a while I stood up and looked around at the room. The walls were hung with a gray close-woven cloth that looked as if it would tear, and I thought of ripping it down in strips, breaking furniture, stuffing carpets and bedding into the oubliette…. But I didn't have the heart for it. I was too tired. Thirty years…. They had given me all the kingdoms of the world, and the glory thereof, thirty years ago. It was more than one man alone could bear, for thirty years.

At last I stooped and picked up the figurine, and the paper that was supposed to go under it—crumpled now, with the forlorn look of a message that someone has thrown away unread.

I sighed bitterly.

I smoothed it out and read the last part.

YOU CAN SHARE THE WORLD WITH ME. THEY CAN'T STOP YOU. STRIKE NOW—PICK UP A SHARP THING AND STAB, OR A HEAVY THING AND CRUSH. THAT'S ALL. THAT WILL MAKE YOU FREE. ANYONE CAN DO IT.

Anyone. Someone. Anyone.

The Anything Box (1956)

ZENNA HENDERSON

ZENNA HENDERSON (1917–1983) was an Arizona schoolteacher for most of her adult life. Her stories of "the People"—humanoids who are here on Earth because their home planet was destroyed—were among *F&SF*'s most popular stories for decades. All of them are collected in one volume, titled *Ingathering*. Most of her other stories are collected in *Holding Wonder* and *The Anything Box*.

"The Anything Box," like many of her tales, concerns subjects she knew well: schoolteachers and children in the American Southwest. And, like many of her tales, "The Anything Box" is moving and memorable.

I SUPPOSE IT was about the second week of school that I noticed Sue-lynn particularly. Of course, I'd noticed her name before and checked her out automatically for maturity and ability and probable performance the way most teachers do with their students during the first weeks of school. She had checked out mature and capable and no worry as to performance as I had pigeonholed her—setting aside for the moment the little nudge that said, "Too quiet"—with my other no-worrys until the fluster and flurry of the first days had died down a little.

I remember my noticing day. I had collapsed into my chair for a brief respite from guiding hot little hands through the intricacies of keeping a Crayola within reasonable bounds and the room was full of the relaxed, happy hum of a pleased class as they worked away, not realizing that they were rubbing "blue" into their memories as well as onto their papers. I was meditating on how individual personalities were beginning to emerge among the thirty-five or so heterogeneous first graders I had, when I noticed Sue-lynn—really noticed her—for the first time.

She had finished her paper—far ahead of the others as usual—and was sitting at her table facing me. She had her thumbs touching in front of her on the table and her fingers curving as though they held something between them—something large enough to keep her fingertips apart and angular enough to bend her fingers as if for corners. It was something pleasant that she held—pleasant and precious. You could tell that by the softness of her hold. She was leaning forward a little, her lower ribs pressed against the table, and she was looking, completely absorbed, at the table between her hands. Her face was relaxed and happy. Her mouth curved in a tender half-smile, and as I watched, her lashes lifted and she looked at me with a warm share-the-pleasure look. Then her eyes blinked and the shutters came down inside them. Her hand flicked into the desk and out. She pressed her thumbs to her forefingers and rubbed them slowly together. Then she laid one hand over the other on the table and looked down at them with the air of complete denial and ignorance children can assume so devastatingly.

The incident caught my fancy and I began to notice Sue-lynn. As I consciously watched her, I saw that she spent most of her free time staring at the table between her hands, much too unobtrusively to catch my busy attention. She hurried through even the fun-est of fun papers and then lost herself in looking. When Davie pushed her down at recess, and blood streamed from her knee to her ankle, she took her bandages and her tear-smudged face to that comfort she had so readily—if you'll pardon the expression—at hand, and emerged minutes later, serene and dry-eyed. I think Davie pushed her down because of her Looking. I know the day before he had come up to me, red-faced and squirming.

"Teacher," he blurted. "She Looks!"

"Who looks?" I asked absently, checking the vocabulary list in my book, wondering how on earth I'd missed *where,* one of those annoying *wh* words that throw the children for a loss.

"Sue-lynn. She Looks and Looks!"

"At you?" I asked.

"Well…" He rubbed a forefinger below his nose, leaving a clean streak on his upper lip, accepted the proffered Kleenex and put it in his pocket. "She looks at her desk and tells lies. She says she can see…"

"Can see what?" My curiosity picked up its ears.

"Anything," said Davie. "It's her Anything Box. She can see anything she wants to."

"Does it hurt you for her to Look?"

"Well," he squirmed. Then he burst out. "She says she saw me with a dog biting me because I took her pencil—she said." He started a pellmell verbal retreat. "She *thinks* I took her pencil. I only found—" His eyes dropped. "I'll give it back."

"I hope so," I smiled. "If you don't want her to look at you, then don't do things like that."

"Dern girls," he muttered and clomped back to his seat.

So I think he pushed her down the next day to get back at her for the dog-bite.

Several times after that I wandered to the back of the room, casually in her vicinity, but always she either saw or felt me coming and the quick sketch of her hand disposed of the evidence. Only once I thought I caught a glimmer of something—but her thumb and forefinger brushed in sunlight, and it must have been just that.

Children don't retreat for no reason at all, and, though Sue-lynn did not follow any overt pattern of withdrawal, I started to wonder about her. I watched her on the playground, to see how she tracked there. That only confused me more.

She had a very regular pattern. When the avalanche of children first descended at recess, she avalanched along with them and nothing in the shrieking, running, dodging mass resolved itself into a withdrawn Sue-lynn. But after ten minutes or so, she emerged from the crowd, tousle-haired, rosy-cheeked, smutched with dust, one shoelace dangling and, through some alchemy that I coveted for myself, she suddenly became untousled, undusty and unsmutched. And there she was, serene and composed on the narrow little step at the side of the flight of stairs just where they disappeared into the base of the pseudo-Corinthian column that graced Our Door and her cupped hands received whatever they received and her absorption in what she saw became so complete that the bell came as a shock every time.

And each time, before she joined the rush to Our Door, her hand would sketch a gesture to her pocket, if she had one, or to the tiny ledge that extended between the hedge and the building. Apparently she always had to put the Anything Box away, but never had to go back to get it.

I was so intrigued by her putting whatever it was on the ledge that once I actually went over and felt along the grimy little outset. I sheepishly followed my children into the hall, wiping the dust from my fingertips, and Sue-lynn's eyes brimmed amusement at me without her mouth's smiling. Her hands mischievously squared in front of her and her thumbs caressed a solidness as the line of children swept into the room.

I smiled too because she was so pleased with having outwitted me. This seemed to be such a gay withdrawal that I let my worry die down. Better this manifestation than any number of other ones that I could name.

Someday, perhaps, I'll learn to keep my mouth shut. I wish I had before that long afternoon when we primary teachers worked together in a heavy cloud of ditto fumes, the acrid smell of India ink, drifting cigarette smoke and the constant current of chatter, and I let Alpha get me started on what to do with our behavior problems. She was all raunched up about the usual rowdy loudness of her boys and the eternal clack of her girls, and I—bless my stupidity—gave her Sue-lynn as an example of what should be our deepest concern rather than the outbursts from our active ones.

"You mean she just sits and looks at nothing?" Alpha's voice grated into her questioning tone.

"Well, I can't see anything," I admitted. "But apparently she can."

"But that's having hallucinations!" Her voice went up a notch. "I read a book once—"

"Yes." Marlene leaned across the desk to flick ashes in the ashtray. "So we have heard and heard and heard."

"Well!" sniffed Alpha. "It's better than *never* reading a book."

"We're waiting," Marlene leaked smoke from her nostrils, "for the day when you read another book. This one must have been uncommonly long."

"Oh, I don't know." Alpha's forehead wrinkled with concentration. "It was only about—" Then she reddened and turned her face angrily away from Marlene.

"Apropos of *our* discussion—" she said pointedly. "It sounds to me like that child has a deep personality disturbance. Maybe even a psychotic— whatever—" Her eyes glistened faintly as she turned the thought over.

"Oh, I don't know," I said, surprised into echoing her words at my sudden need to defend Sue-lynn. "There's something about her. She doesn't have that apprehensive, hunched-shoulder, don't-hit-me-again air about her that so many withdrawn children have." And I thought achingly of one of mine from last year that Alpha had now and was verbally bludgeoning back into silence after all my work with him. "She seems to have a happy, adjusted personality, only with this odd little...*plus.*"

"Well, I'd be worried if she were mine," said Alpha. "I'm glad all my kids are so normal." She sighed complacently. "I guess I really haven't anything to kick about. I seldom ever have problem children except wigglers and yakkers, and a holler and a smack can straighten them out."

Marlene caught my eye mockingly, tallying Alpha's class with me, and I turned away with a sigh. To be so happy—well, I suppose ignorance does help.

"You'd better do something about that girl," Alpha shrilled as she left the room. "She'll probably get worse and worse as time goes on. Deteriorating, I think the book said."

I had known Alpha a long time and I thought I knew how much of her talk to discount, but I began to worry about Sue-lynn. Maybe this *was* a disturbance that was more fundamental than the usual run-of-the-mill that I had met up with. Maybe a child *can* smile a soft, contented smile and still have little maggots of madness flourishing somewhere inside.

Or, by gorry! I said to myself defiantly, maybe she *does* have an Anything Box. Maybe she *is* looking at something precious. Who am I to say no to anything like that?

An Anything Box! What could you see in an Anything Box? Heart's desire? I felt my own heart lurch—just a little—the next time Sue-lynn's hands curved. I breathed deeply to hold me in my chair. If it was *her* Anything Box, I wouldn't be able to see my heart's desire in it. Or would I? I propped my cheek up on my hand and doodled aimlessly on my time schedule sheet. How on earth, I wondered—not for the first time—do I manage to get myself off on these tangents?

Then I felt a small presence at my elbow and turned to meet Sue-lynn's wide eyes.

"Teacher?" The word was hardly more than a breath.

"Yes?" I could tell that for some reason Sue-lynn was loving me dearly at the moment. Maybe because her group had gone into new books that morning. Maybe because I had noticed her new dress, the ruffles of which made her feel very feminine and lovable, or maybe just because the late autumn sun lay so golden across her desk. Anyway, she was loving me to overflowing, and since, unlike most of the children, she had no casual hugs or easy moist kisses, she was bringing her love to me in her encompassing hands.

"See my box, Teacher? It's my Anything Box."

"Oh, my!" I said. "May I hold it?"

After all, I have held—tenderly or apprehensively or bravely—tiger magic, live rattlesnakes, dragon's teeth, poor little dead butterflies and two ears and a nose that dropped off Sojie one cold morning—none of which I could see any more than I could the Anything Box. But I took the squareness from her carefully, my tenderness showing in my fingers and my face.

And I received weight and substance and actuality!

Almost I let it slip out of my surprised fingers, but Sue-lynn's apprehensive breath helped me catch it and I curved my fingers around the precious warmness and looked down, down, past a faint shimmering, down into Sue-lynn's Anything Box.

I was running barefoot through the whispering grass. The swirl of my shirts caught the daisies as I rounded the gnarled apple tree at the corner. The warm wind lay along each of my cheeks and chuckled in my ears. My heart outstripped my flying feet and melted with a rush of delight into warmness as his arms—

I closed my eyes and swallowed hard, my palms tight against the Anything Box. "It's beautiful!" I whispered. "It's wonderful, Sue-lynn. Where did you get it?"

Her hands took it back hastily. "It's mine," she said defiantly. "It's mine."

"Of course," I said. "Be careful now. Don't drop it."

She smiled faintly as she sketched a motion to her pocket. "I won't." She patted the flat pocket on her way back to her seat.

Next day she was afraid to look at me at first for fear I might say something or look something or in some way remind her of what must seem like a betrayal to her now, but after I only smiled my usual smile, with no added secret knowledge, she relaxed.

A night or so later when I leaned over my moon-drenched window sill and let the shadow of my hair hide my face from such ebullient glory, I remembered about the Anything Box. Could I make one for myself? Could I square off this aching waiting, this out-reaching, this silent cry inside me, and make it into an Anything Box? I freed my hands and brought them together, thumb to thumb, framing a part of the horizon's darkness between my upright forefingers. I stared into the empty square until my eyes watered. I sighed, and laughed a little, and let my hands frame my face as I leaned out into the night. To have magic so near—to feel it tingle off my fingertips and then to be so bound that I couldn't receive it. I turned away from the window—turning my back on brightness.

It wasn't long after this that Alpha succeeded in putting sharp points of worry back in my thoughts of Sue-lynn. We had ground duty together, and one morning when we shivered while the kids ran themselves rosy in the crisp air, she sizzed in my ear,

"Which one is it? The abnormal one, I mean."

"I don't have any abnormal children," I said, my voice sharpening before the sentence ended because I suddenly realized whom she meant.

"Well, I call it abnormal to stare at nothing." You could almost taste the acid in her words. "Who is it?"

"Sue-lynn," I said reluctantly. "She's playing on the bars now."

Alpha surveyed the upside-down Sue-lynn whose brief skirts were belled down from her bare pink legs and half covered her face as she swung from one of the bars by her knees. Alpha clutched her wizened, blue hands together and breathed on them. "She looks normal enough," she said.

"She *is* normal!" I snapped.

"*Well,* bite my head off!" cried Alpha. "You're the one that said she wasn't, not me—or is it 'not I'? I never could remember. Not me? Not I?"

The bell saved Alpha from a horrible end. I never knew a person so serenely unaware of essentials and so sensitive to trivia.

But she had succeeded in making me worry about Sue-lynn again, and the worry exploded into distress a few days later.

Sue-lynn came to school sleepy-eyed and quiet. She didn't finish any of her work and she fell asleep during rest time. I cussed TV and Drive-Ins and assumed a night's sleep would put it right. But next day Sue-lynn burst into tears and slapped Davie clear off his chair.

"Why Sue-lynn!" I gathered Davie up in all his astonishment and took Sue-lynn's hand. She jerked it away from me and flung herself at Davie again. She got two handfuls of his hair and had him out of my grasp before I knew it. She threw him bodily against the wall with a flip of her hands, then doubled up her fists and pressed them to her streaming eyes. In the shocked silence of the room, she stumbled over to Isolation and seating herself, back to the class, on the little chair, she leaned her head into the corner and sobbed quietly in big gulping sobs.

"What on earth goes on?" I asked the stupefied Davie who sat spraddle-legged on the floor fingering a detached tuft of hair. "What did you do?"

"I only said 'Robber Daughter,'" said Davie. "It said so in the paper. My mama said her daddy's a robber. They put him in jail cause he robbered a gas station." His bewildered face was trying to decide whether or not to cry. Everything had happened so fast that he didn't know yet if he was hurt.

"It isn't nice to call names," I said weakly. "Get back into your seat. I'll take care of Sue-lynn later."

He got up and sat gingerly down in his chair, rubbing his ruffled hair, wanting to make more of a production of the situation but not knowing how. He twisted his face experimentally to see if he had tears available and had none.

"Dern girls," he muttered and tried to shake his fingers free of a wisp of hair.

I kept my eye on Sue-lynn for the next half hour as I busied myself with the class. Her sobs soon stopped and her rigid shoulders relaxed. Her hands were softly in her lap and I knew she was taking comfort from her Anything Box. We had our talk together later, but she was so completely sealed off from me by her misery that there was no communication between us. She sat quietly watching me as I talked, her hands trembling in her lap. It shakes the heart, somehow, to see the hands of a little child quiver like that.

That afternoon I looked up from my reading group, startled, as though by a cry, to catch Sue-lynn's frightened eyes. She looked around bewildered and then down at her hands again—her empty hands. Then she darted to the Isolation corner and reached under the chair. She went back to her seat slowly, her hands squared to an unseen weight. For the first time, apparently, she had had to go get the Anything Box. It troubled me with a vague unease for the rest of the afternoon.

Through the days that followed while the trial hung fire, I had Sue-lynn in attendance bodily, but that was all. She sank into her Anything Box at every opportunity. And always, if she had put it away somewhere, she had to go back for it. She roused more and more reluctantly from these waking dreams, and there finally came a day when I had to shake her to waken her.

I went to her mother, but she couldn't or wouldn't understand me, and made me feel like a frivolous gossip-monger taking her mind away from her husband, despite the fact that I didn't even mention him—or maybe because I didn't mention him.

"If she's being a bad girl, spank her," she finally said, wearily shifting the weight of a whining baby from one hip to another and pushing her tousled hair off her forehead. "Whatever you do is all right by me. My worrier is all used up. I haven't got any left for the kids right now."

Well, Sue-lynn's father was found guilty and sentenced to the State Penitentiary and school was less than an hour old the next day when Davie came up, clumsily a-tiptoe, braving my wrath for interrupting a reading group, and whispered hoarsely, "Sue-lynn's asleep with her eyes open again, Teacher."

We went back to the table and Davie slid into his chair next to a completely unaware Sue-lynn. He poked her with a warning finger. "I told you I'd tell on you."

And before our horrified eyes, she toppled, as rigidly as a doll, sideways off the chair. The thud of her landing relaxed her and she lay limp on the green asphalt tile—a thin paper-doll of a girl, one hand still clenched open around something. I pried her fingers loose and almost wept to feel enchantment dissolve under my heavy touch. I carried her down to the nurse's room and we worked over her with wet towels and prayer and she finally opened her eyes.

"Teacher," she whispered weakly.

"Yes, Sue-lynn." I took her cold hands in mine.

"Teacher, I almost got in my Anything Box."

"No," I answered. "You couldn't. You're too big."

"Daddy's there," she said. "And where we used to live."

I took a long, long look at her wan face. I hope it was genuine concern for her that prompted my next words. I hope it wasn't envy or the memory of the niggling nagging of Alpha's voice that put firmness in my voice as I went on. "That's play-like," I said. "Just for fun."

Her hands jerked protestingly in mine. "Your Anything Box is just for fun. It's like Davie's cowpony that he keeps in his desk or Sojie's jet plane, or when the big bear chases all of you at recess. It's fun-for-play, but it's not for real. You mustn't think it's for real. It's only play."

"No!" she denied. "No!" she cried frantically and, hunching herself up on the cot, peering through her tear-swollen eyes, she scrabbled under the pillow and down beneath the rough blanket that covered her.

"Where is it?" she cried. "Where is it? Give it back to me, Teacher!"

She flung herself toward me and pulled open both my clenched hands.

"Where did you put it? Where did you put it?"

"There is no Anything Box," I said flatly, trying to hold her to me and feeling my heart breaking along with hers.

"You took it!" she sobbed. "You took it away from me!" And she wrenched herself out of my arms.

"Can't you give it back to her?" whispered the nurse. "If it makes her feel so bad? Whatever it is—"

"It's just imagination," I said, almost sullenly. "I can't give her back something that doesn't exist."

Too young! I thought bitterly. Too young to learn that heart's desire is only play-like.

Of course the doctor found nothing wrong. Her mother dismissed the matter as a fainting spell and Sue-lynn came back to class next day, thin and listless, staring blankly out the window, her hands palm down on the desk. I swore by the pale hollow of her cheek that never, *never* again would I take any belief from anyone without replacing it with something better. What had I given Sue-lynn? What had she better than I had taken from her? How did I know but that her Anything Box was on purpose to tide her over rough spots in her life like this? And what now, now that I had taken it from her?

Well, after a time she began to work again, and later, to play. She came back to smiles, but not to laughter. She puttered along quite satisfactorily except that she was a candle blown out. The flame was gone wherever the brightness of belief goes. And she had no more sharing smiles for me, no overflowing love to bring to me. And her shoulder shrugged subtly away from my touch.

Then one day I suddenly realized that Sue-lynn was searching our class room. Stealthily, casually, day by day she was searching, covering every inch of the room. She went through every puzzle box, every lump of clay, every shelf and cupboard, every box and bag. Methodically she checked behind every row of books and in every child's desk until finally, after almost a week, she had been through everything in the place except my desk. Then she began to materialize suddenly at my elbow every time I opened a drawer. And her eyes would probe quickly and sharply before I slid it shut again. But if I tried to intercept her looks, they slid away and she had some legitimate errand that had brought her up to the vicinity of the desk.

She believes it again, I thought hopefully. She won't accept the fact that her Anything Box is gone. She wants it again.

But it *is* gone. I thought drearily. It's really-for-true gone.

My head was heavy from troubled sleep, and sorrow was a weariness in all my movements. Waiting is sometimes a burden almost too heavy to carry. While my children hummed happily over their fun-stuff, I brooded silently out the window until I managed a laugh at myself. It was a shaky laugh that threatened to dissolve into something else, so I brisked back to my desk.

As good a time as any to throw out useless things, I thought, and to see if I can find that colored chalk I put away so carefully. I plunged my hands into the wilderness of the bottom right-hand drawer of my desk. It was deep with a huge accumulation of anything—just anything—that might need a tempo-rary hiding place. I knelt to pull out left-over Jack Frost pictures, and a broken bean shooter, a chewed red ribbon, a roll of capgun ammunition, one striped sock, six Numbers papers, a rubber dagger, a copy of *The Gospel According to St. Luke,* a miniature coal shovel, patterns for jack-o'-lanterns, and a pink plastic pelican. I retrieved my Irish linen hankie I thought lost forever and Sojie's report card that he had told me solemnly had blown out of his hand and landed on a jet and broke the sound barrier so loud that it busted all to flitters. Under the welter of miscellany, I felt a squareness. Oh, happy! I thought, this *is* where I put the colored chalk! I cascaded papers off both sides of my lifting hands and shook the box free.

We were together again. Outside, the world was an enchanting wilderness of white, the wind shouting softly through the windows, tapping wet, white fingers against the warm light. Inside all the worry and waiting, the apartness and loneliness were over and forgotten, their hugeness dwindled by the comfort of a shoulder, the warmth of clasping hands—and nowhere, nowhere was the fear of parting, nowhere the need to do without again. This was the happy ending. This was—

This was Sue-lynn's Anything Box!

My racing heart slowed as the dream faded…and rushed again at the realization. I had it here! In my junk drawer! It had been here all the time!

I stood up shakily, concealing the invisible box in the flare of my skirts. I sat down and put the box carefully in the center of my desk, covering the top of it with my palms lest I should drown again in delight. I looked at Sue-lynn. She was finishing her fun paper, competently but unjoyously. Now would come her patient sitting with quiet hands until told to do something else.

Alpha would approve. And very possibly, I thought, Alpha would, for once in her limited life, be right. We may need "hallucinations" to keep us going—

all of us but the Alphas—but when we go so far as to try to force ourselves, physically, into the Neverneverland of heart's desire...

I remembered Sue-lynn's thin rigid body toppling doll-like off its chair. Out of her deep need she had found—or created? Who could tell?—something too dangerous for a child. I could so easily bring the brimming happiness back to her eyes—but at what a possible price!

No, I had a duty to protect Sue-lynn. Only maturity—the maturity born of the sorrow and loneliness that Sue-lynn was only beginning to know—could be trusted to use an Anything Box safely and wisely.

My heart thudded as I began to move my hands, letting the palms slip down from the top to shape the sides of—

I had moved them back again before I really saw, and I have now learned almost to forget that glimpse of what heart's desire is like when won at the cost of another's heart.

I sat there at the desk trembling and breathless, my palms moist, feeling as if I had been on a long journey away from the little schoolroom. Perhaps I had. Perhaps I had been shown all the kingdoms of the world in a moment of time.

"Sue-lynn," I called. "Will you come up here when you're through?"

She nodded unsmilingly and snipped off the last paper from the edge of Mistress Mary's dress. Without another look at her handiwork, she carried the scissors safely to the scissors box, crumpled the scraps of paper in her hand and came up to the waste basket by the desk.

"I have something for you, Sue-lynn," I said, uncovering the box.

Her eyes dropped to the desk top. She looked indifferently up at me. "I did my fun paper already."

"Did you like it?"

"Yes." It was a flat lie.

"Good," I lied right back. "But look here." I squared my hands around the Anything Box.

She took a deep breath and the whole of her little body stiffened.

"I found it," I said hastily, fearing anger. "I found it in the bottom drawer."

She leaned her chest against my desk, her hands caught tightly between, her eyes intent on the box, her face white with the aching want you see on children's faces pressed to Christmas windows.

"Can I have it?" she whispered.

"It's yours," I said, holding it out.

Still she leaned against her hands her eyes searching my face.

"Can I have it?" she asked again.

"Yes!" I was impatient with this anticlimax. "But—"

Her eyes flickered. She had sensed my reservation before I had. "But you must never try to get into it again."

"OK," she said, the word coming out on a long relieved sigh. "OK, Teacher."

She took the box and tucked it lovingly into her small pocket. She turned from the desk and started back to her table. My mouth quirked with a small smile. It seemed to me that everything about her had suddenly turned upwards—even the ends of her straight taffy-colored hair. The subtle flame about her that made her Sue-lynn was there again. She scarcely touched the floor as she walked.

I sighed heavily and traced on the desk top with my finger a probable size for an Anything Box. What would Sue-lynn choose to see first? How like a drink after a drought it would seem to her.

I was startled as a small figure materialized at my elbow. It was Sue-lynn, her fingers carefully squared before her.

"Teacher," she said softly, all the flat emptiness gone from her voice. "Any time you want to take my Anything Box, you just say so."

I groped through my astonishment and incredulity for words. She couldn't possibly have had time to look into the Box yet.

"Why, thank you, Sue-lynn," I managed. "Thanks a lot. I would like very much to borrow it some time."

"Would you like it now?" she asked, proffering it.

"No, thank you," I said, around the lump in my throat. "I've had a turn already. You go ahead."

"OK," she murmured. Then—"Teacher?"

"Yes?"

Shyly she leaned against me, her cheek on my shoulder. She looked up at me with her warm, unshuttered eyes, then both arms were suddenly around my neck in a brief awkward embrace.

"Watch out!" I whispered laughing into the collar of her blue dress. "You'll lose it again!"

"No I won't," she laughed back, patting the flat pocket of her dress. "Not ever, ever again!"

The Prize of Peril (1958)

ROBERT SHECKLEY

ROBERT SHECKLEY (1928–2005) is the author of about two dozen novels and scores of short stories, including *The Status Civilization*, *The 10th Victim*, and *Mindswap*. Much of his work is comic or satiric in tone; he gave us the notion that "I must not lesner-ize." Many people believe that Sheckley's stories paved the way for Douglas Adams's *Hitchhiker's Guide to the Galaxy*.

Sheckley wrote for television and radio in the 1950s, and perhaps doing so inspired "The Prize of Peril." This story was adapted for film as *Le Prix du Danger*, and there was also an earlier German television movie version of it.

R AEDER LIFTED HIS head cautiously above the window sill. He saw the fire escape, and below it a narrow alley. There was a weather-beaten baby carriage in the alley, and three garbage cans. As he watched, a black-sleeved arm moved from behind the furthest can, with something shiny in its fist. Raeder ducked down. A bullet smashed through the window above his head and punctured the ceiling, showering him with plaster.

Now he knew about the alley. It was guarded, just like the door.

He lay at full length on the cracked linoleum, staring at the bullet hole in the ceiling, listening to the sounds outside the door. He was a tall man with bloodshot eyes and a two-day stubble. Grime and fatigue had etched lines into his face. Fear had touched his features, tightening a muscle here and twitching a nerve there. The results were startling. His face had character now, for it was reshaped by the expectation of death.

There was a gunman in the alley and two on the stairs. He was trapped. He was dead.

Sure, Raeder thought, he still moved and breathed; but that was only because of death's inefficiency. Death would take care of him in a few minutes.

Death would poke holes in his face and body, artistically dab his clothes with blood, arrange his limbs in some grotesque position of the graveyard ballet...

Raeder bit his lip sharply. He wanted to live. There had to be a way.

He rolled onto his stomach and surveyed the dingy cold-water apartment into which the killers had driven him. It was a perfect little one-room coffin. It had a door, which was watched, and a fire escape, which was watched. And it had a tiny windowless bathroom.

He crawled to the bathroom and stood up. There was a ragged hole in the ceiling, almost four inches wide. If he could enlarge it, crawl through into the apartment above...

He heard a muffled thud. The killers were impatient. They were beginning to break down the door.

He studied the hole in the ceiling. No use even considering it. He could never enlarge it in time.

They were smashing against the door, grunting each time they struck. Soon the lock would tear out, or the hinges would pull out of the rotting wood. The door would go down, and the two blank-faced men would enter, dusting off their jackets...

But surely someone would help him! He took the tiny television set from his pocket. The picture was blurred, and he didn't bother to adjust it. The audio was clear and precise.

He listened to the well-modulated voice of Mike Terry addressing his vast audience.

"...terrible spot," Terry was saying. *"Yes, folks, Jim Raeder is in a truly terrible predicament. He had been hiding, you'll remember, in a third-rate Broadway hotel under an assumed name. It seemed safe enough. But the bellhop recognized him, and gave that information to the Thompson gang."*

The door creaked under repeated blows. Raeder clutched the little television set and listened.

"Jim Raeder just managed to escape from the hotel! Closely pursued, he entered a brownstone at one fifty-six West End Avenue. His intention was to go over the roofs. And it might have worked, folks, it just might have worked. But the roof door was locked. It looked like the end.... But Raeder found that apartment seven was unoccupied and unlocked. He entered..."

Terry paused for emphasis, then cried: *"—and now he's trapped there, trapped like a rat in a cage! The Thompson gang is breaking down the door! The fire escape is guarded! Our camera crew, situated in a nearby building, is giving you a close-up now. Look, folks, just look! Is there no hope for Jim Raeder?"*

Is there no hope, Raeder silently echoed, perspiration pouring from him as he stood in the dark, stifling little bathroom, listening to the steady thud against the door.

"Wait a minute!" Mike Terry cried. *"Hang on, Jim Raeder, hang on a little longer. Perhaps there is hope! I have an urgent call from one of our viewers, a call on the Good Samaritan Line! Here's someone who thinks he can help you, Jim. Are you listening, Jim Raeder?"*

Raeder waited, and heard the hinges tearing out of rotten wood.

"Go right ahead, sir," said Mike Terry. *"What is your name, sir?"*

"Er-Felix Bartholemow."

"Don't be nervous, Mr. Bartholemow. Go right ahead."

"Well, OK. Mr. Raeder," said an old man's shaking voice, *"I used to live at one five six West End Avenue. Same apartment you're trapped in, Mr. Raeder—fact! Look, that bathroom has got a window, Mr. Raeder. It's been painted over, but it has got a—"*

Raeder pushed the television set into his pocket. He located the outlines of the window and kicked. Glass shattered, and daylight poured startlingly in. He cleared the jagged sill and quickly peered down.

Below was a long drop to a concrete courtyard.

The hinges tore free. He heard the door opening. Quickly Raeder climbed through the window, hung by his fingertips for a moment, and dropped.

The shock was stunning. Groggily he stood up. A face appeared at the bathroom window.

"Tough luck," said the man, leaning out and taking careful aim with a snub-nosed .38.

At that moment a smoke bomb exploded inside the bathroom.

The killer's shot went wide. He turned, cursing. More smoke bombs burst in the courtyard, obscuring Raeder's figure.

He could hear Mike Terry's frenzied voice over the TV set in his pocket. *"Now run for it!"* Terry was screaming. *"Run, Jim Raeder, run for your life. Run* now, *while the killers' eyes are filled with smoke. And thank Good Samaritan Sarah Winters, of three four one two Edgar Street, Brockton, Mass, for donating five smoke bombs and employing the services of a man to throw them!"*

In a quieter voice, Terry continued: *"You've saved a man's life today, Mrs. Winters. Would you tell our audience how it—"*

Raeder wasn't able to hear any more. He was running through the smoke-filled courtyard, past clothes lines, into the open street.

He walked down 63rd Street, slouching to minimize his height, staggering slightly from exertion, dizzy from lack of food and sleep.

"Hey you!"

Raeder turned. A middle-aged woman was sitting on the steps of a brownstone, frowning at him.

"You're Raeder, aren't you? The one they're trying to kill?"

Raeder started to walk away.

"Come inside here, Raeder," the woman said.

Perhaps it was a trap. But Raeder knew that he had to depend upon the generosity and good-heartedness of the people. He was their representative, a projection of themselves, an average guy in trouble. Without them, he was lost. With them, nothing could harm him.

Trust in the people, Mike Terry had told him. They'll never let you down.

He followed the woman into her parlor. She told him to sit down and left the room, returning almost immediately with a plate of stew. She stood watching him while he ate, as one would watch an ape in the zoo eat peanuts.

Two children came out of the kitchen and stared at him. Three over-alled men came out of the bedroom and focused a television camera on him. There was a big television set in the parlor. As he gulped his food, Raeder watched the image of Mike Terry, and listened to the man's strong, sincere, worried voice.

"*There he is, folks,*" Terry was saying. "*There's Jim Raeder now, eating his first square meal in two days. Our camera crews have really been working to cover this for you! Thanks, boys.... Folks, Jim Raeder has been given a brief sanctuary by Mrs. Velma O'Dell, of three forty-three Sixty-Third Street. Thank you, Good Samaritan O'Dell. It's really wonderful, how people from all walks of life have taken Jim Raeder to their hearts!*"

"You better hurry," Mrs. O'Dell said.

"Yes ma'am," Raeder said.

"I don't want no gunplay in my apartment."

"I'm almost finished, ma'am."

One of the children asked, "Aren't they going to kill him?"

"Shut up," said Mrs. O'Dell.

"Yes, Jim," chanted Mike Terry, "you'd better hurry. Your killers aren't far behind. They aren't stupid men, Jim. Vicious, warped, insane—yes! But not stupid. They're following a trail of blood—blood from your torn hand, Jim!"

Raeder hadn't realized until now that he'd cut his hand on the window sill.

"Here, I'll bandage that," Mrs. O'Dell said. Raeder stood up and let her bandage his hand. Then she gave him a brown jacket and a gray slouch hat.

"My husband's stuff," she said.

"He has a disguise, folks!" Mike Terry cried delightedly. "This is something new! A disguise! With seven hours to go until he's safe!"

"Now get out of here," Mrs. O'Dell said.

"I'm going, ma'am," Raeder said. "Thanks."

"I think you're stupid," she said. "I think you're stupid to be involved in this."

"Yes ma'am."

"It just isn't worth it."

Raeder thanked her and left. He walked to Broadway, caught a subway to 59th Street, then an uptown local to 86th. There he bought a newspaper and changed for the Manhasset thru-express.

He glanced at his watch. He had six and a half hours to go.

The subway roared under Manhattan. Raeder dozed, his bandaged hand concealed under the newspaper, the hat pulled over his face. Had he been recognized yet? Had he shaken the Thompson gang? Or was someone telephoning them now?

Dreamily he wondered if he had escaped death. Or was he still a cleverly animated corpse, moving around because of death's inefficiency? (My dear, death is so *laggard* these days! Jim Raeder walked about for hours after he died, and actually answered people's *questions* before he could be decently buried!)

Raeder's eyes snapped open. He had dreamed something…unpleasant. He couldn't remember what.

He closed his eyes again and remembered, with mild astonishment, a time when he had been in no trouble.

That was two years ago. He had been a big, pleasant young man working as a truck driver's helper. He had no talents. He was too modest to have dreams.

The tight-faced little truck driver had the dreams for him. "Why not try for a television show, Jim? I would if I had your looks. They like nice average guys with nothing much on the ball. As contestants. Everybody likes guys like that. Why not look into it?"

So he had looked into it. The owner of the local television store had explained it further.

"You see, Jim, the public is sick of highly trained athletes with their trick reflexes and their professional courage. Who can feel for guys like that? Who can identify? People want to watch exciting things, sure. But not when some joker is making it his business for fifty thousand a year. That's why organized sports are in a slump. That's why the thrill shows are booming."

"I see," said Raeder.

"Six years ago, Jim, Congress passed the Voluntary Suicide Act. Those old senators talked a lot about free will and self-determinism at the time. But that's all crap. You know what the Act really means? It means that amateurs can risk their lives for the big loot, not just professionals. In the old days you had to be a professional boxer or footballer or hockey player if you wanted your brains beaten out legally for money. But now that opportunity is open to ordinary people like you, Jim."

"I see," Raeder said again.

"It's a marvelous opportunity. Take you. You're no better than anyone, Jim. Anything you can do, anyone can do. You're *average*. I think the thrill shows would go for you."

Raeder permitted himself to dream. Television shows looked like a sure road to riches for a pleasant young fellow with no particular talent or training. He wrote a letter to a show called *Hazard* and enclosed a photograph of himself.

Hazard was interested in him. The JBC network investigated, and found that he was average enough to satisfy the wariest viewer. His parentage and affiliations were checked. At last he was summoned to New York, and interviewed by Mr. Moulian.

Moulian was dark and intense, and chewed gum as he talked. "You'll do," he snapped. "But not for *Hazard*. You'll appear on *Spills*. It's a half-hour daytime show on Channel Three."

"Gee," said Raeder.

"Don't thank me. There's a thousand dollars if you win or place second, and a consolation prize of a hundred dollars if you lose. But that's not important."

"No sir."

"*Spills* is a *little* show. The JBC network uses it as a testing ground. First-

and second-place winners on *Spills* move on to *Emergency*. The prizes are much bigger on *Emergency*."

"I know they are, sir."

"And if you do well on *Emergency* there are the first-class thrill shows, like *Hazard* and *Underwater Perils*, with their nationwide coverage and enormous prizes. And then comes the really big time. How far you go is up to you."

"I'll do my best, sir," Raeder said.

Moulian stopped chewing gum for a moment and said, almost reverently, "You can do it, Jim. Just remember. You're *the people,* and *the people* can do anything."

The way he said it made Raeder feel momentarily sorry for Mr. Moulian, who was dark and frizzy-haired and pop-eyed, and was obviously not *the people*.

They shook hands. Then Raeder signed a paper absolving the JBC of all responsibility should he lose his life, limbs or reason during the contest. And he signed another paper exercising his rights under the Voluntary Suicide Act. The law required this, and it was a mere formality.

In three weeks, he appeared on *Spills*.

The program followed the classic form of the automobile race. Untrained drivers climbed into powerful American and European competition cars and raced over a murderous twenty-mile course. Raeder was shaking with fear as he slid his big Maserati into the wrong gear and took off.

The race was a screaming, tire-burning nightmare. Raeder stayed back, letting the early leaders smash themselves up on the counter-banked hairpin turns. He crept into third place when a Jaguar in front of him swerved against an Alfa-Romeo, and the two cars roared into a plowed field. Raeder gunned for second place on the last three miles, but couldn't find passing room. An S-curve almost took him, but he fought the car back on the road, still holding third. Then the lead driver broke a crankshaft in the final fifty yards, and Jim ended in second place.

He was now a thousand dollars ahead. He received four fan letters, and a lady in Oshkosh sent him a pair of argyles. He was invited to appear on *Emergency*.

Unlike the others, *Emergency* was not a competition-type program. It stressed individual initiative. For the show, Raeder was knocked out with a non-habit-forming narcotic. He awoke in the cockpit of a small airplane, cruising on autopilot at ten thousand feet. His fuel gauge showed nearly empty. He had no parachute. He was supposed to land the plane.

Of course, he had never flown before.

He experimented gingerly with the controls, remembering that last week's participant had recovered consciousness in a submarine, had opened the wrong valve, and had drowned.

Thousands of viewers watched spellbound as this average man, a man just like themselves, struggled with the situation just as they would do. Jim Raeder was *them*. Anything he could do, they could do. He was representative of *the people*.

Raeder managed to bring the ship down in some semblance of a landing. He flipped over a few times, but his seat belt held. And the engine, contrary to expectation, did not burst into flames.

He staggered out with two broken ribs, three thousand dollars, and a chance, when he healed, to appear on *Torero*.

At last, a first-class thrill show!

Torero paid ten thousand dollars. All you had to do was kill a black Miura bull with a sword, just like a real trained matador.

The fight was held in Madrid, since bullfighting was still illegal in the United States. It was nationally televised.

Raeder had a good cuadrilla. They liked the big, slow-moving American. The picadors really leaned into their lances, trying to slow the bull for him. The banderilleros tried to run the beast off his feet before driving in their banderillas. And the second matador, a mournful man from Algeciras, almost broke the bull's neck with fancy capework.

But when all was said and done it was Jim Raeder on the sand, a red muleta clumsily gripped in his left hand, a sword in his right, facing a ton of black, blood-streaked, wide-horned bull.

Someone was shouting, "Try for the lung, *hombre*. Don't be a hero, stick him in the lung." But Jim only knew what the technical adviser in New York had told him: Aim with the sword and go in over the horns.

Over he went. The sword bounced off bone, and the bull tossed him over its back. He stood up, miraculously ungouged, took another sword and went over the horns again with his eyes closed. The god who protects children and fools must have been watching, for the sword slid in like a needle through butter, and the bull looked startled, stared at him unbelievingly, and dropped like a deflated balloon.

They paid him ten thousand dollars, and his broken collar bone healed in practically no time. He received twenty-three fan letters, including a passionate invitation from a girl in Atlantic City, which he ignored. And they asked him if he wanted to appear on another show.

He had lost some of his innocence. He was now fully aware that he had been almost killed for pocket money. The big loot lay ahead. Now he wanted to be almost killed for something worthwhile.

So he appeared on *Underwater Perils,* sponsored by Fairlady's Soap. In face mask, respirator, weighted belt, flippers and knife, he slipped into the warm waters of the Caribbean with four other contestants, followed by a cage-protected camera crew. The idea was to locate and bring up a treasure which the sponsor had hidden there.

Mask diving isn't especially hazardous. But the sponsor had added some frills for public interest. The area was sown with giant clams, moray eels, sharks of several species, giant octopuses, poison coral, and other dangers of the deep.

It was a stirring contest. A man from Florida found the treasure in a deep crevice, but a moray eel found him. Another diver took the treasure, and a shark took him. The brilliant blue-green water became cloudy with blood, which photographed well on color TV. The treasure slipped to the bottom and Raeder plunged after it, popping an eardrum in the process. He plucked it from the coral, jettisoned his weighted belt and made for the surface. Thirty feet from the top he had to fight another diver for the treasure.

They feinted back and forth with their knives. The man struck, slashing Raeder across the chest. But Raeder, with the self-possession of an old contestant, dropped his knife and tore the man's respirator out of his mouth.

That did it. Raeder surfaced, and presented the treasure at the standby boat. It turned out to be a package of Fairlady's Soap—"The Greatest Treasure of All."

That netted him twenty-two thousand dollars in cash and prizes, and three hundred and eight fan letters, and an interesting proposition from a girl in Macon, which he seriously considered. He received free hospitalization for his knife slash and burst eardrum, and injections for coral infection.

But best of all, he was invited to appear on the biggest of the thrill shows. *The Prize of Peril.*

And that was when the real trouble began....

The subway came to a stop, jolting him out of his reverie. Raeder pushed back his hat and observed, across the aisle, a man staring at him and whispering to a stout woman. Had they recognized him?

He stood up as soon as the doors opened, and glanced at his watch. He had five hours to go.

At the Manhasset station he stepped into a taxi and told the driver to take him to New Salem.

"New Salem?" the driver asked, looking at him in the rear-vision mirror.

"That's right."

The driver snapped on his radio. "Fare to New Salem. Yep, that's right. *New Salem.*"

They drove off. Raeder frowned, wondering if it had been a signal. It was perfectly usual for taxi drivers to report to their dispatchers, of course. But something about the man's voice…

"Let me off here," Raeder said.

He paid the driver and began walking down a narrow country road that curved through sparse woods. The trees were too small and too widely separated for shelter. Raeder walked on, looking for a place to hide.

There was a heavy truck approaching. He kept on walking, pulling his hat low on his forehead. But as the truck drew near, he heard a voice from the television set in his pocket. It cried, *"Watch out!"*

He flung himself into the ditch. The truck careened past, narrowly missing him, and screeched to a stop. The driver was shouting, "There he goes! Shoot, Harry, shoot!"

Bullets clipped leaves from the trees as Raeder sprinted into the woods.

"It's happened again!" Mike Terry was saying, his voice high-pitched with excitement. *"I'm afraid Jim Raeder let himself be lulled into a false sense of security. You can't do that, Jim! Not with your* life *at stake! Not with* killers *pursuing you! Be careful, Jim, you still have four and a half hours to go!"*

The driver was saying, "Claude, Harry, go around with the truck. We got him boxed."

"They've got you boxed, Jim Raeder!" Mike Terry cried. *"But they haven't got you yet! And you can thank Good Samaritan Susy Peters of twelve Elm Street, South Orange, New Jersey, for that warning shout just when the truck was bearing down on you. We'll have little Susy on stage in just a moment.… Look, folks, our studio helicopter has arrived on the scene. Now you can see Jim Raeder running, and the killers pursuing, surrounding him…"*

Raeder ran through a hundred yards of woods and found himself on a concrete highway, with open woods beyond. One of the killers was trotting through the woods behind him. The truck had driven to a connecting road, and was now a mile away, coming toward him.

A car was approaching from the other direction. Raeder ran into the highway, waving frantically. The car came to a stop.

"Hurry!" cried the blond young woman driving it.

Raeder dived in. The woman made a U-turn on the highway. A bullet smashed through the windshield. She stamped on the accelerator, almost running down the lone killer who stood in the way.

The car surged away before the truck was within firing range.

Raeder leaned back and shut his eyes tightly. The woman concentrated on her driving, watching for the truck in her rear-vision mirror.

"It's happened again!" cried Mike Terry, his voice ecstatic. *"Jim Raeder has been plucked again from the jaws of death, thanks to Good Samaritan Janice Morrow of four three three Lexington Avenue, New York City. Did you ever see anything like it, folks? The way Miss Morrow drove through a fusillade of bullets and plucked Jim Raeder from the mouth of doom! Later we'll interview Miss Morrow and get her reactions. Now, while Jim Raeder speeds away—perhaps to safety, perhaps to further peril—we'll have a short announcement from our sponsor. Don't go away! Jim's got four hours and ten minutes until he's safe. Anything* can *happen!"*

"OK," the girl said. "We're off the air now. Raeder, what in the hell is the matter with you?"

"Eh?" Raeder asked. The girl was in her early twenties. She looked efficient, attractive, untouchable. Raeder noticed that she had good features, a trim figure. And he noticed that she seemed angry.

"Miss," he said, "I don't know how to thank you for—"

"Talk straight," Janice Morrow said. "I'm no Good Samaritan. I'm employed by the JBC network."

"So the program had me rescued!"

"Cleverly reasoned," she said.

"But why?"

"Look, this is an expensive show, Raeder. We have to turn in a good performance. If our rating slips, we'll all be in the street selling candy apples. And you aren't cooperating."

"What? Why?"

"Because you're terrible," the girl said bitterly. "You're a flop, a fiasco. Are you trying to commit suicide? Haven't you learned *anything* about survival?"

"I'm doing the best I can."

"The Thompsons could have had you a dozen times by now. We told them to take it easy, stretch it out. But it's like shooting a clay pigeon six feet tall. The Thompsons are cooperating, but they can only fake so far. If I hadn't come along, they'd have had to kill you—air-time or not."

Raeder stared at her, wondering how such a pretty girl could talk that way. She glanced at him, then quickly looked back to the road.

"Don't give me that look!" she said. "You chose to risk your life for money, buster. And plenty of money! You knew the score. Don't act like some innocent little grocer who finds the nasty hoods are after him. That's a different plot."

"I know," Raeder said.

"If you can't live well, at least try to die well."

"You don't mean that," Raeder said.

"Don't be too sure.... You've got three hours and forty minutes until the end of the show. If you can stay alive, fine. The boodle's yours. But if you can't at least try to give them a run for the money."

Raeder nodded, staring intently at her.

"In a few moments we're back on the air. I develop engine trouble, let you off. The Thompsons go all out now. They kill you when and if they can, as soon as they can. Understand?"

"Yes," Raeder said. "If I make it, can I see you some time?"

She bit her lip angrily. "Are you trying to kid me?"

"No. I'd like to see you again. May I?"

She looked at him curiously. "I don't know. Forget it. We're almost on. I think your best bet is the woods to the right. Ready?"

"Yes. Where can I get in touch with you? Afterward, I mean."

"Oh, Raeder, you aren't paying attention. Go through the woods until you find a washed-out ravine. It isn't much, but it'll give you some cover."

"Where can I get in touch with you?" Raeder asked again.

"I'm in the Manhattan telephone book." She stopped the car. "OK, Raeder, start running."

He opened the door.

"Wait." She leaned over and kissed him on the lips. "Good luck, you idiot. Call me if you make it."

And then he was on foot, running into the woods.

He ran through birch and pine, past an occasional split-level house with staring faces at the big picture window. Some occupant of those houses must have called the gang, for they were close behind him when he reached the washed-out little ravine. Those quiet, mannerly, law-abiding people didn't want him to escape, Raeder thought sadly. They wanted to see a killing. Or perhaps they wanted to see him *narrowly escape* a killing.

It came to the same thing, really.

He entered the ravine, burrowed into the thick underbrush and lay still. The Thompsons appeared on both ridges, moving slowly, watching for any movement. Raeder held his breath as they came parallel to him.

He heard the quick explosion of a revolver. But the killer had only shot a squirrel. It squirmed for a moment, then lay still.

Lying in the underbrush, Raeder heard the studio helicopter overhead. He wondered if any cameras were focused on him. It was possible. And if someone were watching, perhaps some Good Samaritan would help.

So looking upward, toward the helicopter, Raeder arranged his face in a reverent expression, clasped his hands and prayed. He prayed silently, for the audience didn't like religious ostentation. But his lips moved. That was every man's privilege.

And a real prayer was on his lips. Once, a lipreader in the audience had detected a fugitive *pretending* to pray, but actually just reciting multiplication tables. No help for that man!

Raeder finished his prayer. Glancing at his watch, he saw that he had nearly two hours to go.

And he didn't want to die! It wasn't worth it, no matter how much they paid! He must have been crazy, absolutely insane to agree to such a thing....

But he knew that wasn't true. And he remembered just how sane he had been.

One week ago he had been on *The Prize of Peril* stage, blinking in the spotlight, and Mike Terry had shaken his hand.

"Now Mr. Raeder," Terry had said solemnly, "do you understand the rules of the game you are about to play?"

Raeder nodded.

"If you accept, Jim Raeder, you will be a *hunted man* for a week. *Killers* will follow you, Jim. *Trained* killers, men wanted by the law for other crimes, granted immunity for this single killing under the Voluntary Suicide Act. They will be trying to kill *you,* Jim. Do you understand?"

"I understand," Raeder said. He also understood the two hundred thousand dollars he would receive if he could live out the week.

"I ask you again, Jim Raeder. We force no man to play for stakes of death."

"I want to play," Raeder said.

Mike Terry turned to the audience. "Ladies and gentlemen, I have here a copy of an exhaustive psychological test which an impartial psychological testing firm made on Jim Raeder at our request. Copies will be sent to anyone who desires them for twenty-five cents to cover the cost of mailing. The test shows that Jim Raeder is sane, well-balanced, and fully responsible in every way." He turned to Raeder.

"Do you still want to enter the contest, Jim?"

"Yes, I do."

"Very well!" cried Mike Terry. "Jim Raeder, meet your would-be killers!"

The Thompson gang moved on stage, booed by the audience.

"Look at them, folks," said Mike Terry, with undisguised contempt. "Just look at them! Antisocial, thoroughly vicious, completely amoral. These men have no code but the criminal's warped code, no honor but the honor of the cowardly hired killer. They are doomed men, doomed by our society which will not sanction their activities for long, fated to an early and unglamorous death."

The audience shouted enthusiastically.

"What have you to say, Claude Thompson?" Terry asked.

Claude, the spokesman of the Thompsons, stepped up to the microphone. He was a thin, clean-shaven man, conservatively dressed.

"I figure," Claude Thompson said hoarsely, "I figure we're no worse than anybody. I mean, like soldiers in a war, *they* kill. And look at the graft in government, and the unions. Everybody's got their graft."

That was Thompson's tenuous code. But how quickly, with what precision, Mike Terry destroyed the killer's rationalizations! Terry's questions pierced straight to the filthy soul of the man.

At the end of the interview Claude Thompson was perspiring, mopping his face with a silk handkerchief and casting quick glances at his men.

Mike Terry put a hand on Raeder's shoulder. "Here is the man who has agreed to become your victim—if you can catch him."

"We'll catch him," Thompson said, his confidence returning.

"Don't be too sure," said Terry. "Jim Raeder has fought wild bulls—now he battles jackals. He's an average man. He's *the people*—who mean ultimate doom to you and your kind."

"We'll get him," Thompson said.

"And one thing more," Terry said, very softly. "Jim Raeder does not stand alone. The folks of America are for him. Good Samaritans from all corners of our great nation stand ready to assist him. Unarmed, defenseless, Jim Raeder can count on the aid and goodheartedness of *the people,* whose representative he is. So don't be too sure, Claude Thompson! The average men are for Jim Raeder—and there are a lot of average men!"

Raeder thought about it, lying motionless in the underbrush. Yes, *the people* had helped him. But they had helped the killers, too.

A tremor ran through him. He had chosen, he reminded himself. He alone was responsible. The psychological test had proved that.

And yet, how responsible were the psychologists who had given him the test? How responsible was Mike Terry for offering a poor man so much money? Society had woven the noose and put it around his neck, and he was hanging himself with it, and calling it free will.

Whose fault?

"Aha!" someone cried.

Raeder looked up and saw a portly man standing near him. The man wore a loud tweed jacket. He had binoculars around his neck, and a cane in his hand.

"Mister," Raeder whispered, "please don't tell—"

"Hi!" shouted the portly man, pointing at Raeder with his cane. "Here he is!"

A madman, thought Raeder. The damned fool must think he's playing Hare and Hounds.

"Right over here!" the man screamed.

Cursing, Raeder sprang to his feet and began running. He came out of the ravine and saw a white building in the distance. He turned toward it. Behind him he could still hear the man.

"That way, over there. Look, you fools, can't you see him yet?"

The killers were shooting again. Raeder ran, stumbling over uneven ground, past three children playing in a tree house.

"Here he is!" the children screamed. "Here he is!"

Raeder groaned and ran on. He reached the steps of the building, and saw that it was a church.

As he opened the door, a bullet struck him behind the right kneecap.

He fell, and crawled inside the church.

The television set in his pocket was saying, *"What a finish, folks, what a finish! Raeder's been hit! He's been hit, folks, he's crawling now, he's in pain, but he hasn't given up! Not Jim Raeder!"*

Raeder lay in the aisle near the altar. He could hear a child's eager voice saying, "He went in there, Mr. Thompson. Hurry, you can still catch him!"

Wasn't a church considered a sanctuary, Raeder wondered.

Then the door was flung open, and Raeder realized that the custom was no longer observed. He gathered himself together and crawled past the altar, out the back door of the church.

He was in an old graveyard. He crawled past crosses and stars, past slabs of marble and granite, past stone tombs and rude wooden markers. A bullet exploded on a tombstone near his head, showering him with fragments. He crawled to the edge of an open grave.

They had deceived him, he thought. All of those nice average normal people. Hadn't they said he was their representative? Hadn't they sworn to protect their own? But no, they loathed him. Why hadn't he seen it? Their hero was the cold, blank-eyed gunman, Thompson, Capone, Billy the Kid, Young Lochinvar, El Cid, Cuchulain, the man without human hopes or fears. They worshiped him, that dead, implacable robot gunman, and lusted to feel his foot in their face.

Raeder tried to move, and slid helplessly into the open grave.

He lay on his back, looking at the blue sky. Presently a black silhouette loomed above him, blotting out the sky. Metal twinkled. The silhouette slowly took aim.

And Raeder gave up all hope forever.

"WAIT, THOMPSON!" roared the amplified voice of Mike Terry.

The revolver wavered.

"It is one second past five o'clock! The week is up! JIM RAEDER HAS WON!"

There was a pandemonium of cheering from the studio audience.

The Thompson gang, gathered around the grave, looked sullen.

"He's won, friends, he's won!" Mike Terry cried. *"Look, look on your screen! The police have arrived, they're taking the Thompsons away from their victim— the victim they could not kill. And all this is thanks to* you, *Good Samaritans of America. Look folks, tender hands are lifting Jim Raeder from the open grave that was his final refuge. Good Samaritan Janice Morrow is there. Could this be the beginning of a romance? Jim seems to have fainted, friends, they're giving him a stimulant. He's won two hundred thousand dollars! Now we'll have a few words from Jim Raeder!"*

There was a short silence.

"That's odd," said Mike Terry. *"Folks, I'm afraid we can't hear from Jim just now. The doctors are examining him. Just one moment..."*

There was a silence. Mike Terry wiped his forehead and smiled.

"It's the strain, folks, the terrible strain. The doctor tells me... Well, folks, Jim Raeder is temporarily not himself. But it's only temporary! JBC is hiring the best psychiatrists and psychoanalysts in the country. We're going to do everything humanly possible for this gallant boy. And entirely at our own expense."

Mike Terry glanced at the studio clock. *"Well, it's about time to sign off, folks. Watch for the announcement of our next great thrill show. And don't worry, I'm sure that very soon we'll have Jim Raeder back with us."*

Mike Terry smiled, and winked at the audience. *"He's bound to get well, friends. After all, we're all pulling for him!"*

"'—All You Zombies—'" (1959)

ROBERT A. HEINLEIN

ROBERT A. HEINLEIN (1907–1988) was one of science fiction's giants. His books include *Starship Troopers*, *The Door into Summer*, *The Man Who Sold the Moon*, *The Puppet Masters*, and *Stranger in a Strange Land*. He was the first writer honored with the Grand Master Award by the Science Fiction Writers of America. Volume two of William Patterson's biography of Heinlein is due to be published soon.

"'—All You Zombies—'" remains a classic on the theme of time travel and its paradoxes. This story has recently been adapted into a feature film entitled *Predestination*.

2217 Time Zone V (EST) 7 Nov 1970 NYC-"Pop's Place": I was polishing a brandy snifter when the Unmarried Mother came in. I noted the time—10:17 p.m. zone five, or eastern time, November 7th, 1970. Temporal agents always notice time & date; we must.

The Unmarried Mother was a man twenty-five years old, no taller than I am, childish features and a touchy temper. I didn't like his looks—I never had—but he was a lad I was here to recruit, he was my boy. I gave him my best barkeep's smile.

Maybe I'm too critical. He wasn't swish; his nickname came from what he always said when some nosy type asked him his line: "I'm an unmarried mother." If he felt less than murderous he would add: "—at four cents a word. I write confession stories."

If he felt nasty, he would wait for somebody to make something of it. He had a lethal style of infighting, like a female cop—one reason I wanted him. Not the only one.

He had a load on and his face showed that he despised people more than usual. Silently I poured a double shot of Old Underwear and left the bottle. He drank it, poured another.

I wiped the bar top. "How's the 'Unmarried Mother' racket?"

His fingers tightened on the glass and he seemed about to throw it at me; I felt for the sap under the bar. In temporal manipulation you try to figure everything, but there are so many factors that you never take needless risks.

I saw him relax that tiny amount they teach you to watch for in the Bureau's training school. "Sorry," I said. "Just asking, 'How's business?' Make it 'How's the weather?'"

He looked sour. "Business is okay. I write 'em, they print 'em, I eat."

I poured myself one, leaned toward him. "Matter of fact," I said, "you write a nice stick—I've sampled a few. You have an amazingly sure touch with the woman's angle."

It was a slip I had to risk; he never admitted what pen-names he used. But he was boiled enough to pick up only the last: "'Woman's angle'!" he repeated with a snort. "Yeah, I know the woman's angle. I should."

"So?" I said doubtfully. "Sisters?"

"No. You wouldn't believe me if I told you."

"Now, now," I answered mildly, "bartenders and psychiatrists learn that nothing is stranger than truth. Why, son, if you heard the stories I do—well, you'd make yourself rich. Incredible."

"You don't know what 'incredible' means!"

"So? Nothing astonishes me. I've always heard worse."

He snorted again. "Want to bet the rest of the bottle?"

"I'll bet a full bottle." I placed one on the bar.

"Well—" I signaled my other bartender to handle the trade. We were at the far end, a single-stool space that I kept private by loading the bar top by it with jars of pickled eggs and other clutter. A few were at the other end watching the fights and somebody was playing the juke box—private as a bed where we were.

"Okay," he began, "to start with, I'm a bastard."

"No distinction around here," I said.

"I mean it," he snapped, "My parents weren't married."

"Still no distinction," I insisted. "Neither were mine."

"When—" He stopped, gave me the first warm look I ever saw on him. "You mean that?"

"I do. A one-hundred-percent bastard. In fact," I added, "no one in my family ever marries. All bastards."

"Oh, that." I showed it to him. "It just looks like a wedding ring; I wear it to keep women off." It is an antique I bought in 1985 from a fellow operative—he had fetched it from pre-Christian Crete. "The Worm Ouroboros…the World Snake that eats its own tail, forever without end. A symbol of the Great Paradox."

He barely glanced at it. "If you're really a bastard, you know how it feels. When I was a little girl—"

"Wups!" I said. "Did I hear you correctly?"

"Who's telling this story? When I was a little girl—Look, ever hear of Christine Jorgensen? Or Roberta Cowell?"

"Uh, sex-change cases? You're trying to tell me—"

"Don't interrupt or swelp me, I won't talk. I was a foundling, left at an orphanage in Cleveland in 1945 when I was a month old. When I was a little girl, I envied kids with parents. Then, when I learned about sex—and, believe me, Pop, you learn fast in an orphanage—"

"I know."

"—I made a solemn vow that any kid of mine would have both a pop and a mom. It kept me 'pure,' quite a feat in that vicinity—I had to learn to fight to manage it. Then I got older and realized I stood darn little chance of getting married—for the same reason I hadn't been adopted." He scowled. "I was horse-faced and buck-toothed, flat-chested and straight-haired."

"You don't look any worse than I do."

"Who cares how a barkeep looks? Or a writer? But people wanting to adopt pick little blue-eyed golden-haired morons. Later on, the boys want bulging breasts, a cute face, and an Oh-you-wonderful-male manner." He shrugged. "I couldn't compete. So I decided to join the W.E.N.C.H.E.S."

"Eh?"

"Women's Emergency National Corps, Hospitality & Entertainment Section, what they now call 'Space Angels'—Auxiliary Nursing Group, Extraterrestrial Legions."

I knew both terms, once I had them chronized. We use still a third name, it's that elite military service corps: Women's Hospitality Order Refortifying & Encouraging Spacemen. Vocabulary shift is the worst hurdle in time-jumps—did you know that "service station" once meant a dispensary for petroleum fractions? Once on an assignment in the Churchill Era, a woman said to me, "Meet me at the service station next door"—which is not what it sounds; a "service station" (then) wouldn't have a bed in it.

He went on: "It was when they first admitted you can't send men into space for months and years and not relieve the tension. You remember how the wowsers screamed?—that improved my chance since volunteers were scarce. A gal had to be respectable, preferably virgin (they liked to train them from scratch), above average mentally, and stable emotionally. But most volunteers were old hookers, or neurotics who would crack up ten days off Earth. So I didn't need looks; if they accepted me, they would fix my buck teeth, put a wave in my hair, teach me to walk and dance and how to listen to a man pleasingly, and everything else—plus training for the prime duties. They would even use plastic surgery if it would help—nothing too good for Our Boys.

"Best yet, they made sure you didn't get pregnant during your enlistment— and you were almost certain to marry at the end of your hitch. Same way today, A.N.G.E.L.S. marry spacers—they talk the language.

"When I was eighteen I was placed as a 'mother's helper.' This family simply wanted a cheap servant but I didn't mind as I couldn't enlist till I was twenty-one. I did housework and went to night school—pretending to continue my high school typing and shorthand but going to a charm class instead, to better my chances for enlistment.

"Then I met this city slicker with his hundred dollar bills." He scowled. "The no-good actually did have a wad of hundred-dollar bills. He showed me one night, told me to help myself.

"But I didn't. I liked him. He was the first man I ever met who was nice to me without trying games with me. I quit night school to see him oftener. It was the happiest time of my life.

"Then one night in the park the games began."

He stopped. I said, "And then?"

"And then *nothing!* I never saw him again. He walked me home and told me he loved me—and kissed me good-night and never came back." He looked grim. "If I could find him, I'd kill him!"

"Well," I sympathize, "I know how you feel. But killing him—just for doing what comes naturally—hmm… Did you struggle?"

"Huh? What's that got to do with it?"

"Quite a bit. Maybe he deserves a couple of broken arms for running out on you, but—"

"He deserves worse than that! Wait till you hear. Somehow I kept anyone from suspecting and decided it was all for the best. I hadn't really loved him and probably would never love anybody—and I was more eager to join the W.E.N.C.H.E.S. than ever. I wasn't disqualified, they didn't insist on virgins. I cheered up.

"It wasn't until my skirts got tight that I realized."

"Pregnant?"

"He had me higher 'n a kite! Those skinflints I lived with ignored it as long as I could work—then kicked me out and the orphanage wouldn't take me back. I landed in a charity ward surrounded by other big bellies and trotted bedpans until my time came.

"One night I found myself on an operating table, with a nurse saying, 'Relax. Now breathe deeply.'

"I woke up in bed, numb from the chest down. My surgeon came in. 'How do you feel?' he says cheerfully.

"'Like a mummy.'

"'Naturally. You're wrapped like one and full of dope to keep you numb. You'll get well—but a Caesarian isn't a hangnail.'

"'Caesarian,' I said. 'Doc—*did I lose the baby?*'

"'Oh, no. Your baby's fine.'

"'Oh. Boy or girl?'

"'A healthy little girl. Five pounds, three ounces.'

"I relaxed. It's something, to have made a baby. I told myself I would go somewhere and tack 'Mrs.' on my name and let the kid think her papa was dead—no orphanage for *my* kid!

"But the surgeon was talking. 'Tell me, uh—' He avoided my name, '—did you ever think your glandular setup was odd?'

"I said, 'Huh? Of course not. What are you driving at?'

"He hesitated. 'I'll give you this in one dose, then a hypo to let you sleep off your jitters. You'll have 'em.'

"'Why?' I demanded.

"'Ever hear of that Scottish physician who was female until she was thirty-five?—then had surgery and became legally and medically a man? Got married. All okay.'

"'What's that got to do with me?'

"'That's what I'm saying. You're a man.'

"I tried to sit up. *'What?'*

"'Take it easy. When I opened you, I found a mess. I sent for the Chief of Surgery while I got the baby out, then we held a consultation with you on the table—and worked for hours to salvage what we could. You had two full sets of organs, both immature, but with the female set well enough developed for you to have a baby. They could never be any use to you again, so we took them out and rearranged things so that you can develop properly as a man.' He put a hand on me. 'Don't worry. You're young, your bones will readjust, we'll watch your glandular balance—and make a fine young man out of you.'

"I started to cry. 'What about my *baby?*'

"Well, you can't nurse her, you haven't milk enough for a kitten. If I were you, I wouldn't see her—put her up for adoption.'

"'*No!*'

"He shrugged. 'The choice is yours; you're her mother—well, her parent. But don't worry now; we'll get you well first.'

"Next day they let me see the kid and I saw her daily—trying to get used to her. I had never seen a brand-new baby and had no idea how awful they look—my daughter looked like an orange monkey. My feeling changed to cold determination to do right by her. But four weeks later that didn't mean anything."

"Eh?"

"She was snatched."

"'Snatched'?"

The Unmarried Mother almost knocked over the bottle we had bet. "Kidnapped—stolen from the hospital nursery!" He breathed hard. "How's that for taking the last a man's got to live for?"

"A bad deal," I agreed. "Let's pour you another. No clues?"

"Nothing the police could trace. Somebody came to see her, claimed to be her uncle. While the nurse had her back turned, he walked out with her."

"Description?"

"Just a man, with a face-shaped face, like yours or mine." He frowned. "I think it was the baby's father. The nurse swore it was an older man but he probably used makeup. Who else would swipe my baby? Childless women pull such stunts—but whoever heard of a man doing it?"

"What happened to you then?"

"Eleven more months of that grim place and three operations. In four months I started to grow a beard; before I was out I was shaving regularly…

and no longer doubted that I was male." He grinned wryly. "I was staring down nurses' necklines."

"Well," I said, "seems to me you came through okay. Here you are, a normal man, making good money, no real troubles. And the life of a female is not an easy one."

He glared at me. "A lot you know about it!"

"So?"

"Ever hear the expression 'a ruined woman'?"

"Mmm, years ago. Doesn't mean much today."

"I was as ruined as a woman can be; that bum *really* ruined me—I was no longer a woman...and I didn't know *how* to be a man."

"Takes getting used to, I suppose."

"You have no idea. I don't mean learning how to dress, or not walking into the wrong restroom; I learned those in the hospital. But how could I *live?* What job could I get? Hell, I couldn't even drive a car. I didn't know a trade; I couldn't do manual labor—too much scar tissue, too tender.

"I hated him for having ruined me for the W.E.N.C.H.E.S., too, but I didn't know how much until I tried to join the Space Corps instead. One look at my belly and I was marked unfit for military service. The medical officer spent time on me just from curiosity; he had read about my case.

"So I changed my name and came to New York. I got by as a fry cook, then rented a typewriter and set myself up as a public stenographer—what a laugh! In four months I typed four letters and one manuscript. The manuscript was for *Real Life Tales* and a waste of paper, but the goof who wrote it, sold it. Which gave me an idea; I bought a stack of confession magazines and studied them." He looked cynical. "Now you know how I get the authentic woman's angle on an unmarried-mother story...through the only version I haven't sold—the true one. Do I win the bottle?"

I pushed it toward him. I was upset myself, but there was work to do. I said, "Son, you still want to lay hands on that so-and-so?"

His eyes lighted up—a feral gleam.

"Hold it!" I said. "You wouldn't kill him?"

He chuckled nastily. "Try me."

"Take it easy. I know more about it than you think I do. I can help you. I know where he is."

He reached across the bar. *"Where is he?"*

I said softly, "Let go my shirt, sonny—or you'll land in the alley and we'll tell the cops you fainted." I showed him the sap.

He let go. "Sorry. But where is he?" He looked at me. "And how do you know so much?"

"All in good time. There are records—hospital records, orphanage records, medical records. The matron of your orphanage was Mrs. Fetherage—right? She was followed by Mrs. Gruenstein—right? Your name, as a girl, was 'Jane'—right? And you didn't tell me any of this—right?"

I had him baffled and a bit scared. "What's this? You trying to make trouble for me?"

"No indeed. I've your welfare at heart. I can put this character in your lap. You do to him as you see fit—and I guarantee that you'll get away with it. But I don't think you'll kill him. You'd be nuts to—and you aren't nuts. Not quite."

He brushed it aside. "Cut the noise. *Where is he?*"

I poured him a short one; he was drunk but anger was offsetting it. "Not so fast. I do something for you—you do something for me."

"Uh…what?"

"You don't like your work. What would you say to high pay, steady work, unlimited expense account, your own boss on the job, and lots of variety and adventure?"

He stared. "I'd say, 'Get those goddam reindeer off my roof!' Shove it, Pop—there's no such job."

"Okay, put it this way: I hand him to you, you settle with him, then try my job. If it's not all I claim—well, I can't hold you."

He was wavering; the last drink did it. "When d'yuh d'liver 'im?" he said thickly.

"If it's a deal—*right now!*"

He shoved out his hand. "It's a deal!"

I nodded to my assistant to watch both ends, noted the time—2300—started to duck through the gate under the bar—when the juke box blared out: "I'm My Own Granpaw!" The service man had orders to load it with old Americana and classics because I couldn't stomach the "music" of 1970, but I hadn't known that tape was in it. I called out, "Shut that off! Give the customer his money back." I added, "Storeroom, back in a moment," and headed there with my Unmarried Mother following.

It was down the passage across from the Johns, a steel door to which no one but my day manager and myself had a key; inside was a door to an inner room to which only I had a key. We went there.

He looked blearily around at windowless walls. "Where is 'e?"

"Right away." I opened a case, the only thing in the room; it was a U.S.F.F. Co-ordinates Transformer Field Kit, series 1992, Mod. II—a beauty, no moving parts, weight twenty-three kilos fully charged, and shaped to pass as a suitcase. I had adjusted it precisely earlier that day; all I had to do was to shake out the metal net which limits the transformation field.

Which I did. "Wha's that?" he demanded.

"Time machine," I said and tossed the net over us.

"Hey!" he yelled and stepped back. There is a technique to this; the net has to be thrown so that the subject will instinctively step back *onto* the metal mesh, then you close the net with both of you inside completely—else you might leave shoe soles behind or a piece of foot, or scoop up a slice of floor. But that's all the skill it takes. Some agents con a subject into the net; I tell the truth and use that instant of utter astonishment to flip the switch. Which I did.

1030-VI-3 April 1963-Cleveland, Ohio-Apex Bldg.: "Hey!" he repeated. "Take this damn thing off!"

"Sorry," I apologized and did so, stuffed the net into the case, closed it. "You said you wanted to find him."

"But—You said that was a time machine!"

I pointed out a window. "Does that look like November? Or New York?" While he was gawking at new buds and spring weather, I reopened the case, took out a packet of hundred-dollar bills, checked that the numbers and signatures were compatible with 1963. The Temporal Bureau doesn't care how much you spend (it costs nothing) but they don't like unnecessary anachronisms. Too many mistakes, and a general court martial will exile you for a year in a nasty period, say 1974 with its strict rationing and forced labor. I never make such mistakes, the money was okay.

He turned around and said, "What happened?"

"He's here. Go outside and take him. Here's expense money."

I shoved it at him and added, "Settle him, then I'll pick you up."

Hundred-dollar bills have a hypnotic effect on a person not used to them. He was thumbing them unbelievingly as I eased him into the hall, locked him out. The next jump was easy, a small shift in era.

7100-VI-10 March 1964-Cleveland-Apex Bldg.: There was a notice under the door saying that my lease expired next week; otherwise the room looked as it had a moment before. Outside, trees were bare and snow threatened; I hurried, stopping only for contemporary money and a coat, hat, and topcoat I had left there when I leased the room. I hired a car, went to the hospital. It took twenty minutes to bore the nursery attendant to the point where I could swipe the baby without being noticed. We went back to the Apex Building. This dial setting was more involved as the building did not yet exist in 1945. But I had precalculated it.

0100-VI-20 Sept 1945-Cleveland-Skyview Motel: Field kit, baby, and I arrived in a motel outside town. Earlier I had registered as "Gregory Johnson, Warren, Ohio," so we arrived in a room with curtains closed, windows locked, and doors bolted, and the floor cleared to allow for waver as the machine hunts. You can get a nasty bruise from a chair where it shouldn't be—not the chair of course, but backlash from the field.

No trouble. Jane was sleeping soundly; I carried her out, put her in a grocery box on the seat of a car I had provided earlier, drove to the orphanage, put her on the steps, drove two blocks to a "service station" (the petroleum products sort) and phoned the orphanage, drove back in time to see them taking the box inside, kept going and abandoned the car near the motel—walked to it and jumped forward to the Apex Building in 1963.

2200-VI-24 April 1963-Cleveland-Apex Bldg.: I had cut the time rather fine— temporal accuracy depends on span, except on return to zero. If I had it right, Jane was discovering, out in the park this balmy spring night, that she wasn't quite as "nice" a girl as she had thought, I grabbed a taxi to the home of those skinflints, had the hackie wait around a corner while I lurked in shadows.

Presently I spotted them down the street, arms around each other. He took her up on the porch and made a long job of kissing her good-night—longer than I thought. Then she went in and he came down the walk, turned away. I slid into step and hooked an arm in his. "That's all, son," I announced quietly. "I'm back to pick you up."

"You!" He gasped and caught his breath.

"Me. Now you know who *he* is—and after you think it over you'll know who you are...and if you think hard enough, you'll figure out who the baby is...and who *I* am."

He didn't answer, he was badly shaken. It's a shock to have it proved to you that you can't resist seducing yourself. I took him to the Apex Building and we jumped again.

2300-VII-12 Aug 1985-Sub Rockies Base: I woke the duty sergeant, showed my I.D., told the sergeant to bed my companion down with a happy pill and recruit him in the morning. The sergeant looked sour, but rank is rank, regardless of era; he did what I said—thinking, no doubt, that the next time we met he might be the colonel and I the sergeant Which can happen in our corps: "What name?" he asked.

I wrote it out. He raised his eyebrows. "Like so, eh? *Hmm*—"

"You just do your job, Sergeant." I turned to my companion.

"Son, your troubles are over. You're about to start the best job a man ever held—and you'll do well. *I know*."

"That you will!" agreed the sergeant. "Look at me—born in 1917—still around, still young, still enjoying life." I went back to the jump room, set everything on pre-selected zero.

2301-V-7 Nov 1970-NYC "Pop's Place": I came out of the storeroom carrying a fifth of Drambuie to account for the minute I had been gone. My assistant was arguing with the customer who had been playing "I'm My Own Granpaw!" I said, "Oh, let him play it, then unplug it." I was very tired.

It's rough, but somebody must do it and it's very hard to recruit anyone in the later years, since the Mistake of 1972. Can you think of a better source than to pick people all fouled up where they are and give them well-paid, interesting (even though dangerous) work in a necessary cause? Everybody knows now why the Fizzle War of 1963 fizzled. The bomb with New York's number on it didn't go off, a hundred other things didn't go as planned—all arranged by the likes of me.

But not the Mistake of '72; that one is not our fault—and can't be undone; there's no paradox to resolve. A thing either is, or it isn't, now and forever amen. But there won't be another like it; an order dated "1992" takes precedence any year.

I closed five minutes early, leaving a letter in the cash register telling my day manager that I was accepting his offer to buy me out, so see my lawyer as I was leaving on a long vacation. The Bureau might or might not pick up his payments, but they want things left tidy. I went to the room back of the storeroom and forward to 1993.

2200-VII-12 Jan 1993-Sub Rockies Annex-HQ Temporal DOL: I checked in with the duty officer and went to my quarters, intending to sleep for a week. I had fetched the bottle we bet (after all, I won it) and took a drink before I wrote my report. It tasted foul and I wondered why I had ever liked Old Underwear. But it was better than nothing; I don't like to be cold sober, I think too much. But I don't really hit the bottle either; other people have snakes—I have people.

I dictated my report; forty recruitments all okayed by the Psych Bureau—counting my own, which I knew would be okayed, I was here, wasn't I? Then I taped a request for assignment to operations; I was sick of recruiting. I dropped both in the slot and headed for bed.

My eye fell on "The By-Laws of Time," over my bed:

Never Do Yesterday What Should Be Done Tomorrow.
If At Last You Do Succeed, Never Try Again.
A Stitch in Time Saves Nine Billion.
A Paradox May Be Paradoctored.
It Is Earlier When You Think.
Ancestors Are Just People.
Even Jove Nods.

They didn't inspire me the way they had when I was a recruit; thirty subjective-years of time-jumping wears you down. I undressed and when I got down to the hide I looked at my belly. A Caesarian leaves a big scar but I'm so hairy now that I don't notice it unless I look for it.

Then I glanced at the ring on my finger.

The Snake That Eats Its Own Tail, Forever and Ever...I *know* where *I* came from—but *where did all you zombies come from?*

I felt a headache coming on, but a headache powder is one thing I do not take. I did once—and you all went away.

So I crawled into bed and whistled out the light.

You aren't really there at all. There isn't anybody but me—Jane—here alone in the dark.

I miss you dreadfully!

A Kind of Artistry (1962)

BRIAN W. ALDISS

BRIAN ALDISS (b. 1925) began publishing fiction in the 1950s and quickly established himself as one of science fiction's preeminent writers. His many novels include *Hothouse*, *Greybeard*, *The Malacia Tapestry*, and the Helliconia trilogy. Various works of his have been adapted for film, including *Brothers of the Head*, *Frankenstein Unbound*, and "Supertoys Last All Summer Long" (which formed the basis for *A.I. Artificial Intelligence*). He lives in Oxford, England, and in 2005 Queen Elizabeth awarded him an OBE (meaning that he was dubbed an *Officer of the Most Excellent Order of the British Empire*).

"A Kind of Artistry" is one of his many stories that ventures far into the future to explore elements of humanity that might possibly be universal. It was incorporated into Aldiss's novel *Starswarm*.

I

A GIANT RISING from the fjord, from the grey arm of sea in the fjord, could have peered over the crown of its sheer cliffs and discovered Endehaaven there on the edge, sprawling at the very start of the island.

Derek Flamifew Ende saw much of this sprawl from his high window; indeed, a growing ill-ease, apprehensions of a quarrel, forced him to see everything with particular clarity, just as a landscape takes on an intense actinic visibility before a thunderstorm. Although he was warmseeing with his face, yet his eye vision wandered over the estate.

All was bleakly neat at Endehaaven—as I should know, for its neatness is my care. The gardens are made to support evergreens and shrubs that never flower; this is My Lady's whim, that likes a sobriety to match the furrowed brow of the coastline. The building, gaunt Endehaaven itself, is tall and lank and severe; earlier ages would have found its structure impossible: for its thousand built-in paragravity units ensure the support of masonry the mass of which is largely an illusion.

Between the building and the fjord, where the garden contrived itself into a parade, stood My Lady's laboratory, and My Lady's pets—and, indeed, My Lady herself at this time, her long hands busy with the minicoypu and the agoutinis. I stood with her, attending the animals' cages or passing her instruments or stirring the tanks, doing always what she asked. And the eyes of Derek Ende looked down on us; no, they looked down on her only.

Derek Flamifew Ende stood with his face over the receptor bowl, reading the message from Star One. It played lightly over his countenance and over the boscises of his forehead. Though he stared down across that achingly familiar stage of his life outside, he still warmsaw the communication clearly. When it was finished, he negated the receptor, pressed his face to it, and flexed his message back.

"I will do as you message, Star One. I will go at once to Festi XV in the Veil Nebula and enter liaison with the being you call the Cliff. If possible I will also obey your order to take some of its substance to Pyrylyn. Thank you for your greetings; I return them in good faith. Good-bye."

He straightened and massaged his face: warmlooking over great light distances was always tiring, as if the sensitive muscles of the countenance knew that they delivered up their tiny electrostatic charges to parsecs of vacuum, and were appalled. Slowly his boscises also relaxed, as slowly he gathered together his gear. It would be a long flight to the Veil, and the task that had been set him would daunt the stoutest heart on Earth; yet it was for another reason he lingered: before he could be away, he had to say a farewell to his Mistress.

Dilating the door, he stepped out into the corridor, walked along it with a steady tread—feet covering mosaics of a pattern learnt long ago in his childhood—and walked into the paragravity shaft. Moments later, he was leaving the main hall, approaching My Lady as she stood gaunt, with her rodents scuttling at beast level before her and Vatna Jokull's heights rising behind her, grey with the impurities of distance.

"Go indoors and fetch me the box of name rings, Hols," she said to me; so I passed him, My Lord, as he went to her. He noticed me no more than he noticed any of the other parthenos.

When I returned, she had not turned towards him, though he was speaking urgently to her.

"You know I have my duty to perform, Mistress," I heard him saying. "Nobody else but a normal-born Earthborn can be entrusted with this sort of task."

"This sort of task! The galaxy is loaded inexhaustibly with such tasks! You can excuse yourself forever with such excursions."

He said to her remote back, pleadingly: "You can't talk of them like that. You know of the nature of the Cliff—I told you all about it. You know this isn't an excursion: it requires all the courage I have. And you know that only Earthborns, for some reason, have such courage...Don't you, Mistress?"

Although I had come up to them, threading my subservient way between cage and tank, they noticed me not enough even to lower their voices. My Lady stood gazing at the grey heights inland, her countenance as formidable as they; one boscis twitched as she said, "You think you are so big and brave, don't you?"

Knowing the power of sympathetic magic, she never spoke his name when she was angry; it was as if she wished him to disappear.

"It isn't that," he said humbly. "Please be reasonable, Mistress; you know I must go; a man cannot be forever at home. Don't be angry."

She turned to him at last.

Her face was high and stern; it did not receive. Yet she had a beauty of some dreadful kind I cannot describe, if weariness and knowledge can together knead beauty. Her eyes were as grey and distant as the frieze of snow-covered volcano behind her, O My Lady! She was a century older than Derek: though the difference showed not in her skin—which would stay fresh yet a thousand years—but in her authority.

"I'm not angry. I'm only hurt. You know how you have the power to hurt me."

"Mistress—" he said, taking a step towards her.

"Don't touch me," she said. "Go if you must, but don't make a mockery of it by touching me."

He took her elbow. She held one of the minicoypus quiet in the crook of her arm—animals were always docile at her touch—and strained it closer.

"I don't mean to hurt you, Mistress. You know we owe allegiance to Star One; I must work for them, or how else do we hold this estate? Let me go for once with an affectionate parting."

"Affection! You go off and leave me alone with a handful of parthenos and you talk of affection! Don't pretend you don't rejoice to get away from me. You're tired of me, aren't you?"

Wearily he said, as if nothing else would come, "It's not that..."

"You see! You don't even attempt to sound sincere. Why don't you go? It doesn't matter what happens to me."

"Oh, if you could only hear your own self-pity."

Now she had a tear on the icy slope of one cheek. Turning, she flashed it for his inspection.

"Who else should pity me? You don't, or you wouldn't go away from me as you do. Suppose you get killed by this Cliff, what will happen to me?"

"I shall be back, Mistress," he said. "Never fear."

"It's easy to say. Why don't you have the courage to admit that you're only too glad to leave me?"

"Because I'm not going to be provoked into a quarrel."

"Pah, you sound like a child again. You won't answer, will you? Instead you're going to run away, evading your responsibilities."

"I'm not running away!"

"Of course you are, whatever you pretend. You're just immature."

"I'm not, I'm not! And I'm not running away! It takes real courage to do what I'm going to do."

"You think so well of yourself!"

He turned away then, petulantly, without dignity. He began to head towards the landing platform. He began to run.

"Derek!" she called.

He did not answer.

She took the squatting minicoypu by the scruff of its neck. Angrily she flung it into the nearby tank of water. It turned into a fish and swam down into the depths.

II

Derek journeyed towards the Veil Nebula in his fast lightpusher. Lonely it sailed, a great fin shaped like an archer's bow, barnacled all over with the photon cells that sucked its motive power from the dense and dusty emptiness of space. Midway along the trailing edge was the blister in which Derek lay, senseless over most of his voyage.

He woke in the therapeutic bed, called to another resurrection day that was no day, with gentle machine hands easing the stiffness from his muscles. Soup gurgled in a retort, bubbling up towards a nipple only two inches from his mouth. He drank. He slept again, tired from his long inactivity.

When he woke again, he climbed slowly from the bed and exercised for fifteen minutes. Then he moved forward to the controls. My friend Jon was there.

"How is everything?" Derek asked.

"Everything is in order, My Lord," Jon replied. "We are swinging into the orbit of Festi XV now." He gave the coordinates and retired to eat. Jon's job was the loneliest any partheno could have. We are hatched according to strictly controlled formulae, without the inbred organisations of DNA that assure true Earthborns of their amazing longevity; five more long hauls and Jon will be old and worn out, fit only for the transmuter.

Derek sat at the controls. Did he see, superimposed on the face of Festi, the face he loved and feared? I think he did. I think there were no swirling clouds for him that could erase the clouding of her brow.

Whatever he saw, he settled the lightpusher into a fast low orbit about the desolate planet. The sun Festi was little more than a blazing point some eight hundred million miles away. Like the riding light of a ship it bobbed above a turbulent sea of cloud as they went in.

For a long while, Derek sat with his face in a receptor bowl, checking ground heats far below. Since he was dealing with temperatures approaching absolute zero, this was not simple; yet when the Cliff moved into a position directly below, there was no mistaking its bulk; it stood out as clearly on his senses as if outlined on a radar screen.

"There she goes!" Derek exclaimed.

Jon had come forward again. He fed the time coordinates into the lightpusher's brain, waited, and read off the time when the Cliff would be below them again.

Nodding, Derek began to prepare to jump. Without haste, he assumed his special suit, checking each item as he took it up, opening the paragravs until he floated, then closing them again, clicking down every snap-fastener until he was entirely encased.

"395 seconds to next zenith, My Lord," Jon said.

"You know all about collecting me?"

"Yes, sir."

"I shall not activate the radio beacon till I'm back in orbit."

"I fully understand, sir."

"Right. I'll be moving."

A little animated prison, he walked ponderously into the air lock.

Three minutes before they were next above the Cliff, Derek opened the outer door and dived into the sea of cloud. A brief blast of his suit jets set him free from the lightpusher's orbit. Cloud engulfed him like death as he fell.

The twenty surly planets that swung round Festi held only an infinitesimal fraction of the mysteries of the galaxy. Every globe in the universe huddled its own secret purpose to itself. On some of those globes, as on Earth, the purpose manifested itself in a type of being that could shape itself, burst into the space lanes, and rough-hew its aims in a civilized extra-planetary environment. On others, the purpose remained aloof and dark; only Earthborns, weaving their obscure patterns of will and compulsion, challenged those alien beings, to wrest from them new knowledge that might be added to the pool of the old.

All knowledge has its influence. Over the millennia since interstellar flight had become practicable, mankind was insensibly moulded by its own findings; together with its lost innocence, its genetic stability went out of the galactic window. As man fell like rain over other planets, so his strain lost its original hereditary design: each centre of civilization bred new ways of thought, of feeling, of shape—of life. Only on old Earth itself did man still somewhat resemble the men of pre-stellar days.

That was why it was an Earthborn who dived head-first to meet an entity called the Cliff.

The Cliff had destroyed each of the few spaceships or lightpushers that had landed on its desolate globe. After long study of the being from safe orbits, the wise men of Star One evolved the theory that it destroyed any considerable source of power, as a man will swat a buzzing fly. Derek Ende, going alone with no powering but his suit motors, would be safe—or so the theory went.

Riding down on the paragravs, he sank more and more slowly into planetary night. The last of the cloud was whipped from about his shoulders and a high wind thrummed and whistled round the supporters of his suit. Beneath him, the ground loomed. So as not to be blown across it, he speeded his rate of fall; next moment he sprawled full length on Festi XV. For a while he lay there, resting and letting his suit cool.

The darkness was not complete. Though almost no solar light touched this continent, green flares grew from the earth, illuminating its barren contours. Wishing to accustom his eyes to the gloom, he did not switch on his head, shoulder, stomach, or hand lights.

Something like a stream of fire flowed to his left. Because its radiance was poor and guttering, it confused itself with its own shadows, so that the smoke it gave off, distorted into bars by the bulk of the 4G planet, appeared to roll along its course like burning tumbleweed. Further off were larger sources of fire, impure ethane and methane most probably, burning with a sound that came like frying steak to Derek's ears, and spouting upwards with an energy that licked the lowering cloud race with blue light. At another point, blazing on an eminence, a geyser of flame wrapped itself in a thickly swirling mantle of brown smoke, a pall that spread upwards as slowly as porridge. Elsewhere, a pillar of white fire burnt without motion or smoke; it stood to the right of where Derek lay, like a floodlit sword in its perfection.

He nodded approval to himself. His drop had been successfully placed. This was the Region of Fire, where the Cliff lived.

To lie there was content enough, to gaze on a scene never closely viewed by man fulfillment enough—until he realised that a wide segment of landscape offered not the slightest glimmer of illumination. He looked into it with a keen warmsight, and found it was the Cliff.

The immense bulk of the thing blotted out all light from the ground and rose to eclipse the cloud over its crest.

At the mere sight of it, Derek's primary and secondary hearts began to beat out a hastening pulse of awe. Stretched flat on the ground, his paragravs keeping him level to 1G, he peered ahead at it; he swallowed to clear his choked throat; his eyes strained through the mosaic of dull light in an effort to define the Cliff.

One thing was sure: it was large! He cursed that although photosistors allowed him to use his warmsight on objects beyond the suit he wore, this sense was distorted by the eternal firework display. Then in a moment of good seeing he had an accurate fix: the Cliff was three-quarters of a mile away! From first observations, he had thought it to be no more than a hundred yards distant.

Now he knew how large it was. It was enormous!

Momentarily he gloated. The only sort of tasks worth being set were impossible ones. Star One's astrophysicists held the notion that the Cliff was in some sense aware, so they required Derek to take them a pound of its flesh. How do you carve a being the size of a small moon?

All the time he lay there, the wind jarred along the veins and supporters of his suit. Gradually, it occurred to Derek that the vibration he felt from this constant motion was changed. It carried a new note and a new strength. He looked about, placed his gloved hand outstretched on the ground.

The wind was no longer vibrating. It was the earth that shook, Festi itself that trembled. The Cliff was moving!

When he looked back up at it with both his senses, he saw which way it headed. Jarring steadily, it bore down on him.

"If it has intelligence, then it will reason—if it has detected me—that I am too small to offer it harm. So it will offer me none and I have nothing to fear," Derek told himself. The logic did not reassure him.

An absorbent pseudopod, activated by a simple humidity gland in the brow of his helmet, slid across his forehead and removed the sweat that formed there.

Visibility fluttered like a rag in a cellar. The slow forward surge of the Cliff was still something Derek sensed rather than saw. Now the rolling mattresses of cloud blotted the thing's crest, as it in its turn eclipsed the fountains of fire. To the jar of its approach even the marrow of Derek's bones raised a response.

Something else also responded.

The legs of Derek's suit began to move. The arms moved. The body wriggled.

Puzzled, Derek stiffened his legs. Irresistibly, the knees of the suit hinged, forcing his own to do likewise. And not only his knees: his arms too, stiffly though he braced them on the ground before him, were made to bend to the whim of the suit. He could not keep still without breaking bones.

Thoroughly alarmed he lay there, flexing contortedly to keep rhythm with his suit, performing the gestures of an idiot.

As if it had suddenly learnt to crawl, the suit began to move forward. It shuffled forward over the ground; Derek inside went willy-nilly with it.

One ironic thought struck him. Not only was the mountain coming to Mohammed; Mohammed was perforce going to the mountain…

III

Nothing he could do checked his progress; he was no longer master of his movements; his will was useless. With the realisation rode a sense of relief. His Mistress could hardly blame him for anything that happened now.

Through the darkness he went on hands and knees, blundering in the direction of the oncoming Cliff, prisoner in an animated prison.

The only constructive thought that came to him was that his suit had somehow become subject to the Cliff. How, he did not know or try to guess.

He crawled. He was almost relaxed now, letting his limbs move limply with the suit movements.

Smoke furled him about. The vibrations ceased, telling him that the Cliff was stationary again. Raising his head, he could see nothing but smoke—produced perhaps by the Cliff's mass as it scraped over the ground. When the blur parted, he glimpsed only darkness. The thing was directly ahead!

He blundered on. Abruptly he began to climb, still involuntarily aping the movements of his suit.

Beneath him was a doughy substance, tough yet yielding. The suit worked its way heavily upwards at an angle of something like sixty-five degrees; the stiffeners creaked, the paragravs throbbed. He was ascending the Cliff.

By this time there was no doubt in Derek's mind that the thing possessed what might be termed volition, if not consciousness. It possessed too a power no man could claim: it could impart that volition to an inanimate object like his suit. Helpless inside it, he carried his considerations a stage further. This power to impart volition seemed to have a limited range: otherwise the Cliff would surely not have bothered to move its gigantic mass at all, but would have forced the suit to traverse all the distance between them. If this reasoning were sound, then the lightpusher was safe from capture in orbit.

The movement of his arms distracted him. His suit was tunneling. Giving it no aid, he lay and let his hands make swimming motions. If it was going to bore into the Cliff, then he could only conclude he was about to be digested: yet he stilled his impulse to struggle, knowing that struggle was fruitless.

Thrusting against the doughy stuff, the suit burrowed into it and made a sibilant little world of movement and friction which stopped directly it stopped, leaving Derek embedded in the most solid kind of isolation.

To ward off growing claustrophobia, he attempted to switch on his headlight; his suit arms remained so stiff he could not bend them enough to reach the toggle. All he could do was lie there helplessly in his shell and stare into the featureless darkness of the Cliff.

But the darkness was not entirely featureless. His ears detected a constant *slither* along the outside surfaces of his suit. His warmsight discerned a meaningless pattern beyond his helmet. Though he focussed his boscises, he could make no sense of the pattern; it had neither symmetry nor meaning for him…

Yet for his body it seemed to have some meaning. Derek felt his limbs tremble, was aware of pulses and phantom impressions within himself that he had not known before. The realisation percolated through to him that he was in touch with powers of which he had no cognisance—and, conversely, that something was in touch with him that had no cognisance of his powers.

An immense heaviness overcame him. The forces of life laboured within him. He sensed more vividly than before the vast bulk of the Cliff. Though it was dwarfed by the mass of Festi XV, it was as large as a good-sized asteroid... He could picture an asteroid, formed from a jetting explosion of gas on the face of Festi the sun. Half-solid, half-molten, it swung about its parent on an eccentric orbit. Cooling under an interplay of pressures, its interior crystallised into a unique form. So, with its surface semi-plastic, it existed for many millions of years, gradually accumulating an electrostatic charge that poised... and waited...and brewed the life acids about its crystalline heart.

Festi was a stable system, but once in every so many thousands of millions of years, the giant first, second, and third planets achieved perihelion with the sun and with each other simultaneously. This happened coincidentally with the asteroid's nearest approach; it was wrenched from its orbit and all but grazed the three lined-up planets. Vast electrical and gravitational forces were unleashed. The asteroid glowed: and woke to consciousness. Life was not born on it: it was born to life, born in one cataclysmic clash!

Before it had more than mutely savoured the sad-sharp-sweet sensation of consciousness, it was in trouble. Plunging away from the sun on its new course, it found itself snared in the gravitational pull of the 4G planet, Festi XV. It knew no shaping force but gravity; gravity was to it all that oxygen was to cellular life on Earth; yet it had no wish to exchange its flight for captivity; yet it was too puny to resist. For the first time, the asteroid recognised that its consciousness had a use, in that it could to some extent control its environment outside itself. Rather than risk being broken up in Festi's orbit, it sped inwards, and by retarding its own fall performed its first act of volition, an act that brought it down shaken but entire on the planet's surface.

For an immeasurable period, the asteroid—but now it was the Cliff—lay in the shallow crater formed by its impact, speculating without thought. It knew nothing except the inorganic scene about it, and could visualise nothing else, but that scene it knew well. Gradually it came to some kind of terms with the scene. Formed by gravity, it used gravity as thoughtlessly as a man uses breath; it began to move other things, and it began to move itself.

That it should be other than alone in the universe had never occurred to the Cliff. Now it knew there was other life, it accepted the fact. The other life was not as it was; that it accepted. The other life had its own requirements; that it accepted. Of questions, of doubt, it did not know. It had a need; so did the other life; they should both be accommodated, for accommodation was the adjustment to pressure, and that response it comprehended.

Derek Ende's suit began to move again under external volition. Carefully it worked its way backwards. It was ejected from the Cliff. It lay still.

Derek himself lay still. He was barely conscious.

In a half daze, he was piecing together what had happened.

The Cliff had communicated with him; if he ever doubted that, the evidence of it lay clutched in the crook of his left arm.

"Yet it did not—yet it could not communicate with me!" he murmured. But it had communicated: he was still faint with the burden of it.

The Cliff had nothing like a brain. It had not "recognised" Derek's brain. Instead, it had communicated with the only part of him it could recognise; it had communicated direct to his cell organisation, and in particular probably to those cytoplasmic structures, the mitochondria, the power sources of the cell. His brain had been bypassed, his own cells had taken in the information offered.

He recognised his feeling of weakness. The Cliff had drained him of power. Even that could not drain his feeling of triumph. For the Cliff had taken information even as it gave it. The Cliff had learnt that other life existed in other parts of the universe.

Without hesitation, without debate, it had given a fragment of itself to be taken to those other parts of the universe. Derek's mission was completed.

In the Cliff's gesture, Derek read one of the deepest urges of living things: the urge to make an impression on another living thing. Smiling wryly, he pulled himself to his feet.

He was alone in the Region of Fire. The occasional mournful flame still confronted its surrounding dark, but the Cliff had disappeared; he had lain on the threshold of consciousness longer than he thought. He looked at his chronometer, to find it was high time he moved towards his rendezvous with the lightpusher. Stepping up his suit heating to combat the cold that began to seep through his bones, he revved up the paragrav unit and rose. The noisome clouds came down and engulfed him; Festi was lost to view. Soon he had risen beyond cloud or atmosphere.

Under Jon's direction, the space craft homed onto Derek's radio beacon. After a few tricky minutes, they matched velocities and Derek climbed aboard.

"Are you all right?" the partheno asked, as his master staggered into a flight seat.

"Fine—just weak. I'll tell you all about it as I do a report on spool for Pyrylyn. They're going to be pleased with us."

He produced a yellow grey blob of matter that had expanded to the size of a large turkey and held it out to Jon.

"Don't touch this with your bare hands. Put it in one of the low-temperature lockers under 4Gs. It's a little souvenir from Festi XV."

IV

The Eyebright in Pynnati, one of Pyrylyn's capital cities, was where you went to enjoy yourself on the most lavish scale possible. This was where Derek Ende's hosts took him, with Jon in self-effacing attendance.

They lay in a nest of couches which slowly revolved, giving them a full view of other dance and couch parties. The room itself moved. Its walls were transparent; through them could be seen an ever-changing view as the room slid up and down and about the great metal framework of the Eyebright. First they were on the outside of the structure, with the bright night lights of Pynnati winking up at them as if intimately involved in their delight. Then they slipped inwards in the slow evagination of the building, to be surrounded by other pleasure rooms, their revelers clearly visible as they moved grandly up or down or along.

Uneasily, Derek lay on his couch. A vision of his Mistress's face was before him; he could imagine how she would treat all this harmless festivity: with cool contempt. His own pleasure was consequently reduced to ashes.

"I suppose you'll be moving back to Earth as soon as possible?"

"Eh?" Derek grunted.

"I said, I supposed you would soon be going home again." The speaker was Belix Ix Sappose, Chief Administrator of High Gee Research at Star One; as Derek's host of the evening, he lay next to him.

"I'm sorry, Belix, yes—I shall have to head back for home soon."

"No 'have to' about it. You have discovered an entirely new life form; we can now attempt communication with the Festi XV entity, with goodness knows what extension of knowledge. The government can easily show its gratitude by awarding you any sort of post here you care to name; I am not without influence in that respect, as you are aware. I don't imagine that Earth in its senescent stage has much to offer a man of your calibre."

Derek thought of what it had to offer. He was bound to it. These decadent people did not understand how anything could be binding.

"Well, what do you say, Ende? I'm not speaking idly." Belix Ix Sappose tapped his antler system impatiently.

"Er…Oh, they will discover a great deal from the Cliff. That doesn't concern me. My part of the work is over. I'm just a field worker, not an intellectual."

"You don't reply to my suggestion."

He looked at Belix with only slight vexation. Belix was an unglaat, one of a species that had done as much as any to bring about the peaceful concourse of the galaxy. His backbone branched into an elaborate antler system, from which six sloe-dark eyes surveyed Derek with unblinking irritation. Other members of the party, including Jupkey, Belix's female, were also looking at him.

"I must get back to Earth soon," Derek said. What had Belix said? Offered some sort of post? Restlessly he shifted on his couch, under pressure as always when surrounded by people he knew none too well.

"You are bored, Mr. Ende."

"No, not at all. My apologies, Belix. I'm overcome as always by the luxury of Eyebright. I was watching the nude dancers."

"I fear you are bored."

"Not at all, I assure you."

"May I get you a woman?"

"No, thank you."

"A boy, perhaps?"

"No, thank you."

"Have you ever tried the flowering asexuals from the Cphids?"

"Not at present, thank you."

"Then perhaps you will excuse us if Jupkey and I remove our clothes and join the dance," Belix said stiffly.

As they moved out onto the dance floor to greet the strepent trumpets, Derek heard Jupkey say something of which he caught only the words "arrogant Earthborn." His eyes met Jon's; he saw that the partheno had overheard also.

In an instinctive dismissive gesture of his left hand, Derek revealed his mortification. He rose and began to pace round the room. Often he shouldered his way through a knot of naked dancers, ignoring their complaints.

At one of the doors, a staircase was floating by. He stepped onto it to escape from the crowds.

Four young women were passing down the stairs. They were gaily dressed, with sonant-stones pulsing on their costumes. In their faces youth kept its lantern, lighting them as they laughed and chattered. Derek stopped and beheld the girls. One of them he recognised. Instinctively he called her name: "Eva!"

She had already seen him. Waving her companions on, she came back to him, dancing up the intervening steps.

"So the brave Earthborn climbs once more the golden stairs of Pynnati! Well, Derek Ende, your eyes are as dark as ever, and your brow as high!"

As he looked at her, the strepent trumpets were in tune for him for the first time that evening, and his delight rose up in his throat.

"Eva!…And your eyes as bright as ever…And you have no man with you."

"The powers of coincidence work on your behalf." She laughed—yes, he remembered that sound!—and then said more seriously, "I heard you were here with Belix Sappose and his female; so I was making the grandly foolish gesture of coming to see you. You remember how devoted I am to foolish gestures."

"So foolish?"

"Probably. You have less change in you, Derek Ende, than the core of Pyrylyn. To suppose otherwise is foolish, to know how unalterable you are and still to see you doubly foolish."

He took her hand, beginning to lead her up the staircase; the rooms moving by them on either side were blurs to his eyes.

"Must you still bring up that old charge, Eva?"

"It lies between us; I do not have to touch it. I fear your unchangeability because I am a butterfly against your grey castle."

"You are beautiful, Eva, so beautiful!—And may a butterfly not rest unharmed on a castle wall?" He fitted into her allusive way of speech with difficulty.

"Walls! I cannot bear your walls, Derek! Am I a bulldozer that I should want to come up against walls? To be either inside or outside them is to be a prisoner."

"Let us not quarrel until we have found some point of agreement," he said. "Here are the stars. Can't we agree about them?"

"If we are both indifferent to them," she said, looking out and impudently winding his arm about her. The staircase had reached the zenith of its travels and moved slowly sideways along the upper edge of Eyebright. They stood on the top step with night flashing their images back at them from the glass.

Eva Coll-Kennerley was a human, but not of Earthborn stock. She was a velure, born on the y-cluster worlds of the dense Third Arm of the galaxy, and her skin was richly covered with the brown fur of her kind. Her mercurial talents were employed in the same research department that enjoyed Belix Sappose's more sober ones; Derek had met her there on an earlier visit to Pyrylyn. Their love had been an affair of swords.

He looked at her now and touched her and could say not one word for himself. When she flashed a liquid eye at him, he essayed an awkward smile.

"Because I am oriented like a compass towards strong men, my lavish offer to you still holds good. Is it not bait enough?" she asked him.

"I don't think of you as a trap, Eva."

"Then for how many more centuries are you going to refrigerate your nature on Earth? You still remain faithful, if I recall your euphemism for slavery, to your Mistress, to her cold lips and locked heart?"

"I have no choice!"

"Ah yes, my debate on that motion was defeated: and more than once. Is she still pursuing her researches into the trans-mutability of species?"

"Oh yes, indeed. The mediaeval idea that one species can turn into another was foolish in the Middle Ages; now, with the gradual accumulation of cosmic radiation in planetary bodies, it is correct to a certain definable extent. She is endeavouring to show that cellular bondage can be—"

"Yes, yes, and this serious talk is an eyesore in Eyebright! You are locked away, Derek, doing your sterile deeds of heroism and never entering the real world. If you imagine you can live with her much longer and then come to me, you are mistaken. Your walls grow higher about your ears every century, till I cannot, cannot—oh, it's the wrong metaphor!—cannot scale you!"

Even in his pain, the texture of her fur was joy to his warmsight. Helplessly he shook his head in an effort to shake her clattering words away.

"Look at you being big and brave and silent even now! You're so arrogant," she said—and then, without perceptible change of tone, "Because I still love the bit of you inside the castle, I'll make once more my monstrous and petty offer to you."

"No, please, Eva!—"

"But yes! Forget this tedious bondage of Earth, forget this ghastly matriarchy, live here with me. I don't want you forever. You know I am a eudemonist and judge by standards of pleasure—our liaison need be only for a century or two. In that time, I will deny you nothing your senses may require."

"Eva!"

"After that, our demands will be satisfied. You may then go back to the Lady Mother of Endehaaven for all I care."

"Eva, you know how I spurn this belief, this eudemonism."

"Forget your creed! I'm asking you nothing difficult. Who are you to haggle? Am I fish, to be bought by the kilo, this bit selected, this rejected?"

He was silent.

"*You* don't really need me," he said at last. "You have everything already: beauty, wit, sense, warmth, feeling, balance, comfort. *She* has nothing. She is shallow, haunted, cold—oh, she needs me, Eva…"

"You are apologising for yourself, not her."

She had already turned with the supple movement of a velure and was running down the staircase. Lighted chambers drifted up about them like bubbles.

His laboured attempt to explain his heart turned to exasperation. He ran down after her, grasping her arm.

"Listen to me, will you, damn you!"

"Nobody in Pyrylyn would listen to such masochistic nonsense as yours! You are an arrogant fool, Derek, and I am a weak-willed one. Now release me!"

As the next room came up, she jumped through its entrance and disappeared into the crowd.

V

Not all the drifting chambers of Eyebright were lighted. Some pleasures come more delightfully with the dark, and these pleasures were coaxed and cossetted into fruition in shrouded halls where illumination cast only the gentlest ripple on the ceiling and the gloom was sensuous with ylang-ylang and other perfumes. Here Derek found a place to weep.

Sections of his life slid before him as if impelled by the same mechanisms that moved Eyebright. Always, one presence was there.

Angrily he related to himself how he always laboured to satisfy her—yes, in every sphere laboured to satisfy her! And how when that satisfaction was accorded him it came as though riven from her, as a spring sometimes trickles down the split face of a rock. Undeniably there was satisfaction for him in drinking from that cool source—but no, where was the satisfaction when pleasure depended on such extreme disciplining and subduing of himself?

Mistress, I love and hate your needs!

And the discipline had been such...so long, also...that now when he might enjoy himself far from her, he could scarcely strike a trickle from his own rock. He had walked here before, in this city where the hedonists and eudemonists reigned, walked among the scents of pleasure, walked among the ioblepharous women, the beautiful guests and celebrated beauties, with My Lady always in him, feeling that she showed even on his countenance. People spoke to him: somehow he replied. They manifested gaiety: he tried to do so. They opened to him: he attempted a response. All the time, he hoped they would understand that his arrogance masked only shyness—or did he hope that it was his shyness which masked arrogance? He did not know.

Who could presume to know? The one quality holds much of the other. Both refuse to come forward and share.

He roused from his meditation knowing that Eva Coll-Kennerley was again somewhere near. She had not left the building, then! She was seeking him out!

Derek half-rose from his position in a shrouded alcove. He was baffled to think how she could have traced him here. On entering Eyebright, visitors were given sonant-stones, by which they could be traced from room to room; but judging that nobody would wish to trace him, Derek had switched his stone off even before leaving Belix Sappose's party.

He heard Eva's voice, its unmistakable overtones not near, not far...

"You find the most impenetrable bushels to hide your light under..."

He caught no more. She had sunk down among tapestries with someone else. She was not after him at all! Waves of relief and regret rolled over him... and when he paid attention again, she was speaking his name.

With shame on him, like a wolf creeping towards a camp fire, he crouched forward to listen. At once his warmsight told him to whom Eva spoke. He recognised the pattern of the antlers; Belix was there, with Jupkey sprawled beside him on some elaborate kind of bed.

"…useless to try again. Derek is too far entombed within himself," Eva said.

"Entombed rather within his conditioning," Belix said. "We found the same. It's conditioning, my dear."

"However he became entombed, I still admire him enough to want to understand him." Eva's voice was a note or two astray from its usual controlled timbre.

"Look at it scientifically," Belix said, with the weighty inflections of a man about to produce truth out of a hat. "Earth is the last bastion of a bankrupt culture. The Earthborns number less than a couple of millions now. They disdain social graces and occasions. They are served by parthenogenetically bred slaves, all of which are built on the same controlled genetic formula. They are inbred. In consequence, they have become practically a species apart. You can see it all in friend Ende. As I say, he's entombed in his conditioning. A tragedy, Eva, but you must face up to it."

"You're probably right, you pontifical old pop," Jupkey said lazily. "Who but an Earthborn would do what Derek did on Festi?"

"No, no!" Eva said. "Derek's ruled by a woman, not by conditioning. He's—"

"In Ende's case they are one and the same thing, my dear, believe me. Consider Earth's social organisation. The partheno slaves have replaced all but a comparative handful of true Earthborns. That handful has parcelled out Earth into great estates which it holds by a sinister matriarchalism."

"Yes, I know, but Derek—"

"Derek is caught in the system. The Earthborns have fallen into a mating pattern for which there is no precedent. The sons of a family marry their mothers, not only to perpetuate their line but because the productive Earthborn female is scarce now that Earth itself is senescent. This is what the Endes have done; this is what Derek Ende has done. His 'mistress' is both mother and wife to him. Given the factor of longevity as well—well, naturally you ensure an excessive emotional rigidity that almost nothing can break. Not even you, my sweet-coated Eva!"

"He was on the point of breaking tonight!"

"I doubt it," Belix said. "Ende may want to get away from his claustrophobic home, but the same forces that drive him off will eventually lure him back."

"I tell you he was on the point of breaking—only I broke first."

"Well, as Teer Ruche said to me many centuries ago, only a pleasure-hater knows how to shape a pleasure-hater. I would say you were lucky he did not break; you would only have had a baby on your hands."

Her answering laugh did not ring true.

"My Lady of Endehaaven, then, must be the one to do it. I will never try again—though he seems under too much stress to stand for long. Oh, it's really immoral! He deserves better!"

"A moral judgement from you, Eva!" Jupkey exclaimed amusedly to the fragrant gloom.

"My advice to you, Eva, is to forget all about the poor fellow. Apart from anything else, he is barely articulate—which would not suit you for a season."

The unseen listener could bear no more. A sudden rage—as much against himself for hearing as against them for speaking—burst over him, freeing him to act. Straightening up, he seized the arm of the couch on which Belix and Jupkey nestled, wildly supposing he could tip them onto the floor.

Too late, his warmsight warned him of the real nature of the couch. Instead of tipping, it swivelled, sending a wave of liquid over him. The two unglaats were lying in a warm bath scented with ylang-ylang and other essences.

Jupkey squealed in anger and fright. Kicking out, she caught Derek on the shin with a hoof; he slipped in the oily liquid and fell. Belix, unaided by warmsight, jumped out of the bath, entangled himself with Derek's legs, and also fell.

Eva was shouting for lights. Other occupants of the hall cried back that darkness must prevail at all costs.

Picking himself up—leaving only his dignity behind—Derek ran for the exit, abandoning the confusion to sort itself out as it would.

Burningly, disgustedly, he made his way dripping from Eyebright. The hastening footsteps of Jon followed him like an echo all the way to the space field.

Soon he would be back at Endehaaven. Though he would always be a failure in his dealings with other humans, there at least he knew every inch of his bleak allotted territory.

ENVOI

Had there been a spell over all Endehaaven, it could have been no quieter when My Lord Derek Ende arrived home.

I informed My Lady of the moment when his lightpusher arrived and rode at orbit. In the receptor bowl I watched him and Jon come home, cutting northwest across the emaciated wilds of Europe, across Denmark, over the Shetlands, the Faroes, the sea, alighting by the very edge of the island, by the fjord with its silent waters.

All the while the wind lay low as if under some stunning malediction, and none of our tall trees stirred.

"Where is my Mistress, Hols?" Derek asked me, as I went to greet him and assist him out of his suit.

"She asked me to tell you that she is confined to her chambers and cannot see you, My Lord."

He looked me in the eyes as he did so rarely.

"Is she ill?"

"No."

Without waiting to remove his suit, he hurried on into the building.

Over the next two days, he was about but little, preferring to remain in his room. Once he wandered among the experimental tanks and cages. I saw him net a fish and toss it into the air, watching it while it struggled into new form and flew away until it was lost in a jumbled background of cumulus; but it was plain he was less interested in the riddles of stress and transmutation than in the symbolism of the carp's flight.

Mostly he sat compiling the spools on which he imposed the tale of his life. All one wall was covered with files full of these spools: the arrested drumbeats of past centuries. From the later spools I have secretly compiled this record; for all his unspoken self-pity, he never knew the sickness of merely observing.

We parthenos will never understand the luxuries of a divided mind. Surely suffering as much as happiness is a kind of artistry?

On the day that he received a summons from Star One to go upon another quest for them, Derek met My Lady in the Blue Corridor.

"It is good to see you about again, Mistress," he said, kissing her cheek.

She stroked his hair. On her nervous hand she wore one ring with an amber stone; her gown was of olive and umber.

"I was very upset to have you go away from me. The Earth is dying, Derek, and I fear its loneliness. You have left me alone too much. However, I have recovered myself and am glad to see you back."

"You know I am glad to see you. Smile for me and come outside for some fresh air. The sun is shining."

"It's so long since it shone. Do you remember how once it always shone? I can't bear to quarrel any more. Take my arm and be kind to me."

"Mistress, I always wish to be kind to you. And I have all sorts of things to discuss with you. You'll want to hear what I have been doing, and—"

"You won't leave me any more?"

He felt her hand tighten on his arm. She spoke very loudly.

"That was one of the things I wished to discuss—later," he said. "First let me tell you about the wonderful life form with which I made contact on Festi."

As they left the corridor and descended the paragravity shaft, My Lady said wearily, "I suppose that's a polite way of telling me that you are bored here."

He clutched her hands as they floated down. Then he released them and clutched her face instead.

"Understand this. Mistress mine, I love you and want to serve you. You are in my blood; wherever I go I never can forget you. My dearest wish is to make you happy—this you must know. But equally you must know that I have needs of my own."

Grumpily she said, withdrawing her face, "Oh, I know that all right. And I know those needs will always come first with you. Whatever you say or pretend, you don't care a rap about me. You make that all too clear."

She moved ahead of him, shaking off the hand he put on her arm. He had a vision of himself running down a golden staircase and stretching out that same detaining hand to another girl. The indignity of having to repeat oneself, century after century.

"You're lying! You're faking! You're being cruel!" he said.

Gleaming, she turned.

"Am I? Then answer me this—aren't you already planning to leave Endehaaven and me soon?"

He smote his forehead.

He said inarticulately, "Look, you must try to stop this recrimination. Yes, yes, it's true I am thinking… But I have to—I reproach myself. I could be kinder. But you shut yourself away when I come back, you don't welcome me—"

"Trust you to find excuses rather than face up to your own nature," she said contemptuously, walking briskly into the garden. Amber and olive and umber, and sable of hair, she walked down the path, her outlines sharp in the winter air; in the perspectives of his mind she did not dwindle.

For some minutes he stood in the threshold, immobilized by antagonistic emotions.

Finally he pushed himself out into the sunlight.

She was in her favourite spot by the fjord, feeding an old badger from her hand. Only her increased attention to the badger suggested that she heard him approach.

His boscises twitched as he said, "If you will forgive a cliché, I apologise."

"I don't mind what you do."

Walking backwards and forwards behind her, he said, "When I was away, I heard some people talking. On Pyrylyn this was. They were discussing the mores of our matrimonial system."

"It's no business of theirs."

"Perhaps not. But what they said suggested a new line of thought to me."

She put the old badger back in his cage without comment.

"Are you listening, Mistress?"

"Do go on."

"Try to listen sympathetically. Consider all the history of galactic exploration—or even before that, consider the explorers of Earth in the pre-space age, men like Shackleton and so on. They were brave men, of course, but wouldn't it be strange if most of them only ventured where they did because the struggle at home was too much for them?"

He stopped. She had turned to him; the half-smile was whipped off his face by her look of fury.

"And you're trying to tell me that that's how you see yourself—a martyr? Derek, how you must hate me! Not only do you go away, you secretly blame me because you go away. It doesn't matter that I tell you a thousand times I want you here—no, it's all my fault! I drive you away! That's what you tell your charming friends on Pyrylyn, isn't it? Oh, how you must hate me!"

Savagely he grasped her wrists. She screamed to me for aid and struggled. I came near but halted, playing my usual impotent part. He swore at her, bellowed for her to be silent, whereupon she cried the louder, shaking furiously in his arms.

He struck her across the face.

At once she was quiet. Her eyes closed: almost, it would seem, in ecstasy.

Standing there, she had the pose of a woman offering herself.

"Go on, hit me! You want to hit me!" she whispered.

With the words, with the look of her, he too was altered. As if realising for the first time her true nature, he dropped his fists and stepped back, staring at her sick-mouthed. His heel met no resistance. He twisted suddenly, spread out his arms as if to fly, and fell over the cliff edge.

Her scream pursued him down.

Even as his body hit the waters of the fjord, it began to change. A flurry of foam marked some sort of painful struggle beneath the surface. Then a seal plunged into view, dived below the next wave, and swam towards open sea over which already a freshening breeze blew.

Green Magic (1963)

JACK VANCE

JACK VANCE (1916–2013) authored dozens of novels over the course of his long career, including *To Live Forever*, *The Languages of Pao*, *Big Planet*, *The Last Castle*, and many more. His works variously won the Hugo, Nebula, Edgar, and World Fantasy awards.

Over the years, *F&SF* has published a lot of stories involving magic but, this one remains one of the best tales about the discipline of study. According to Gary Gygax, Vance's work was a big influence on *Dungeons & Dragons*.

HOWARD FAIR, LOOKING over the relics of his great uncle Gerald McIntyre, found a large ledger entitled:
WORKBOOK & JOURNAL
Open at Peril!

Fair read the journal with interest, although his own work went far beyond ideas treated only gingerly by Gerald McIntyre.

"The existence of disciplines concentric to the elementary magics must now be admitted without further controversy," wrote McIntyre. "Guided by a set of analogies from the white and black magics (to be detailed in due course), I have delineated the basic extension of purple magic, as well as its corollary, Dynamic Nomism."

Fair read on, remarking the careful charts, the projections and expansions, the transpolations and transformations by which Gerald McIntyre had conceived his systemology. So swiftly had the technical arts advanced that McIntyre's expositions, highly controversial sixty years before, now seemed pedantic and overly rigorous.

"Whereas benign creatures: angels, white sprites, merrihews, sandestins—are typical of the white cycle; whereas demons, magners, trolls and warlocks are evinced by black magic; so do the purple and green cycles sponsor their own particulars, but these are neither good nor evil, bearing, rather, the same relation to the black and white provinces that these latter do to our own basic realm."

Fair re-read the passage. The "green cycle"? Had Gerald McIntyre wandered into regions overlooked by modern workers?

He reviewed the journal in the light of this suspicion, and discovered additional hints and references. Especially provocative was a bit of scribbled marginalia: "More concerning my latest researches I may not state, having been promised an infinite reward for this forbearance."

The passage was dated a day before Gerald McIntyre's death, which had occurred on March 21, 1898, the first day of spring. McIntyre had enjoyed very little of his "infinite reward," whatever had been its nature… Fair returned to a consideration of the journal, which, in a sentence or two, had opened a chink on an entire, new panorama. McIntyre provided no further illumination, and Fair set out to make a fuller investigation.

His first steps were routine. He performed two divinations, searched the standard indexes, concordances, handbooks and formularies, evoked a demon whom he had previously found knowledgeable: all without success. He found no direct reference to cycles beyond the purple; the demon refused even to speculate.

Fair was by no means discouraged; if anything, the intensity of his interest increased. He re-read the journal, with particular care to the justification for purple magic, reasoning that McIntyre, groping for a lore beyond the purple, might well have used the methods which had yielded results before. Applying stains and ultraviolet light to the pages, Fair made legible a number of notes McIntyre had jotted down, then erased.

Fair was immensely stimulated. The notes assured him that he was on the right track, and further indicated a number of blind alleys which Fair profited by avoiding. He applied himself so successfully that before the week was out he had evoked a sprite of the green cycle.

It appeared in the semblance of a man with green glass eyes and a thatch of young eucalyptus leaves in the place of hair. It greeted Fair with cool courtesy, would not seat itself, and ignored Fair's proffer of coffee.

After wandering around the apartment inspecting Fair's books and curios with an air of negligent amusement, it agreed to respond to Fair's questions.

Fair asked permission to use his tape recorder, which the sprite allowed, and Fair set the apparatus in motion. (When subsequently he replayed the interview, no sound could be heard.)

"What realms of magic lie beyond the green?" asked Fair.

"I can't give you an exact answer," replied the sprite, "because I don't know. There are at least two more, corresponding to the colors we call rawn and pallow, and very likely others."

Fair arranged the microphone where it would more directly intercept the voice of the sprite.

"What," he asked, "is the green cycle like? What is its physical semblance?"

The sprite paused to consider. Glistening mother-of-pearl films wandered across its face, reflecting the tinge of its thoughts. "I'm rather severely restricted by your use of the word 'physical.' And 'semblance' involves a subjective interpretation, which changes with the rise and fall of the seconds."

"By all means," Fair said hastily, "describe it in your own words."

"Well—we have four different regions, two of which floresce from the basic skeleton of the universe, and so subsede the others. The first of these is compressed and isthiated, but is notable for its wide pools of mottle which we use sometimes for deranging stations. We've transplanted club-mosses from Earth's Devonian and a few ice-fires from Perdition. They climb among the rods which we call devil-hair—" He went on for several minutes but the meaning almost entirely escaped Fair. And it seemed as if the question by which he had hoped to break the ice might run away with the entire interview. He introduced another idea.

"'Can we freely manipulate the physical extensions of Earth?'" The sprite seemed amused. "You refer, so I assume, to the various aspects of space, time, mass, energy, life, thought and recollection."

"Exactly."

The sprite raised its green corn-silk eyebrows. "I might as sensibly ask can you break an egg by striking it with a club? The response is on a similar level of seriousness."

Fair had expected a certain amount of condescension and impatience, and was not abashed. "How may I learn these techniques?"

"In the usual manner: through diligent study."

"Ah, indeed—but where could I study? Who would teach me?"

The sprite made an easy gesture, and whorls of green smoke trailed from his fingers to spin through the air. "I could arrange the matter, but since I bear you no particular animosity, I'll do nothing of the sort. And now, I must be gone."

"Where do you go?" Fair asked in wonder and longing. "May I go with you?"

The sprite, swirling a drape of bright green dust over its shoulders, shook his head. "You would be less than comfortable."

"Other men have explored the worlds of magic!"

"True: your uncle Gerald McIntyre, for instance."

"My uncle Gerald learned green magic?"

"To the limit of his capabilities. He found no pleasure in his learning. You would do well to profit by his experience and modify your ambitions." The sprite turned and walked away.

Fair watched it depart. The sprite receded in space and dimension, but never reached the wall of Fair's room. At a distance which might have been fifty yards, the sprite glanced back, as if to make sure that Fair was not following, then stepped off at another angle and disappeared.

Fair's first impulse was to take heed and limit his explorations. He was an adept in white magic, and had mastered the black art—occasionally he evoked a demon to liven a social gathering which otherwise threatened to become dull—but he had by no means illuminated every mystery of purple magic, which is the realm of Incarnate Symbols.

Howard Fair might have turned away from the green cycle except for three factors.

First was his physical appearance. He stood rather under medium height, with a swarthy face, sparse black hair, a gnarled nose, a small heavy mouth. He felt no great sensitivity about his appearance, but realized that it might be improved. In his mind's eye he pictured the personified ideal of himself: he was taller by six inches, his nose thin and keen, his skin cleared of its muddy undertone. A striking figure, but still recognizable as Howard Fair. He wanted the love of women, but he wanted it without the interposition of his craft. Many times he had brought beautiful girls to his bed, lips wet and eyes shining; but purple magic had seduced them rather than Howard Fair, and he took limited satisfaction in such conquests.

Here was the first factor which drew Howard Fair back to the green lore; the second was his yearning for extended, perhaps eternal, life; the third was simple thirst for knowledge.

The fact of Gerald McIntyre's death, or dissolution, or disappearance—whatever had happened to him—was naturally a matter of concern. If he had won to a goal so precious, why had he died so quickly? Was the "infinite reward" so miraculous, so exquisite, that the mind failed under its possession? (If such were the case, the reward was hardly a reward.)

Fair could not restrain himself, and by degrees returned to a study of green magic. Rather than again invoke the sprite whose air of indulgent contempt he had found exasperating, he decided to seek knowledge by an indirect method, employing the most advanced concepts of technical and cabalistic science.

He obtained a portable television transmitter which he loaded into his panel truck along with a receiver. On a Monday night in early May, he drove to an abandoned graveyard far out in the wooded hills, and there, by the light of a waning moon, he buried the television camera in graveyard clay until only the lens protruded from the soil.

With a sharp alder twig he scratched on the ground a monstrous outline. The television lens served for one eye, a beer bottle pushed neck-first into the soil the other.

During the middle hours, while the moon died behind wisps of pale cloud, he carved a word on the dark forehead; then recited the activating incantation.

The ground rumbled and moaned, the golem heaved up to blot out the stars.

The glass eyes stared down at Fair, secure in his pentagon.

"Speak!" called out Fair. *"Enteresthes, Akmai Adonai Bidemgir! Elohim, pa rahulli! Enteresthes, HVOI!* Speak!"

"Return me to earth, return my clay to the quiet clay from whence you roused me."

"First you must serve."

The golem stumbled forward to crush Fair, but was halted by the pang of protective magic.

"Serve you I will, if serve you I must."

Fair stepped boldly forth from the pentagon, strung from yards of green ribbon down the road in the shape of a narrow V. "Go forth into the realm of green magic," he told the monster. "The ribbons reach forty miles, walk to the end, turn about, return, and then fall back, return to the earth from which you rose."

The golem turned, shuffled into the V of green ribbon, shaking off clods of mold, jarring the ground with its ponderous tread.

Fair watched the squat shape dwindle, recede, yet never reach the angle of the magic V. He returned to his panel truck, tuned the television receiver to the golem's eye, and surveyed the fantastic vistas of the green realm.

Two elementals of the green realm met on a spun-silver landscape. They were Jaadian and Misthemar, and they fell to discussing the earthen monster which had stalked forty miles through the region known as Cil; which then, turning in tracks, had retraced its steps, gradually increasing its pace until at the end it moved in a shambling rush, leaving a trail of clods on the fragile moth-wing mosaics.

"Events, events, events," Misthemar fretted, "they crowd the chute of time till the bounds bulge. Or then again, the course is as lean and spare as a stretched tendon... But in regard to this incursion..." He paused for a period of reflection, and silver clouds moved over his head and under his feet.

Jaadian remarked, "You are aware that I conversed with Howard Fair; he is so obsessed to escape the squalor of his world that he acts with recklessness."

"The man Gerald McIntyre was his uncle," mused Misthemar. "McIntyre besought, we yielded; as perhaps now we must yield to Howard Fair."

Jaadian uneasily opened his hand, shook off a spray of emerald fire. "Events press, both in and out. I find myself unable to act in this regard."

"I likewise do not care to be the agent of tragedy."

A Meaning came fluttering up from below: "A disturbance among the spiral towers! A caterpillar of glass and metal has come clanking; it has thrust electric eyes into the Portinone and broke open the Egg of Innocence. Howard Fair is the fault."

Jaadian and Misthemar consulted each other with wry disinclination. "Very well, both of us will go; such a duty needs two souls in support."

They impinged upon Earth and found Howard Fair in a wall booth at a cocktail bar. He looked up at the two strangers and one of them asked, "May we join you?"

Fair examined the two men. Both wore conservative suits and carried cashmere topcoats over their arms. Fair noticed that the left thumb-nail of each man glistened green.

Fair rose politely to his feet. "Will you sit down?"

The green sprites hung up their overcoats and slid into the booth. Fair looked from one to the other. He addressed Jaadian. "Aren't you he whom I interviewed several weeks ago?"

Jaadian assented. "You have not accepted my advice."

Fair shrugged. "You asked me to remain ignorant, to accept my stupidity and ineptitude."

"And why should you not?" asked Jaadian gently. "You are a primitive in a primitive realm; nevertheless not one man in a thousand can match your achievements."

Fair agreed, smiling faintly. "But knowledge creates a craving for further knowledge. Where is the harm in knowledge?"

Misthemar, the more mercurial of the sprites, spoke angrily. "Where is the harm? Consider your earthen monster! It befouled forty miles of delicacy, the record of ten million years. Consider your caterpillar! It trampled our pillars of carved milk, our dreaming towers, damaged the nerve-skeins which extrude and waft us our Meanings."

"I'm dreadfully sorry," said Fair. "I meant no destruction."

The sprites nodded. "But your apology conveys no guarantee of restraint."

Fair toyed with his glass. A waiter approached the table, addressed the two sprites. "Something for you two gentlemen?"

Jaadian ordered a glass of charged water, as did Misthemar. Fair called for another highball.

"What do you hope to gain from this activity?" inquired Misthemar. "Destructive forays teach you nothing!"

Fair agreed. "I have learned little. But I have seen miraculous sights. I am more than ever anxious to learn."

The green sprites glumly watched the bubbles rising in their glasses. Jaadian at last drew a deep sigh. "Perhaps we can obviate toil on your part and disturbance on ours. Explicitly, what gains or advantages do you hope to derive from green magic?"

Fair, smiling, leaned back into the red imitation-leather cushions. "I want many things. Extended life—mobility in time—comprehensive memory—augmented perception, with vision across the whole spectrum. I want physical charm and magnetism, the semblance of youth, muscular endurance... Then there are qualities more or less speculative, such as—"

Jaadian interrupted. "These qualities and characteristics we will confer upon you. In return you will undertake never again to disturb the green realm. You will evade centuries of toil; we will be spared the nuisance of your presence, and the inevitable tragedy."

"Tragedy?" inquired Fair in wonder. "Why tragedy?"

Jaadian spoke in a deep reverberating voice. "You are a man of Earth. Your goals are not our goals. Green magic makes you aware of our goals."

Fair thoughtfully sipped his highball. "I can't see that this is a disadvantage. I am willing to submit to the discipline of instruction. Surely a knowledge of green magic will not change me into a different entity?"

"No. And this is the basic tragedy!"

Misthemar spoke in exasperation. "We are forbidden to harm lesser creatures, and so you are fortunate; for to dissolve you into air would end all the annoyance."

Fair laughed. "I apologize again for making such a nuisance of myself. But surely you understand how important this is to me?"

Jaadian asked hopefully, "Then you agree to our offer?"

Fair shook his head. "How could I live, forever young, capable of extended learning, but limited to knowledge which I already see bounds to? I would be bored, restless, miserable."

"That well may be," said Jaadian. "But not so bored, restless and miserable as if you were learned in green magic."

Fair drew himself erect. "I must learn green magic. It is an opportunity which only a person both torpid and stupid could refuse."

Jaadian sighed. "In your place I would make the same response." The sprites rose to their feet. "Come then, we will teach you."

"Don't say we didn't warn you," said Misthemar.

Time passed. Sunset waned and twilight darkened. A man walked up the stairs, entered Howard Fair's apartment. He was tall, unobtrusively muscular. His face was sensitive, keen, humorous; his left thumb-nail glistened green.

Time is a function of vital processes. The people of Earth had perceived the motion of their clocks. On this understanding, two hours had elapsed since Howard Fair had followed the green sprites from the bar.

Howard Fair had perceived other criteria. For him the interval had been seven hundred years, during which he had lived in the green realm, learning to the utmost capacity of his brain.

He had occupied two years training his senses to the new conditions. Gradually he learned to walk in the six basic three-dimensional directions, and accustomed himself to the fourth-dimensional short-cuts. By easy stages the blinds over his eyes were removed, so that the dazzling over-human intricacy of the landscape never completely confounded him.

Another year was spent training him to the use of a code-language— an intermediate step between the vocalizations of Earth and the meaning-patterns of the green realm, where a hundred symbol-flakes (each a flitting spot of delicate iridescence) might be displayed in a single swirl of import. During this time Howard Fair's eyes and brain were altered, to allow him the use of the many new colors, without which the meaning-flakes could not be recognized.

These were preliminary steps. For forty years he studied the flakes, of which there were almost a million. Another forty years was given to elementary permutations and shifts, and another forty to parallels, attenuation, diminishments and extensions; and during this time he was introduced to flake patterns, and certain of the more obvious displays.

Now he was able to study without recourse to the code-language, and his progress became more marked. Another twenty years found him able to recognize more complicated Meanings, and he was introduced to a more varied program. He floated over the field of moth-wing mosaics, which still showed the footprints of the golem. He sweated in embarrassment, the extent of his wicked willfulness now clear to him.

So passed the years. Howard Fair learned as much green magic as his brain could encompass.

He explored much of the green realm, finding so much beauty that he feared his brain might burst. He tasted, he heard, he felt, he sensed, and each one of his senses was a hundred times more discriminating than before. Nourishment came in a thousand different forms: from pink eggs which burst into a hot sweet gas, suffusing his entire body; from passing through a rain of stinging metal crystals; from simple contemplation of the proper symbol.

Homesickness for Earth waxed and waned. Sometimes it was insupportable and he was ready to forsake all he had learned and abandon his hopes for the future. At other times the magnificence of the green realm permeated him, and the thought of departure seemed like the threat of death itself.

By stages so gradual he never realized them he learned green magic.

But the new faculty gave him no pride: between his crude ineptitudes and the poetic elegance of the sprites remained a tremendous gap—and he felt his innate inferiority much more keenly than he ever had in his old state. Worse, his most earnest efforts failed to improve his technique, and sometimes, observing the singing joy of an improvised manifestation by one of the sprites, and contrasting it to his own labored constructions, he felt futility and shame.

The longer he remained in the green realm, the stronger grew the sense of his own maladroitness, and he began to long for the easy environment of Earth, where each of his acts would not shout aloud of vulgarity and crassness. At times he would watch the sprites (in the gossamer forms natural to them) at play among the pearl-petals, or twining like quick flashes of music through the forest of pink spirals. The contrast between their verve and his brutish fumbling could not be borne and he would turn away. His self-respect dwindled with each passing hour, and instead of pride in his learning, he felt a sullen ache for what he was not and could never become. The first few hundred years he worked with the enthusiasm of ignorance, for the next few he was buoyed by hope. During the last part of his time, only dogged obstinacy kept him plodding through what now he knew for infantile exercises.

In one terrible bitter-sweet spasm, he gave up. He found Jaadian weaving tinkling fragments of various magics into a warp of shining long splines. With grave courtesy, Jaadian gave Fair his attention, and Fair laboriously set forth his meaning.

Jaadian returned a message. "I recognize your discomfort, and extend my sympathy. It is best that you now return to your native home."

He put aside his weaving and conveyed Fair down through the requisite vortices. Along the way they passed Misthemar. No flicker of meaning was expressed or exchanged, but Howard Fair thought to feel a tinge of faintly malicious amusement.

Howard Fair sat in his apartment. His perceptions, augmented and sharpened by his sojourn in the green realm, took note of the surroundings. Only two hours before, by the clocks of Earth, he had found them both restful and stimulating; now they were neither. His books: superstition, spuriousness, earnest nonsense. His private journals and workbooks: a pathetic scrawl of infantilisms. Gravity tugged at his feet, held him rigid. The shoddy construction of the house, which heretofore he never had noticed, oppressed him. Everywhere he looked he saw slipshod disorder, primitive filth. The thought of the food he must now eat revolted him.

He went out on his little balcony which overlooked the street. The air was impregnated with organic smells. Across the street he could look into windows where his fellow humans lived in stupid squalor.

Fair smiled sadly. He had tried to prepare himself for these reactions, but now was surprised by their intensity. He returned into his apartment. He must accustom himself to the old environment. And after all there were compensations. The most desirable commodities of the world were now his to enjoy.

Howard Fair plunged into the enjoyment of these pleasures. He forced himself to drink quantities of expensive wines, brandies, liqueurs, even though they offended his palate. Hunger overcame his nausea, he forced himself to the consumption of what he thought of as fried animal tissue, the hypertrophied sexual organs of plants. He experimented with erotic sensations, but found that beautiful women no longer seemed different from the plain ones, and that he could barely steel himself to the untidy contacts. He bought libraries of erudite books, glanced through them with contempt. He tried to amuse himself with his old magics; they seemed ridiculous.

He forced himself to enjoy these pleasures for a month; then he fled the city and established a crystal bubble on a crag in the Andes. To nourish himself, he contrived a thick liquid, which, while by no means as exhilarating as the substances of the green realm, was innocent of organic contamination.

After a certain degree of improvisation and make-shift, he arranged his life to its minimum discomfort. The view was one of austere grandeur; not even the condors came to disturb him. He sat back to ponder the chain of events which had started with his discovery of Gerald McIntyre's workbook. He frowned. Gerald McIntyre? He jumped to his feet, looked far off over the crags.

He found Gerald McIntyre at a wayside service station in the heart of the South Dakota prairie. McIntyre was sitting in an old wooden chair, tilted back against the peeling yellow paint of the service station, a straw hat shading his eyes from the sun.

He was a magnetically handsome man, blond of hair, brown of skin, with blue eyes whose gaze stung like the touch of icicle. His left thumb-nail glistened green.

Fair greeted him casually; the two men surveyed each other with wry curiosity.

"I see you have adapted yourself," said Howard Fair.

McIntyre shrugged. "As well as possible. I try to maintain a balance between solitude and the pressure of humanity." He looked into the bright blue sky where crows flapped and called. "For many years I lived in isolation. I began to detest the sound of my own breathing."

Along the highway came a glittering automobile, rococo as a hybrid goldfish. With the perceptions now available to them, Fair and McIntyre could see the driver to be red-faced and truculent, his companion a peevish woman in expensive clothes.

"There are other advantages to residence here," said McIntyre. "For instance, I am able to enrich the lives of passers-by with trifles of novel adventure." He made a small gesture; two dozen crows swooped down and flew beside the automobile. They settled on the fenders, strutted back and forth along the hood, fouled the windshield.

The automobile squealed to a halt, the driver jumped out, put the birds to flight. He threw an ineffectual rock, waved his arms in outrage, returned to his car, proceeded.

"A paltry affair," said McIntyre with a sigh. "The truth of the matter is that I am bored." He pursed his mouth and blew forth three bright puffs of smoke: first red, then yellow, then blazing blue. "I have arrived at the estate of foolishness, as you can see."

Fair surveyed his great uncle with a trace of uneasiness. McIntyre laughed. "No more pranks. I predict, however, that you will presently share my malaise."

"I share it already," said Fair. "Sometimes I wish I could abandon all my magic and return to my former innocence."

"I have toyed with the idea," McIntyre replied thoughtfully. "In fact I have made all the necessary arrangements. It is really a simple matter." He led Fair to a small room behind the station. Although the door was open, the interior showed a thick darkness.

McIntyre, standing well back, surveyed the darkness with a quizzical curl to his lip. "You need only enter. All your magic, all your recollections of the green realm will depart. You will be no wiser than the next man you meet. And with your knowledge will go your boredom, your melancholy, your dissatisfaction."

Fair contemplated the dark doorway. A single step would resolve his discomfort.

He glanced at McIntyre; the two surveyed each other with sardonic amusement. They returned to the front of the building.

"Sometimes I stand by the door and look into the darkness," said McIntyre. "Then I am reminded how dearly I cherish my boredom, and what a precious commodity is so much misery."

Fair made himself ready for departure. "I thank you for this new wisdom, which a hundred more years in the green realm would not have taught me. And now—for a time, at least—I go back to my crag in the Andes."

McIntyre tilted his chair against the wall of the service station. "And I—for a time, at least—will wait for the next passer-by."

"Goodby then, Uncle Gerald."

"Goodby, Howard."

Narrow Valley (1966)

R. A. LAFFERTY

It is fair to say that R. A. LAFFERTY (1914–2002) marched to the beat of a different drummer. Just a few of the ways he differed from the majority of science-fiction writers: He did not start writing until he was in his forties, his work had a rural bent to it (Mr. Lafferty lived in Tulsa, Oklahoma, for most of his life), his devout Catholicism informed much of his fiction, and his stories probably owed more to the works of James Joyce than to many of the writers traditionally associated with fantasy fiction. His novels—which include *Past Master, The Reefs of Earth, Arrive at Easterwine*, and *Okla Hannali*—range from the masterful to the nearly incomprehensible to the sublime.

All of which is simply background to help prepare any unsuspecting readers who are about to encounter Lafferty's fiction for the first time. "Narrow Valley" is representative of his fiction in that it is a pure shot of North American fabulism.

I N THE YEAR 1893, land allotments in severalty were made to the remaining eight hundred and twenty-one Pawnee Indians. Each would receive one hundred and sixty acres of land and no more, and thereafter the Pawnees would be expected to pay taxes on their land, the same as the White-Eyes did.

"Kitkehahke!" Clarence Big-Saddle cussed. "You can't kick a dog around proper on a hundred and sixty acres. And I sure am not hear before about this pay taxes on land."

Clarence Big-Saddle selected a nice green valley for his allotment. It was one of the half-dozen plots he had always regarded as his own. He sodded around the summer lodge that he had there and made it an all-season home. But he sure didn't intend to pay taxes on it.

So he burned leaves and bark and made a speech:

"That my valley be always wide and flourish and green and such stuff as that!" he orated in Pawnee chant style. "But that it be narrow if an intruder come."

He didn't have any balsam bark to burn. He threw on a little cedar bark instead. He didn't have any elder leaves. He used a handful of jack-oak leaves. And he forgot the word. How you going to work it if you forget the word?

"Petahauerat!" he howled out with the confidence he hoped would fool the fates.

"That's the same long of a word," he said in a low aside to himself. But he was doubtful. "What am I, a White Man, a burr-tailed jack, a new kind of nut to think it will work?" he asked. "I have to laugh at me. Oh well, we see."

He threw the rest of the bark and the leaves on the fire, and he hollered the wrong word out again.

And he was answered by a dazzling sheet of summer lightning.

"Skidi!" Clarence Big-Saddle swore. "It worked. I didn't think it would."

Clarence Big-Saddle lived on his land for many years, and he paid no taxes. Intruders were unable to come down to his place. The land was sold for taxes three times, but nobody ever came down to claim it. Finally, it was carried as open land on the books. Homesteaders filed on it several times, but none of them fulfilled the qualification of living on the land.

Half a century went by. Clarence Big-Saddle called his son.

"I've had it, boy," he said. "I think I'll just go in the house and die."

"Okay, Dad," the son Clarence Little-Saddle said. "I'm going in to town to shoot a few games of pool with the boys. I'll bury you when I get back this evening."

So the son Clarence Little-Saddle inherited. He also lived on the land for many years without paying taxes.

There was a disturbance in the courthouse one day. The place seemed to be invaded in force, but actually there were but one man, one woman, and five children. "I'm Robert Rampart," said the man, "and we want the Land Office."

"I'm Robert Rampart Junior," said a nine-year-old gangler, "and we want it pretty blamed quick."

"I don't think we have anything like that," the girl at the desk said. "Isn't that something they had a long time ago?"

"Ignorance is no excuse for inefficiency, my dear," said Mary Mabel Rampart, an eight-year-old who could easily pass for eight and a half. "After I make my report, I wonder who will be sitting at your desk tomorrow."

"You people are either in the wrong state or the wrong century," the girl said.

"The Homestead Act still obtains," Robert Rampart insisted. "There is one tract of land carried as open in this county. I want to file on it."

Cecilia Rampart answered the knowing wink of a beefy man at the distant desk. "Hi," she breathed as she slinked over. "I'm Cecilia Rampart, but my stage name is Cecilia San Juan. Do you think that seven is too young to play ingenue roles?"

"Not for you," the man said. "Tell your folks to come over here."

"Do you know where the Land Office is?" Cecilia asked.

"Sure. It's the fourth left-hand drawer of my desk. The smallest office we got in the whole courthouse. We don't use it much any more."

The Ramparts gathered around. The beefy man started to make out the papers.

"This is the land description," Robert Rampart began. "Why, you've got it down already. How did you know?"

"I've been around here a long time," the man answered.

They did the paper work, and Robert Rampart filed on the land.

"You won't be able to come onto the land itself, though," the man said.

"Why won't I?" Rampart demanded. "Isn't the land description accurate?"

"Oh, I suppose so. But nobody's ever been able to get to the land. It's become a sort of joke."

"Well, I intend to get to the bottom of that joke," Rampart insisted. "I will occupy the land, or I will find out why not."

"I'm not sure about that," the beefy man said. "The last man to file on the land, about a dozen years ago, wasn't able to occupy the land. And he wasn't able to say why he couldn't. It's kind of interesting, the look on their faces after they try it for a day or two, and then give it up."

The Ramparts left the courthouse, loaded into their camper, and drove out to find their land. They stopped at the house of a cattle and wheat farmer named Charley Dublin. Dublin met them with a grin which indicated he had been tipped off.

"Come along if you want to, folks," Dublin said. "The easiest way is on foot across my short pasture here. Your land's directly west of mine."

They walked the short distance to the border.

"My name is Tom Rampart, Mr. Dublin." Six-year-old Tom made conversation as they walked. "But my name is really Ramires, and not Tom. I am the issue of an indiscretion of my mother in Mexico several years ago."

"The boy is a kidder, Mr. Dublin," said the mother Nina Rampart, defending herself. "I have never been in Mexico, but sometimes I have the urge to disappear there forever."

"Ah yes, Mrs. Rampart. And what is the name of the youngest boy here?" Charley Dublin asked.

"Fatty," said Fatty Rampart.

"But surely that is not your given name?"

"Audifax," said five-year-old Fatty.

"Ah well, Audifax, Fatty, are you a kidder too?"

"He's getting better at it, Mr. Dublin," Mary Mabel said. "He was a twin till last week. His twin was named Skinny. Mama left Skinny unguarded while she was out tippling, and there were wild dogs in the neighborhood. When Mama got back, do you know what was left of Skinny? Two neck bones and an ankle bone. That was all."

"Poor Skinny," Dublin said. "Well, Rampart, this is the fence and the end of my land. Yours is just beyond."

"Is that ditch on my land?" Rampart asked.

"That ditch is your land."

"I'll have it filled in. It's a dangerous deep cut even if it is narrow. And the other fence looks like a good one, and I sure have a pretty plot of land beyond it."

"No, Rampart, the land beyond the second fence belongs to Hollister Hyde," Charley Dublin said. "That second fence is the end of your land."

"Now, just wait a minute, Dublin! There's something wrong here. My land is one hundred and sixty acres, which would be a half mile on a side. Where's my half-mile width?"

"Between the two fences."

"That's not eight feet."

"Doesn't look like it, does it, Rampart? Tell you what—there's plenty of throwing-sized rocks around. Try to throw one across it."

"I'm not interested in any such boys' games," Rampart exploded. "I want my land."

But the Rampart children were interested in such games. They got with it with those throwing rocks. They winged them out over the little gully. The stones acted funny. They hung in the air, as it were, and diminished in size. And they were small as pebbles when they dropped down, down into the gully.

None of them could throw a stone across that ditch, and they were throwing kids.

"You and your neighbor have conspired to fence open land for your own use," Rampart charged.

"No such thing, Rampart," Dublin said cheerfully. "My land checks perfectly. So does Hyde's. So does yours, if we knew how to check it. It's like one of those trick topological drawings. It really is half a mile from here to there, but the eye gets lost somewhere. It's your land. Crawl through the fence and figure it out."

Rampart crawled through the fence, and drew himself up to jump the gully. Then he hesitated. He got a glimpse of just how deep that gully was. Still, it wasn't five feet across.

There was a heavy fence post on the ground, designed for use as a corner post. Rampart up-ended it with some effort. Then he shoved it to fall and bridge the gully. But it fell short, and it shouldn't have. An eight-foot post should bridge a five-foot gully.

The post fell into the gully, and rolled and rolled and rolled. It spun as though it were rolling outward, but it made no progress except vertically. The post came to rest on a ledge of the gully, so close that Rampart could almost reach out and touch it, but it now appeared no bigger than a match stick.

"There is something wrong with that fence post, or with the world, or with my eyes," Robert Rampart said. "I wish I felt dizzy so I could blame it on that."

"There's a little game that I sometimes play with my neighbor Hyde when we're both out," Dublin said. "I've a heavy rifle and I train it on the middle of his forehead as he stands on the other side of the ditch apparently eight feet away. I fire it off then (I'm a good shot), and I hear it whine across. It'd kill him dead if things were as they seem. But Hyde's in no danger. The shot always bangs into that little scuff of rocks and boulders about thirty feet below him. I can see it kick up the rock dust there, and the sound of it rattling into those little boulders comes back to me in about two and a half seconds."

A bull-bat (poor people call it the night-hawk) raveled around in the air and zoomed out over the narrow ditch, but it did not reach the other side. The bird dropped below ground level and could be seen against the background of the other side of the ditch. It grew smaller and hazier as though at a distance of three or four hundred yards. The white bars on its wings could no longer be discerned; then the bird itself could hardly be discerned; but it was far short of the other side of the five-foot ditch.

A man identified by Charley Dublin as the neighbor Hollister Hyde had appeared on the other side of the little ditch. Hyde grinned and waved. He shouted something, but could not be heard.

"Hyde and I both read mouths," Dublin said, "so we can talk across the ditch easy enough. Which kid wants to play chicken? Hyde will barrel a good-sized rock right at your head, and if you duck or flinch you're chicken."

"Me! Me!" Audifax Rampart challenged. And Hyde, a big man with big hands, did barrel a fearsome jagged rock right at the head of the boy. It would have killed him if things had been as they appeared. But the rock diminished to nothing and disappeared into the ditch. Here was a phenomenon: things seemed real-sized on either side of the ditch, but they diminished coming out over the ditch either way.

"Everybody game for it?" Robert Rampart Junior asked.

"We won't get down there by standing here," Mary Mabel said.

"Nothing wenchered, nothing gained," said Cecilia. "I got that from an ad for a sex comedy."

Then the five Rampart kids ran down into the gully. Ran down is right. It was almost as if they ran down the vertical face of a cliff. They couldn't do that. The gully was no wider than the stride of the biggest kids. But the gully diminished those children, it ate them alive. They were doll-sized. They were acorn-sized. They were running for minute after minute across a ditch that was only five feet across. They were going, deeper in it, and getting smaller. Robert Rampart was roaring his alarm, and his wife Nina was screaming. Then she stopped. "What am I carrying on so loud about?" she asked herself. "It looks like fun. I'll do it too."

She plunged into the gully, diminished in size as the children had done, and ran at a pace to carry her a hundred yards away across a gully only five feet wide.

That Robert Rampart stirred things up for a while then. He got the sheriff there, and the highway patrolmen. A ditch had stolen his wife and five children, he said, and maybe had killed them. And if anybody laughs, there may be another killing. He got the colonel of the State National Guard there, and a command post set up. He got a couple of airplane pilots. Robert Rampart had one quality: when he hollered, people came.

He got the newsmen out from T-Town, and the eminent scientists Dr. Velikof Vonk, Arpad Arkabaranan, and Willy McGilly. That bunch turns up every time you get on a good one. They just happen to be in that part of the country where something interesting is going on.

They attacked the thing from all four sides and the top, and by inner and outer theory. If a thing measures half a mile on each side, and the sides are straight, there just has to be something in the middle of it. They took pictures from the air, and they turned out perfect. They proved that Robert Rampart had the prettiest hundred and sixty acres in the country, the larger part of it being a lush green valley, and all of it being half a mile on a side, and situated just where it should be. They took ground-level photos then, and it showed a beautiful half-mile stretch of land between the boundaries of Charley Dublin and Hollister Hyde. But a man isn't a camera. None of them could see that beautiful spread with the eyes in their heads. Where was it?

Down in the valley itself everything was normal. It really was half a mile wide and no more than eighty feet deep with a very gentle slope. It was warm and sweet, and beautiful with grass and grain.

Nina and the kids loved it, and they rushed to see what squatter had built that little house on their land. A house, or a shack. It had never known paint, but paint would have spoiled it. It was built of split timbers dressed near smooth with ax and draw knife, chinked with white clay, and sodded up to about half its height. And there was an interloper standing by the little lodge.

"Here, here what are you doing on our land?" Robert Rampart Junior demanded of the man. "Now you just shamble off again wherever you came from. I'll bet you're a thief too, and those cattle are stolen."

"Only the black-and-white calf," Clarence Little-Saddle said. "I couldn't resist him, but the rest are mine. I guess I'll just stay around and see that you folks get settled all right."

"Is there any wild Indians around here?" Fatty Rampart asked.

"No, not really. I go on a bender about every three months and get a little bit wild, and there's a couple Osage boys from Gray Horse that get noisy sometimes, but that's about all," Clarence Little-Saddle said.

"You certainly don't intend to palm yourself off on us as an Indian," Mary Mabel challenged. "You'll find us a little too knowledgeable for that."

"Little girl, you might as well tell this cow there's no room for her to be a cow since you're so knowledgeable. She thinks she's a short-horn cow named Sweet Virginia. I think I'm a Pawnee Indian named Clarence. Break it to us real gentle if we're not."

"If you're an Indian where's your war bonnet? There's not a feather on you anywhere."

"How you be sure? There's a story that we got feathers instead of hair on— Aw, I can't tell a joke like that to a little girl! How come you're not wearing the Iron Crown of Lombardy if you're a white girl? How you expect me to believe you're a little white girl and your folks came from Europe a couple hundred years ago if you don't wear it? There are six hundred tribes, and only one of them, the Oglala Sioux, had the war bonnet, and only the big leaders, never more than two or three of them alive at one time, wore it."

"Your analogy is a little strained," Mary Mabel said. "Those Indians we saw in Florida and the ones at Atlantic City had war bonnets, and they couldn't very well have been the kind of Sioux you said. And just last night on the TV in the motel, those Massachusetts Indians put a war bonnet on the President and called him the Great White Father. You mean to tell me that they were all phonies? Hey, who's laughing at who here?"

"If you're an Indian where's your bow and arrow?" Tom Rampart interrupted. "I bet you can't even shoot one."

"You're sure right there," Clarence admitted. "I never shot one of those things but once in my life. They used to have an archery range in Boulder Park over in T-Town, and you could rent the things and shoot at targets tied to hay bales. Hey, I barked my whole forearm and nearly broke my thumb when the bow-string thwacked home. I couldn't shoot that thing at all. I don't see how anybody ever could shoot one of them."

"Okay, kids," Nina Rampart called to her brood. "Let's start pitching this junk out of the shack so we can move in. Is there any way we can drive our camper down here, Clarence?"

"Sure, there's a pretty good dirt road, and it's a lot wider than it looks from the top. I got a bunch of green bills in an old night charley in the shack. Let me get them, and then I'll clear out for a while. The shack hasn't been cleaned out for seven years, since the last time this happened. I'll show you the road to the top, and you can bring your car down it."

"Hey, you old Indian, you lied!" Cecilia Rampart shrilled from the doorway of the shack. "You do have a war bonnet. Can I have it?"

"I didn't mean to lie, I forgot about that thing," Clarence Little-Saddle said. "My son Clarence Bare-Back sent that to me from Japan for a joke a long time ago. Sure, you can have it."

All the children were assigned tasks carrying the junk out of the shack and setting fire to it. Nina Rampart and Clarence Little-Saddle ambled up to the rim of the valley by the vehicle road that was wider than it looked from the top.

"Nina, you're back! I thought you were gone forever," Robert Rampart jittered at seeing her again. "What—where are the children?"

"Why, I left them down in the valley, Robert. That is, ah, down in that little ditch right there. Now you've got me worried again. I'm going to drive the camper down there and unload it. You'd better go on down and lend a hand too, Robert, and quit talking to all these funny-looking men here."

And Nina went back to Dublin's place for the camper.

"It would be easier for a camel to go through the eye of a needle than for that intrepid woman to drive a car down into that narrow ditch," the eminent scientist Dr Velikof Vonk said.

"You know how that camel does it?" Clarence Little-Saddle offered, appearing of a sudden from nowhere. "He just closes one of his own eyes and flops back his ears and plunges right through. A camel is mighty narrow when he closes one eye and flops back his ears. Besides, they use a big-eyed needle in the act."

"Where'd this crazy man come from?" Robert Rampart demanded, jumping three feet in the air. "Things are coming out of the ground now. I want my land! I want my children! I want my wife! Whoops, here she comes driving it. Nina, you can't drive a loaded camper into a little ditch like that! You'll be killed or collapsed!"

Nina Rampart drove the loaded camper into the little ditch at a pretty good rate of speed. The best of belief is that she just closed one eye and plunged right through. The car diminished and dropped, and it was smaller than a toy car. But it raised a pretty good cloud of dust as it bumped for several hundred yards across a ditch that was only five feet wide.

"Rampart, it's akin to the phenomenon known as looming, only in reverse," the eminent scientist Arpad Arkabaranan explained as he attempted to throw a rock across the narrow ditch. The rock rose very high in the air, seemed to hang at its apex while it diminished to the size of a grain of sand, and then fell into the ditch not six inches of the way across. There isn't anybody going to throw across a half-mile valley even if it looks five feet. "Look at a rising moon sometimes, Rampart. It appears very large, as though covering a great sector of the horizon, but it only covers one-half of a degree. It is hard to believe that you could set seven hundred and twenty of such large moons side by side around the horizon, or that it would take one hundred and eighty of the big things to reach from the horizon to a point overhead. It is also hard to believe that your valley is five hundred times as wide as it appears, but it has been surveyed, and it is."

"I want my land. I want my children. I want my wife," Robert chanted dully. "Damn, I let her get away again."

"I tell you, Rampy," Clarence Little-Saddle squared on him, "a man that lets his wife get away twice doesn't deserve to keep her. I give you till nightfall; then you forfeit. I've taken a liking to the brood. One of us is going to be down there tonight."

After a while a bunch of them were off in that little tavern on the road between Cleveland and Osage. It was only half a mile away. If the valley had run in the other direction, it would have been only six feet away.

"It is a psychic nexus in the form of an elongated dome," said the eminent scientist Dr. Velikof Vonk. "It is maintained subconsciously by the concatenation of at least two minds, the stronger of them belonging to a man dead for many years. It has apparently existed for a little less than a hundred years, and in another hundred years it will be considerably weakened. We know from our checking out folk tales of Europe as well as Cambodia that these ensorceled areas seldom survive for more than two hundred and fifty years. The person who first set such a thing in being will usually lose interest in it, and in all worldly things, within a hundred years of his own death. This is a simple thanato-psychic limitation. As a short-term device, the thing has been used several times as a military tactic.

"This psychic nexus, as long as it maintains itself, causes group illusion, but it is really a simple thing. It doesn't fool birds or rabbits or cattle or cameras, only humans. There is nothing meteorological about it. It is strictly psychological. I'm glad I was able to give a scientific explanation to it or it would have worried me."

"It is a continental fault coinciding with a noospheric fault," said the eminent scientist Arpad Arkabaranan. "The valley really is half a mile wide, and at the same time it really is only five feet wide. If we measured correctly, we would get these dual measurements. Of course it is meteorological! Everything including dreams is meteorological. It is the animals and cameras which are fooled, as lacking a true dimension; it is only humans who see the true duality. The phenomenon should be common along the whole continental fault where the Earth gains or loses half a mile that has to go somewhere. Likely it extends through the whole sweep of the Cross Timbers. Many of those trees appear twice, and many do not appear at all. A man in the proper state of mind could farm that land or raise cattle on it, but it doesn't really exist. There is a clear parallel in the Luftspiegelungthal sector in the Black Forest of Germany which exists, or does not exist, according to the circumstances and to the attitude of the beholder. Then we have the case of Mad Mountain in Morgan County, Tennessee, which isn't there all the time, and also the Little Lobo Mirage south of Presidio, Texas, from which twenty thousand barrels of water were pumped in one two-and-a-half-year period before the mirage reverted to mirage status. I'm glad I was able to give a scientific explanation to this or it would have worried me."

"I just don't understand how he worked it," said the eminent scientist Willy McGilly. "Cedar bark, jack-oak leaves, and the world 'Petahauerat.' The thing's impossible! When I was a boy and we wanted to make a hideout, we used bark from the skunk-spruce tree, the leaves of a box-elder, and the word was 'Boadicea.' All three elements are wrong here. I cannot find a scientific explanation for it, and it does worry me."

They went back to Narrow Valley. Robert Rampart was still chanting dully: "I want my land. I want my children. I want my wife."

Nina Rampart came chugging up out of the narrow ditch in the camper and emerged through that little gate a few yards down the fence row.

"Supper's ready and we're tired of waiting for you, Robert," she said. "A fine homesteader you are! Afraid to come onto your own land! Come along now; I'm tired of waiting for you."

"I want my land! I want my children! I want my wife!" Robert Rampart still chanted. "Oh, there you are, Nina. You stay here this time. I want my land! I want my children! I want an answer to this terrible thing."

"It is time we decided who wears the pants in this family," Nina said stoutly. She picked up her husband, slung him over her shoulder, carried him to the camper and dumped him in, slammed (as it seemed) a dozen doors at once, and drove furiously down into the Narrow Valley, which already seemed wider.

Why, that place was getting normaler and normaler by the minute! Pretty soon it looked almost as wide as it was supposed to be. The psychic nexus in the form of an elongated dome had collapsed. The continental fault that coincided with the noospheric fault had faced facts and decided to conform. The Ramparts were in effective possession of their homestead, and Narrow Valley was as normal as any place anywhere.

"I have lost my land," Clarence Little-Saddle moaned. "It was the land of my father Clarence Big-Saddle, and I meant it to be the land of my son Clarence Bare-Back. It looked so narrow that people did not notice how wide it was, and people did not try to enter it. Now I have lost it."

Clarence Little-Saddle and the eminent scientist Willy McGilly were standing on the edge of Narrow Valley, which now appeared its true half-mile extent. The moon was just rising, so big that it filled a third of the sky. Who would have imagined that it would take a hundred and eight of such monstrous things to reach from the horizon to a point overhead, and yet you could sight it with sighters and figure it so.

"I had a little bear-cat by the tail and I let go," Clarence groaned. "I had a fine valley for free, and I have lost it. I am like that hard-luck guy in the funny-paper or Job in the Bible. Destitution is my lot."

Willy McGilly looked around furtively. They were alone on the edge of the half-mile-wide valley.

"Let's give it a booster shot," Willy McGilly said.

Hey, those two got with it! They started a snapping fire and began to throw the stuff onto it. Bark from the dog-elm tree—how do you know it won't work?

It was working! Already the other side of the valley seemed a hundred yards closer, and there were alarmed noises coming up from the people in the valley.

Leaves from a black locust tree—and the valley narrowed still more! There was, moreover, terrified screaming of both children and big people from the depths of Narrow Valley, and the happy voice of Mary Mabel Rampart chanting, "Earthquake! Earthquake!"

"That my valley be always wide and flourish and such stuff, and green with money and grass!" Clarence Little-Saddle orated in Pawnee chant style, "but that it be narrow if intruders come, smash them like bugs!"

People, that valley wasn't over a hundred feet wide now, and the screaming of the people in the bottom of the valley had been joined by the hysterical coughing of the camper car starting up.

Willy and Clarence threw everything that was left on the fire. But the word? The word? Who remembers the word?

"Corsicanatexas!" Clarence Little-Saddle howled out with confidence he hoped would fool the fates.

He was answered not only by a dazzling sheet of summer lightning, but also by thunder and raindrops.

"Chahiksi!" Clarence Little-Saddle swore. "It worked. I didn't think it would. It will be all right now. I can use the rain."

The valley was again a ditch only five feet wide.

The camper car struggled out of Narrow Valley through the little gate. It was smashed flat as a sheet of paper, and the screaming kids and people in it had only one dimension.

"It's closing in! It's closing in!" Robert Rampart roared, and he was no thicker than if he had been made out of cardboard.

"We're smashed like bugs," the Rampart boys intoned. "We're thin like paper."

"Mort, ruine, écrasement!" spoke-acted Cecilia Rampart like the great tragedienne she was.

"Help! Help!" Nina Rampart croaked, but she winked at Willy and Clarence as they rolled by. "This homesteading jag always did leave me a little flat."

"Don't throw those paper dolls away. They might be the Ramparts," Mary Mabel called.

The camper car coughed again and bumped along on level ground. This couldn't last forever. The car was widening out as it bumped along.

"Did we overdo it, Clarence?" Willy McGilly asked. "What did one flatlander say to the other?"

"Dimension of us never got around," Clarence said. "No, I don't think we overdid it, Willy. That car must be eighteen inches wide already, and they all ought to be normal by the time they reach the main road. The next time I do it, I think I'll throw wood-grain plastic on the fire to see who's kidding who."

Sundance (1969)

ROBERT SILVERBERG

ROBERT SILVERBERG (b. 1935) began publishing science-fiction stories while he was an undergraduate at Columbia University in the early 1950s, and by the time he made his first sale to *F&SF* three years later (in 1957), he already had scores of publications to his credit. Over the years, his prolificity has matched his erudition, and he has published hundreds of books on a wide variety of subjects. It is indicative of his science-fiction oeuvre that several different collections have appeared with some version of "The Best of Robert Silverberg" in the title but with very little overlap in the contents.

It happens that "Sundance" appeared in two of those "Best of" collections, and with good reason—it is the work of a virtuoso at the height of his skills.

TODAY YOU LIQUIDATED about 50,000 Eaters in Sector A, and now you are spending an uneasy night. You and Herndon flew east at dawn, with the green-gold sunrise at your backs, and sprayed the neural pellets over a thousand hectares along the Forked River. You flew on into the prairie beyond the river, where the Eaters have already been wiped out, and had lunch sprawled on that thick, soft carpet of grass where the first settlement is expected to rise. Herndon picked some juiceflowers, and you enjoyed half an hour of mild hallucinations. Then, as you headed toward the copter to begin an afternoon of further pellet spraying, he said suddenly, "Tom, how would you feel about this if it turned out that the Eaters weren't just animal pests? That they were people, say, with a language and rites and a history and all?"

You thought of how it had been for your own people.

"They aren't," you said.

"Suppose they were. Suppose the Eaters—"

"They aren't. Drop it."

Herndon has this streak of cruelty in him that leads him to ask such questions. He goes for the vulnerabilities; it amuses him. All night now his casual remark has echoed in your mind. Suppose the Eaters...suppose the Eaters...suppose...suppose...

You sleep for a while, and dream, and in your dreams you swim through rivers of blood.

Foolishness. A feverish fantasy. You know how important it is to exterminate the Eaters fast, before the settlers get here. They're just animals, and not even harmless animals at that; ecology-wreckers is what they are, devourers of oxygen-liberating plants, and they have to go. A few have been saved for zoological study. The rest must be destroyed. Ritual extirpation of undesirable beings, the old, old story. But let's not complicate our job with moral qualms, you tell yourself. Let's not dream of rivers of blood.

The Eaters don't even *have* blood, none that could flow in rivers, anyway. What they have is, well, a kind of lymph that permeates every tissue and transmits nourishment along the interfaces. Waste products go out the same way, osmotically. In terms of process, it's structurally analogous to your own kind of circulatory system, except there's no network of blood vessels hooked to a master pump. The life-stuff just oozes through their bodies as though they were amoebas or sponges or some other low-phylum form. Yet they're definitely high-phylum in nervous system, digestive setup, limb-and-organ template, etc. Odd, you think. The thing about aliens is that they're alien, you tell yourself, not for the first time.

The beauty of their biology for you and your companions is that it lets you exterminate them so neatly.

You fly over the grazing grounds and drop the neural pellets. The Eaters find and ingest them. Within an hour the poison has reached all sectors of the body. Life ceases; a rapid breakdown of cellular matter follows, the Eater literally falling apart molecule by molecule the instant that nutrition is cut off; the lymph-like stuff works like acid; a universal lysis occurs; flesh and even the bones, which are cartilaginous, dissolve. In two hours, a puddle on the ground. In four, nothing at all left. Considering how many millions of Eaters you've scheduled for extermination here, it's sweet of the bodies to be self-disposing. Otherwise what a charnel house this world would become!

Suppose the Eaters...

Damn Herndon. You almost feel like getting a memory-editing in the morning. Scrape his stupid speculations out of your head. If you dared. If you dared.

In the morning he does not dare. Memory-editing frightens him; he will try to shake free of his newfound guilt without it. The Eaters, he explains to himself, are mindless herbivores, the unfortunate victims of human expansionism, but not really deserving of passionate defense. Their extermination is not tragic; it's just too bad. If Earthmen are to have this world, the Eaters must relinquish it. There's a difference, he tells himself, between the elimination of the Plains Indians from the American prairie in the nineteenth century and the destruction of the bison on that same prairie. One feels a little wistful about the slaughter of the thundering herds; one regrets the butchering of millions of the noble brown woolly beasts, yes. But one feels outrage, not mere wistful regret, at what was done to the Sioux. There's a difference. Reserve your passions for the proper cause.

He walks from his bubble at the edge of the camp toward the center of things. The flagstone path is moist and glistening. The morning fog has not yet lifted, and every tree is bowed, the long, notched leaves heavy with droplets of water. He pauses, crouching, to observe a spider-analog spinning its asymmetrical web. As he watches, a small amphibian, delicately shaded turquoise, glides as inconspicuously as possible over the mossy ground. Not inconspicuously enough; he gently lifts the little creature and puts it on the back of his hand. The gills flutter in anguish, and the amphibian's sides quiver. Slowly, cunningly, its color changes until it matches the coppery tone of the hand. The camouflage is excellent. He lowers his hand and the amphibian scurries into a puddle. He walks on.

He is forty years old, shorter than most of the other members of the expedition, with wide shoulders, a heavy chest, dark glossy hair, a blunt, spreading nose. He is a biologist. This is his third career, for he has failed as an anthropologist and as a developer of real estate. His name is Tom Two Ribbons. He has been married twice but has had no children. His great-grandfather died of alcoholism; his grandfather was addicted to hallucinogens; his father had compulsively visited cheap memory-editing parlors. Tom Two Ribbons is conscious that he is failing a family tradition, but he has not found his own mode of self-destruction.

In the main building he discovers Herndon, Julia, Ellen, Schwartz, Chang, Michaelson, and Nichols. They are eating breakfast; the others are already at work. Ellen rises and comes to him and kisses him. Her short soft yellow hair tickles his cheeks. "I love you," she whispers. She has spent the night in Michaelson's bubble. "I love you," he tells her, and draws a quick vertical line of affection between her small pale breasts. He winks at Michaelson, who nods, touches the tops of two fingers to his lips, and blows them a kiss. We are all good friends here, Tom Two Ribbons thinks.

"Who drops pellets today?" he asks.

"Mike and Chang," says Julia. "Sector C."

Schwartz says, "Eleven more days and we ought to have the whole peninsula clear. Then we can move inland."

"If our pellet supply holds up," Chang points out.

Herndon says, "Did you sleep well, Tom?"

"No," says Tom. He sits down and taps out his breakfast requisition. In the west, the fog is beginning to burn off the mountains. Something throbs in the back of his neck. He has been on this world nine weeks now, and in that time it has undergone its only change of season, shading from dry weather to foggy. The mists will remain for many months. Before the plains parch again, the Eaters will be gone and the settlers will begin to arrive. His food slides down the chute and he seizes it. Ellen sits beside him. She is a little more than half his age; this is her first voyage; she is their keeper of records, but she is also skilled at editing. "You look troubled," Ellen tells him. "Can I help you?"

"No. Thank you."

"I hate it when you get gloomy."

"It's a racial trait," says Tom Two Ribbons.

"I doubt that very much."

"The truth is that maybe my personality reconstruct is wearing thin. The trauma level was so close to the surface. I'm just a walking veneer, you know."

Ellen laughs prettily. She wears only a sprayon half-wrap. Her skin looks damp; she and Michaelson have had a swim at dawn. Tom Two Ribbons is thinking of asking her to marry him, when this job is over. He has not been married since the collapse of the real estate business. The therapist suggested divorce as part of the reconstruct. He sometimes wonders where Terry has gone and whom she lives with now. Ellen says, "You seem pretty stable to me, Tom."

"Thank you," he says. She is young. She does not know.

"If it's just a passing gloom I can edit it out in one quick snip."

"Thank you," he says. "No."

"I forgot. You don't like editing."

"My father—"

"Yes?"

"In fifty years he pared himself down to a thread," Tom Two Ribbons says. "He had his ancestors edited away, his whole heritage, his religion, his wife, his sons, finally his name. Then he sat and smiled all day. Thank you, no editing."

"Where are you working today?" Ellen asks.

"In the compound, running tests."

"Want company? I'm off all morning."

"Thank you, no," he says, too quickly. She looks hurt. He tries to remedy his unintended cruelty by touching her arm lightly and saying, "Maybe this afternoon, all right? I need to commune a while. Yes?"

"Yes," she says, and smiles, and shapes a kiss with her lips.

After breakfast he goes to the compound. It covers a thousand hectares east of the base; they have bordered it with neutral-field projectors at intervals of eighty meters, and this is a sufficient fence to keep the captive population of two hundred Eaters from straying. When all the others have been exterminated, this study group will remain. At the southwest corner of the compound stands a lab bubble from which the experiments are run: metabolic, psychological, physiological, ecological. A stream crosses the compound diagonally. There is a low ridge of grassy hills at its eastern edge. Five distinct copses of tightly clustered knifeblade trees are separated by patches of dense savanna. Sheltered beneath the glass are the oxygen-plants, almost completely hidden except for the photosynthetic spikes that jut to heights of three or four meters at regular intervals, and the lemon-colored respiratory bodies, chest high, that make the grassland sweet and dizzying with exhaled gases. Through the fields move the Eaters in a straggling herd, nibbling delicately at the respiratory bodies.

Tom Two Ribbons spies the herd beside the stream and goes toward it. He stumbles over an oxygen-plant hidden in the grass but deftly recovers his balance and, seizing the puckered orifice of the respiratory body, inhales deeply. His despair lifts. He approaches the Eaters. They are spherical, bulky, slow-moving creatures, covered by masses of coarse orange fur. Saucer-like eyes protrude above narrow rubbery lips. Their legs are thin and scaly, like a chicken's, and their arms are short and held close to their bodies. They regard him with bland lack of curiosity. "Good morning, brothers!" is the way he greets them this time, and he wonders why.

I noticed something strange today. Perhaps I simply sniffed too much oxygen in the fields; maybe I was succumbing to a suggestion Herndon planted; or possibly it's the family masochism cropping out. But while I was observing the Eaters in the compound, it seemed to me, for the first time, that they were behaving intelligently, that they were functioning in a ritualized way.

I followed them around for three hours. During that time they uncovered half a dozen outcroppings of oxygen-plants. In each case they went through a stylized pattern of action before starting to munch. They:

Formed a straggly circle around the plants.

Looked toward the sun.

Looked toward their neighbors on left and right around the circle.

Made fuzzy neighing sounds only after having done the foregoing.

Looked toward the sun again.

Moved in and ate.

If this wasn't a prayer of thanksgiving, a saying of grace, then what was it? And if they're advanced enough spiritually to say grace, are we not therefore committing genocide here? Do chimpanzees say grace? Christ, we wouldn't even wipe out chimps the way we're cleaning out the Eaters! Of course, chimps don't interfere with human crops, and some kind of coexistence would be possible, whereas Eaters and human agriculturalists simply can't function on the same planet. Nevertheless, there's a moral issue here. The liquidation effort is predicated on the assumption that the intelligence level of the Eaters is about on par with that of oysters, or, at best, sheep. Our consciences stay clear because our poison is quick and painless and because the Eaters thoughtfully dissolve upon dying, sparing us the mess of incinerating millions of corpses. But if they pray—

I won't say anything to the others just yet. I want more evidence, hard, objective. Films, tapes, record cubes. Then we'll see. What if I can show that we're exterminating intelligent beings? My family knows a little about genocide, after all, having been on the receiving end just a few centuries back. I doubt that I could halt what's going on here. But at the very least I could withdraw from the operation. Head back to Earth and stir up public outcries.

I hope I'm imagining this.

I'm not imagining a thing. They gather in circles; they look to the sun; they neigh and pray. They're only balls of jelly on chicken-legs, but they give thanks for their food. Those big round eyes now seem to stare accusingly at me. Our tame herd here knows what's going on: that we have descended from the stars to eradicate their kind, and that they alone will be spared. They have no way of fighting back or even of communicating their displeasure, but they *know*. And hate us. Jesus, we have killed two million of them since we got here, and in a metaphorical sense I'm stained with blood, and what will I do, what can I do?

I must move very carefully, or I'll end up drugged and edited.

I can't let myself seem like a crank, a quack, an agitator. I can't stand up and *denounce!* I have to find allies. Herndon, first. He surely is onto the truth; he's the one who nudged me to it, that day we dropped pellets. And I thought he was merely being vicious in his usual way!

I'll talk to him tonight.

He says, "I've been thinking about that suggestion you made. About the Eaters. Perhaps we haven't made sufficiently close psychological studies. I mean, if they really *are* intelligent—"

Herndon blinks. He is a tall man with glossy dark hair, a heavy beard, sharp cheekbones. "Who says they are, Tom?"

"You did. On the far side of the Forked River, you said—"

"It was just a speculative hypothesis. To make conversation."

"No, I think it was more than that. You really believed it."

Herndon looks troubled. "Tom, I don't know what you're trying to start, but don't start it. If I for a moment believed we were killing intelligent creatures, I'd run for an editor so fast I'd start an implosion wave."

"Why did you ask me that thing, then?" Tom Two Ribbons says.

"Idle chatter."

"Amusing yourself by kindling guilts in somebody else? You're a bastard, Herndon. I mean it."

"Well, look, Tom, if I had any idea that you'd get so worked up about a hypothetical suggestion—" Herndon shakes his head. "The Eaters aren't intelligent beings. Obviously. Otherwise we wouldn't be under orders to liquidate them."

"Obviously," says Tom Two Ribbons.

Ellen said, "No, I don't know what Tom's up to. But I'm pretty sure he needs a rest. It's only a year and a half since his personality reconstruct, and he had a pretty bad breakdown back then."

Michaelson consulted a chart. "He's refused three times in a row to make his pellet-dropping run. Claiming he can't take time away from his research. Hell, we can fill in for him, but it's the idea that he's ducking chores that bothers me."

"What kind of research is he doing?" Nichols wanted to know.

"Not biological," said Julia. "He's with the Eaters in the compound all the time, but I don't see him making any tests on them. He just watches them."

"And talks to them," Chang observed.

"And talks, yes," Julia said.

"About what?" Nichols asked.

"Who knows?"

Everyone looked at Ellen. "You're closest to him," Michaelson said. "Can't you bring him out of it?"

"I've got to know what he's in, first," Ellen said. "He isn't saying a thing."

You know that you must be very careful, for they outnumber you, and their concern for your welfare can be deadly. Already they realize you are disturbed, and Ellen has begun to probe for the source of the disturbance. Last night you lay in her arms and she questioned you, obliquely, skillfully, and you knew what she is trying to find out. When the moons appeared she suggested that you and she stroll in the compound, among the sleeping Eaters. You declined, but she sees that you have become involved with the creatures.

You have done probing of your own—subtly, you hope. And you are aware that you can do nothing to save the Eaters. An irrevocable commitment has been made. It is 1876 all over again; these are the bison, these are the Sioux, and they must be destroyed, for the railroad is on its way. If you speak out here, your friends will calm you and pacify you and edit you, for they do not see what you see. If you return to Earth to agitate, you will be mocked and recommended for another reconstruct. You can do nothing. You can do nothing.

You cannot save, but perhaps you can record.

Go out into the prairie. Live with the Eaters; make yourself their friend; learn their ways. Set it down, a full account of their culture, so that at least that much will not be lost. You know the techniques of field anthropology. As was done for your people in the old days, do now for the Eaters.

He finds Michaelson. "Can you spare me for a few weeks?" he asks.

"Spare you, Tom? What do you mean?"

"I've got some field studies to do. I'd like to leave the base and work with Eaters in the wild."

"What's wrong with the ones in the compound?"

"It's the last chance with wild ones, Mike. I've got to go."

"Alone, or with Ellen?"

"Alone."

Michaelson nods slowly. "All right, Tom. Whatever you want. Go. I won't hold you here."

I dance in the prairie under the green-gold sun. About me the Eaters gather. I am stripped; sweat makes my skin glisten; my heart pounds. I talk to them with my feet, and they understand.

They understand.

They have a language of soft sounds. They have a god. They know love and awe and rapture. They have rites. They have names. They have a history. Of all this I am convinced.

I dance on thick grass.

How can I reach them? With my feet, with my hands, with my grunts, with my sweat. They gather by the hundreds, by the thousands, and I dance. I must not stop. They cluster about me and make their sounds. I am a conduit for strange forces. My great-grandfather should see me now! Sitting on his porch in Wyoming, the firewater in his hand, his brain rotting—see me now, old one! See the dance of Tom Two Ribbons! I talk to these strange ones with my feet under a sun that is the wrong color. I dance. I dance.

"Listen to me," I say. "I am your friend, I alone, the only one you can trust. Trust me, talk to me, teach me. Let me preserve your ways, for soon the destruction will come."

I dance, and the sun climbs, and the Eaters murmur.

There is the chief. I dance toward him, back, toward, I bow, I point to the sun, I imagine the being that lives in that ball of flame, I imitate the sounds of these people, I kneel, I rise, I dance. Tom Two Ribbons dances for you.

I summon skills my ancestors forgot. I feel the power flowing in me. As they danced in the days of the bison, I dance now, beyond the Forked River.

I dance, and now the Eaters dance too. Slowly, uncertainly, they move toward me, they shift their weight, lift leg and leg, sway about. "Yes, like that!" I cry. "Dance!"

We dance together as the sun reaches noon height.

Now their eyes are no longer accusing. I see warmth and kinship. I am their brother, their redskinned tribesman, he who dances with them. No longer do they seem clumsy to me. There is a strange ponderous grace in their movements. They dance. They dance. They caper about me. Closer, closer, closer!

We move in holy frenzy.

They sing, now, a blurred hymn of joy. They throw forth their arms, unclench their little claws. In unison they shift weight, left foot forward, right, left, right. Dance, brothers, dance, dance, dance! They press against me. Their flesh quivers; their smell is a sweet one. They gently thrust me across the field, to a part of the meadow where the grass is deep and untrampled. Still dancing, we seek for the oxygen-plants, and find clumps of them beneath the grass, and they make their prayer and seize them with their awkward arms, separating the respiratory bodies from the photosynthetic spikes. The plants, in anguish, release floods of oxygen. My mind reels. I laugh and sing. The Eaters are nibbling the lemon-colored perforated globes, nibbling the stalks as well. They thrust their plants at me. It is a religious ceremony, I see. Take from us, eat with us, join with us, this is the body, this is the blood, take, eat, join. I bend forward and put a lemon-colored globe to my lips. I do not bite; I nibble, as they do, my teeth slicing away the skin of the globe. Juice spurts into my mouth while oxygen drenches my nostrils. The Eaters sing hosannas. I should be in full paint for this, paint of my forefathers, feathers too, meeting their religion in the regalia of what should have been mine. Take, eat, join. The juice of the oxygen-plant flows in my veins. I embrace my brothers. I sing, and as my voice leaves my lips it becomes an arch that glistens like new steel, and I pitch my song lower, and the arch turns to tarnished silver. The Eaters crowd close. The scent of their bodies is fiery red to me. Their soft cries are puffs of steam. The sun is very warm; its rays are tiny jagged pings of puckered sound, close to the top of my range of hearing, plink! plink! plink! The thick grass hums to me, deep and rich, and the wind hurls points of flame along the prairie. I devour another oxygen-plant, and then a third. My brothers laugh and shout. They tell me of their gods, the god of warmth, the god of food, the god of pleasure, the god of death, the god of holiness, the god of wrongness, and the others. They recite for me the names of their kings, and I hear their voices as splashes of green mold on the clean sheet of the sky. They instruct me in their holy rites. I must remember this, I tell myself, for when it is gone it will never come again. I continue to dance. They continue to dance. The color of the hills becomes rough and coarse, like abrasive gas. Take, eat, join. Dance. They are so gentle!

I hear the drone of the copter, suddenly.

It hovers far overhead. I am unable to see who flies in it. "No!" I scream. "Not here! Not these people! Listen to me! This is Tom Ribbons! Can't you hear me? I'm doing a field study here! You've no right—!"

My voice makes spirals of blue moss edged with red sparks. They drift upward and are scattered by the breeze.

I yell, I shout, I bellow. I dance and shake my fists. From the wings of the copter the jointed arms of the pellet-distributors unfold. The gleaming spigots extend and whirl. The neural pellets rain down into the meadow, each tracing a blazing track that lingers in the sky. The sound of the copter becomes a furry carpet stretching to the horizon, and my shrill voice is lost in it.

The Eaters drift away from me, seeking the pellets, scratching at the roots of the grass to find them. Still dancing, I leap into their midst, striking the pellets from their hands, hurling them into the stream, crushing them to powder. The Eaters growl black needles at me. They turn away and search for more pellets. The copter turns and flies off, leaving a trail of dense oily sound. My brothers are gobbling the pellets eagerly.

There is no way to prevent it.

Joy consumes them and they topple and lie still. Occasionally a limb twitches; then even this stops. They begin to dissolve. Thousands of them melt on the prairie, sinking into shapelessness, losing spherical forms, flattening, ebbing into the ground. The bonds of the molecules will no longer hold. It is the twilight of protoplasm. They perish. They vanish. For hours I walk the prairie. Now I inhale oxygen; now I eat a lemon-colored globe. Sunset begins with the ringing of leaden chimes. Black clouds make brazen trumpet calls in the east and the deepening wind is a swirl of coaly bristles. Silence comes. Night falls. I dance. I am alone.

The copter comes again, and they find you, and you do not resist as they gather you in. You are beyond bitterness. Quietly you explain what you have done and what you have learned, and why it is wrong to exterminate these people. You describe the plant you have eaten and the way it affects your senses, and as you talk of the blessed synesthesia, the texture of the wind and the sound of the clouds and the timbre of the sunlight, they nod and smile and tell you not to worry, that everything will be all right soon, and they touch something cold to your forearm, so cold that it is a whir and a buzz and the deintoxicant sinks into your vein and soon the ecstasy drains away, leaving only the exhaustion and the grief.

He says, "We never learn a thing, do we? We export all our horrors to the stars. Wipe out the Armenians, wipe out the Jews, wipe out the Tasmanians, wipe out the Indians, wipe out everyone who's in our way, and do the same damned murderous thing. You weren't with me out there. You didn't dance with them. You didn't see what a rich, complex culture the Eaters have. Let me tell you about their tribal structure. It's dense: seven levels of matrimonial relationships, to begin with, and an exogamy factor that requires—"

Softly Ellen says, "Tom, darling, nobody's going to harm the Eaters."

"And the religion," he goes on. "Nine gods, each one an aspect of *the* god. Holiness and wrongness both worshiped. They have hymns, prayers, a theology. And we, the emissaries of the god of wrongness—"

"We're not exterminating them," Michaelson says. "Won't you understand that, Tom? This is all a fantasy of yours. You've been under the influence of drugs, but now we're clearing you out. You'll be clean in a little while. You'll have perspective again."

"A fantasy?" he says bitterly. "A drug dream? I stood out in the prairie and saw you drop pellets. And I watched them die and melt away. I didn't dream that."

"How can we convince you?" Chang asks earnestly. "What will make you believe? Shall we fly over the Eater country with you and show you how many millions there are?"

"But how many millions have been destroyed?" he demands.

They insist that he is wrong. Ellen tells him again that no one has ever desired to harm the Eaters. "This is a scientific expedition, Tom. We're here to *study* them. It's a violation of all we stand for to injure intelligent lifeforms."

"You admit that they're intelligent?"

"Of course. That's never been in doubt."

"Then why drop the pellets?" he asks. "Why slaughter them?"

"None of that has happened, Tom," Ellen says. She takes his hand between her cool palms. "Believe us. Believe us."

He says bitterly, "If you want me to believe you, why don't you do the job properly? Get out the editing machine and go to work on me. You can't simply *talk* me into rejecting the evidence of my own eyes."

"You were under drugs all the time," Michaelson says.

"I've never taken drugs! Except for what I ate in the meadow, when I danced—and that came after I had watched the massacre going on for weeks and weeks. Are you saying that it's a retroactive delusion?"

"No, Tom," Schwartz says. "You've had this delusion all along. It's part of your therapy, your reconstruct. You came here programmed with it."

"Impossible," he says.

Ellen kisses his fevered forehead. "It was done to reconcile you to mankind, you see. You had this terrible resentment of the displacement of your people in the nineteenth century. You were unable to forgive the industrial society for scattering the Sioux, and you were terribly full of hate. Your therapist thought that if you could be made to participate in an imaginary modern extermination, if you could come to see it as a necessary operation, you'd be purged of your resentment and able to take your place in society as—"

He thrusts her away. "Don't talk idiocy! If you knew the first thing about reconstruct therapy, you'd realize that no reputable therapist could be so shallow. There are no one-to-one correlations in reconstructs. No, don't touch me. Keep away. Keep away."

He will not let them persuade him that this is merely a drug-born dream. It is no fantasy, he tells himself, and it is no therapy. He rises. He goes out. They do not follow him. He takes a copter and seeks his brothers.

The sun is much hotter today. The Eaters are more numerous. Today I wear paint, today I wear feathers. My body shines with my sweat. They dance with me, and they have a frenzy in them that I have never seen before. We pound the trampled meadow with our feet. We clutch for the sun with our hands. We sing, we shout, we cry. We will dance until we fall.

This is no fantasy. These people are real, and they are intelligent, and they are doomed. This I know.

We dance. Despite the doom, we dance.

My great-grandfather comes and dances with us. He too is real. His nose is like a hawk's, not blunt like mine, and he wears the big headdress, and his muscles are like cords under his brown skin. He sings, he shouts, he cries.

Others of my family join us.

We eat the oxygen-plants together. We embrace the Eaters. We know, all of us, what it is to be hunted.

The clouds make music and the wind takes on texture and the sun's warmth has color.

We dance. We dance. Our limbs know no weariness.

The sun grows and fills the whole sky, and I see no Eaters now, only my own people, my father's fathers across the centuries, thousands of gleaming skins, thousands of hawks' noses, and we eat the plants, and we find sharp sticks and thrust them into our flesh, and the sweet blood flows and dries in the blaze of the sun, and we dance, and we dance, and some of us fall from weariness, and we dance, and the prairie is a sea of bobbing headdresses, an ocean of feathers, and we dance, and my heart makes thunder, and my knees become water, and the sun's fire engulfs me, and I dance, and I fall, and I dance, and I fall, and I fall, and I fall.

Again they find you and bring you back. They give you the cool snout on your arm to take the oxygen-plant drug from your veins, and then they give you something else so you will rest. You rest and you are very calm. Ellen kisses you and you stroke her soft skin, and then the others come in and they talk to you, saying soothing things, but you do not listen, for you are searching for realities. It is not an easy search. It is like falling through many trapdoors, looking for the one room whose floor is not hinged. Everything that has happened on this planet is your therapy, you tell yourself, designed to reconcile an embittered aborigine to the white man's conquest; nothing is really being exterminated here. You reject that and fall through and realize that this must be the therapy of your friends; they carry the weight of accumulated centuries of guilts and have come here to shed that load, and you are here to ease them of their burden, to draw their sins into yourself and give them forgiveness. Again you fall through, and see that the Eaters are mere animals who threaten the ecology and must be removed; the culture you imagined for them is your hallucination, kindled out of old churnings. You try to withdraw your objections to this necessary extermination, but you fall through again and discover that there is no extermination except in your mind, which is troubled and disordered by your obsession with the crime against your ancestors, and you sit up, for you wish to apologize to these friends of yours, these innocent scientists whom you have called murderers. And you fall through.

The Attack of the Giant Baby (1976)

Kit Reed

Like many of *F&SF*'s best contributors, KIT REED (b. 1932) moves deftly from genre to genre. Her novels have been published as mainstream fiction, fantasy, thriller, and science fiction. They include *Armed Camps, Catholic Girls, Gone* (under the pen name Kit Craig), *The Night Children*, and *Son of Destruction*. Her *F&SF* stories—three dozen of them and counting—include creepy horror, such as "The Vine"; dystopian speculation; surreal fantasias, such as "The Singing Marine"; and gonzo humor like this classic tale. *The Story Until Now*, a great big collection of her short stories, has recently been published.

NEW YORK CITY, 9 A.M. SATURDAY, SEPT. 16, 197-

Dr. Jonas Freibourg is at a particularly delicate point in his experiment with electrolytes, certain plant molds and the man within. Freibourg (who, like many scientists, insists on being called Doctor although he is in fact a Ph.D.) has also been left in charge of Leonard, the Freibourg baby, while Dilys Freibourg attends her regular weekly class in Zen Cookery. Dr. Freibourg has driven in from New Jersey with Leonard, and now the baby sits on a pink blanket in a corner of the laboratory. Leonard, aged fourteen months, has been supplied with a box of Mallomars and a plastic rattle; he is supposed to play quietly while Daddy works.

9:20

Leonard has eaten all the Mallomars and is tired of the rattle; he leaves the blanket, hitching along the laboratory floor. Instead of crawling on all fours, he likes to pull himself along with his arms, putting his weight on his hands and hitching in a semi-sitting position.

9:30

Dr. Freibourg scrapes an unsatisfactory culture out of the petri dish. He is not aware that part of the mess misses the bin marked for special disposal problems, and lands on the floor.

9:30 1/2

Leonard finds the mess, and like all good babies investigating foreign matter, puts it in his mouth.

9:31

On his way back from the autoclave, Dr. Freibourg trips on Leonard. Leonard cries and the doctor picks him up.

"Whussamadda, Lennie, whussamadda, there, there, what's that in your mouth?" Something crunches. "Ick ick, spit it out, Lennie, Aaaaaaaa, Aaaaaaaa, AAAAAAA."

At last the baby imitates its father: "Aaaaaaaa."

"That's a good boy, Lennie, spit it into Daddy's hand, that's a *good* boy, yeugh." Dr. Freibourg scrapes the mess off the baby's tongue. "Oh, yeugh, Mallomar, it's okay, Lennie, OK?"

"Ggg.nnn. K" The baby ingests the brown mess and then grabs for the doctor's nose and tries to put that in his mouth.

Despairing of his work, Dr. Freibourg throws a cover over his experiment, stashes Leonard in his stroller and heads across the hall to insert his key in the self-service elevator, going down and away from the secret laboratory. Although he is one block from Riverside Park it is a fine day and so Dr. Freibourg walks several blocks east to join the other Saturday parents and their charges on the benches in Central Park.

10:15

The Freibourgs reach the park. Although he has some difficulty extracting Leonard from the stroller, Dr. Freibourg notices nothing untoward. He sets the baby on the grass. The baby picks up a discarded tennis ball and almost fits it in his mouth.

10:31

Leonard is definitely swelling. Everything he has on stretches, up to a point: T-shirt, knitted diaper, rubber pants, so that, seen from a distance, he may still deceive the inattentive. His father is deep in conversation with a pretty divorcee with twin poodles, and although he checks on Leonard from time to time, Dr. Freibourg is satisfied that the baby is safe.

10:35
Leonard spots something bright in the bushes on the far side of the clearing. He hitches over to look at it. It is, indeed, the glint of sunlight on the fender of a moving bicycle and as he approaches it recedes, so he has to keep approaching.

10:37
Leonard is gone. It may be just as well because his father would most certainly be alarmed by the growing expanse of pink flesh to be seen between his shrinking T-shirt and the straining waistband of his rubber pants.

10:50
Dr. Freibourg looks up from his conversation to discover that Leonard has disappeared. He calls.
"Leonard. Lennie."

10:51
Leonard does not come. Dr. Freibourg excuses himself to hunt for Leonard.

11:52
After an hour of hunting, Dr. Freibourg has to conclude that Leonard hasn't just wandered away, he is either lost or stolen. He summons park police.

1 P.M.
Leonard is still missing.

In another part of the park, a would-be mugger approaches a favorite glen. He spies something large and pink: it half-fills the tiny clearing. Before he can run, the pink phenomenon pulls itself up, clutching at a pine for support, topples, and accidentally sits on him.

1:45
Two lovers are frightened by unexplained noises in the woods, sounds of crackling brush and heavy thuddings accompanied by a huge, wordless maundering. They flee as the thing approaches, gasping out their stories to an

incredulous policeman who detains them until the ambulance arrives to take them to Bellevue.

At the sound of what they take to be a thunder crack, a picnicking family returns to the picnic site to find their food missing, plates and all. They assume this is the work of a bicycle thief but are puzzled by a pink rag left by the marauder: it is a baby's shirt, stretched beyond recognition, and ripped as if by a giant, angry hand.

2 P.M.

Extra units join park police to widen the search for missing Leonard Freibourg, aged fourteen months. The baby's mother arrives and after a pause for recriminations leaves her husband's side to augment the official description: that was a sailboat on the pink shirt, and those are puppy-dogs printed on the Carter's dress-up rubber pants. The search is complicated by the fact that police have no way of knowing the baby they are looking for is not the baby they are going to find.

4:45

Leonard is hungry. Fired by adventure, he has been chirping and happy up till now, playing doggie with a stray Newfoundland which is the same relative size as his favorite stuffed Scottie at home. Now the Newfoundland has used its last remaining strength to steal away, and Leonard remembers he is hungry. What's more, he's getting cranky because he has missed his nap. He begins to whimper.

4:45 1/60

With preternatural acuity, the distraught mother hears. "It's Leonard," she says.

At the sound, park police break out regulation slickers and cap covers and put them on. One alert patrolman feels the ground for tremors. Another says, "I'd put up my umbrella if I was you, lady, there's going to be a helluva storm."

"Don't be ridiculous," Mrs. Freibourg says. "It's only Leonard. I'd know him anywhere." Calls, "Leonard, it's Mommy."

"I don't know what it is, lady, but it don't sound like any baby."

"Don't you think I know my own child?" She picks up a bullhorn. "Leonard, it's me, Mommy. Leonard. Leonard…"

From across the park, Leonard hears.

5 P.M.

The WNEW traffic control helicopter reports a pale, strange shape moving in a remote corner of Central Park. Because of its apparent size, nobody in the helicopter links this with the story of the missing Freibourg baby. As the excited reporter radios the particulars and the men in the control room giggle at what they take to be the first manifestations of an enormous hoax, the mass begins to move.

5:10

In the main playing area, police check their weapons as the air fills with the sound of crackling brush and the earth begins to tremble as something huge approaches. At the station houses nearest Central Park on both East and West sides, switchboards clog as apartment-dwellers living above the tree line call in to report the incredible thing they've just seen from their front windows.

5:11

Police crouch and raise riot guns; the Freibourgs embrace in anticipation; there is a hideous stench and a sound as if of rushing wind and a huge shape enters the clearing, carrying bits of trees and bushes with it and gurgling with joy.

Police prepare to fire.

Mrs. Freibourg rushes back and forth in front of them, protecting the huge creature with her frantic body. "Stop it, you monsters, it's my baby."

Dr. Freibourg says, "My baby. Leonard," and in the same moment his joy gives way to guilt and despair. "The culture. Dear heaven, the beta culture. And I thought he was eating Mallomars."

Although Leonard has felled several small trees and damaged innumerable automobiles in his passage to join his parents, he is strangely gentle with them. "M.m.m.m.m.m," he says, picking up first his mother and then his father. The Freibourg family exchanges hugs as best it can. Leonard fixes his father with an intent, cross-eyed look that his mother recognizes.

"No no," she says sharply. "Not in the mouth. Put it down."

He puts his father down. Then, musing, he picks up a police sergeant, studies and puts his head in his mouth. Because Leonard has very few teeth, the sergeant emerges physically unharmed, but flushed and jabbering with fear.

"Put it down," says Mrs. Freibourg. Then, to the lieutenant: "You'd better get him something to eat. And you'd better find some way for me to change him," she adds, referring obliquely to the appalling stench. The sergeant looks puzzled until she points out a soiled mass clinging to the big toe of the left foot. "His diaper is a mess." She turns to her husband. "You didn't even change him. And what did you do to him while my back was turned?"

"The beta culture," Dr. Freibourg says miserably. He is pale and shaken. "It works."

"Well you'd better find some way to reverse it," Mrs. Freibourg says. "And you'd better do it soon."

"Of course, my dear," Dr. Freibourg says, with more confidence than he actually feels. He steps into the police car waiting to rush him to the laboratory. "I'll stay up all night if I have to."

The mother looks at Leonard appraisingly. "You may have to stay up all week."

Meanwhile, the semi filled with unwrapped Wonder Bread and the tank truck have arrived with Leonard's dinner. His diaper has been arranged by one of the Cherokee crews that helped build the Verrazano-Narrows Bridge, with preliminary cleansing done by hoses trained on him by the Auxiliary Fire Department. Officials at Madison Square Garden have loaned a tarpaulin to cover Leonard in his hastily constructed crib of hoardings, and graffitists are at work on the outsides. "Paint a duck," Mrs. Freibourg says to one of the minority groups with spray cans, "I want him to be happy here." Leonard cuddles the life-sized Steiff rhinoceros loaned by FAO Schwarz, and goes to sleep.

His mother stands vigil until almost midnight, in case Leonard cries in the night, and across town, in his secret laboratory, Dr. Freibourg has assembled some of the best brains in contemporary science to help him in his search for the antidote.

Meanwhile all the major television networks have established prime-time coverage, with camera crews remaining on the site to record late developments.

At the mother's insistence, riot-trained police have been withdrawn to the vicinity of the Plaza. The mood in the park is one of quiet confidence. Despite the lights and the magnified sound of heavy breathing, fatigue seizes Mrs. Freibourg and, some time near dawn, she sleeps.

5 A.M. SUNDAY, SEPT. 17
Unfortunately, like most babies, Leonard is an early riser. Secure in a mother's love, he wakes up early and sneaks out of his crib, heading across 79th Street

and out of the park, making for the river. Although the people at the site are roused by the creak as he levels the hoardings and the crash of a trailer accidentally toppled and then carefully righted, it is too late to head him off. He has escaped the park in the nick of time, because he has grown in the night, and there is some question as to whether he would have fit between the buildings on East 79th Street in another few hours.

5:10 A.M.
Leonard mashes a portion of the East River Drive on the way into the water. Picking up a taxi, he runs it back and forth on the remaining portion of the road, going, "Rmmmm, RMRMMMMM."

5:11 A.M.
Leonard's mother arrives. She is unable to attract his attention because he has put down the taxi and is splashing his hands in the water, swamping boats for several miles on either side of him.

Across town, Dr. Freibourg has succeeded in shrinking a cat to half-size but he can't find any way to multiply the dosage without emptying laboratories all over the nation to make enough of the salient ingredient. He is frantic because he knows there isn't any time.

5:29 A.M.
In the absence of any other way to manage the problem, fire hoses are squirting milk at Leonard, hit-or-miss. He is enraged by the misses and starts throwing his toys.

The National Guard, summoned when Leonard started down 79th Street to the river, attempts to deter the infant with light artillery.

Naturally, the baby starts to cry.

5:30 A.M.
Despite his mother's best efforts to silence him with bullhorn and Steiff rhinoceros proffered at the end of a giant crane, Leonard is still bellowing.

The Joint Chiefs of Staff arrive, and attempt to survey the problem. Leonard has more or less filled the river at the point where he is sitting. His tears have raised the water level, threatening to inundate portions of the FDR Drive. Speaker trucks simultaneously broadcasting recordings of "Chitty

Chitty Bang Bang" have reduced his bellows to sobs, so the immediate threat of buildings collapsing from the vibrations has been minimized, but there is still the problem of shipping, as he plays boat with tugs and barges but, because of his age, is bored easily, and has thrown several toys into the harbor, causing shipping disasters along the entire Eastern Seaboard. Now he is lifting the top off a building and has begun to examine its contents, picking out the parts that look good to eat and swallowing them whole. After an abbreviated debate, the Joint Chiefs discuss the feasibility of nuclear weaponry of the limited type. They have ruled out tranquilizer cannon because of the size of the problem, and there is some question as to whether massive doses of poison would have any effect.

Overhearing some of the top-level planning, the distraught mother has seized Channel Five's recording equipment to make a nationwide appeal. Now militant mothers from all of the boroughs are marching on the site, threatening massive retaliation if the baby is harmed in any way.

Pollution problems are becoming acute.

The UN is meeting around the clock.

The premiers of all the major nations have sent messages of concern with guarded offers of help.

6:30 A.M.

Leonard has picked the last good bits out of his building and now he has tired of playing fire truck and he is bored. Just as the tanks rumble down East 79th Street, leveling their cannon, and the SAC bombers take off from their secret base, the baby plops on his hands and starts hitching out to sea.

6:34

The baby has reached deep water now. SAC planes report that Leonard, made buoyant by the enormous quantities of fat he carries, is floating happily; he has made his breakfast on a whale.

Dr. Freibourg arrives. "Substitute ingredients. I've found the antidote."

Dilys Freibourg says, "Too little and too late."

"But our baby!"

"He's not our baby any more. He belongs to the ages now."

The Joint Chiefs are discussing alternatives. "I wonder if we should look for him."

Mrs. Freibourg says, "I wouldn't if I were you."

The Supreme Commander looks from mother to Joint Chiefs. "Oh well, he's already in international waters."

The Joint Chiefs exchange looks of relief. "Then it's not our problem."

Suffused by guilt, Dr. Freibourg looks out to sea. "I wonder what will become of him."

His wife says, "Wherever he goes, my heart will go with him, but I wonder if all that salt water will be good for his skin."

COMING SOON: THE ATTACK OF THE GIANT TODDLER

The Hundredth Dove (1977)

Jane Yolen

One of the most gifted storytellers of our day, JANE YOLEN (b. 1939) is the author of hundreds of books for children and adults. Among her best-known works are *The Devil's Arithmetic*; *Sister Light, Sister Dark*; and the Commander Toad stories. She divides her time between homes in Scotland and in western Massachussetts.

As Michael Dirda notes in this book's introduction, "The Hundredth Dove" has the feel of a story you've known all your life—yet our records clearly show that it saw first publication in 1977.

T HERE ONCE LIVED in the forest of old England a fowler named Hugh who supplied all the gamebirds for the high king's table.

The larger birds he hunted with a bow, and it was said of him that he never shot but that a bird fell, and sometimes two. But for the smaller birds that flocked like gray clouds over the forest, he used only a silken net he wove himself. This net was soft and fine and did not injure the birds though it held them fast. Then Hugh the fowler could pick and chose the plumpest of the doves for the high king's table and set the others free.

One day in early summer, Hugh was summoned to court and brought into the throne room.

Hugh bowed low, for it was not often that he was called into the king's own presence. And indeed he felt uncomfortable in the palace, as though caught in a stone cage.

"Rise, fowler, and listen," said the king. "In one week's time I am to be married." Then, turning with a smile to the woman who sat by him, the king held out her hand to the fowler.

The fowler stared up at her. She was neat as a bird, slim and fair, with black eyes. There was a quiet in her, but a restlessness too. He had never seen anyone so beautiful.

Hugh took the tiny hand offered him and put his lips to it, but he only dared to kiss the gold ring that glittered on her finger.

The king looked carefully at the fowler and saw how he trembled. It made the king smile. "See, my lady, how your beauty turns the head of even my fowler. And he is a man who lives as solitary as a monk in his wooded cell."

The lady smiled and said nothing, but she drew her hand away from Hugh.

The king then turned again to the fowler. "In honor of my bride, the Lady Columba, whose name means dove and whose beauty is celebrated in all the world, I wish to serve one hundred of the birds at our wedding feast."

Lady Columba gasped and held up her hand. "Please do not serve them, sire."

But the king spoke to the fowler. "I have spoken. Do not fail me, fowler."

"As you command," said Hugh and he bowed again. He touched his hand to his tunic where his motto *Servo,* "I serve," was sewn over the heart.

Then the fowler went back to the cottage deep in the forest where he lived.

There he took out the silken net and spread it upon the floor. Slowly he searched the net for snags and snarls and weakened threads. These he rewove with great care, sitting straight-backed at his wooden loom.

After a night and a day he was done. The net was as strong as his own stout heart. He laid the net down on the hearth and slept a dreamless sleep.

Before dawn Hugh set out into the forest clearing which only he knew. The trails he followed were less than deer runs, for the fowler needed no paths to show him the way. He knew every tree, every stone in the forest as a lover knows the form of his beloved. And he served the forest easily as well as he served the high king.

The clearing was full of life; yet so silent did the fowler move, neither bird nor insect remarked his coming. He crouched at the edge, his brown and green clothes a part of the wood. Then he waited.

A long patience was his strength, and he waited the whole of the day, neither moving nor sleeping. At dusk the doves came, settling over the clearing like a gray mist. And when they were down and greedily feeding, Hugh leapt up and swung the net over the nearest ones in a single swift motion.

He counted twenty-one doves in his net, all but one gray-blue and meaty. The last was a dove that was slim, elegant, and white as milk. Yet even as Hugh watched, the white dove slipped through the silken strands that bound it and flew away into the darkening air.

Since Hugh was not the kind of hunter to curse his bad luck but rather praise his good, he gathered up the twenty and went home. He placed the doves in a large wooden cage whose bars he had carved out of white oak.

Then he looked at his net. There was not a single break in it, no way for the white dove to have escaped. Hugh thought long and hard about this, but at last he lay down to the cooing of the captured birds and slept.

In the morning the fowler was up at dawn. Again he crept to the forest clearing and waited, quieter than any stone, for the doves. And again he threw his net at dusk and caught twenty fat gray doves and the single white one.

But, as before, the white dove slipped through his net as easily as air.

The fowler carried the gray doves home and caged them with the rest. But his mind was filled with the sight of the white bird, slim and fair. He was determined to capture it.

For five days and nights it was the same except for this one thing: on the fifth night there were only nineteen gray doves in his net. He was short of the hundred by one. Yet he had taken all of the birds in the flock but the white dove.

Hugh looked into the hearthfire but he felt no warmth. He placed his hand upon the motto above his heart. "I swear by the king whom I serve and by the lady who will be his queen that I will capture that bird," he said. "I will bring the hundred doves to them. I shall not fail."

So the sixth day, well before dawn, the fowler arose. He checked the net one final time and saw it was tight. Then he was away to the clearing.

All that day Hugh sat at the clearing's edge, still as a stone. The meadow was full of life. Songbirds sang that had never sung there before. Strange flowers grew and blossomed and died at his feet; yet he never looked at them. Animals that were once and were no longer came out of the forest shadows and passed him by: the hippocampus, the gryphon, and the silken swift unicorn. But he never moved. It was for the white dove he waited, and at last she came.

In the quickening dark she floated down, feather light and luminous at the clearing's edge. Slowly she moved, eating and cooing and calling for her missing flock. She came in the end to where Hugh sat and began to feed at his feet.

He moved his hands once and the net was over her; then his hands were over her, too. The dove twisted and pecked, but he held her close, palms upon wings, fingers on neck.

When the white dove saw she could not move, she turned her bright black eyes on the fowler and spoke to him in a cooing woman's voice:

> Master fowler, set me free,
> Gold and silver I'll give thee.

"Neither gold nor silver tempt me," said Hugh. "*Servo* is my motto. I serve my master. And my master is the king."

Then the white dove spoke again:

> Master fowler, set me free,
> Fame and fortune follow thee.

But the fowler shook his head and held on tight. "After the king, I serve the forest," he said. "Fame and fortune are not masters here." He rose with the white dove in his hands and made ready to return to his house.

Then the bird shook itself all over and spoke for a third time. Its voice was low and beguiling:

> Master fowler, free this dove,
> The Queen will be your own true love.

For the first time, then, the fowler noticed the golden ring that glittered and shone on the dove's foot though night was almost on them. As if in a vision, he saw the Lady Columba again, slim and neat and fair. He heard her voice and felt her hand in his.

He began to tremble and his heart began to pulse madly. He felt a burning in his chest and limbs. Then he looked down at the dove and it seemed to be smiling at him, its black eyes glittering.

"*Servo*," he cried out, his voice shaking and dead. "*Servo*." He closed his eyes and twisted the dove's neck. Then he touched the motto on his tunic. He could feel the word *Servo* impress itself coldly on his fingertips. One quick rip and the motto was torn from his breast. He flung it to the meadow floor, put the limp dove in his pouch, and went through the forest to his home.

The next day the fowler brought the hundred doves—the ninety-nine live ones and the one dead—to the king's kitchen. But there was never a wedding. The Lady Columba came neither to the chapel nor the castle, and her name was never spoken of again in the kingdom.

The fowler gave up hunting and lived on berries and fruit the rest of his life. Every day he made his way to the clearing to throw out grain for the birds. Around his neck, from a chain, a gold ring glittered. And occasionally he would touch the spot on his tunic above his heart, which was shredded and torn.

But though songbirds and sparrows ate his grain, and swallows came at his calling, he never saw another dove.

Jeffty Is Five (1977)

Harlan Ellison®

HARLAN ELLISON® (b. 1934) says he was at a party, talking to the hosts' young son, when he overheard a snatch of conversation that was probably "Jeff is fine, he's always fine." But what he heard was slightly different—he heard "five," not "fine"—and thus did a masterpiece of fantasy get its start.

WHEN I WAS five years old, there was a little kid I played with: Jeffty. His real name was Jeff Kinzer, and everyone who played with him called him Jeffty. We were five years old together, and we had good times playing together.

When I was five, a Clark Bar was as fat around as the gripping end of a Louisville Slugger, and pretty nearly six inches long, and they used real chocolate to coat it, and it crunched very nicely when you bit into the center, and the paper it came wrapped in smelled fresh and good when you peeled off one end to hold the bar so it wouldn't melt onto your fingers. Today, a Clark Bar is as thin as a credit card, they use something artificial and awful-tasting instead of pure chocolate, the thing is soft and soggy, it costs fifteen or twenty cents instead of a decent, correct nickel, and they wrap it so you think it's the same size it was twenty years ago, only it isn't; it's slim and ugly and nasty-tasting and not worth a penny, much less fifteen or twenty cents.

When I was that age, five years old, I was sent away to my Aunt Patricia's home in Buffalo, New York, for two years. My father was going through "bad times" and Aunt Patricia was very beautiful and had married a stockbroker. They took care of me for two years. When I was seven, I came back home and went to find Jeffty, so we could play together.

I was seven. Jeffty was still five. I didn't notice any difference. I didn't know: I was only seven.

When I was seven years old I used to lie on my stomach in front of our Atwater Kent radio and listen to swell stuff. I had tied the ground wire to the radiator, and I would lie there with my coloring books and my Crayolas (when there were only sixteen colors in the big box), and listen to the NBC Red network: Jack Benny on the *Jell-O Program*, *Amos 'n' Andy*, Edgar Bergen and Charlie McCarthy on the *Chase and Sanborn Program*, *One Man's Family*, *First Nighter*; the NBC Blue network: *Easy Aces*, the *Jergens Journal* with Walter Winchell, *Information Please*, *Death Valley Days*; and best of all, the Mutual Network with *The Green Hornet*, *The Lone Ranger*, *The Shadow* and *Quiet, Please*. Today, I turn on my car radio and go from one end of the dial to the other and all I get is 100 strings orchestras, banal housewives and insipid truckers discussing their kinky sex lives with arrogant talk show hosts, country and western drivel and rock music so loud it hurts my ears.

When I was ten, my grandfather died of old age and I was "a troublesome kid," and they sent me off to military school, so I could be "taken in hand."

I came back when I was fourteen. Jeffty was still five.

When I was fourteen years old, I used to go to the movies on Saturday afternoons and a matinee was ten cents and they used real butter on the popcorn and I could always be sure of seeing a western like Lash LaRue, or Wild Bill Elliott as Red Ryder with Bobby Blake as Little Beaver, or Roy Rogers, or Johnny Mack Brown; a scary picture like *House of Horrors* with Rondo Hatton as the Creeper, or *Cat People,* or *The Mummy,* or *I Married a Witch* with Fredric March and Veronica Lake; plus an episode of a great serial like *The Shadow* with Victor Jory, or *Dick Tracy* or *Flash Gordon*; and three cartoons; a James Fitzpatrick TravelTalk; Movietone News; a sing-along and, if I stayed on till evening, Bingo or Keno; and free dishes. Today, I go to movies and see Clint Eastwood blowing people's heads apart like ripe cantaloupes.

At eighteen, I went to college. Jeffty was still five. I came back during the summers, to work at my Uncle Joe's jewelry store. Jeffty hadn't changed. Now I knew there was something different about him, something wrong, something weird. Jeffty was still five years old, not a day older.

At twenty-two I came home for keeps. To open a Sony television franchise in town, the first one. I saw Jeffty from time to time. He was five.

Things are better in a lot of ways. People don't die from some of the old diseases any more. Cars go faster and get you there more quickly on better roads. Shirts are softer and silkier. We have paperback books even though they cost as much as a good hardcover used to. When I'm running short in the bank I can live off credit cards till things even out. But I still think we've lost a lot of good stuff. Did you know you can't buy linoleum any more, only vinyl floor covering? There's no such thing as oilcloth any more; you'll never again smell that special, sweet smell from your grandmother's kitchen. Furniture isn't made to last thirty years or longer because they took a survey and found that young homemakers like to throw their furniture out and bring in all new color-coded borax every seven years. Records don't feel right; they're not thick and solid like the old ones, they're thin and you can bend them…that doesn't seem right to me. Restaurants don't serve cream in pitchers any more, just that artificial glop in little plastic tubs, and one is never enough to get coffee the right color. Everywhere you go, all the towns look the same with Burger Kings and McDonald's and 7-Elevens and Taco Bells and motels and shopping centers. Things may be better, but why do I keep thinking about the past?

What I mean by five years old is not that Jeffty was retarded. I don't think that's what it was. Smart as a whip for five years old; very bright, quick, cute, a funny kid.

But he was three feet tall, small for his age, and perfectly formed, no big head, no strange jaw, none of that. A nice, normal-looking five-year-old kid. Except that he was the same age as I was: twenty-two.

When he spoke, it was with the squeaking, soprano voice of a five-year-old; when he walked it was with the little hops and shuffles of a five-year-old; when he talked to you, it was about the concerns of a five-year-old…comic books, playing soldier, using a clothes pin to attach a stiff piece of cardboard to the front fork of his bike so the sound it made when the spokes hit was like a motorboat, asking questions like *why does that thing do that like that,* how high is up, how old is old, why is grass green, what's an elephant look like? At twenty-two, he was five.

Jeffty's parents were a sad pair. Because I was still a friend of Jeffty's, still let him hang around with me, sometimes took him to the county fair or miniature golf or the movies, I wound up spending time with *them.* Not that I much cared for them, because they were so awfully depressing. But then, I suppose one couldn't expect much more from the poor devils. They had an alien thing in their home, a child who had grown no older than five in twenty-two years, who provided the treasure of that special childlike state indefinitely, but who also denied them the joys of watching the child grow into a normal adult.

Five is a wonderful time of life for a little kid...or it *can* be, if the child is relatively free of the monstrous beastliness other children indulge in. It is a time when the eyes are wide open and the patterns are not yet set; a time when one has not yet been hammered into accepting everything as immutable and hopeless; a time when the hands cannot do enough, the mind cannot learn enough, the world is infinite and colorful and filled with mysteries. Five is a special time before they take the questing, unquenchable, quixotic soul of the young dreamer and thrust it into dreary schoolroom boxes. A time before they take the trembling hands that want to hold everything, touch everything, figure everything out, and make them lie still on desktops. A time before people begin saying "act your age" and "grow up" or "you're behaving like a baby." It is a time when a child who acts adolescent is still cute and responsive and everyone's pet. A time of delight, of wonder, of innocence.

Jeffty had been stuck in that time, just five, just so.

But for his parents it was an ongoing nightmare from which no one—not social workers, not priests, not child psychologists, not teachers, not friends, not medical wizards, not psychiatrists, no one—could slap or shake them awake. For seventeen years their sorrow had grown through stages of parental dotage to concern, from concern to worry, from worry to fear, from fear to confusion, from confusion to anger, from anger to dislike, from dislike to naked hatred, and finally, from deepest loathing and revulsion to a stolid, depressive acceptance.

John Kinzer was a shift foreman at the Balder Tool & Die plant. He was a thirty-year man. To everyone but the man living it, his was a spectacularly uneventful life. In no way was he remarkable...save that he had fathered a twenty-two-year-old five-year-old.

John Kinzer was a small man, soft, with no sharp angles, with pale eyes that never seemed to hold mine for longer than a few seconds. He continually shifted in his chair during conversations, and seemed to see things in the upper corners of the room, things no one else could see...or wanted to see. I suppose the word that best suited him was *haunted*. What his life had become...well, *haunted* suited him.

Leona Kinzer tried valiantly to compensate. No matter what hour of the day I visited, she always tried to foist food on me. And when Jeffty was in the house she was always at *him* about eating: "Honey, would you like an orange? A nice orange? Or a tangerine? I have tangerines. I could peel a tangerine for you." But there was clearly such fear in her, fear of her own child, that the offers of sustenance always had a faintly ominous tone.

Leona Kinzer had been a tall woman, but the years had bent her. She seemed always to be seeking some area of wallpapered wall or storage niche into which she could fade, adopt some chintz or rose-patterned protective coloration and hide forever in plain sight of the child's big brown eyes, pass her a hundred times a day and never realize she was there, holding her breath, invisible. She always had an apron tied around her waist. And her hands were red from cleaning. As if by maintaining the environment immaculately she could pay off her imagined sin: having given birth to this strange creature.

Neither of them watched television very much. The house was usually dead silent, not even the sibilant whispering of water in the pipes, the creaking of timbers settling, the humming of the refrigerator. Awfully silent, as if time itself had taken a detour around that house.

As for Jeffty, he was inoffensive. He lived in that atmosphere of gentle dread and dulled loathing, and if he understood it, he never remarked in any way. He played, as a child plays, and seemed happy. But he must have sensed, in the way of a five-year-old, just how alien he was in their presence.

Alien. No, that wasn't right. He was *too* human, if anything. But out of phase, out of synch with the world around him, and resonating to a different vibration than his parents, God knows. Nor would other children play with him. As they grew past him, they found him at first childish, then uninteresting, then simply frightening as their perceptions of aging became clear and they could see he was not affected by time as they were. Even the little ones, his own age, who might wander into the neighborhood, quickly came to shy away from him like a dog in the street when a car backfires.

Thus, I remained his only friend. A friend of many years. Five years. Twenty-two years. I liked him; more than I can say. And never knew exactly why. But I did, without reserve.

But because we spent time together, I found I was also—polite society—spending time with John and Leona Kinzer. Dinner, Saturday afternoons sometimes, an hour or so when I'd bring Jeffty back from a movie. They were grateful: slavishly so. It relieved them of the embarrassing chore of going out with him, of having to pretend before the world that they were loving parents with a perfectly normal, happy, attractive child. And their gratitude extended to hosting me. Hideous, every moment of their depression, hideous.

I felt sorry for the poor devils, but I despised them for their inability to love Jeffty, who was eminently lovable.

I never let on, even during the evenings in their company that were awkward beyond belief.

We would sit there in the darkening living room—*always* dark or darkening, as if kept in shadow to hold back what the light might reveal to the world outside through the bright eyes of the house—we would sit and silently stare at one another. They never knew what to say to me.

"So how are things down at the plant," I'd say to John Kinzer.

He would shrug. Neither conversation nor life suited him with any ease or grace. "Fine, just fine," he would say, finally.

And we would sit in silence again.

"Would you like a nice piece of coffee cake?" Leona would say. "I made it fresh just this morning." Or deep dish green apple pie. Or milk and toll house cookies. Or a brown betty pudding.

"No, no, thank you, Mrs. Kinzer; Jeffty and I grabbed a couple of cheeseburgers on the way home." And again, silence.

Then, when the stillness and the awkwardness became too much even for them (and who knew how long that total silence reigned when they were alone, with that thing they never talked about any more, hanging between them), Leona Kinzer would say, "I think he's asleep."

John Kinzer would say, "I don't hear the radio playing."

Just so, it would go on like that, until I could politely find an excuse to bolt away on some flimsy pretext. Yes, that was the way it would go on, every time, just the same…except once.

"I don't know what to do any more," Leona said. She began crying. "There's no change, not one day of peace."

Her husband managed to drag himself out of the old easy chair and went to her. He bent and tried to soothe her, but it was clear from the graceless way in which he touched her graying hair that the ability to be compassionate had been stunned in him. "Shhh, Leona, it's all right. Shhh." But she continued crying. Her hands scraped gently at the antimacassars on the arms of the chair.

Then she said, "Sometimes I wish he had been stillborn."

John looked up into the corners of the room. For the nameless shadows that were always watching him? Was it God he was seeking in those spaces? "You don't mean that," he said to her, softly, pathetically, urging her with body tension and trembling in his voice to recant before God took notice of the terrible thought. But she meant it; she meant it very much.

I managed to get away quickly that evening. They didn't want witnesses to their shame. I was glad to go.

And for a week I stayed away. From them, from Jeffty, from their street, even from that end of town.

I had my own life. The store, accounts, suppliers' conferences, poker with friends, pretty women I took to well-lit restaurants, my own parents, putting anti-freeze in the car, complaining to the laundry about too much starch in the collars and cuffs, working out at the gym, taxes, catching Jan or David (whichever one it was) stealing from the cash register. I had my own life.

But not even *that* evening could keep me from Jeffty. He called me at the store and asked me to take him to the rodeo. We chummed it up as best a twenty-two-year-old with other interests *could*...with a five-year-old. I never dwelled on what bound us together; I always thought it was simply the years. That, and affection for a kid who could have been the little brother I never had. (Except I *remembered* when we had played together, when we had both been the same age; I *remembered* that period, and Jeffty was still the same.)

And then, one Saturday afternoon, I came to take him to a double feature, and things I should have noticed so many times before, I first began to notice only that afternoon.

I came walking up to the Kinzer house, expecting Jeffty to be sitting on the front porch steps, or in the porch glider, waiting for me. But he was nowhere in sight.

Going inside, into that darkness and silence, in the midst of May sunshine, was unthinkable. I stood on the front walk for a few moments, then cupped my hands around my mouth and yelled, "Jeffty? Hey, Jeffty, come on out, let's go. We'll be late."

His voice came faintly, as if from under the ground.

"Here I am, Donny."

I could hear him, but I couldn't see him. It was Jeffty, no question about it: as Donald H. Horton, President and Sole Owner of The Horton TV & Sound Center, no one but Jeffty called me Donny. He had never called me anything else.

(Actually, it isn't a lie. I *am,* as far as the public is concerned, Sole Owner of the Center. The partnership with my Aunt Patricia is only to repay the loan she made me, to supplement the money I came into when I was twenty-one, left to me when I was ten by my grandfather. It wasn't a very big loan, only eighteen thousand, but I asked her to be a silent partner, because of when she had taken care of me as a child.)

"Where are you, Jeffty?"

"Under the porch in my secret place."

I walked around the side of the porch, and stooped down and pulled away the wicker grating. Back in there, on the pressed dirt, Jeffty had built himself a secret place. He had comics in orange crates, he had a little table and some pillows, it was lit by big fat candles, and we used to hide there when we were both...five.

"What'cha up to?" I asked, crawling in and pulling the grate closed behind me. It was cool under the porch, and the dirt smelled comfortable, the candles smelled clubby and familiar. Any kid would feel at home in such a secret place: there's never been a kid who didn't spend the happiest, most productive, most deliciously mysterious times of his life in such a secret place.

"Playin'," he said. He was holding something golden and round. It filled the palm of his little hand.

"You forget we were going to the movies?"

"Nope. I was just waitin' for you here."

"Your mom and dad home?"

"Momma."

I understood why he was waiting under the porch. I didn't push it any further. "What've you got there?"

"Captain Midnight Secret Decoder Badge," he said, showing it to me on his flattened palm.

I realized I was looking at it without comprehending what it was for a long time. Then it dawned on me what a miracle Jeffty had in his hand. A miracle that simply could *not* exist.

"Jeffty," I said softly, with wonder in my voice, "where'd you get that?"

"Came in the mail today. I sent away for it."

"It must have cost a lot of money."

"Not so much. Ten cents an' two inner wax seals from two jars of Ovaltine."

"May I see it?" My voice was trembling, and so was the hand I extended. He gave it to me and I held the miracle in the palm of my hand. It was *wonderful*.

You remember. *Captain Midnight* went on the radio nationwide in 1940. It was sponsored by Ovaltine. And every year they issued a Secret Squadron Decoder Badge. And every day at the end of the program, they would give you a clue to the next day's installment in a code that only kids with the official badge could decipher. They stopped making those wonderful Decoder Badges in 1949. I remember the one I had in 1945: it was beautiful. It had a magnifying glass in the center of the code dial. *Captain Midnight* went off the air in 1950, and though it was a short-lived television series in the mid-fifties, and though they issued Decoder Badges in 1955 and 1956, as far as the *real* badges were concerned, they never made one after 1949.

The Captain Midnight Code-O-Graph I held in my hand, the one Jeffty said he had gotten in the mail for ten cents (*ten cents!!!*) and two Ovaltine labels, was brand new, shiny gold metal, not a dent or a spot of rust on it like the old ones you can find at exorbitant prices in collectible shoppes from time to time...it was a *new* Decoder. And the date on it was *this* year.

But *Captain Midnight* no longer existed. Nothing like it existed on the radio. I'd listened to the one or two weak imitations of old-time radio the networks were currently airing, and the stories were dull, the sound effects bland, the whole feel of it wrong, out of date, cornball. Yet I held a *new* Code-O-Graph.

"Jeffty, tell me about this," I said.

"Tell you what, Donny? It's my new Capt'n Midnight Secret Decoder Badge. I use it to figger out what's gonna happen tomorrow."

"Tomorrow how?"

"On the program."

"*What* program?!"

He stared at me as if I was being purposely stupid. "On Capt'n *Mid*night! Boy!" I was being dumb.

I still couldn't get it straight. It was right there, right out in the open, and I still didn't know what was happening. "You mean one of those records they made of the old-time radio programs? Is that what you mean, Jeffty?"

"What records?" he asked. He didn't know what *I* meant.

We stared at each other, there under the porch. And then I said, very slowly, almost afraid of the answer, "Jeffty, how do you hear *Captain Midnight?*"

"Every day. On the radio. On my radio. Every day at five-thirty."

News. Music, dumb music, and news. That's what was on the radio every day at five-thirty. Not *Captain Midnight*. The Secret Squadron hadn't been on the air in twenty years.

"Can we hear it tonight?" I asked.

"Boy!" he said. I was being dumb. I knew it from the way he said it; but I didn't know *why*. Then it dawned on me: this was Saturday. *Captain Midnight* was on Monday through Friday. Not on Saturday or Sunday.

"We goin' to the movies?"

He had to repeat himself twice. My mind was somewhere else. Nothing definite. No conclusions. No wild assumptions leapt to. Just off somewhere trying to figure it out, and concluding—as *you* would have concluded, as *any*one would have concluded rather than accepting the truth, the impossible and wonderful truth—just finally concluding there was a simple explanation I didn't yet perceive. Something mundane and dull, like the passage of time that steals all good, old things from us, packratting trinkets and plastic in exchange. And all in the name of Progress.

"We goin' to the movies, Donny?"

"You bet your boots we are, kiddo," I said. And I smiled. And I handed him the Code-O-Graph. And he put it in his side pants pocket. And we crawled out from under the porch. And we went to the movies. And neither of us said anything about *Captain Midnight* all the rest of that day. And there wasn't a ten-minute stretch, all the rest of that day, that I didn't think about it.

It was inventory all that next week. I didn't see Jeffty till late Thursday. I confess I left the store in the hands of Jan and David, told them I had some errands to run, and left early. At 4:00. I got to the Kinzers' right around 4:45. Leona answered the door, looking exhausted and distant. "Is Jeffty around?" She said he was upstairs in his room...

...listening to the radio.

I climbed the stairs two at a time.

All right, I had finally made that impossible, illogical leap. Had the stretch of belief involved anyone but Jeffty, adult or child, I would have reasoned out more explicable answers. But it *was* Jeffty, clearly another kind of vessel of life, and what he might experience should not be expected to fit into the ordered scheme.

I admit it: I *wanted* to hear what I heard.

Even with the door closed, I recognized the program:

"There he goes, Tennessee! Get him!"

There was the heavy report of a squirrel rifle and the keening whine of the slug ricocheting, and then the same voice yelled triumphantly, *"Got him! D-e-a-a-a-a-d center!"*

He was listening to the American Broadcasting Company, 790 kilocycles, and he was hearing *Tennessee Jed,* one of my most favorite programs from the forties, a western adventure I had not heard in twenty years, because it had not existed for twenty years.

I sat down on the top step of the stairs, there in the upstairs hall of the Kinzer home, and I listened to the show. It wasn't a rerun of an old program; I dimly remembered every one of *them* by heart. I had never missed an episode. And even more convincing evidence than childhood memory that this was a *new* installment were the occasional references during the commercials to current cultural and technological developments, and phrases that had not existed in common usage in the forties: aerosol spray cans, laserasing of tattoos, Tanzania, the word "uptight."

I could not ignore the fact. Jeffty was listening to a *new* segment of *Tennessee Jed.*

I ran downstairs and out the front door to my car. Leona must have been in the kitchen. I turned the key and punched on the radio and spun the dial to 790 kilohertz. The ABC station. Rock music.

I sat there for a few moments, then ran the dial slowly from one end to the other. Music, news, talk shows. No *Tennessee Jed.* And it was a Blaupunkt, the best radio I could get. I wasn't missing some perimeter station. It simply was not there!

After a few moments I turned off the radio and the ignition and went back upstairs quietly. I sat down on the top step and listened to the entire program. It was *wonderful.*

Exciting, imaginative, filled with everything I remembered as being most innovative about radio drama. But it was modern. It wasn't an antique, rebroadcast to assuage the need of that dwindling listenership who longed for the old days. It was a new show, with all the old voices, but still young and bright. Even the commercials were for currently available products, but they weren't as loud or as insulting as the screamer ads one heard on radio these days.

And when *Tennessee Jed* went off at 5:00, I heard Jeffty spin the dial on his radio till I heard the familiar voice of the announcer Glenn Riggs proclaim, *"Presenting Hop Harrigan! America's ace of the airwaves!"* There was the sound of an airplane in flight. It was a prop plane, *not* a jet! Not the sound kids today have grown up with, but the sound *I* grew up with, the *real* sound of an airplane, the growling, revving, throaty sound of the kind of airplanes G-8 and His Battle Aces flew, the kind Captain Midnight flew, the kind Hop Harrigan flew. And then I heard Hop say, *"CX-4 calling control tower. CX-4 calling control tower. Standing by!"* A pause, then, *"Okay, this is Hop Harrigan…coming in!"*

And Jeffty, who had the same problem all of us kids had had in the forties with programming that pitted equal favorites against one another on different stations, having paid his respects to Hop Harrigan and Tank Tinker, spun the dial and went back to ABC where I heard the stroke of a gong, the wild cacophony of nonsense Chinese chatter, and the announcer yelled, *"T-e-e-e-rry and the Pirates!"*

I sat there on the top step and listened to Terry and Connie and Flip Corkin and, so help me God, Agnes Moorehead as The Dragon Lady, all of them in a new adventure that took place in a Red China that had not existed in the days of Milton Caniff's 1937 version of the Orient, with river pirates and Chiang Kai-shek and warlords and the naive Imperialism of American gunboat diplomacy.

Sat, and listened to the whole show, and sat even longer to hear *Superman* and part of *Jack Armstrong, the All-American Boy,* and part of *Captain Midnight,* and John Kinzer came home and neither he nor Leona came upstairs to find out what had happened to me, or where Jeffty was, and sat longer, and found I had started crying, and could not stop, just sat there with tears running down my face, into the corners of my mouth, sitting and crying until Jeffty heard me and opened his door and saw me and came out and looked at me in childish confusion as I heard the station break for the Mutual Network and they began the theme music of *Tom Mix,* "When It's Round-up Time in Texas and the Bloom Is on the Sage," and Jeffty touched my shoulder and smiled at me, with his mouth and his big brown eyes, and said, "Hi, Donny. Wanna come in an' listen to the radio with me?"

Hume denied the existence of an absolute space, in which each thing has its place; Borges denies the existence of one single time, in which all events are linked.

Jeffty received radio programs from a place that could not, in logic, in the natural scheme of the space-time universe as conceived by Einstein, exist. But that wasn't all he received. He got mail-order premiums that no one was manufacturing. He read comic books that had been defunct for three decades. He saw movies with actors who had been dead for twenty years. He was the receiving terminal for endless joys and pleasures of the past that the world had dropped along the way. On its headlong suicidal flight toward New Tomorrows, the world had razed its treasure house of simple happiness, had poured concrete over its playgrounds, had abandoned its elfin stragglers, and all of it was being impossibly, miraculously shunted back into the present through Jeffty. Revivified, updated, the traditions maintained but contemporaneous. Jeffty was the unbidding Aladdin whose very nature formed the magic lampness of his reality.

And he took me into his world with him.

Because he trusted me.

We had breakfast of Quaker Puffed Wheat Sparkies and warm Ovaltine we drank out of *this* year's little Orphan Annie Shake-Up Mugs. We went to the movies and while everyone else was seeing a comedy starring Goldie Hawn and Ryan O'Neal, Jeffty and I were enjoying Humphrey Bogart as the professional thief Parker in John Huston's brilliant adaptation of the Donald Westlake novel, SLAYGROUND. The second feature was Spencer Tracy, Carole Lombard and Laird Cregar in the Val Lewton-produced film of *Leiningen Versus the Ants*.

Twice a month we went down to the newsstand and bought the current pulp issues of *The Shadow, Doc Savage* and *Startling Stories*. Jeffty and I sat together and I read to him from the magazines. He particularly liked the new short novel by Henry Kuttner, "The Dreams of Achilles," and the new Stanley G. Weinbaum series of short stories set in the subatomic particle universe of Redurna. In September we enjoyed the first installment of the new Robert E. Howard Conan novel, ISLE OF THE BLACK ONES, in *Weird Tales*; and in August we were only mildly disappointed by Edgar Rice Burroughs' fourth novella in the Jupiter series featuring John Carter of Barsoom—"Corsairs of

Jupiter." But the editor of *Argosy All-Story Weekly* promised there would be two more stories in the series, and it was such an unexpected revelation for Jeffty and me, that it dimmed our disappointment at the lessened quality of the current story.

We read comics together, and Jeffty and I both decided—separately, before we came together to discuss it—that our favorite characters were Doll Man, Airboy and The Heap. We also adored the George Carlson strips in *Jingle Jangle Comics,* particularly the Pie-Face Prince of Old Pretzleburg stories, which we read together and laughed over, even though I had to explain some of the subtler puns to Jeffty, who was too young to have that kind of subtle wit.

How to explain it? I can't. I had enough physics in college to make some offhand guesses, but I'm more likely wrong than right. The laws of the conservation of energy occasionally break. These are laws that physicists call "weakly violated." Perhaps Jeffty was a catalyst for the weak violation of conservation laws we're only now beginning to realize exist. I tried doing some reading in the area—muon decay of the "forbidden" kind: gamma decay that doesn't include the muon neutrino among its products—but nothing I encountered, not even the latest readings from the Swiss Institute for Nuclear Research near Zurich gave me an insight. I was thrown back on a vague acceptance of the philosophy that the real name for "science" is *magic.*

No explanations, but enormous good times.

The happiest time of my life.

I had the "real" world, the world of my store and my friends and my family, the world of profit&loss, of taxes and evenings with young women who talked about going shopping, or the United Nations, or the rising cost of coffee and microwave ovens. And I had Jeffty's world, in which I existed only when I was with him. The things of the past he knew as fresh and new, I could experience only when in his company. And the membrane between the two worlds grew ever thinner, more luminous and transparent. I had the best of both worlds. And knew, somehow, that I could carry nothing from one to the other.

Forgetting that, for just a moment, betraying Jeffty by forgetting, brought an end to it all.

Enjoying myself so much, I grew careless and failed to consider how fragile the relationship between Jeffty's world and my world really was. There is a reason why the Present begrudges the existence of the Past. I never really understood. Nowhere in the beast books, where survival is shown in battles between claw and fang, tentacle and poison sac, is there recognition of the ferocity the Present always brings to bear on the Past. Nowhere is there a detailed statement of how the Present lies in wait for What-Was, waiting for it to become Now-This-Moment so it can shred it with its merciless jaws.

Who could know such a thing…at any age…and certainly not at my age… who could understand such a thing?

I'm trying to exculpate myself. I can't. It was my fault.

It was another Saturday afternoon.

"What's playing today?" I asked him, in the car, on the way downtown.

He looked up at me from the other side of the front seat and smiled one of his best smiles. "Ken Maynard in *Bullwhip Justice* an' *The Demolished Man*." He kept smiling, as if he'd really put one over on me. I looked at him with disbelief.

"You're *kid*ding!" I said, delighted. Bester's THE DEMOLISHED MAN?" He nodded his head, delighted at my being delighted. He knew it was one of my favorite books. "Oh, that's super!"

"Super *duper*," he said.

"Who's in it?"

"Franchot Tone, Evelyn Keyes, Lionel Barrymore and Elisha Cook, Jr." He was much more knowledgeable about movie actors than I'd ever been. He could name the character actors in any movie he'd ever seen. Even the crowd scenes.

"And cartoons?" I asked.

"Three of 'em, a *Little Lulu,* a *Donald Duck* and a *Bugs Bunny.* An' a *Pete Smith Specialty* an' a *Lew Lehr Monkeys is da C-r-r-r-aziest Peoples*."

"Oh boy!" I said. I was grinning from ear to ear. And then I looked down and saw the pad of purchase order forms on the seat. I'd forgotten to drop it off at the store.

"Gotta stop by the Center," I said. "Gotta drop off something. It'll only take a minute."

"Okay," Jeffty said. "But we won't be late, will we?"

"Not on your tintype, kiddo," I said.

When I pulled into the parking lot behind the Center, he decided to come in with me and we'd walk over to the theater. It's not a large town. There are only two movie houses, the Utopia and the Lyric. We were going to the Utopia and it was only three blocks from the Center.

I walked into the store with the pad of forms, and it was bedlam. David and Jan were handling two customers each, and there were people standing around waiting to be helped. Jan turned a look on me and her face was a horror-mask of pleading. David was running from the stockroom to the showroom and all he could murmur as he whipped past was "Help!" and then he was gone.

"Jeffty," I said, crouching down, "listen, give me a few minutes. Jan and David are in trouble with all these people. We won't be late, I promise. Just let me get rid of a couple of these customers." He looked nervous, but nodded okay.

I motioned to a chair and said, "Just sit down for a while and I'll be right with you."

He went to the chair, good as you please, though he knew what was happening, and he sat down.

I started taking care of people who wanted color television sets. This was the first really substantial batch of units we'd gotten in—color television was only now becoming reasonably priced and this was Sony's first promotion— and it was bonanza time for me. I could see paying off the loan and being out in front for the first time with the Center. It was business.

In my world, good business comes first.

Jeffty sat there and stared at the wall. Let me tell you about the wall.

Stanchion and bracket designs had been rigged from floor to within two feet of the ceiling. Television sets had been stacked artfully on the wall. Thirty-three television sets. All playing at the same time. Black and white, color, little ones, big ones, all going at the same time.

Jeffty sat and watched thirty-three television sets, on a Saturday afternoon. We can pick up a total of thirteen channels including the UHF educational stations. Golf was on one channel; baseball was on a second; celebrity bowling was on a third; the fourth channel was a religious seminar; a teenage dance show was on the fifth; the sixth was a rerun of a situation comedy; the seventh was a rerun of a police show; eighth was a nature program showing a man fly-casting endlessly; ninth was news and conversation; tenth was a stock car race; eleventh was a man doing logarithms on a blackboard; twelfth was a woman in a leotard doing setting-up exercises; and on the thirteenth channel was a badly animated cartoon show in Spanish. All but six of the shows were repeated on three sets. Jeffty sat and watched that wall of television on a Saturday afternoon while I sold as fast and as hard as I could, to pay back my Aunt Patricia and stay in touch with my world. It was business.

I should have known better. I should have understood about the Present and the way it kills the Past. But I was selling with both hands. And when I finally glanced over at Jeffty, half an hour later, he looked like another child.

He was sweating. That terrible fever sweat when you have stomach flu. He was pale, as pasty and pale as a worm, and his little hands were gripping the arms of the chair so tightly I could see his knuckles in bold relief. I dashed over to him, excusing myself from the middle-aged couple looking at the new 21" Mediterranean model.

"Jeffty!"

He looked at me, but his eyes didn't track. He was in absolute terror. I pulled him out of the chair and started toward the front door with him, but the customers I'd deserted yelled at me, "Hey!" The middle-aged man said, "You wanna sell me this thing or don't you?"

I looked from him to Jeffty and back again. Jeffty was like a zombie. He had come where I'd pulled him. His legs were rubbery and his feet dragged. The past, being eaten by the present, the sound of something in pain.

I clawed some money out of my pants pocket and jammed it into Jeffty's hand. "Kiddo...listen to me...get out of here right now!" He still couldn't focus properly. "*Jeffty*," I said as tightly as I could, "*listen* to me!" The middle-aged customer and his wife were walking toward us. "Listen, kiddo, get out of here right this minute. Walk over to the Utopia and buy the tickets. I'll be right behind you." The middle-aged man and his wife were almost on us. I shoved Jeffty through the door and watched him stumble away in the wrong direction, then stop as if gathering his wits, turn and go back past the front of the Center and in the direction of the Utopia. "Yes, sir," I said, straightening up and facing them, "yes, ma'am, that is one terrific set with some sen*sa*tional features! If you'll just step back here with me..."

There was a terrible sound of something hurting, but I couldn't tell from which channel, or from which set, it was coming.

Most of it I learned later, from the girl in the ticket booth, and from some people I knew who came to me to tell me what had happened. By the time I got to the Utopia, nearly twenty minutes later, Jeffty was already beaten to a pulp and had been taken to the Manager's office.

"Did you see a very little boy, about five years old, with big brown eyes and straight brown hair…he was waiting for me?"

"Oh, I think that's the little boy those kids beat up?"

"What!?! *Where is he?*"

"They took him to the Manager's office. No one knew who he was or where to find his parents—"

A young girl wearing an usher's uniform was placing a wet paper towel on his face.

I took the towel away from her and ordered her out of the office.

She looked insulted and she snorted something rude; but she left. I sat on the edge of the couch and tried to swab away the blood from the lacerations without opening the wounds where the blood had caked. Both his eyes were swollen shut. His mouth was ripped badly. His hair was matted with dried blood.

He had been standing in line behind two kids in their teens. They started selling tickets at 12:30 and the show started at 1:00. The doors weren't opened till 12:45. He had been waiting, and the kids in front of him had had a portable radio. They were listening to the ball game. Jeffty had wanted to hear some program, God knows what it might have been, *Grand Central Station*, *Let's Pretend*, *The Land of the Lost*, God only knows which one it might have been.

He had asked if he could borrow their radio to hear the program for a minute, and it had been a commercial break or something, and the kids had given him the radio, probably out of some malicious kind of courtesy that would permit them to take offense and rag the little boy. He had changed the station…and they'd been unable to get it to go back to the ball game. It was locked into the past, on a station that was broadcasting a program that didn't exist for anyone but Jeffty.

They had beaten him badly…as everyone watched.

And then they had run away.

I had left him alone, left him to fight off the present without sufficient weaponry. I had betrayed him for the sale of a 21" Mediterranean console television, and now his face was pulped meat. He moaned something inaudible and sobbed softly.

"Shhh, it's okay, kiddo, it's Donny. I'm here. I'll get you home, it'll be okay."

I should have taken him straight to the hospital. I don't know why I didn't. I should have. I should have done that.

When I carried him through the door, John and Leona Kinzer just stared at me. They didn't move to take him from my arms. One of his hands was hanging down. He was conscious, but just barely. They stared, there in the semi-darkness of a Saturday afternoon in the present. I looked at them. "A couple of kids beat him up at the theater." I raised him a few inches in my arms and extended him. They stared at me, at both of us, with nothing in their eyes, without movement. "Jesus Christ," I shouted, "he's been beaten! He's your son! Don't you even want to touch him? What the hell kind of people are you?!"

Then Leona moved toward me very slowly. She stood in front of us for a few seconds, and there was a leaden stoicism in her face that was terrible to see. It said, *I have been in this place before, many times, and I cannot bear to be in it again; but I am here now.*

So I gave him to her. God help me, I gave him over to her.

And she took him upstairs to bathe away his blood and his pain.

John Kinzer and I stood in our separate places in the dim living room of their home, and we stared at each other. He had nothing to say to me.

I shoved past him and fell into a chair. I was shaking.

I heard the bath water running upstairs.

After what seemed a very long time Leona came downstairs, wiping her hands on her apron. She sat down on the sofa and after a moment John sat down beside her. I heard the sound of rock music from upstairs.

"Would you like a piece of nice pound cake?" Leona said.

I didn't answer. I was listening to the sound of the music. Rock music. On the radio. There was a table lamp on the end table beside the sofa. It cast a dim and futile light in the shadowed living room. *Rock music from the present, on a radio upstairs?* I started to say something, and then *knew*... Oh God... *No!*

I jumped up just as the sound of hideous crackling blotted out the music, and the table lamp dimmed and dimmed and flickered. I screamed something, I don't know what it was, and ran for the stairs.

Jeffty's parents did not move. They sat there with their hands folded, in that place they had been for so many years.

I fell twice rushing up the stairs.

There isn't much on television that can hold my interest. I bought an old cathedral-shaped Philco radio in a second-hand store, and I replaced all the burnt-out parts with the original tubes from old radios I could cannibalize that still worked. I don't use transistors or printed circuits. They wouldn't work. I've sat in front of that set for hours sometimes, running the dial back and forth as slowly as you can imagine, so slowly it doesn't look as if it's moving at all sometimes.

But I can't find *Captain Midnight* or *The Land of the Lost* or *The Shadow* or *Quiet, Please*.

So she did love him, still, a little bit, even after all those years. I can't hate them: they only wanted to live in the present world again. That isn't such a terrible thing.

It's a good world, all things considered. It's much better than it used to be, in a lot of ways. People don't die from the old diseases any more. They die from new ones, but that's Progress, isn't it?

Isn't it?

Tell me.

Somebody please tell me.

Salvador (1984)

LUCIUS SHEPARD

Among the most gifted stylists ever to grace the pages of *F&SF*, LUCIUS SHEPARD (1943–2014) typically applied that writing style to tales that are both hard-edged and hallucinatory. His many novels include *The Golden, Floater, Viator,* and *A Handbook of American Prayer,* and he published roughly a dozen collections of short fiction, including *The Ends of the Earth, The Jaguar Hunter, Beast of the Heartland and Other Stories,* and *The Best of Lucius Shepard.* That last volume, not surprisingly, includes the hallucinatory tale of a soldier in Central America that you are about to read.

THREE WEEKS BEFORE they wasted Tecolutla, Dantzler had his baptism of fire. The platoon was crossing a meadow at the foot of an emerald-green volcano, and being a dreamy sort, he was idling along, swatting tall grasses with his rifle barrel and thinking how it might have been a first-grader with crayons who had devised this elementary landscape of a perfect cone rising into a cloudless sky, when cap-pistol noises sounded on the slope. Someone screamed for the medic, and Dantzler dove into the grass, fumbling for his ampules. He slipped one from the dispenser and popped it under his nose, inhaling frantically; then, to be on the safe side, he popped another—"A double helpin' of martial arts," as DT would say—and lay with his head down until the drugs had worked their magic. There was dirt in his mouth, and he was very afraid.

Gradually his arms and legs lost their heaviness, and his heart rate slowed. His vision sharpened to the point that he could see not only the pinpricks of fire blooming on the slope, but also the figures behind them, half-obscured by brush. A bubble of grim anger welled up in his brain, hardened to a fierce resolve, and he started moving towards the volcano. By the time he reached the base of the cone, he was all rage and reflexes. He spent the next forty minutes spinning acrobatically through the thickets, spraying shadows with bursts of his M-18; yet part of his mind remained distant from the action, marveling at his efficiency, at the comic-strip enthusiasm he felt for the task of killing. He shouted at the men he shot, and he shot them many more times than was necessary, like a child playing soldier.

"Playin' my ass!" DT would say. "You just actin' natural."

DT was a firm believer in the ampules; though the official line was that they contained tailored RNA compounds and pseudoendorphins modified to an inhalant form, he held the opinion that they opened a man up to his inner nature. He was big, black, with heavily muscled arms and crudely stamped features, and he had come to the Special Forces direct from prison, where he had done a stretch for attempted murder; the palms of his hands were covered by jail tattoos—a pentagram and a horned monster. The words DIE HIGH were painted on his helmet. This was his second tour in Salvador, and Moody—who was Dantzler's buddy—said the drugs had addled DT's brains, that he was crazy and gone to hell.

"He collects trophies," Moody had said. "And not just ears like they done in 'Nam."

When Dantzler had finally gotten a glimpse of the trophies, he had been appalled. They were kept in a tin box in DT's pack and were nearly unrecognizable; they looked like withered brown orchids. But despite his revulsion, despite the fact that he was afraid of DT, he admired the man's capacity for survival and had taken to heart his advice to rely on the drugs.

On the way back down the slope they discovered a live casualty, an Indian kid about Dantzler's age, nineteen or twenty. Black hair, adobe skin, and heavy-lidded brown eyes. Dantzler, whose father was an anthropologist and had done fieldwork in Salvador, figured him for a Santa Ana tribesman; before leaving the States, Dantzler had pored over his father's notes, hoping this would give him an edge, and had learned to identify the various regional types. The kid had a minor leg wound and was wearing fatigue pants and a faded COKE ADDS LIFE T-shirt. This T-shirt irritated DT no end.

"What the hell you know 'bout Coke?" he asked the kid as they headed for the chopper that was to carry them deeper into Morazán Province. "You think it's funny or somethin'?" He whacked the kid in the back with his rifle butt, and when they reached the chopper, he slung him inside and had him sit by the door. He sat beside him, tapped out a joint from a pack of Kools, and asked, "Where's Infante?"

"Dead," said the medic.

"Shit!" DT licked the joint so it would burn evenly. "Goddamn beaner ain't no use 'cept somebody else know Spanish."

"I know a little," Dantzler volunteered.

Staring at Dantzler, DT's eyes went empty and unfocused. "Naw," he said. "You don't know no Spanish."

Dantzler ducked his head to avoid DT's stare and said nothing; he thought he understood what DT meant, but he ducked away from the understanding as well. The chopper bore them aloft, and DT lit the joint. He let the smoke out his nostrils and passed the joint to the kid, who accepted gratefully.

"*Qué sabor!*" he said, exhaling a billow; he smiled and nodded, wanting to be friends.

Dantzler turned his gaze to the open door. They were flying low between the hills, and looking at the deep bays of shadow in their folds acted to drain away the residue of the drugs, leaving him weary and frazzled. Sunlight poured in, dazzling the oil-smeared floor.

"Hey, Dantzler!" DT had to shout over the noise of the rotors. "Ask him whass his name!"

The kid's eyelids were drooping from the joint, but on hearing Spanish he perked up; he shook his head, though, refusing to answer. Dantzler smiled and told him not to be afraid.

"Ricardo Quu," said the kid.

"Kool!" said DT with false heartiness. "Thass my brand!" He offered his pack to the kid.

"*Gracias,* no." The kid waved the joint and grinned.

"Dude's named for a goddamn cigarette," said DT disparagingly, as if this were the height of insanity.

Dantzler asked the kid if there were more soldiers nearby, and once again received no reply; but, apparently sensing in Dantzler a kindred soul, the kid leaned forward and spoke rapidly, saying that his village was Santander Jiménez, that his father was—he hesitated—a man of power. He asked where they were taking him. Dantzler returned a stony glare. He found it easy to reject the kid, and he realized later this was because he had already given up on him.

Latching his hands behind his head, DT began to sing—a wordless melody. His voice was discordant, barely audible above the rotors; but the tune had a familiar ring and Dantzler soon placed it. The theme from *Star Trek*. It brought back memories of watching TV with his sister, laughing at the low-budget aliens and Scotty's Actors' Equity accent. He gazed out the door again. The sun was behind the hills, and the hillsides were unfeatured blurs of dark green smoke. Oh, God, he wanted to be home, to be anywhere but Salvador! A couple of the guys joined in the singing at DT's urging, and as the volume swelled, Dantzler's emotion peaked. He was on the verge of tears, remembering tastes and sights, the way his girl Jeanine had smelled, so clean and fresh, not reeking of sweat and perfume like the whores around Ilopango—finding all this substance in the banal touchstone of his culture and the illusions of the hillsides rushing past. Then Moody tensed beside him, and he glanced up to learn the reason why.

In the gloom of the chopper's belly, DT was as unfeatured as the hills—a black presence ruling them, more the leader of a coven than a platoon. The other two guys were singing their lungs out, and even the kid was getting into the spirit of things. *"Música!"* he said at one point, smiling at everybody, trying to fan the flame of good feeling. He swayed to the rhythm and essayed a "la-la" now and again. But no one else was responding.

The singing stopped, and Dantzler saw that the whole platoon was staring at the kid, their expressions slack and dispirited.

"Space!" shouted DT, giving the kid a little shove. "The final frontier!"

The smile had not yet left the kid's face when he toppled out the door. DT peered after him; a few seconds later he smacked his hand against the floor and sat back, grinning. Dantzler felt like screaming, the stupid horror of the joke was so at odds with the languor of his homesickness. He looked to the others for reaction. They were sitting with their heads down, fiddling with trigger guards and pack straps, studying their bootlaces, and seeing this, he quickly imitated them.

Morazán Province was spook country. Santa Ana spooks. Flights of birds had been reported to attack patrols; animals appeared at the perimeters of campsites and vanished when you shot at them; dreams afflicted everyone who ventured there. Dantzler could not testify to the birds and animals, but he did have a recurring dream. In it the kid DT had killed was pinwheeling down through a golden fog, his T-shirt visible against the roiling backdrop, and sometimes a voice would boom out of the fog, saying, "You are killing my son." No, no, Dantzler would reply, it wasn't me, and besides, he's already dead. Then he would wake covered with sweat, groping for his rifle, his heart racing.

But the dream was not an important terror, and he assigned it no significance. The land was far more terrifying. Pine-forested ridges that stood out against the sky like fringes of electrified hair; little trails winding off into thickets and petering out, as if what they led to had been magicked away; gray rock faces along which they were forced to walk, hopelessly exposed to ambush. There were innumerable booby traps set by the guerrillas, and they lost several men to rockfalls. It was the emptiest place of Dantzler's experience. No people, no animals, just a few hawks circling the solitudes between the ridges. Once in a while they found tunnels, and these they blew with the new gas grenades; the gas ignited the rich concentrations of hydrocarbons and sent flame sweeping through the entire system. DT would praise whoever had discovered the tunnel and would estimate in a loud voice how many beaners they had "refried." But Dantzler knew they were traversing pure emptiness and burning empty holes. Days, under debilitating heat, they humped the mountains, traveling seven, eight, even ten klicks up trails so steep that frequently the feet of the guy ahead of you would be on a level with your face; nights, it was cold, the darkness absolute, the silence so profound that Dantzler imagined he could hear the great humming vibration of the earth. They might have been anywhere or nowhere. Their fear was nourished by the isolation, and the only remedy was "martial arts."

Dantzler took to popping the pills without the excuse of combat. Moody cautioned him against abusing the drugs, citing rumors of bad side effects and DT's madness; but even he was using them more and more often. During basic training, Dantzler's DI had told the boots that the drugs were available only to the Special Forces, that their use was optional; but there had been too many instances of lackluster battlefield performance in the last war, and this was to prevent a reoccurrence.

"The chickenshit infantry take 'em," the DI had said. "You bastards are brave already. You're born killers, right?"

"Right, sir!" they had shouted.

"What are you?"

"Born killers, sir!"

But Dantzler was not a born killer; he was not even clear as to how he had been drafted, less clear as to how he had been manipulated into the Special Forces, and he had learned that nothing was optional in Salvador, with the possible exception of life itself.

The platoon's mission was reconnaissance and mop-up. Along with other Special Forces platoons, they were to secure Morazán prior to the invasion of Nicaragua; specifically, they were to proceed to the village of Tecolutla, where a Sandinista patrol had recently been spotted, and following that they were to join up with the First Infantry and take part in the offensive against León, a provincial capital just across the Nicaraguan border. As Dantzler and Moody walked together, they frequently talked about the offensive, how it would be good to get down into flat country; occasionally they talked about the possibility of reporting DT, and once, after he had led them on a forced night march, they toyed with the idea of killing him. But most often they discussed the ways of the Indians and the land, since this was what had caused them to become buddies.

Moody was slightly built, freckled, and red-haired; his eyes had the "thousand-yard stare" that came from too much war. Dantzler had seen winos with such vacant, lusterless stares. Moody's father had been in 'Nam, and Moody said it had been worse than Salvador because there had been no real commitment to win; but he thought Nicaragua and Guatemala might be the worst of all, especially if the Cubans sent in troops as they had threatened. He was adept at locating tunnels and detecting booby traps, and it was for this reason Dantzler had cultivated his friendship. Essentially a loner, Moody had resisted all advances until learning of Dantzler's father; thereafter he had buddied up, eager to hear about the field notes, believing they might give him an edge.

"They think the land has animal traits," said Dantzler one day as they climbed along a ridgetop. "Just like some kinds of fish look like plants or sea bottom, parts of the land look like plain ground, jungle…whatever. But when you enter them, you find you've entered the spirit world, the world of *Sukias*."

"What's *Sukias*?" asked Moody.

"Magicians." A twig snapped behind Dantzler, and he spun around, twitching off the safety of his rifle. It was only Hodge—a lanky kid with the beginnings of a beer gut. He stared hollow-eyed at Dantzler and popped an ampule.

Moody made a noise of disbelief. "If they got magicians, why ain't they winnin'? Why ain't they zappin' us off the cliffs?"

"It's not their business," said Dantzler. "They don't believe in messing with worldly affairs unless it concerns them directly. Anyway, these places—the ones that look like normal land but aren't—they're called…" He drew a blank on the name. *"Aya*-something. I can't remember. But they have different laws. They're where your spirit goes to die after your body dies."

"Don't they got no Heaven?"

"Nope. It just takes longer for your spirit to die, and so it goes to one of these places that's between everything and nothing."

"Nothin'," said Moody disconsolately, as if all his hopes for an afterlife had been dashed. "Don't make no sense to have spirits and not have no Heaven."

"Hey," said Dantzler, tensing as wind rustled the pine boughs. "They're just a bunch of damn primitives. You know what their sacred drink is? Hot chocolate! My old man was a guest at one of their funerals, and he said they carried cups of hot chocolate balanced on these little red towers and acted like drinking it was going to wake them to the secrets of the universe." He laughed, and the laughter sounded tinny and psychotic to his own ears. "So you're going to worry about fools who think hot chocolate's holy water?"

"Maybe they just like it," said Moody. "Maybe somebody dyin' just give 'em an excuse to drink it."

But Dantzler was no longer listening. A moment before, as they emerged from pine cover onto the highest point of the ridge, a stony scarp open to the winds and providing a view of rumpled mountains and valleys extending to the horizon, he had popped an ampule. He felt so strong, so full of righteous purpose and controlled fury, it seemed only the sky was around him, that he was still ascending, preparing to do battle with the gods themselves.

Tecolutla was a village of whitewashed stone tucked into a notch between two hills. From above, the houses—with their shadow-blackened windows and doorways—looked like an unlucky throw of dice. The streets ran uphill and down, diverging around boulders. Bougainvilleas and hibiscuses speckled the hillsides, and there were tilled fields on the gentler slopes. It was a sweet, peaceful place when they arrived, and after they had gone it was once again peaceful; but its sweetness had been permanently banished. The reports of Sandinistas had proved accurate, and though they were casualties left behind to recuperate, DT had decided their presence called for extreme measures. Fu gas, frag grenades, and such. He had fired an M-60 until the barrel melted down, and then had manned the flamethrower. Afterward, as they rested atop the next ridge, exhausted and begrimed, having radioed in a chopper for resupply, he could not get over how one of the houses he had torched had come to resemble a toasted marshmallow.

"Ain't that how it was, man?" he asked, striding up and down the line. He did not care if they agreed about the house; it was a deeper question he was asking, one concerning the ethics of their actions.

"Yeah," said Dantzler, forcing a smile. "Sure did."

DT grunted with laughter. "You *know* I'm right, don'tcha man?"

The sun hung directly behind his head, a golden corona rimming a black oval, and Dantzler could not turn his eyes away. He felt weak and weakening, as if threads of himself were being spun loose and sucked into the blackness. He had popped three ampules prior to the firefight, and his experience of Tecolutla had been a kind of mad whirling dance through the streets, spraying erratic bursts that appeared to be writing weird names on the walls. The leader of the Sandinistas had worn a mask—a gray face with a surprised hole of a mouth and pink circles around the eyes. A ghost face. Dantzler had been afraid of the mask and had poured round after round into it. Then, leaving the village, he had seen a small girl standing beside the shell of the last house, watching them, her colorless rag of a dress tattering in the breeze. She had been a victim of that malnutrition disease, the one that paled your skin and whitened your hair and left you retarded. He could not recall the name of the disease—things like names were slipping away from him—nor could he believe anyone had survived, and for a moment he had thought the spirit of the village had come out to mark their trail.

That was all he could remember of Tecolutla, all he wanted to remember. But he knew he had been brave.

Four days later, they headed up into a cloud forest. It was the dry season, but dry season or not, blackish gray clouds always shrouded these peaks. They were shot through by ugly glimmers of lightning, making it seem that malfunctioning neon signs were hidden beneath them, advertisements for evil. Everyone was jittery, and Jerry LeDoux—a slim dark-haired Cajun kid—flat-out refused to go.

"It ain't reasonable," he said. "Be easier to go through the passes."

"We're on recon, man! You think the beaners be waitin' in the passes, wavin' their white flags?" DT whipped his rifle into firing position and pointed it at LeDoux. "C'mon, Louisiana man. Pop a few, and you feel different."

As LeDoux popped the ampules, DT talked to him.

"Look at it this way, man. This is your big adventure. Up there it be like all them animal shows on the tube. The savage kingdom, the unknown. Could be like Mars or somethin'. Monsters and shit, with big red eyes and tentacles. You wanna miss that, man? You wanna miss bein' the first grunt on Mars?"

Soon LeDoux was raring to go, giggling at DT's rap.

Moody kept his mouth shut, but he fingered the safety of his rifle and glared at DT's back. When DT turned to him, however, he relaxed. Since Tecolutla he had grown taciturn, and there seemed to be a shifting of lights and darks in his eyes, as if something were scurrying back and forth behind them. He had taken to wearing banana leaves on his head, arranging them under his helmet so the frayed ends stuck out the side like strange green hair. He said this was camouflage, but Dantzler was certain it bespoke some secretive irrational purpose. Of course DT had noticed Moody's spiritual erosion, and as they prepared to move out, he called Dantzler aside.

"He done found someplace inside his head that feel good to him," said DT. "He's tryin' to curl up into it, and once he do that he ain't gon' be responsible. Keep an eye on him."

Dantzler mumbled his assent, but was not enthused.

"I know he your fren', man, but that don't mean shit. Not the way things are. Now me, I don't give a damn 'bout you personally. But I'm your brother-in-arms, and thass somethin' you can count on...y'understand."

To Dantzler's shame, he did understand.

They had planned on negotiating the cloud forest by nightfall, but they had underestimated the difficulty. The vegetation beneath the clouds was lush—thick, juicy leaves that mashed underfoot, tangles of vines, trees with slick, pale bark and waxy leaves—and the visibility was only about fifteen feet. They were gray wraiths passing through grayness. The vague shapes of the foliage reminded Dantzler of fancifully engraved letters, and for a while he entertained himself with the notion that they were walking among the half-formed phrases of a constitution not yet manifest in the land. They barged off the trail, losing it completely, becoming veiled in spiderwebs and drenched by spills of water; their voices were oddly muffled, the tag ends of words swallowed up. After seven hours of this, DT reluctantly gave the order to pitch camp. They set electric lamps around the perimeter so they could see to string the jungle hammocks; the beam of light illuminated the moisture in the air, piercing the murk with jeweled blades. They talked in hushed tones, alarmed by the eerie atmosphere. When they had done with the hammocks, DT posted four sentries—Moody, LeDoux, Dantzler, and himself. Then they switched off the lamps.

It grew pitch-dark, and the darkness was picked out by plips and plops, the entire spectrum of dripping sounds. To Dantzler's ears they blended into a gabbling speech. He imagined tiny Santa Ana demons talking about him, and to stave off paranoia he popped two ampules. He continued to pop them, trying to limit himself to one every half hour; but he was uneasy, unsure where to train his rifle in the dark, and he exceeded his limit. Soon it began to grow light again, and he assumed that more time had passed than he had thought. That often happened with the ampules—it was easy to lose yourself in being alert, in the wealth of perceptual detail available to your sharpened senses. Yet on checking his watch, he saw it was only a few minutes after two o'clock. His system was too inundated with the drugs to allow panic, but he twitched his head from side to side in tight little arcs to determine the source of the brightness. There did not appear to be a single source; it was simply that filaments of the cloud were gleaming, casting a diffuse golden glow, as if they were elements of a nervous system coming to life. He started to call out, then held back. The others must have seen the light, and they had given no cry; they probably had a good reason for their silence. He scrunched down flat, pointing his rifle out from the campsite.

Bathed in the golden mist, the forest had acquired an alchemic beauty. Beads of water glittered with gemmy brilliance; the leaves and vines and bark were gilded. Every surface shimmered with light…everything except a fleck of blackness hovering between two of the trunks, its size gradually increasing. As it swelled in his vision, he saw it had the shape of a bird, its wings beating, flying toward him from an inconceivable distance—inconceivable, because the dense vegetation did not permit you to see very far in a straight line, and yet the bird was growing larger with such slowness that it must have been coming from a long way off. It was not really flying, he realized; rather, it was as if the forest were painted on a piece of paper, as if someone were holding a lit match behind it and burning a hole, a hole that maintained the shape of a bird as it spread. He was transfixed, unable to react. Even when it had blotted out half the light, when he lay before it no bigger than a mote in relation to its huge span, he could not move or squeeze the trigger. And then the blackness swept over him. He had the sensation of being borne along at incredible speed, and he could no longer hear the dripping of the forest.

"Moody!" he shouted. "DT!"

But the voice that answered belonged to neither of them. It was hoarse, issuing from every part of the surrounding blackness, and he recognized it as the voice of his recurring dream.

"You are killing my son," it said. "I have led you here, to this *ayahuamaco*, so he may judge you."

Dantzler knew to his bones the voice was that of the Sukia of the village of Santander Jiménez. He wanted to offer a denial, to explain his innocence, but all he could manage was, "No." He said it tearfully, hopelessly, his forehead resting on his rifle barrel. Then his mind gave a savage twist, and his soldiery self regained control. He ejected an ampule from his dispenser and popped it.

The voice laughed—malefic, damning laughter whose vibrations shuddered Dantzler. He opened up with the rifle, spraying fire in all directions. Filigrees of golden holes appeared in the blackness, tendrils of mist coiled through them. He kept on firing until the blackness shattered and fell in jagged sections toward him. Slowly. Like shards of black glass dropping through water. He emptied the rifle and flung himself flat, shielding his head with his arms, expecting to be sliced into bits; but nothing touched him. At last he peeked between his arms; then—amazed, because the forest was now a uniform lustrous yellow—he rose to his knees. He scraped his hands on one of the crushed leaves beneath him, and blood welled from the cut. The broken fibers of the leaf were as stiff as wires. He stood, a giddy trickle of hysteria leaking up from the bottom of his soul. It was no forest, but a building of solid gold worked to resemble a forest—the sort of conceit that might have been fabricated for the child of an emperor. Canopied by golden leaves, columned by slender golden trunks, carpeted by golden grasses. The water beads were diamonds. All the gleam and glitter soothed his apprehension; here was something out of a myth, a habitat for princesses and wizards and dragons. Almost gleeful, he turned to the campsite to see how the others were reacting.

Once, when he was nine years old, he had sneaked into the attic to rummage through the boxes and trunks, and he had run across an old morocco-bound copy of *Gulliver's Travels*. He had been taught to treasure old books, and so he had opened it eagerly to look at the illustrations, only to find that the centers of the pages had been eaten away, and there, right in the heart of the fiction, was a nest of larvae. Pulpy, horrid things. It had been an awful sight, but one unique in his experience, and he might have studied those crawling scraps of life for a very long time if his father had not interrupted. Such a sight was now before him, and he was numb with it.

They were all dead. He should have guessed they would be; he had given no thought to them while firing his rifle. They had been struggling out of their hammocks when the bullets hit, and as a result they were hanging half-in, half-out, their limbs dangling, blood pooled beneath them. The veils of golden mist made them look dark and mysterious and malformed, like monsters killed as they emerged from their cocoons. Dantzler could not stop staring, but he was shrinking inside himself. It was not his fault. That thought kept swooping in and out of a flock of less acceptable thoughts; he wanted it to stay put, to be true, to alleviate the sick horror he was beginning to feel.

"What's your name?" asked a girl's voice behind him.

She was sitting on a stone about twenty feet away. Her hair was a tawny shade of gold, her skin a half-tone lighter, and her dress was cunningly formed out of the mist. Only her eyes were real. Brown heavy-lidded eyes—they were at variance with the rest of her face, which had the fresh, unaffected beauty of an American teenager.

"Don't be afraid," she said, and patted the ground, inviting him to sit beside her.

He recognized the eyes, but it was no matter. He badly needed the consolation she could offer; he walked over and sat down. She let him lean his head against her thigh.

"What's your name?" she repeated.

"Dantzler," he said. "John Dantzler." And then he added, "I'm from Boston. My father's..." It would be too difficult to explain about anthropology. "He's a teacher."

"Are there many soldiers in Boston?" She stroked his cheek with a golden finger.

The caress made Dantzler happy. "Oh, no," he said. "They hardly know there's a war going on."

"This is true?" she said, incredulous.

"Well, they *do* know about it, but it's just news on the TV to them. They've got more pressing problems. Their jobs, families."

"Will you let them know about the war when you return home?" she asked. "Will you do that for me?"

Dantzler had given up hope of returning home, of surviving, and her assumption that he would do both acted to awaken his gratitude. "Yes," he said fervently. "I will."

"You must hurry," she said. "If you stay in the *ayahuamaco* too long, you will never leave. You must find the way out. It is a way not of directions or trails, but of events."

"Where is this place?" he asked, suddenly aware of how much he had taken it for granted.

She shifted her leg away, and if he had not caught himself on the stone, he would have fallen. When he looked up, she had vanished. He was surprised that her disappearance did not alarm him; in reflex he slipped out a couple of ampules, but after a moment's reflection he decided not to use them. It was impossible to slip them back into the dispenser, so he tucked them into the interior webbing of his helmet for later. He doubted he would need them, though. He felt strong, competent and unafraid.

Dantzler stepped carefully between the hammocks; not wanting to brush against them; it might have been his imagination, but they seemed to be bulged down lower than before, as if death had weighed out heavier than life. That heaviness was in the air, pressuring him. Mist rose like golden steam from the corpses, but the sight no longer affected him—perhaps because the mist gave the illusion of being their souls. He picked up a rifle with a full magazine and headed off into the forest.

The tips of the golden leaves were sharp, and he had to ease past them to avoid being cut; but he was at the top of his form, moving gracefully, and the obstacles barely slowed his pace. He was not even anxious about the girl's warning to hurry; he was certain the way out would soon present itself. After a minute or so he heard voices, and after another few seconds he came to a clearing divided by a stream, one so perfectly reflecting that its banks appeared to enclose a wedge of golden mist. Moody was squatting to the left of the stream, staring at the blade of his survival knife and singing under his breath—a wordless melody that had the erratic rhythm of a trapped fly. Beside him lay Jerry

LeDoux, his throat slashed from ear to ear. DT was sitting on the other side of the stream; he had been shot just above the knee, and though he had ripped up his shirt for bandages and tied off the leg with a tourniquet, he was not in good shape. He was sweating, and a gray chalky pallor infused his skin. The entire scene had the weird vitality of something that had materialized in a magic mirror, a bubble of reality enclosed within a gilt frame.

DT heard Dantzler's footfalls and glanced up. "Waste him!" he shouted, pointing to Moody.

Moody did not turn from contemplation of the knife. "No," he said, as if speaking to someone whose image was held in the blade.

"Waste him, man!" screamed DT. "He killed LeDoux!"

"Please," said Moody to the knife. "I don't want to."

There was blood clotted on his face, more blood on the banana leaves sticking out of his helmet.

"Did you kill Jerry?" asked Dantzler; while he addressed the question to Moody, he did not relate to him as an individual, only as part of a design whose message he had to unravel.

"Jesus Christ! Waste him!" DT smashed his fist against the ground in frustration.

"Okay," said Moody. With an apologetic look, he sprang to his feet and charged Dantzler, swinging the knife.

Emotionless, Dantzler stitched a line of fire across Moody's chest; he went sideways into the bushes and down.

"What the hell was you waitin' for!" DT tried to rise, but winced and fell back. "Damn! Don't know if I can walk."

"Pop a few," Dantzler suggested mildly.

"Yeah. Good thinkin', man." DT fumbled for his dispenser.

Dantzler peered into the bushes to see where Moody had fallen. He felt nothing, and this pleased him. He was weary of feeling.

DT popped an ampule with a flourish, as if making a toast, and inhaled. "Ain't you gon' to do some, man?"

"I don't need them," said Dantzler. "I'm fine."

The stream interested him; it did not reflect the mist, as he had supposed, but was itself a seam of the mist.

"How many you think they was?" asked DT.

"How many what?"

"Beaners, man! I wasted three or four after they hit us, but I couldn't tell how many they was."

Dantzler considered this in light of his own interpretation of events and Moody's conversation with the knife. It made sense. A Santa Ana kind of sense.

"Beats me," he said. "But I guess there's less than there used to be."

DT snorted. "You got *that* right!" He heaved to his feet and limped to the edge of the stream. "Gimme a hand across."

Dantzler reached out to him, but instead of taking his hand, he grabbed his wrist and pulled him off-balance. DT teetered on his good leg, then toppled and vanished beneath the mist. Dantzler had expected him to fall, but he surfaced instantly, mist clinging to his skin. Of course, thought Dantzler; his body would have to die before his spirit would fall.

"What you doin', man?" DT was more disbelieving than enraged.

Dantzler planted a foot in the middle of his back and pushed him down until his head was submerged. DT bucked and clawed at the foot and managed to come to his hands and knees. Mist slithered from his eyes, his nose, and he choked out the words "...kill you...." Dantzler pushed him down again; he got into pushing him down and letting him up, over and over. Not so as to torture him. Not really. It was because he had suddenly understood the nature of the *ayahuamaco*'s laws, that they were approximations of normal laws, and he further understood that his actions had to approximate those of someone jiggling a key in a lock. DT was the key to the way out, and Dantzler was jiggling him, making sure all the tumblers were engaged.

Some of the vessels in DT's eyes had burst, and the whites were occluded by films of blood. When he tried to speak, mist curled from his mouth. Gradually his struggles subsided; he clawed runnels in the gleaming yellow dirt of the bank and shuddered. His shoulders were knobs of black land foundering in a mystic sea.

For a long time after DT sank from view. Dantzler stood beside the stream, uncertain of what was left to do and unable to remember a lesson he had been taught. Finally he shouldered his rifle and walked away from the clearing. Morning had broken, the mist had thinned, and the forest had regained its usual coloration. But he scarcely noticed these changes, still troubled by his faulty memory. Eventually, he let it slide—it would all come clear sooner or later. He was just happy to be alive. After a while he began to kick the stones as he went, and to swing his rifle in a carefree fashion against the weeds.

When the First Infantry poured across the Nicaraguan border and wasted León, Dantzler was having a quiet time at the VA hospital in Ann Arbor, Michigan; and at the precise moment the bulletin was flashed nationwide, he was sitting in the lounge, watching the American League playoffs between Detroit and Texas. Some of the patients ranted at the interruption, while others shouted them down, wanting to hear the details. Dantzler expressed no reaction whatsoever. He was solely concerned with being a model patient; however, noticing that one of the staff was giving him a clinical stare, he added his weight on the side of the baseball fans. He did not want to appear too controlled. The doctors were as suspicious of that sort of behavior as they were of its contrary. But the funny thing was—at least it was funny to Dantzler—that his feigned annoyance at the bulletin was an exemplary proof of his control, his expertise at moving through life the way he had moved through the golden leaves of the cloud forest. Cautiously, gracefully, efficiently. Touching nothing, and being touched by nothing. That was the lesson he had learned—to be as perfect a counterfeit of a man as the *ayahuamaco* had been of the land; to adopt the various stances of a man, and yet, by virtue of his distance from things human, to be all the more prepared for the onset of crisis or a call to action. He saw nothing aberrant in this; even the doctors would admit that men were little more than organized pretense. If he was different from other men, it was only that he had a deeper awareness of the principles on which his personality was founded.

When the battle of Managua was joined, Dantzler was living at home. His parents had urged him to go easy in readjusting to civilian life, but he had immediately gotten a job as a management trainee in a bank. Each morning he would drive to work and spend a controlled, quiet eight hours; each night he would watch TV with his mother, and before going to bed, he would climb to the attic and inspect the trunk containing his souvenirs of war—helmet, fatigues, knife, boots. The doctors had insisted he face his experiences, and this ritual was his way of following their instructions. All in all, he was quite pleased with his progress, but he still had problems. He had not been able to force himself to venture out at night, remembering too well the darkness in the cloud forest, and he had rejected his friends, refusing to see them or answer their calls—he was not secure with the idea of friendship. Further, despite his methodical approach to life, he was prone to a nagging restlessness, the feeling of a chore left undone.

One night his mother came into his room and told him that an old friend, Phil Curry, was on the phone. "Please talk to him, Johnny," she said. "He's been drafted, and I think he's a little scared."

The word *drafted* struck a responsive chord in Dantzler's soul, and after brief deliberation he went downstairs and picked up the receiver.

"Hey," said Phil. "What's the story, man? Three months, and you don't even give me a call."

"I'm sorry," said Dantzler. "I haven't been feeling so hot."

"Yeah, I understand." Phil was silent a moment. "Listen, man. I'm leavin', y'know, and we're havin' a big send-off at Sparky's. It's goin' on right now. Why don't you come down?"

"I don't know."

"Jeanine's here, man. Y'know, she's still crazy 'bout you, talks 'bout you alla time. She don't go out with nobody."

Dantzler was unable to think of anything to say.

"Look," said Phil, "I'm pretty weirded out by this soldier shit. I hear it's pretty bad down there. If you got anything you can tell me 'bout what it's like, man, I'd 'preciate it."

Dantzler could relate to Phil's concern, his desire for an edge, and besides, it felt right to go. Very right. He would take some precautions against the darkness.

"I'll be there," he said.

It was a foul night, spitting snow, but Sparky's parking lot was jammed. Dantzler's mind was flurried like the snow, crowded like the lot—thoughts whirling in, jockeying for position, melting away. He hoped his mother would not wait up, he wondered if Jeanine still wore her hair long, he was worried because the palms of his hands were unnaturally warm. Even with the car windows rolled up, he could hear loud music coming from inside the club. Above the door the words SPARKY'S ROCK CITY were being spelled out a letter at a time in red neon, and when the spelling was complete, the letters flashed off and on and a golden neon explosion bloomed around them. After the explosion, the entire sign went dark for a split second, and the big ramshackle building seemed to grow large and merge with the black sky. He had an idea it was watching him, and he shuddered—one of those sudden lurches downward of the kind that take you just before you fall asleep. He knew the people inside did not intend him any harm, but he also knew that places have a way of changing people's intent, and he did not want to be caught off-guard. Sparky's might be such a place, might be a huge black presence camouflaged by neon, its true substance one with the abyss of the sky, the phosphorescent snowflakes, jittering in his headlights, the wind keening through the side vent. He would have liked very much to drive home and forget about his promise to Phil; however, he felt a responsibility to explain about the war. More than a responsibility, an evangelistic urge. He would tell them about the kid falling out of the chopper, the white-haired girl in Tecolutla, the emptiness. God, yes! How you went down chock-full of ordinary American thoughts and dreams, memories of smoking weed and chasing tail and hanging out and freeway flying with a case of something cold, and how you smuggled back a human-shaped container of pure Salvadorian emptiness. Primo grade. Smuggled it back to the land of silk and money, of mindfuck video games and topless tennis matches and fast-food solutions to the nutritional problem. Just a taste of Salvador would banish all those trivial obsessions. Just a taste. It would be easy to explain.

Of course, some things beggared explanation.

He bent down and adjusted the survival knife in his boot so the hilt would not rub against his calf. From the coat pocket he withdrew the two ampules he had secreted in his helmet that long-ago night in the cloud forest. As the neon explosion flashed once more, glimmers of gold coursed along their shiny surfaces. He did not think he would need them; his hand was steady, and his purpose was clear. But to be on the safe side, he popped them both.

The Aliens Who Knew, I Mean, *Everything*
(1984)

GEORGE ALEC EFFINGER

GEORGE ALEC EFFINGER (1947–2002) began publishing science-fiction and fantasy stories in the early 1970s and soon thereafter published his first novel, *What Entropy Means to Me*. He went on to publish more than two dozen books, including several collections of short fiction and such novels as *Relatives*, *The Nick of Time*, and the Marîd Audran books: *When Gravity Fails*, *A Fire in the Sun*, and *The Exile Kiss*. Much of his writing is marked by his strong sense of humor, which is in full flower in "The Aliens Who Knew, I Mean, *Everything*."

I WAS SITTING at my desk, reading a report on the brown pelican situation, when the secretary of state burst in. "Mr. President," he said, his eyes wide, "the aliens are here!" Just like that. "The aliens are here!" As if I had any idea what to do about them.

"I see," I said. I learned early in my first term that "I see" was one of the safest and most useful comments I could possibly make in any situation. When I said, "I see," it indicated that I had digested the news and was waiting intelligently and calmly for further data. That knocked the ball back into my advisers' court. I looked at the secretary of state expectantly. I was all prepared with my next utterance, in the event that he had nothing further to add. My next utterance would be, "Well?" That would indicate that I was on top of the problem, but that I couldn't be expected to make an executive decision without sufficient information, and that he should have known better than to burst into the Oval Office unless he had that information. That's why we had protocol; that's why we had proper channels; that's why I had advisers. The voters out there didn't want me to make decisions without sufficient information. If the secretary didn't have anything more to tell me, he shouldn't have burst in in the first place. I looked at him awhile longer. "Well?" I asked at last.

"That's about all we have at the moment," he said uncomfortably. I looked at him sternly for a few seconds, scoring a couple of points while he stood there all flustered. I turned back to the pelican report, dismissing him. I certainly wasn't going to get all flustered. I could think of only one president in recent memory who was ever flustered in office, and we all know what happened to him. As the secretary of state closed the door to my office behind him, I smiled. The aliens were probably going to be a bitch of a problem eventually, but it wasn't my problem yet. I had a little time.

But I found that I couldn't really keep my mind on the pelican question. Even the president of the United States has *some* imagination, and if the secretary of state was correct, I was going to have to confront these aliens pretty damn soon. I'd read stories about aliens when I was a kid, I'd seen all sorts of aliens in movies and television, but these were the first aliens who'd actually stopped by for a chat. Well, I wasn't going to be the first American president to make a fool of himself in front of visitors from another world. I was going to be briefed. I telephoned the secretary of defense. "We must have some contingency plans drawn up for this," I told him. "We have plans for every other possible situation." This was true; the Defense Department has scenarios for such bizarre events as the rise of an imperialist fascist regime in Liechtenstein or the spontaneous depletion of all the world's selenium.

"Just a second, Mr. President," said the secretary. I could hear him muttering to someone else. I held the phone and stared out the window. There were crowds of people running around hysterically out there. Probably because of the aliens. "Mr. President?" came the voice of the secretary of defense. "I have one of the aliens here, and he suggests that we use the same plan that President Eisenhower used."

I closed my eyes and sighed. I hated it when they said stuff like that. I wanted information, and they told me these things knowing that I would have to ask four or five more questions just to understand the answer to the first one. "You have an alien with you?" I said in a pleasant enough voice.

"Yes, sir. They prefer not to be called 'aliens.' He tells me he's a 'nuhp.'"

"Thank you, Luis. Tell me, why do you have an al—Why do you have a nuhp and I don't?"

Luis muttered the question to his nuhp. "He says it's because they wanted to go through proper channels. They learned about all that from President Eisenhower."

"Very good, Luis." This was going to take all day, I could see that; and I had a photo session with Mick Jagger's granddaughter. "My second question, Luis, is what the hell does he mean by 'the same plan that President Eisenhower used'?"

Another muffled consultation. "He says that this isn't the first time that the nuhp have landed on Earth. A scout ship with two nuhp aboard landed at Edwards Air Force Base in 1954. The two nuhp met with President Eisenhower. It was apparently a very cordial occasion, and President Eisenhower impressed the nuhp as a warm and sincere old gentleman. They've been planning to return to Earth ever since, but they've been very busy, what with one thing and another. President Eisenhower requested that the nuhp not reveal themselves to the people of Earth in general, until our government decided how to control the inevitable hysteria. My guess is that the government never got around to that, and when the nuhp departed, the matter was studied and then shelved. As the years passed, few people were even aware that the first meeting ever occurred. The nuhp have returned now in great numbers, expecting that we'd have prepared the populace by now. It's not their fault that we haven't. They just sort of took it for granted that they'd be welcome."

"Uh-huh," I said. That was my usual utterance when I didn't know what the hell else to say. "Assure them that they are, indeed, welcome. I don't suppose the study they did during the Eisenhower administration was ever completed. I don't suppose there really is a plan to break the news to the public."

"Unfortunately, Mr. President, that seems to be the case."

"Uh-huh," That's Republicans for you, I thought. "Ask your nuhp something for me, Luis. Ask him if he knows what they told Eisenhower. They must be full of outer-space wisdom. Maybe they have some ideas about how we should deal with this."

There was yet another pause. "Mr. President, he says all they discussed with Mr. Eisenhower was his golf game. They helped to correct his putting stroke. But they are definitely full of wisdom. They know all sorts of things. My nuhp—that is, his name is Hurv—anyway, he says that they'd be happy to give you some advice."

"Tell him that I'm grateful, Luis. Can they have someone meet with me in, say, half an hour?"

"There are three nuhp on their way to the Oval Office at this moment. One of them is the leader of their expedition, and one of the others is the commander of their mother ship."

"Mother ship?" I asked.

"You haven't seen it? It's tethered on the Mall. They're real sorry about what they did to the Washington Monument. They say they can take care of it tomorrow."

I just shuddered and hung up the phone. I called my secretary. "There are going to be three—"

"They're here now, Mr. President."

I sighed. "Send them in." And that's how I met the nuhp. Just as President Eisenhower had.

They were handsome people. Likable, too. They smiled and shook hands and suggested that photographs be taken of the historic moment, so we called in the media; and then I had to sort of wing the most important diplomatic meeting of my entire political career. I welcomed the nuhp to Earth. "Welcome to Earth," I said, "and welcome to the United States."

"Thank you," said the nuhp I would come to know as Pleen. "We're glad to be here."

"How long do you plan to be with us?" I hated myself when I said that, in front of the Associated Press and UPI and all the network news people. I sounded like a room clerk at a Holiday Inn.

"We don't know, exactly," said Pleen. "We don't have to be back to work until a week from Monday."

"Uh-huh," I said. Then I just posed for pictures and kept my mouth shut. I wasn't going to say or do another goddamn thing until my advisers showed up and started advising.

Well, of course, the people panicked. Pleen told me to expect that, but I had figured it out for myself. We've seen too many movies about visitors from space. Sometimes they come with a message of peace and universal brotherhood and just the inside information mankind has been needing for thousands of years. More often, though, the aliens come to enslave and murder us because the visual effects are better, and so when the nuhp arrived, everyone was all prepared to hate them. People didn't trust their good looks. People were suspicious of their nice manners and their quietly tasteful clothing. When the nuhp offered to solve all our problems for us, we all said, sure, solve our problems—*but at what cost?*

That first week, Pleen and I spent a lot of time together, just getting to know one another and trying to understand what the other one wanted. I invited him and Commander Toag and the other nuhp bigwigs to a reception at the White House. We had a church choir from Alabama singing gospel music, and a high school band from Michigan playing a medley of favorite collegiate fight songs, and talented clones of the original stars nostalgically re-creating the Steve and Eydie Experience, and an improvisational comedy troupe from Los Angeles or someplace, and the New York Philharmonic under the baton of a twelve-year-old girl genius. They played Beethoven's Ninth Symphony in an attempt to impress the nuhp with how marvelous Earth culture was.

Pleen enjoyed it all very much. "Men are as varied in their expressions of joy as we nuhp," he said, applauding vigorously. "We are all very fond of human music. We think Beethoven composed some of the most beautiful melodies we've ever heard, anywhere in our galactic travels."

I smiled. "I'm sure we are all pleased to hear that," I said.

"Although the Ninth Symphony is certainly not the best of his work."

I faltered in my clapping. "Excuse me?" I said.

Pleen gave me a gracious smile. "It is well known among us that Beethoven's finest composition is his Piano Concerto No. 5 in E-flat major."

I let out my breath. "Of course, that's a matter of opinion. Perhaps the standards of the nuhp—"

"Oh, no," Pleen hastened to assure me, "taste does not enter into it at all. The Concerto No. 5 is Beethoven's best, according to very rigorous and definite critical principles. And even that lovely piece is by no means the best music ever produced by mankind."

I felt just a trifle annoyed. What could this nuhp, who came from some weirdo planet God alone knows how far away, from some society with not the slightest connection to our heritage and culture, what could this nuhp know of what Beethoven's Ninth Symphony aroused in our human souls? "Tell me, then, Pleen," I said in my ominously soft voice, "what *is* the best human musical composition?"

"The score from the motion picture *Ben-Hur*, by Miklós Rózsa," he said simply. What could I do but nod my head in silence? It wasn't worth starting an interplanetary incident over.

So from fear our reaction to the nuhp changed to distrust. We kept waiting for them to reveal their real selves; we waited for the pleasant masks to slip off and show us the true nightmarish faces we all suspected lurked beneath. The nuhp did not go home a week from Monday, after all. They liked Earth, and they liked us. They decided to stay a little longer. We told them about ourselves and our centuries of trouble; and they mentioned, in an offhand nuhp way, that they could take care of a few little things, make some small adjustments, and life would be a whole lot better for everybody on Earth. They didn't want anything in return. They wanted to give us these things in gratitude for our hospitality: for letting them park their mother ship on the Mall and for all the free refills of coffee they were getting all around the world. We hesitated, but our vanity and our greed won out. "Go ahead," we said, "make our deserts bloom. Go ahead, end war and poverty and disease. Show us twenty exciting new things to do with leftovers. Call us when you're done."

The fear changed to distrust, but soon the distrust changed to hope. The nuhp made the deserts bloom, all right. They asked for four months. We were perfectly willing to let them have all the time they needed. They put a tall fence all around the Namib and wouldn't let anyone in to watch what they were doing. Four months later, they had a big cocktail party and invited the whole world to see what they'd accomplished. I sent the secretary of state as my personal representative. He brought back some wonderful slides: the vast desert had been turned into a botanical miracle. There were miles and miles of flowering plants now, instead of the monotonous dead sand and gravel sea. Of course, the immense garden contained nothing but hollyhocks, many millions of hollyhocks. I mentioned to Pleen that the people of Earth had been hoping for a little more in the way of variety, and something just a trifle more practical, too.

"What do yon mean, 'practical'?" he asked.

"You know," I said, "food."

"Don't worry about food," said Pleen. "We're going to take care of hunger pretty soon."

"Good, good. But hollyhocks?"

"What's wrong with hollyhocks?"

"Nothing," I admitted.

"Hollyhocks are the single prettiest flower grown on Earth."

"Some people like orchids," I said. "Some people like roses."

"No," said Pleen firmly. "Hollyhocks are it. I wouldn't kid you."

So we thanked the nuhp for a Namibia full of hollyhocks and stopped them before they did the same thing to the Sahara, the Mojave, and the Gobi.

～

On the whole, everyone began to like the nuhp, although they took just a little getting used to. They had very definite opinions about everything, and they wouldn't admit that what they had were *opinions*. To hear a nuhp talk, he had a direct line to some categorical imperative that spelled everything out in terms that were unflinchingly black and white. Hollyhocks were the best flowers. Alexander Dumas was the greatest novelist. Powder blue was the prettiest color. Melancholy was the most ennobling emotion. *Grand Hotel* was the finest movie. The best car ever built was the 1956 Chevy Bel Air, but it had to be aqua and white. And there just wasn't room for discussion: the nuhp made these pronouncements with the force of divine revelation.

I asked Pleen once about the American presidency. I asked him who the nuhp thought was the best president in our history. I felt sort of like the Wicked Queen in *Snow White*. Mirror, mirror, on the wall. I didn't really believe Pleen would tell me that I was the best president, but my heart pounded while I waited for his answer; you never know, right? To tell the truth, I expected him to say Washington, Lincoln, Roosevelt, or Akiwara. His answer surprised me: James K. Polk.

"Polk?" I asked. I wasn't even sure I could recognize Polk's portrait.

"He's not the most familiar," said Pleen, "but he was an honest if unexciting president. He fought the Mexican War and added a great amount of territory to the United States. He saw every bit of his platform become law. He was a good, hardworking man who deserves a better reputation."

"What about Thomas Jefferson?" I asked.

Pleen just shrugged. "He was O.K., too, but he was no James Polk."

My wife, the First Lady, became very good friends with the wife of Commander Toag, whose name was Doim. They often went shopping together, and Doim would make suggestions to the First Lady about fashion and hair care. Doim told my wife which rooms in the White House needed redecoration, and which charities were worthy of official support. It was Doim who negotiated the First Lady's recording contract, and it was Doim who introduced her to the Philadelphia cheese steak, one of the nuhp's favorite treats (although they asserted that the best cuisine on Earth was Tex-Mex).

One day, Doim and my wife were having lunch. They sat at a small table in a chic Washington restaurant, with a couple of dozen Secret Service people and nuhp security agents disguised elsewhere among the patrons. "I've noticed that there seem to be more nuhp here in Washington every week," said the First Lady.

"Yes," said Doim, "new mother ships arrive daily. We think Earth is one of the most pleasant planets we've ever visited."

"We're glad to have you, of course," said my wife, "and it seems that our people have gotten over their initial fears."

"The hollyhocks did the trick," said Doim.

"I guess so. How many nuhp are there on Earth now?"

"About five or six million, I'd say."

The First Lady was startled. "I didn't think it would be that many."

Doim laughed. "We're not just here in America, you know. We're all over. We really like Earth. Although, of course, Earth isn't absolutely the best planet. Our own home, Nupworld, is still Number One; but Earth would certainly be on any Top Ten list."

"Uh-huh." (My wife has learned many important oratorical tricks from me.)

"That's why we're so glad to help you beautify and modernize your world."

"The hollyhocks were nice," said the First Lady. "But when are you going to tackle the really vital questions?"

"Don't worry about that," said Doim, turning her attention to her cottage cheese salad.

"When are you going to take care of world hunger?"

"Pretty soon. Don't worry."

"Urban blight?"

"Pretty soon."

"Man's inhumanity to man?"

Doim gave my wife an impatient look. "We haven't even been here for six months yet. What do you want, miracles? We've already done more than your husband accomplished in his entire first term."

"Hollyhocks," muttered the First Lady.

"I heard that," said Doim. "The rest of the universe absolutely *adores* hollyhocks. We can't help it if humans have no taste."

They finished their lunch in silence, and my wife came back to the White House fuming.

That same week, one of my advisers showed me a letter that had been sent by a young man in New Mexico. Several nuhp had moved into a condo next door to him and had begun advising him about the best investment possibilities (urban respiratory spas), the best fabrics and colors to wear to show off his coloring, the best holo system on the market (the Esmeraldas F-64 with hex-phased Libertad screens and a Ruy Challenger argon solipsizer), the best place to watch sunsets (the revolving restaurant on top of the Weyerhaeuser Building in Yellowstone City), the best wines to go with everything (too numerous to mention—send SASE for list), and which of the two women he was dating to marry (Candi Marie Esterhazy). "Mr. President," said the bewildered young man, "I realize that we must be gracious hosts to our benefactors from space, but I am having some difficulty keeping my temper. The nuhp are certainly knowledgeable and willing to share the benefits of their wisdom, but they don't even wait to be asked. If they were people, regular human beings who lived next door, I would have punched their lights out by now. Please advise. And hurry: they are taking me downtown next Friday to pick out an engagement ring and new living room furniture. I don't even *want* new living room furniture!"

Luis, my secretary of defense, talked to Hurv about the ultimate goals of the nuhp. "We don't have any goals," he said. "We're just taking it easy."

"Then why did you come to Earth?" asked Luis.

"Why do you go bowling?"

"I don't go bowling."

"You should," said Hurv. "Bowling is the most enjoyable thing a person can do."

"What about sex?"

"Bowling *is* sex. Bowling is a symbolic form of intercourse, except you don't have to bother about the feelings of some other person. Bowling is sex without guilt. Bowling is what people have wanted down through all the millennia: sex without the slightest responsibility. It's the very distillation of the essence of sex. Bowling is sex without fear and shame."

"Bowling is sex without pleasure," said Luis.

There was a brief silence. "You mean," said Hurv, "that when you put that ball right into the pocket and see those pins explode off the alley, you don't have an orgasm?"

"Nope," said Luis.

"*That's* your problem, then. I can't help you there, you'll have to see some kind of therapist. It's obvious this subject embarrasses you. Let's talk about something else."

"Fine with me," said Luis moodily. "When are we going to receive the real benefits of your technological superiority? When are you going to unlock the final secrets of the atom? When are you going to free mankind from drudgery?"

"What do you mean, 'technological superiority'?" asked Hurv.

"There must be scientific wonders beyond our imagining aboard your mother ships."

"Not so's you'd notice. We're not even so advanced as you people here on Earth. We've learned all sorts of wonderful things since we've been here."

"What?" Luis couldn't imagine what Hurv was trying to say.

"We don't have anything like your astonishing bubble memories or silicon chips. We never invented anything comparable to the transistor, even. You know why the mother ships are so big?"

"My God."

"That's right," said Hurv, "vacuum tubes. All our spacecraft operate on vacuum tubes. They take up a hell of a lot of space. And they burn out. Do you know how long it takes to find the goddamn tube when it burns out? Remember how people used to take bags of vacuum tubes from their television sets down to the drugstore to use the tube tester? Think of doing that with something the size of our mother ships. And we can't just zip off into space when we feel like it. We have let a mother ship warm up first. You have to turn the key and let the thing warm up for a couple of minutes, *then* you can zip off into space. It's a goddamn pain in the neck."

"I don't understand," said Luis, stunned. "If your technology is so primitive, how did you come here? If we're so far ahead of you, we should have discovered your planet, instead of the other way around."

Hurv gave a gentle laugh. "Don't pat yourself on the back, Luis. Just because your electronics are better than ours, you aren't necessarily superior in any way. Look, imagine that you humans are a man in Los Angeles with a brand-new Trujillo and we are a nuhp in New York with a beat-up old Ford. The two fellows start driving toward St. Louis. Now, the guy in the Trujillo is doing 120 on the interstates, and the guy in the Ford is putting along at 55; but the human in the Trujillo stops in Vegas and puts all of his gas money down the hole of a blackjack table, and the determined little nuhp cruises along for days until at last he reaches his goal. It's all a matter of superior intellect and the will to succeed. Your people talk a lot about going to the stars, but you just keep putting your money into other projects, like war and popular music and international athletic events and resurrecting the fashions of previous decades. If you wanted to go into space, you would have."

"But we *do* want to go."

"Then we'll help you. We'll give you the secrets. And you can explain your electronics to our engineers, and together we'll build wonderful new mother ships that will open the universe to both humans and nuhp."

Luis let out his breath. "Sounds good to me," he said.

Everyone agreed that this looked better than hollyhocks. We all hoped that we could keep from kicking their collective asses long enough to collect on that promise.

When I was in college, my roommate in my sophomore year was a tall, skinny guy named Barry Rintz. Barry had wild, wavy black hair and a sharp face that looked like a handsome, normal face that had been sat on and folded in the middle. He squinted a lot, not because he had any defect in his eyesight, but because he wanted to give the impression that he was constantly evaluating the world. This was true. Barry could tell you the actual and market values of any object you happened to come across.

We had a double date one football weekend with two girls from another college in the same city. Before the game, we met the girls and took them to the university's art museum, which was pretty large and owned an impressive collection. My date, a pretty elementary ed. major named Brigid, and I wandered from gallery to gallery, remarking that our tastes in art were very similar. We both liked the Impressionists, and we both liked Surrealism. There were a couple of little Renoirs that we admired for almost half an hour, and then we made a lot of silly sophomoric jokes about what was happening in the Magritte and Dali and de Chirico paintings.

Barry and his date, Dixie, ran across us by accident as all four of us passed through the sculpture gallery. "There's a terrific Seurat down there," Brigid told her girlfriend.

"Seurat," Barry said. There was a lot of amused disbelief in his voice.

"I like Seurat," said Dixie.

"Well, of course," said Barry, "there's nothing really *wrong* with Seurat."

"What do you mean by that?"

"Do you know F. E. Church?" he asked.

"Who?" I said.

"Come here." He practically dragged us to a gallery of American paintings. F. E. Church was a remarkable American landscape painter (1826–1900) who achieved an astonishing and lovely luminance in his works. "Look at that light!" cried Barry. "Look at that space! Look at that air!"

Brigid glanced at Dixie. "Look at that air?" she whispered.

It was a fine painting and we all said so, but Barry was insistent. F. E. Church was the greatest artist in American history, and one of the best the world has ever known. "I'd put him right up there with Van Dyck and Canaletto."

"Canaletto?" said Dixie. "The one who did all those pictures of Venice?"

"Those skies!" murmured Barry ecstatically. He wore the drunken expression of the satisfied voluptuary.

"Some people like paintings of puppies or naked women," I offered. "Barry likes light and air."

We left the museum and had lunch. Barry told us which things on the menu were worth ordering, and which things were an abomination. He made us all drink an obscure imported beer from Ecuador. To Barry, the world was divided up into masterpieces and abominations. It made life so much simpler for him, except that he never understood why his friends could never tell one from the other.

At the football game, Barry compared our school's quarterback to Y. A. Tittle. He compared the other team's punter to Ngoc Van Vinh. He compared the halftime show to the Ohio State band's Script Ohio formation. Before the end of the third quarter, it was very obvious to me that Barry was going to have absolutely no luck at all with Dixie. Before the clock ran out in the fourth quarter, Brigid and I had made whispered plans to dump the other two as soon as possible and sneak away by ourselves. Dixie would probably find an excuse to ride the bus back to her dorm before suppertime. Barry, as usual, would spend the evening in our room, reading *The Making of the President 1996*.

On other occasions Barry would lecture me about subjects as diverse as American literature (the best poet was Edwin Arlington Robinson, the best novelist James T. Farrell), animals (the only correct pet was the golden retriever), clothing (in anything other than a navy blue jacket and gray slacks a man was just asking for trouble), and even hobbies (Barry collected military decorations of czarist Imperial Russia, he wouldn't talk to me for days after I told him my father collected barbed wire).

Barry was a wealth of information. He was the campus arbiter of good taste. Everyone knew that Barry was the man to ask.

But no one ever did. We all hated his guts. I moved out of our dorm room before the end of the fall semester. Shunned, lonely, and bitter Barry Rintz wound up as a guidance counselor in a high school in Ames, Iowa. The job was absolutely perfect for him; few people are so lucky in finding a career.

If I didn't know better, I might have believed that Barry was the original advance spy for the nuhp.

When the nuhp had been on Earth for a full year, they gave us the gift of interstellar travel. It was surprisingly inexpensive. The nuhp explained their propulsion system, which was cheap and safe and adaptable to all sorts of other earthbound applications. The revelations opened up an entirely new area of scientific speculation. Then the nuhp taught us their navigational methods, and about the "shortcuts" they had discovered in space. People called them space warps, although technically speaking, the shortcuts had nothing to do with Einsteinian theory or curved space or anything like that. Not many humans understood what the nuhp were talking about, but that didn't make very much difference. The nuhp didn't understand the shortcuts, either; they just used them. The matter was presented to us like a Thanksgiving turkey on a platter. We bypassed the whole business of cautious scientific experimentation and leaped right into commercial exploitation. Mitsubishi of La Paz and Martin Marietta used nuhp schematics to begin construction of three luxury passenger ships, each capable of transporting a thousand tourists anywhere in our galaxy. Although man had yet to set foot on the moons of Jupiter, certain selected travel agencies began booking passage for a grand tour of the dozen nearest inhabited worlds.

Yes, it seemed that space was teeming with life, humanoid life on planets circling half the G-type stars in the heavens. "We've been trying to communicate with extraterrestrial intelligence for decades," complained one Soviet scientist. "Why haven't they responded?"

A friendly nuhp merely shrugged. "Everybody's trying to communicate out there," he said. "Your messages are like Publishers Clearing House mail to them." At first, that was a blow to our racial pride, but we got over it. As soon as we joined the interstellar community, they'd begin to take us more seriously. And the nuhp had made that possible.

We were grateful to the nuhp, but that didn't make them any easier to live with. They were still insufferable. As my second term as president came to an end, Pleen began to advise me about my future career. "Don't write a book," he told me (after I had already written the first two hundred pages of *A President Remembers*). "If you want to be an elder statesman, fine; but keep a low profile and wait for the people to come to you."

"What am I supposed to do with my time, then?" I asked.

"Choose a new career," Pleen said. "You're not all that old. Lots of people do it. Have you considered starting a mail-order business? You can operate it from your home. Or go back to school and take courses in some subject that's always interested you. Or become active in church or civic projects. Find a new hobby: raising hollyhocks or collecting military decorations."

"Pleen," I begged, "just leave me alone."

He seemed hurt. "Sure, if that's what you want." I regretted my harsh words.

All over the country, all over the world, everyone was having the same trouble with the nuhp. It seemed that so many of them had come to Earth, every human had his own personal nuhp to make endless suggestions. There hadn't been so much tension in the world since the 1992 Miss Universe contest, when the most votes went to No Award.

That's why it didn't surprise me very much when the first of our own mother ships returned from its 28-day voyage among the stars with only 276 of its 1,000 passengers still aboard. The other 724 had remained behind on one lush, exciting, exotic, friendly world or another. These planets had one thing in common: they were all populated by charming, warm, intelligent, human-like people who had left their own home worlds after being discovered by the nuhp. Many races lived together in peace and harmony on these planets, in spacious cities newly built to house the fed-up expatriates. Perhaps these alien races had experienced the same internal jealousies and hatreds we human beings had known for so long, but no more. Coming together from many planets throughout our galaxy, these various peoples dwelt contentedly beside each other, united by a single common feeling: their dislike for the nuhp.

Within a year of the launching of our first interstellar ship, the population of Earth had declined by 0.5 percent. Within two years, the population had fallen by almost 14 million. The nuhp were too sincere and too eager and too sympathetic to fight with. That didn't make them any less tedious. Rather than make a scene, most people just up and left. There were plenty of really lovely worlds to visit, and it didn't cost very much, and the opportunities in space were unlimited. Many people who were frustrated and disappointed on Earth were able to build new and fulfilling lives for themselves on planets that, until the nuhp arrived, we didn't even know existed.

The nuhp knew this would happen. It had already happened dozens, hundreds of times in the past, wherever their mother ships touched down.

They had made promises to us and they had kept them, although we couldn't have guessed just how things would turn out.

Our cities were no longer decaying warrens imprisoning the impoverished masses. The few people who remained behind could pick and choose among the best housing. Landlords were forced to reduce rents and keep properties in perfect repair just to attract tenants.

Hunger was ended when the ratio of consumers to food producers dropped drastically. Within ten years, the population of Earth was cut in half, and was still falling.

For the same reason, poverty began to disappear. There were plenty of jobs for everyone. When it became apparent that the nuhp weren't going to compete for those jobs, there were more opportunities than people to take advantage of them.

Discrimination and prejudice vanished almost overnight. Everyone cooperated to keep things running smoothly despite the large-scale emigration. The good life was available to everyone, and so resentments melted away. Then, too, whatever enmity people still felt could be focused solely on the nuhp; the nuhp didn't mind, either. They were oblivious to it all.

I am now the mayor and postmaster of the small human community of New Dallas, here on Thir, the fourth planet of a star known in our old catalog as Struve 2398. The various alien races we encountered here call the star by another name, which translates into "God's Pineal." All the aliens here are extremely helpful and charitable, and there are few nuhp.

All through the galaxy, the nuhp are considered the messengers of peace. Their mission is to travel from planet to planet, bringing reconciliation, prosperity, and true civilization. There isn't an intelligent race in the galaxy that doesn't love the nuhp. We all recognize what they've done and what they've given us.

But if the nuhp started moving in down the block, we'd be packed and on our way somewhere else by morning.

Rat (1986)

JAMES PATRICK KELLY

JAMES PATRICK KELLY's (b. 1951) first published fiction appeared in the 1970s, but he hit his stride in the 1980s, and over the following decades he has published many innovative and affecting works of science fiction, including the novels *Wildlife* and *Burn* and a host of short stories, many of which have been collected in *Think Like a Dinosaur and Other Stories* and *Strange but Not a Stranger*. In the past decade, he and John Kessel, his frequent collaborator, have edited a variety of anthologies, including *Rewired: The Post Cyberpunk Anthology* and *The Secret History of Science Fiction*. His story "Rat" was published in the heyday of the cyberpunk movement but reads just as well now as it did when first published.

R AT HAD STASHED the dust in four plastic capsules and then swallowed them. From the stinging at the base of his ribs he guessed they were now squeezing into his duodenum. Still plenty of time. The bullet train had been shooting through the vacuum of the Transatlantic tunnel for almost two hours now; they would arrive at Port Authority/Koch soon. Customs had already been fixed, according to the marechal. All Rat had to do was to get back to his nest, lock the smart door behind him and put the word out on his protected nets. He had enough Algerian Yellow to dust at least half the cerebrums on the East Side. If he could turn this deal he would be rich enough to bathe in Dom Pérignon and dry himself with Gromaire tapestries. Another pang shot down his left flank. Instinctively his hind leg came off the seat and scratched at air.

There was only one problem; Rat had decided to cut the marechal out. That meant he had to lose the old man's spook before he got home.

The spook had attached herself to him at Marseilles. She braided her blonde hair in pigtails. She had freckles, wore braces on her teeth. Tiny breasts nudged a modest silk turtleneck. She looked to be between twelve and fourteen. Cute. She had probably looked that way for twenty years, would stay the same another twenty if she did not stop a slug first or get cut in half by some automated security laser that tracked only heat and could not read—or be troubled by—cuteness. Their passports said they were Mr. Sterling Jaynes and daughter Jessalynn, of Forest Hills, New York. She was typing in her notebook, chubby fingers curled over the keys. Homework? A letter to a boyfriend? More likely she was operating on some corporate database with scalpel code of her own devising.

"Ne fais pas semblant d'etudier, ma petite," Rat said. *"Que fais-tu?"*

"Oh, Daddy," she said, pouting, "can't we go back to plain old English? After all, we're almost home." She tilted her notebook so that he could see the display. It read, "Two rows back, second seat from aisle. Fed. If he knew you were carrying, he'd cut the dust out of you and wipe his ass with your pelt." She tapped the return key and the message disappeared.

"All right, dear." He arched his back, fighting a surge of adrenalin that made his incisors click. "You know, all of a sudden I'm feeling hungry. Should we do something here on the train or wait until we get to New York?" Only the spook saw him gesture back toward the fed.

"Why don't we wait for the station? More choices there."

"As you wish, dear." He wanted her to take the fed out now but there was nothing more he dared say. He licked his hands nervously and groomed the fur behind his short, thick ears to pass the time.

The International Arrivals Hall at Koch Terminal was unusually quiet for a Thursday night. It smelled to Rat like a setup. The passengers from the bullet shuffled through the echoing marble vastness toward the row of customs stations. Rat was unarmed; if they were going to put up a fight the spook would have to provide the firepower. But Rat was not a fighter, he was a runner. Their instructions were to pass through Station Number Four. As they waited in line Rat spotted the federally appointed vigilante behind them. The classic invisible man: neither handsome nor ugly, five-ten, about one-seventy, brown hair, dark suit, white shirt. He looked bored.

"Do you have anything to declare?" The customs agent looked bored too. Everybody looked bored except Rat who had two million new dollars worth of illegal drugs in his gut and a fed ready to carve them out of him.

"We hold these truths to be self-evident," said Rat, "that all men are created equal." He managed a feeble grin—as if this were a witticism and not the password.

"Daddy, please!" The spook feigned embarrassment. "I'm sorry, ma'am; it's his idea of a joke. It's the Declaration of Independence, you know."

The customs agent smiled as she tousled the spook's hair. "I know that, dear. Please put your luggage on the conveyor." She gave a perfunctory glance at her monitor as their suitcases passed through the scanner and then nodded at Rat. "Thank you, sir, and have a pleasant..." The insincere thought died on her lips as she noticed the fed pushing through the line toward them. Rat saw her spin toward the exit at the same moment that the spook thrust her notebook computer into the scanner. The notebook stretched a blue finger of point discharge toward the magnetic lens just before the overhead lights novaed and went dark. The emergency backup failed as well. Rat's snout filled with the acrid smell of electrical fire. Through the darkness came shouts and screams, thumps and cracks—the crazed pounding of a stampede gathering momentum.

He dropped to all fours and skittered across the floor. Koch Terminal was his territory; he had crisscrossed its many levels with scent trails. Even in total darkness he could find his way. But in his haste he cracked his head against a pair of stockinged knees and a squawking weight fell across him, crushing the breath from his lungs. He felt an icy stab on his hindquarters and scrabbled at it with his hind leg. His toes came away wet and he squealed. There was an answering scream and the point of a shoe drove into him, propelling him across the floor. He rolled left and came up running. Up a dead escalator, down a carpeted hall. He stood upright and stretched to his full twenty-six inches, hands scratching until they found the emergency bar across the fire door. He hurled himself at it, a siren shrieked and with a whoosh the door opened, dumping him into an alley. He lay there for a moment, gasping, half in and half out of Koch Terminal. With the certain knowledge that he was bleeding to death he touched the coldness on his back. A sticky purple substance; he sniffed, then tasted it. Ice cream. Rat threw back his head and laughed. The high squeaky sound echoed in the deserted alley.

But there was no time to waste. He could already hear the buzz of police hovers swooping down from the night sky. The blackout might keep them busy for a while; Rat was more worried about the fed. And the spook. They would be out soon enough, looking for him. Rat scurried down the alley toward the street. He glanced quickly at the terminal, now a black hole in the galaxy of bright holographic sleaze that was Forty-Second Street. A few cops with flashlights were trying to fight against the flow of panicky travelers pouring from its open doors. Rat smoothed his ruffled fur and turned away from the disaster, walking crosstown. His instincts said to run but Rat forced himself to dawdle like a hick shopping for big city excitement. He grinned at the pimps and window-shopped the hardware stores. He paused in front of a pair of mirror-image sex stops—GIRLS! LIVE! GIRLS! and LIVE! GIRLS! LIVE!—to sniff the pheromone-scented sweat pouring off an androgynous robot shill which was working the sidewalk. The robot obligingly put its hand to Rat's crotch but he pushed it away with a hiss and continued on. At last, sure that he was not being followed, he powered up his wallet and tapped into the transnet to summon a hovercab. The wallet informed him that the city had cordoned off midtown airspace to facilitate rescue operations at Koch Terminal. It advised trying the subway or a taxi. Since he had no intention of sticking an ID chip—even a false one!—into a subway turnstile, he stepped to the curb and began watching the traffic.

The rebuilt Checker that rattled to a stop beside him was a patchwork of orange ABS and stainless steel armor. "No we leave Manhattan," said a speaker on the roof light. "No we north of a hundred and ten." Rat nodded and the door locks popped. The passenger compartment smelled of chlorobenzylmalononitrile and urine.

"First Avenue Bunker," said Rat, sniffing. "Christ, it stinks back here. Who was your last fare—the circus?"

"Troubleman." The speaker connections were loose, giving a scratchy edge to the cabbie's voice. The locks re-engaged as the Checker pulled away from the curb. "Ha-has get a fullsnoot of tear gas in this hack."

Rat had already spotted the pressure vents in the floor. He peered through the gloom at the registration. A slogan had been lased over it—probably by one of the new Mitsubishi penlights. "Free the dead." Rat smiled: the dead were his customers. People who had chosen the dusty road. Twelve to eighteen months of glorious addiction: synesthetic orgasms, recursive hallucinations leading to a total sensory overload and an ecstatic death experience. One dose was all it took to start down the dusty road. The feds were trying to cut off the supply—with dire consequences for the dead. They could live a few months longer without dust but their joyride down the dusty road was transformed into a grueling marathon of withdrawal pangs and madness. Either way, they were dead. Rat settled back onto the seat. The penlight graffito was a good omen.

He reached into his pocket and pulled out a leather strip that had been soaked with a private blend of fat-soluble amphetamines and began to gnaw at it.

From time to time he could hear the cabbie monitoring NYPD net for flameouts or wildcat tolls set up by street gangs. They had to detour to heavily guarded Park Avenue all the way uptown to Fifty-Ninth before doubling back toward the bunker. Originally built to protect UN diplomats from terrorists, the bunker had gone condo after the dissolution of the United Nations. Its hype was that it was the "safest address in the city." Its rep was that most of the owners' association were prime candidates either for a mindwipe or an extended vacation on a fed punkfarm.

"Hey, Fare," said the cabbie, "net says the dead be rioting front of your door. Crash through or roll away?"

The fur along Rat's backbone went erect. "Cops?"

"Letting them play for now."

"You've got armor for a crash?"

"Shit yes. Park this hack to ground zero for the right fare." The cabbie's laugh was static. "Don't worry, bunkerman. Give those deadboys a shot of old CS gas and they be too busy scratching they eyes out to bother us much."

Rat tried to smooth his fur. He could crash the riot and get stuck. But if he waited either the spook or the fed would be stepping on his tail before long. Rat had no doubt that both had managed to plant locator bugs on him.

"'Course, riot crashing don't come cheap," said the cabbie.

"Triple the meter." The fare was already over two hundred dollars for the fifteen-minute ride. "Shoot for Bay Two—the one with the yellow door." He pulled out his wallet and started tapping its luminescent keys. "I'm sending recognition code now."

He heard the cabbie notify the cops that they were coming through. Rat could feel the Checker accelerate as they passed the cordon, and he had a glimpse of strobing lights, cops in blue body armor, a tank studded with water cannons. Suddenly the cabbie braked and Rat pitched forward against his shoulder harness. The Checker's solid rubber tires squealed and there was a thump of something bouncing off the hood. They had slowed to a crawl and the dead closed around them.

Rat could not see out the front because the cabbie was protected from his passengers by steel plate. But the side windows filled with faces streaming with sweat and tears and blood. Twisted faces, screaming faces, faces etched by the agonies of withdrawal. The soundproofing muffled their howls. Fear and exhilaration filled Rat as he watched them pass. If only they knew how close they were to dust, he thought. He imagined the dead faces gnawing through the cab's armor in a frenzy, pausing only to spit out broken teeth. It was wonderful. The riot was proof that the dust market was still white hot. The dead must be desperate to attack the bunker like this looking for a flash. He decided to bump the price of his dust another ten percent.

Rat heard a clatter on the roof: then someone began to jump up and down. It was like being inside a kettledrum. Rat sank claws into the seat and arched his back. "What are you waiting for? Gas them, damn it!"

"Hey, Fare. Stuff ain't cheap. We be fine—almost there."

A woman with bloody red hair matted to her head pressed her mouth against the window and screamed. Rat reared up on his hind legs and made biting feints at her. Then he saw the penlight in her hand. At the last moment Rat threw himself backwards. The penlight flared and the passenger compartment filled with the stench of melting plastic. A needle of coherent light singed the fur on Rat's left flank; he squealed and flopped onto the floor, twitching.

The cabbie opened the external gas vents and abruptly the faces dropped away from the windows. The cab accelerated, bouncing as it ran over the fallen dead. There was a dazzling transition from the darkness of the violent night to the floodlit calm of Bay Number Two. Rat scrambled back onto the seat and looked out the back window in time to see the hydraulic doors of the outer lock swing shut. Something was caught between them—something that popped and spattered. Then the inner door rolled down on its track like a curtain coming down on a bloody final act.

Rat was almost home. Two security guards in armor approached. The door locks popped and Rat climbed out of the cab. One of the guards leveled a burster at his head; the other wordlessly offered him a printreader. He thumbed it and the bunker's computer verified him immediately.

"Good evening, sir," said one of the guards. "Little rough out there tonight. Did you have luggage?"

The front door of the cab opened and Rat heard the low whine of electric motors as a mechanical arm lowered the cabbie's wheelchair onto the floor of the bay. She was a gray-haired woman with a rheumy stare who looked like she belonged in a rest home in New Jersey. A knitted shawl covered her withered legs. "You said triple." The cab's hoist clicked and released the chair; she rolled toward him. "Six hundred and sixty-nine dollars."

"No luggage, no." Now that he was safe inside the bunker, Rat regretted his panic-stricken generosity. A credit transfer from one of his own accounts was out of the question. He slipped his last thousand dollar bubble chip into his wallet's card reader, dumped three hundred and thirty one dollars from it into a Bahamian laundry loop, and then dropped the chip into her outstretched hand. She accepted it dubiously: for a minute he expected her to bite into it like they did sometimes on fossil TV. Old people made him nervous. Instead she inserted the chip into her own card reader and frowned at him.

"How about a tip?"

Rat sniffed. "Don't pick up strangers."

One of the guards guffawed obligingly. The other pointed but Rat saw the skunk port in the wheelchair a millisecond too late. With a wet plop the chair emitted a gaseous stinkball which bloomed like an evil flower beneath Rat's whiskers. One guard tried to grab at the rear of the chair but the old cabbie backed suddenly over his foot. The other guard aimed his burster.

The cabbie smiled like a grandmother from hell. "Under the pollution index. No law against sharing a little scent, boys. And you wouldn't want to hurt me anyway. The hack monitors my EEG. I go flat and it goes berserk."

The guard with the bad foot stopped hopping. The guard with the gun shrugged. "It's up to you, sir."

Rat batted the side of his head several times and then buried his snout beneath his armpit. All he could smell was rancid burger topped with sulphur sauce. "Forget it. I haven't got time."

"You know," said the cabbie. "I never get out of the hack but I just wanted to see what kind of person would live in a place like this." The lifts whined as the arm fitted its fingers into the chair. "And now I know." She cackled as the arm gathered her back into the cab. "I'll park it by the door. The cops say they're ready to sweep the street."

The guards led Rat to the bank of elevators. He entered the one with the open door, thumbed the print reader and spoke his access code.

"Good evening, sir," said the elevator. "Will you be going straight to your rooms?"

"Yes."

"Very good, sir. Would you like a list of the communal facilities currently open to serve you?"

There was no shutting the sales pitch off so Rat ignored it and began to lick the stink from his fur.

"The pool is open for lap swimmers only," said the elevator as the doors closed. "All environmats except for the weightless room are currently in use. The sensory deprivation tanks will be occupied until eleven. The surrogatorium is temporarily out of female chassis; we apologize for any inconvenience..."

The cab moved down two and a half floors and then stopped just above the subbasement. Rat glanced up and saw a dark gap opening in the array of light diffuser panels. The spook dropped through it.

"...the holo therapist is off line until eight tomorrow morning but the interactive sex booths will stay open until midnight. The drug dispensary..."

She looked as if she had been waterskiing through the sewer. Her blonde hair was wet and smeared with dirt; she had lost the ribbons from her pigtails. Her jeans were torn at the knees and there was an ugly scrape on the side of her face. The silk turtleneck clung wetly to her. Yet despite her dishevelment, the hand that held the penlight was as steady as a jewel cutter's.

"There seems to be a minor problem," said the elevator in a soothing voice. "There is no cause for alarm. This unit is temporarily non-functional. Maintenance has been notified and is now working to correct the problem. In case of emergency, please contact Security. We regret this temporary inconvenience."

The spook fired a burst of light at the floor selector panel; it spat fire at them and went dark. "Where the hell were you?" said the spook. "You said the McDonald's in Times Square if we got separated."

"Where were you?" Rat rose up on his hind legs. "When I got there the place was swarming with cops."

He froze as the tip of the penlight flared. The spook traced a rough outline of Rat on the stainless steel door behind him. "Fuck your lies," she said. The beam came so close that Rat could smell his fur curling away from it. "I want the dust."

"Trespass alert!" screeched the wounded elevator. A note of urgency had crept into its artificial voice. "Security reports unauthorized persons within the complex. Residents are urged to return immediately to their apartments and engage all personal security devices. Do not be alarmed. We regret this temporary inconvenience."

The scales on Rat's tail fluffed. "We have a deal. The marechal needs my networks to move his product. So let's get out of here before..."

"The dust."

Rat sprung at her with a squeal of hatred. His claws caught on her turtleneck and he struck repeatedly at her open collar, gashing her neck with his long red incisors. Taken aback by the swiftness and ferocity of his attack, she dropped the penlight and tried to fling him against the wall. He held fast, worrying at her and chittering rabidly. When she stumbled under the open emergency exit in the ceiling he leapt again. He cleared the suspended ceiling, caught himself on the inductor and scrabbled up onto the hoist cables. Light was pouring into the shaft from above; armored guards had forced the door open and were climbing down toward the stalled car. Rat jumped from the cables across five feet of open space to the counterweight and huddled there, trying to use its bulk to shield himself from the spook's fire. Her stand was short and inglorious. She threw a dazzler out of the hatch, hoping to blind the guards, then tried to pull herself through. Rat could hear the shriek of burster fire. He waited until he could smell the aroma of broiling meat and scorched plastic before he emerged from the shadows and signaled to the security team.

A squad of apologetic guards rode the service elevator with Rat down to the storage subbasement where he lived. When he had first looked at the bunker, the broker had been reluctant to rent him the abandoned rooms, insisting that he live above ground with the other residents. But all of the suites they showed him were unacceptably open, clean and uncluttered. Rat much preferred his musty dungeon, where odors lingered in the still air. He liked to fall asleep to the booming of the ventilation system on the level above him and slept easier knowing that he was as far away from the stink of other people as he could get in the city.

The guards escorted him to the gleaming brass smart door and looked away discreetly as he entered his passcode on the keypad. He had ordered it custom-built from Mosler so that it would recognize high-frequency squeals well beyond the range of human hearing. He called to it and then pressed trembling fingers onto the printreader. His bowels had loosened in terror during the firefight and the capsules had begun to sting terribly. It was all he could do to keep from defecating right there in the hallway. The door sensed the guards and beeped to warn him of their presence. He punched in the override sequence impatiently and the seals broke with a sigh.

"Have a pleasant evening, sir," said one of the guards as he scurried inside. "And don't worry ab—" The door cut him off as it swung shut.

Against all odds, Rat had made it. For a moment he stood, tail switching against the inside of the door, and let the magnificent chaos of his apartment soothe his jangled nerves. He had earned his reward—the dust was all his now. No one could take it away from him. He saw himself in a shard of mirror propped up against an empty THC aerosol and wriggled in self-congratulation. He was the richest rat on the East Side, perhaps in the entire city.

He picked his way through a maze formed by a jumble of overburdened steel shelving left behind years, perhaps decades, ago. The managers of the bunker had offered to remove them and their contents before he moved in; Rat had insisted that they stay. When the fire inspector had come to approve his newly installed sprinkler system she had been horrified at the clutter on the shelves and had threatened to condemn the place. It had cost him plenty to buy her off but it had been worth it. Since then Rat's trove of junk had at least doubled in size. For years no one had seen it but Rat and the occasional cockroach.

Relaxing at last, Rat stopped to pull a mildewed wingtip down from his huge collection of shoes; he loved the bouquet of fine old leather and gnawed it whenever he could. Next to the shoes was a heap of books: his private library. One of Rat's favorite delicacies was the first edition *Leaves of Grass* which he had pilfered from the rare book collection at the New York Public Library. To celebrate his safe arrival he ripped out page 43 for a snack and stuffed it into the wingtip. He dragged the shoe over a pile of broken sheetrock and past shelves filled with scrap electronics: shattered monitors and dead typewriters, microwaves and robot vacuums. He had almost reached his nest when the fed stepped from behind a dirty Hungarian flag that hung from a broken florescent light fixture.

Startled, Rat instinctively hurled himself at the crack in the wall where he had built his nest. But the fed was too quick. Rat did not recognize the weapon; all he knew was that when it hissed Rat lost all feeling in his hindquarters. He landed in a heap but continued to crawl, slowly, painfully.

"You have something I want." The fed kicked him. Rat skidded across the concrete floor toward the crack, leaving a thin gruel of excrement in his wake. Rat continued to crawl until the fed stepped on his tail, pinning him.

"Where's the dust?"

"I…I don't…"

The fed stepped again; Rat's left fibula snapped like cheap plastic. He felt no pain.

"The dust." The fed's voice quavered strangely.

"Not here. Too dangerous."

"Where?" The fed released him. "Where?"

Rat was surprised to see that the fed's gun hand was shaking. For the first time he looked up at the man's eyes and recognized the telltale yellow tint. Rat realized then how badly he had misinterpreted the fed's expression back at Koch. Not bored. Empty. For an instant he could not believe his extraordinary good fortune. Bargain for time, he told himself. There's still a chance. Even though he was cornered he knew his instinct to fight was wrong.

"I can get it for you fast if you let me go," said Rat. "Ten minutes, fifteen. You look like you need it."

"What are you talking about?" The fed's bravado started to crumble and Rat knew he had the man. The fed wanted the dust for himself. He was one of the dead.

"Don't make it hard on yourself," said Rat. "There's a terminal in my nest. By the crack. Ten minutes." He started to pull himself toward the nest. He knew the fed would not dare stop him; the man was already deep into withdrawal. "Only ten minutes and you can have all the dust you want." The poor fool could not hope to fight the flood of neuroregulators pumping crazily across his synapses. He might break any minute, let his weapon slip from trembling hands. Rat reached the crack and scrambled through into comforting darkness.

The nest was built around a century-old shopping cart and a stripped subway bench. Rat had filled the gaps in with pieces of synthetic rubber, a hubcap, plastic greeting cards, barbed wire, disk casings, baggies, a No Parking sign and an assortment of bones. Rat climbed in and lowered himself onto the soft bed of shredded thousand-dollar bills. The profits of six years of deals and betrayals, a few dozen murders and several thousand dusty deaths.

The fed sniffled as Rat powered up his terminal to notify security. "Someone set me up some vicious bastard slipped it to me I don't know when I think it was Barcelona…it would kill Sarah to see…" He began to weep. "I wanted to turn myself in…they keep working on new treatments you know but it's not fair damn it! The success rate is less than…I made my first buy two weeks only two God it seems…killed a man to get some lousy dust…but they're right it's, it's, I can't begin to describe what it's like…"

Rat's fingers flew over the glowing keyboard, describing his situation, the layout of the rooms, a strategy for the assault. He had overridden the smart door's recognition sequence. It would be tricky but security could take the fed out if they were quick and careful. Better to risk a surprise attack than to dicker with an armed and unraveling dead man.

"I really ought to kill myself...would be best but it's not only me...I've seen ten-year-olds...what kind of animal sells dust to kids...I should kill myself. And you." Something changed in the fed's voice as Rat signed off. "And you." He stooped and reached through the crack.

"It's coming," said Rat quickly. "By messenger. Ten doses. By the time you get to the door it should be here." He could see the fed's hand and burrowed into the rotting pile of money. "You wait by the door, you hear? It's coming any minute."

"I don't want it." The hand was so large it blocked the light. Rat's fur went erect and he arched his spine. "Keep your fucking dust."

Rat could hear the guards fighting their way through the clutter. Shelves crashed. So clumsy, these men.

"It's you I want." The hand sifted through the shredded bills, searching for Rat. He had no doubt that the fed could crush the life from him—the hand was huge now. In the darkness he could count the lines on the palm, follow the whorls on the fingertips. They seemed to spin in Rat's brain—he was losing control. He realized then that one of the capsules must have broken, spilling a megadose of first-quality Algerian Yellow dust into his gut. With a hallucinatory clarity he imagined sparks streaming through his blood, igniting neurons like tinder. Suddenly the guards did not matter. Nothing mattered except that he was cornered. When he could no longer fight the instinct to strike, the fed's hand closed around him. The man was stronger than Rat could have imagined. As the fed hauled him—clawing and biting—back into the light, Rat's only thought was of how terrifyingly large a man was. So much larger than a rat.

The Friendship Light (1989)

GENE WOLFE

GENE WOLFE'S (b. 1931) many novels include *Peace*, *The Devil in a Forest*, *Free Live Free*, *Soldier of the Mist*, and, most recently, *The Land Across*. He is possibly best known for the novels that comprise *The Book of the New Sun*, the story of Severian, a member of the Torturer's Guild in a far-future world. Wolfe's storytelling skills sometimes seem sorcerous, and his short fiction—which includes such well-known tales as *The Fifth Head of Cerberus*, "Seven American Nights," and "The Island of Doctor Death and Other Stories"—has often worked a magic spell on readers. Wolfe's stories sometimes draw on mythology, and they are allusive and elusive at times, but casual and close readers find them potent.

FOR MY OWN part I have my journal; for my late brother-in-law's, his tape. I will refer to myself as "Ty" and to him as "Jack." That, I think, with careful concealment of our location, should prove sufficient. Ours is a mountainous—or at least, a hilly—area, more rural than Jack can have liked. My sister's house (I insist upon calling it that, as does the law) is set back two hundred yards from the county road. My own is yet more obscure, being precisely three miles down the gravel road that leaves the county road to the north, three-quarters of a mile west of poor Tessie's drive. I hope that these distances will be of help to you.

It began three months ago, and it was over—properly over, that is to say—in less than a week.

Though I have a telephone, I seldom answer it. Jack knew this; thus I received a note from him in the mail asking me to come to him on the very day on which his note was delivered. Typically, he failed to so much as mention the matter he wished to discuss with me, but wrote that he would be gone for several days. He was to leave that night.

He was a heavy-limbed blond man, large and strong. Tessie says he played football in college, which I can well believe. I know he played baseball professionally for several seasons after graduation, because he never tired of talking about it. For me to specify his team would be counterproductive.

I found him at the end of the drive, eyeing the hole that the men from the gas company had dug; he smiled when he saw me. "I was afraid you weren't coming," he said.

I told him I had received his note only that day.

"I have to go away," he said. "The judge wants to see me." He named the city.

I offered to accompany him.

"No, no. I need you here. To look after the place, and—You see this hole?"

I was very tempted to leave him then and there. To spit, perhaps, and stroll back to my car. Even though he was so much stronger, he would have done nothing. I contented myself with pointing out that it was nearly a yard across, and that we were standing before it. As I ought to have anticipated, it had no effect upon him.

"It's for a friendship light. One of those gas things, you know? Tess ordered it last fall...."

"Before you had her committed," I added helpfully.

"Before she got so sick. Only they wouldn't put it in then because they were busy tuning up furnaces." He paused to wipe the sweat from his forehead with his index finger, flinging the moisture into the hole. I could see he did not like talking to me, and I resolved to stay for as long as I could tolerate him.

"And they don't like doing it in the winter because of the ground's being frozen and hard to dig. Then in the spring it's all mushy."

I said, "But here we are at last. I suppose it will be made to look like a carriage lamp? With a little arm for your name? They're so nice."

He would not look at me. "I would have cancelled the order if I'd remembered it, but some damned woman phoned me about it a couple of days ago, and I don't know—Because Tess ordered it—See that trench there?"

Again, I could hardly have failed to notice it.

"It's for the pipe that'll tap into the gas line. They'll be back tomorrow to run the pipe and put up the lamp and so on. Somebody's got to be here to sign for it. And somebody ought to see to Tess's cats and everything. I've still got them. You're the only one I could think of."

I said that I was flattered that he had so much confidence in me.

"Besides, I want to visit her while I'm away. It's been a couple of months. I'll let her know that you're looking after things. Maybe that will make her happy."

How little he knew of her!

"And I've got some business of my own to take care of."

It would have given me enormous pleasure to have refused, making some excuse. But to see my old home again—the room in which Tessie and I slept as children—I would have done a great deal more. "I'll need a key," I told him. "Do you know when the workmen will come?"

"About nine-thirty or ten, they said." Jack hesitated. "The cats are outside. I don't let them in the house anymore."

"I am certainly not going to take any responsibility for a property I am not allowed to enter," I told him. "What if there was some emergency? I would have to drive back to my own house to use the telephone. Do you keep your cat food outside, too? What about the can-opener? The milk?"

"All right—all right." Reluctantly, he fished his keys from his pocket. I smiled when I saw that there was a rabbit's foot on the ring. I had nearly forgotten how superstitious he was.

I arrived at the house that for so many years had been my home before nine. Tessie's cats seemed as happy to see me as I was to see them—Marmaduke and Millicent "talked" and rubbed my legs, and Princess actually sprang into my arms. Jack had had them neutered, I believe. It struck me that it would be fairly easy to take one of the females—Princess, let us say—home with me, substituting an unaltered female of similar appearance who would doubtless soon present Jack with an unexpected litter of alley kittens. One seal-point Siamese, I reflected, looks very like another; and most of the kittens—possibly all of them—would be black, blacks being exceedingly common when Siamese are outcrossed.

I would have had to pay for the new female, however—fifty dollars at least. I dropped the idea as a practical possibility as I opened the can of cat food and extended it with one of tuna. But it had set my mental wheels in motion, so to speak.

It was after eleven when the men from the gas company came, and after two before their supervisor rang the bell. He asked if I was Jack, and to save trouble I told him I was and prepared to sign whatever paper he might thrust under my nose.

"Come out here for a minute, will you?" he said. "I want to show you how it works."

Docilely, I followed him down the long drive.

"This is the control valve." He tapped it with his pencil. "You turn this knob to raise and lower the flame."

I nodded to show I understood.

"Now when you light it, you've got to hold this button in until it gets hot—otherwise, it'll go out, see? That's so if it goes out somehow, it'll turn off."

He applied his cigarette lighter, and the flame came on with a *whoosh*.

"Don't try to turn it off in the daytime. You'll ruin the mantle if you light it a lot. Just let it burn, and it'll last you maybe ten years. Should be hot enough now."

He removed his hand. The blue and yellow flame seemed to die, blazed up, then appeared almost to die once more.

"Flickering a little."

He paused and glanced at his watch. I could see that he did not want to take the time to change the valve. Thinking of Jack's irritation, I said, "It will probably be all right when it gets a bit hotter." It flared again as I spoke.

"Yeah. I better turn it down a little. I got it set kind of high." The sullen flickering persisted, though in somewhat muted fashion.

The supervisor pointed. "Right over here's your cut-off. You see how long that valve-stem is? When the boys get through filling in the trench, it'll be just about level with the ground so you don't hit it with the mower. But if you've got to put in a new light—like, if somebody wracks up this one with his car—that's where you can turn off the gas."

I lingered in the house. If you knew how spartanly I live, in a house that my grandfather had thought scarcely fit for his tenant farmers, you would understand why. Jack had liquor, and plenty of good food. (Trust him for that.) My sister's books still lined her shelves, and there was an excellent stereo. It was with something of a shock that I glanced up from *À Rebours* and realized that night had fallen. Far away, at the very end of the long, winding driveway, the new friendship light glared fitfully. It was then that I conceived my little plan.

In the morning I found the handle of the cut-off valve that the supervisor had shown me and took it off, employing one of Jack's screwdrivers. Though I am not really mechanically inclined, I had observed that the screws holding the plate over the control valve had shallow heads and poorly formed slots; they had given the supervisor some difficulty when he replaced them. I told a clerk at our hardware store in the village that I frequently had to retighten a screw in my stove which (although there was never any need to take it out) repeatedly worked loose. The product he recommended is called an anaerobic adhesive, I believe. It was available in four grades: Wicking, Medium (General Purposes), High Strength, and Permanent Installation. I selected the last, though the clerk warned me that I would have to heat the screw thoroughly with a propane torch if I ever wished to remove it.

Back at my sister's, I turned the flame higher, treated the screws with adhesive, and tightened them as much as I could. At that time, I did not know that Jack kept a journal of his own on cassette tapes. He had locked them away from my prying ears before he left, you may be sure; but I found the current number when the end-of-tape alarm sounded following his demise, and it may be time now to give old Jack the floor—time for a bit of fun.

"Well, here we are. Nicolette's in the bedroom switching into something a lot more comfortable as they always say, so I'm going to take a minute to wrap things up.

"The judge said okay to selling the beach property, but all the money's got to go into the fund. I'll knock down the price a little and take a finder's fee. Nicolette and I had a couple of good days, and I thought—"

"Jack! Jack!"

"Okay, here's what happened. Nicolette says she was trying out some of Tess's lipsticks, and looking in the mirror, when she saw somebody down at the end of the driveway watching her. I told her she ought to have shut the drapes, but she said she thought way out in the country like this she wouldn't have to. Anyway, she saw this guy, standing there and not moving. Then the gas died down, and when it came back up he was still there, only a little nearer the house. Then it died down again, and when it came back up he was gone. She was looking out of the window by that time, she says in her slip. I went down to the end of the drive with a flashlight and looked around, but there's so many footprints from the guys that put up the friendship light you can't tell anything. If you ask me it was Ty. He stopped to look when he saw lights in the windows. It would be just like that sneaky son of a bitch not to come by or say anything, but I've got to admit I'm glad he didn't.

"Well, when I got back to the house, Nicolette told me she heard the back door open and close again while I was gone. I went back there, and it was shut and locked. I remembered how it was while Tess was here, and I thought, that bastard has let those cats in, so I went, 'Kitty-kitty-kitty,' and sure as hell the big tom came out of the pantry to see if there was anything to eat. I got him by the neck and chucked him out."

"Got some good pix of Nicolette and me by using the bulb with the motor drive. What I did was put the bulb under the mattress. Every once in a while it would get shoved down hard enough to trip the shutter, then the motor would advance the film. Shot up a whole roll of twenty-four that way last night. She laughed and said, 'Put in a big roll tomorrow,' but I don't think so. I'm going to try to get her to go back Thursday—got to think about that. Can't take *this* roll to Berry's in town, that's for sure. I'll wait till I go sign the transfer of title, then turn it in to one of the big camera stores. Maybe they'll mail the prints to me, too.

"She wanted me to call Ty and ask if anything funny went on while we were away. I said okay, thinking he wouldn't answer, but he did. He said there was nothing funny while I was gone, but last night he was driving past, and he saw what looked like lightning at an upstairs window. I said I'd been fooling around with my camera equipment and set off the flash a couple of times to test it out. I said I was calling to thank him and see when I could drop by and get my key back. He said he'd already put it in the mail.

"If you ask me he knows Nicolette's here. That was him out there last night as sure as hell. He's been watching the house, and a few minutes ago on the phone he was playing a little game. Okay by me. I've loaded the Savage and stuck it under the bed. Next time he comes snooping around, he's going to have bullets buzzing around his ears. If he gets hit—Hell, no jury around here's going to blame a man for shooting at trespassers on his property at night.

"Either there's more cats now, or the coons are eating the cat food again."

"Nicolette got real scared tonight as soon as it got dark. I kept saying what's the matter? And she kept saying she didn't know, but there was something out there, moving around. I got the Savage, thinking it would make her feel better. Every so often the phone would ring and keep on ringing, but there'd be nobody on the line when I picked it up. I mixed us a couple of stiff drinks, but it was like she'd never touched hers—when she finished, she was just as scared as ever.

"Finally I got smart and told her, 'Listen, honey, if this old place bothers you so much, why don't I just drive you to the airport tonight and put you on a plane home?' She jumped on it. 'Would you? Oh, Lord, Jack, I love you! Just a minute and I'll run up and get packed.'

"Until then there hadn't really been anything to be scared of that I could see, but then something really spooky happened. The phone rang again. I picked it up out of habit, and instead of nobody being there like before, I heard a car start up—over the goddamned phone! I was mad as hell and banged it down, and right then Nicolette screamed.

"I grabbed the rifle and ran upstairs, only she was crying too much to say what it was. The damn drapes were still open, and I figured she'd seen Ty out by the friendship light again, so I closed them. Later she said it wasn't the guy she'd seen before, but something big with wings. It could have been a big owl, or maybe just her imagination and too much liquor. Anyway we wasted a lot of time before she got straightened out enough to pack.

"Then I heard something moving around downstairs. While I was going down the stairs, I heard it run—I guess to hide, and the sack of garbage falling over. After I saw the mess in the kitchen, I thought sure it was one of those damned cats, and I still do, but it seemed like it made too much noise running to be a cat—more like a dog, maybe.

"Nicolette didn't want to go out to the garage with me, so I said I'd bring the car around and pick her up out front. The car and jeep looked okay when I raised the door and switched on the light, but as soon as I opened the car door I knew something was wrong, because the dome light didn't come on. I tossed the rifle in back, meaning to take a look under the hood, and there was the God-damnedest noise you ever heard in your life. It's a hell of a good thing I wasn't still holding the gun.

"It was a cat, and not one of ours. I guess he was asleep on the back seat and I hit him with the Savage when I tossed it inside.

"He came out of there like a buzz saw and it feels like he peeled off half my face. I yelled—that scared the shit out of Nicolette in the house—and grabbed the hammer off my bench. I was going to kill that son of a bitch if I could find him. The moon was up, and I saw him scooting past the pond. I chucked the hammer at him but missed him a mile. He'd been yowling like crazy, but all of a sudden he shut up, and I went back into the house to get a bandage for my face.

"I was a mess, too. That bastard took a lot of skin off my cheek, and a lot of blood had run onto my shirt and jacket.

"Nicolette was helping me when we heard something fall on the roof. She yelled, 'Where's your gun?' and I told her it was still out in the goddamned car, which it was. She wanted me to go out and get it, and I wanted to find out what had hit on the roof, but I went out first and got the Savage. Everything was O.K., too—the garage light was still on, and the gun was lying on the seat of the car. But when I tried to start the car, it wouldn't turn over. Finally I checked the headlights, and sure enough the switch was pulled out. I must have left the lights on last night. The battery's as dead as a doornail.

"I was pulling out the folding steps to the attic when the phone rang. Nicolette got it, and she said all she could hear was a car starting up, the same as I'd heard.

"I went up into the attic with a flashlight, and opened the window and went out onto the roof. It took a lot of looking to find what had hit. I should have just chucked it out into the yard, but like a jerk I picked it up by the ear and carried it downstairs and scared Nicolette half to death. It's the head of a big tomcat, if you ask me, or maybe a wildcat. Not one of ours, a black one.

"O.K., when I was outside and that cat got quiet all of a sudden, I felt a breeze—only cold like somebody had opened the door of a big freezer. There wasn't a noise, but then owls can fly without making a sound. So it's pretty clear what happened.

"We've got a big owl around here. That was probably what Nicolette saw out the window, and it was sure as hell what got the cat. The cat must have come around to eat our cat food, and got into the garage sometime when I opened the door. None of this has got anything to do with the phone. That's just kids.

"Nicolette wanted me to take her to the airport in the jeep right away, but after all that had happened I didn't feel like doing it, so I told her it would be too late to catch a flight and the jeep wasn't running anyhow. I told her tomorrow we'll call the garage and get somebody to come out and give us a jump.

"We yelled about that for a while until I gave her some of Tess's sleeping pills. She took two or three. Now she's out like a light. I've pulled the jack on every goddamned phone in the house. I took a couple of aspirins, but my cheek still hurt so bad I couldn't sleep, so I got up and fixed a drink and tried to talk all this out. Now I'm going back to bed."

"This is bad—I've called the sheriff, and the ambulance is supposed to come out. It will be all over the damned paper, and the judge will see it as sure as hell, but what else could I do? Just now I mopped up the blood with a couple of dirty shirts. I threw them out back, and as soon as I shut the door I could hear them out there. I should've opened the door and shot. I don't know why I didn't, except Nicolette was making that noise that drives me crazy. I damn near hit her with the rifle. I've done everything I can. She needs an ambulance—a hospital."

"Now, honey, I want you to say—right into here—that it wasn't me, understand?"

"Water...."

"I'll get you plenty of water. You say it, and I'll get it right away. Tell them what happened."

"The tape ran out. Had to turn it over.

"O.K., then I'll say it. It wasn't me—wasn't Jack. Maybe I ought to start right at the beginning.

"Nicolette shot at a coon. I was sound asleep, but I must have jumped damned near through the ceiling. I came up yelling and fighting, and it was dark as hell. I hit the light switch, but the lights wouldn't come on. The only light in the whole place was the little crack between the drapes. I pulled them open. It was just the damned friendship light way down at the end of the drive, but that was better than nothing.

"I saw she had the gun, so I grabbed it. She'd been trying to work it, but she hadn't pulled the lever down far enough to chamber a fresh round. If she had, she'd probably have killed us both.

"I said, 'Listen, the power's just gone off—that happens a lot out here.' She said she got up to go to the bathroom, and she saw eyes, green eyes shining. She turned on the hall light, but it was gone. She tried to wake me up but I just grabbed her, so she got the gun. Pretty soon all the lights went out. She thought she heard it coming and fired.

"I got my flashlight and looked around. The bullet went right through the wall of Tess's room and hit the bed—I think it stopped in the mattress somewhere.

"Nicolette kept saying, 'Give me the keys—I'll go to the airport by myself.' I smacked her good and hard a few times to make her shut up, once with the flashlight.

"Then I saw the green eyes, too, but as soon as I got the light on it, I knew what it was—just a coon, not even a real big one.

"I didn't want to shoot again, because even if I'd hit it would have made a hell of a mess, so I told Nicolette to open the door. She did, and that's when I saw them, two or three of them, flying around down by the friendship light. Jesus!"

"They're outside now. I know they are. I took a shot at one through the big window, but I don't think I hit it.

"Where the hell's the sheriff's guy? He should've been here an hour ago—the ambulance, too. It's starting to get light outside."

"The coon got in through the goddamned cat door. I ought to have guessed. When Ty was here he had the cats in the house with him, so he unbolted it—that was how Marmaduke got in last night.

"I tried to switch this thing off, but I'm shaking too bad. I damn near dropped it. I might as well get on with it anyway. This isn't getting us anywhere. I gave her the keys and I told her, 'O.K., you want to go to the goddamn airport so bad, here. Leave the keys and the ticket in the dash compartment and I'll go out and pick it up when I can.'

"I didn't think she'd do it, but she took the keys and ran outside. I went to the window. I heard the jeep start up, and it sounded like she was tearing out the whole damn transmission. Pretty soon she came roaring down the driveway. I guess she had it in second and the pedal all the way to the floor. I didn't think any were close to her, and all of a sudden there was one right above her, dropping down. The wings made it look like the jeep was blinking on and off, too.

"The jeep went across the road and into the ditch. I never thought I'd see her again, but it dropped her on the front lawn. I shouldn't have gone out to get her. I could've been killed.

"It was looking for something in her, that's what I think. I didn't know there was so much blood when you cut a person open like that. What the hell do the doctors do?

"I think she's dead now."

"The sheriff's men just left. They say the power's off all over. It looks like a plane hit the wires, they said, without crashing. Jesus.

"Here's what I told them. Nicolette and I had a fight. I keep the gun loaded in case of prowlers, and she took a couple of shots at me. They said, 'How do we know you didn't shoot at her?' I said, 'You think I'd miss a woman twice, with my deer rifle, inside the house?' I could see they bought it.

"I said I gave her the keys to the jeep and said to leave it at the airport—the truth in other words. They said, 'Didn't you give her any money?' I told them, 'Not then, but I'd given her some before, back when we were still in the hotel.' I told them she floorboarded it down the drive and couldn't make the turn. I saw her hit and went out and got her, and brought her back into the house.

"They said, 'You ripped her up the belly with a knife.' I said, 'No way. Sure, I slapped her a couple times for shooting at me, but I never knifed her.' I showed them my hunting knife, and they checked out all the kitchen knives. They said, 'How'd she get ripped up the middle like that?' and I said, 'How the hell should I know? She got thrown out of the jeep.'

"I'm not supposed to leave the country, not supposed to stay anyplace but here. They took the Savage, but I've still got my shotgun and the twenty-two."

"Power's back on. The tow truck came out for the jeep and gave me a jump for the Cadillac.

"The way I see it, they've never even tried to get into the house, so if I stay in here I ought to be all right. I'm going to wait until after dark, then see if I can get Ty to come over. If he gets in okay, fine—I'll string him along for a while. If he doesn't, I'll leave tomorrow and the sheriff can go to hell. I'll let his office know where I am, and tell them I'll come in for questioning any time they want to see me."

"I just phoned Ty. I said I'd like to give him something for looking after the place while I was gone. And that I was going away again, this time for quite a while, and I wanted him to take care of things like he did before. I told him I've been using the spare key, but the one he mailed was probably in the box, down by the friendship light, because I haven't picked up my mail yet. I said for him to check the box before he came to the house. He said O.K., he'd be right over. It seems to be taking him...."

Ty again. At this point in the tape, my knock can be heard quite distinctly, followed by Jack's footfalls as he went to the door; it would seem that he was too rattled to turn off his tape recorder. (Liquor, as I have observed several times, does not in fact prevent nervousness, merely allowing it to accumulate.) I would be very happy to transcribe his scream here, if only I knew how to express it by means of the twenty-six letters of the Roman alphabet.

You took him, as you promised, whole and entire. I have no grounds for complaint upon that score, or indeed upon any. And I feel certain he met his well-deserved death firmly convinced that he was in the grip of demons, or some such thing, which I find enormously satisfying.

Why, then, do I write? Permit me to be frank now: I am in need of your assistance. I will not pretend that I deserve it (you would quite correctly care nothing for that), or that it is owed me; I carried out my part of the agreement we made at the friendship light, and you carried out yours. But I find myself in difficulties.

Poor Tessie will probably never be discharged. Even the most progressive of our hospitals are now loath to grant release in cases of her type—there were so many unfortunate incidents earlier, and although society really has very little invested in children aged two to four, it overvalues them absurdly.

As her husband, Jack was charged with administration of the estate in which (though it was by right mine) I shared only to a minuscule degree through the perversity of my mother. Were Jack legally dead, I, as Tessie's brother, would almost certainly be appointed administrator—so my attorney assures me. But as long as Jack is considered by law a fugitive, a suspect in the suspicious death of Nicolette Corso, the entire matter is in abeyance.

True, I have access to the house; but I have been unable to persuade the conservator that I am the obvious person to look after the property. Nor can I vote the stock, complete the sale of the beach acreage, or do any other of many such useful and possibly remunerative things.

Thus I appeal to you. (And to any privileged human being who may read this. Please forward my message to the appropriate recipients.) I urgently require proof of Jack's demise. The nature of that proof I shall leave entirely at your discretion. I venture to point out, however, that identifications based on dental records are in most cases accepted by our courts without question. If

Jack's skull, for example, were discovered some fifty or more miles from here, there should be little difficulty.

In return, I stand ready to do whatever may be of value to you. Let us discuss this matter, openly and in good faith. I will arrange for this account to be reproduced in a variety of media.

It was I, of course, as even old Jack surmised, whom Jack's whore saw the first time near the friendship light. To a human being its morose dance appeared quite threatening, a point I had grasped from the beginning.

It was I also who pulled out Jack's headlight switch and put the black tom—I obtained it from the Humane Society—in his car. And it was I who telephoned; at first I did it merely to annoy him—a symbolic revenge on all those (himself included) who have employed that means to render my existence miserable. Later I permitted him to hear my vehicle start, knowing as I did that his would not. Childish, all of them, to be sure; and yet I dare hope they were of some service to you.

Before I replaced the handle of the valve and extinguished Tessie's friendship light, I contrived that my Coleman lantern should be made to flicker at the signal frequency. Each evening I hoist it high into the branches of the large maple tree in front of my home. Consider it, please, a beacon of welcome. I am most anxious to speak with you again.

The Bone Woman (1993)

CHARLES DE LINT

CHARLES DE LINT (b. 1951) is the author of many novels and stories, including *The Riddle of the Wren*, *Moonheart*, *The Little Country*, and several novels for younger readers, such as *The Painted Boy*, *The Cats of Tanglewood Forest*, and *Seven Wild Sisters*. Many of de Lint's stories, including the novels *Someplace to Be Flying* and *Widdershins*, are set in the fictional North American city of Newford, and de Lint often shares credit with Megan Lindholm, Emma Bull, and Terri Windling for pioneering and popularizing stories that draw on traditionally rural fantasy themes but explore them in a contemporary urban setting. (The term "Urban Fantasy" is often used for such tales, although—like all such labels—there is lots of debate over just what it encompasses.) "The Bone Woman" exemplifies the blend of city life and fantasy that de Lint writes so well.

N O ONE REALLY stops to think of Ellie Spink, and why should they?
   She's no one.
   She has nothing.
   Homely as a child, all that the passing of years did was add to her unattractiveness. Face like a horse, jaw long and square, forehead broad; limpid eyes set bird-wide on either side of a gargantuan nose; hair a nondescript brown, greasy and matted, stuffed up under a woolen tuque lined with a patchwork of metal foil scavenged from discarded cigarette packages. The angularity of her slight frame doesn't get its volume from her meager diet, but from the multiple layers of clothing she wears.

   Raised in foster homes, she's been used, but she's never experienced a kiss. Institutionalized for most of her adult life, she's been medicated, but never treated. Pass her on the street and your gaze slides right on by, never pausing to register the difference between the old woman huddled in the doorway and a bag of garbage.

   Old woman? Though she doesn't know it, Monday, two weeks past, was her thirty-seventh birthday. She looks twice her age.

There's no point in trying to talk to her. Usually no one's home. When there is, the words spill out in a disjointed mumble, a rambling, one-sided dialogue itemizing a litany of misperceived conspiracies and ills that soon leave you feeling as confused as she herself must be.

Normal conversation is impossible and not many bother to try it. The exceptions are few: The odd pitying passerby. A concerned social worker, fresh out of college and new to the streets. Maybe one of the other street people who happens to stumble into her particular haunts.

They talk and she listens or she doesn't—she never makes any sort of a relevant response, so who can tell? Few push the matter. Fewer still, however well-intentioned, have the stamina to make the attempt to do so more than once or twice. It's easier to just walk away; to bury your guilt, or laugh off her confused ranting as the excessive rhetoric it can only be.

I've done it myself.

I used to try to talk to her when I first started seeing her around, but I didn't get far. Angel told me a little about her, but even knowing her name and some of her history didn't help.

"Hey, Ellie. How're you doing?"

Pale eyes, almost translucent, turn towards me, set so far apart it's as though she can only see me with one eye at a time.

"They should test for aliens," she tells me. "You know, like in the Olympics."

"Aliens?"

"I mean, who cares who killed Kennedy? Dead's dead, right?"

"What's Kennedy got to do with aliens?"

"I don't even know why they took down the Berlin Wall. What about the one in China? Shouldn't they have worked on that one first?"

It's like trying to have a conversation with a game of Trivial Pursuit that specializes in information garnered from supermarket tabloids. After a while I'd just pack an extra sandwich whenever I was busking in her neighbourhood. I'd sit beside her, share my lunch and let her talk if she wanted to, but I wouldn't say all that much myself.

That all changed the day I saw her with the Bone Woman.

I didn't call her the Bone Woman at first; the adjective that came more immediately to mind was fat. She couldn't have been much more than five-foot-one, but she had to weigh in at two-fifty, leaving me with the impression that she was wider than she was tall. But she was light on her feet—peculiarly graceful for all her squat bulk.

She had a round face like a full moon, framed by thick black hair that hung in two long braids to her waist. Her eyes were small, almost lost in that expanse of face, and so dark they seemed all pupil. She went barefoot in a shapeless black dress, her only accessory an equally shapeless shoulder-bag made of some kind of animal skin and festooned with dangling thongs from which hung various feathers, beads, bottle-caps and other found objects.

I paused at the far end of the street when I saw the two of them together. I had a sandwich for Ellie in my knapsack, but I hesitated in approaching them. They seemed deep in conversation, real conversation, give and take, and Ellie was—knitting? Talking *and* knitting? The pair of them looked like a couple of old gossips, sitting on the back porch of their building. The sight of Ellie acting so normal was something I didn't want to interrupt.

I sat down on a nearby stoop and watched until Ellie put away her knitting and stood up. She looked down at her companion with an expression in her features that I'd never seen before. It was awareness, I realized. She was completely *here* for a change.

As she came up the street, I stood up and called a greeting to her, but by the time she reached me she wore her usually vacuous expression.

"It's the newspapers," she told me. "They use radiation to print them and that's what makes the news seem so bad."

Before I could take the sandwich I'd brought her out of my knapsack, she'd shuffled off, around the corner, and was gone. I glanced back down the street to where the fat woman was still sitting, and decided to find Ellie later. Right now I wanted to know what the woman had done to get such a positive reaction out of Ellie.

When I approached, the fat woman was sifting through the refuse where the two of them had been sitting. As I watched, she picked up a good-sized bone. What kind, I don't know, but it was as long as my forearm and as big around as the neck of my fiddle. Brushing dirt and a sticky candy-wrapper from it, she gave it a quick polish on the sleeve of her dress and stuffed it away in her shoulder-bag. Then she looked up at me.

My question died stillborn in my throat under the sudden scrutiny of those small dark eyes. She looked right through me—not the drifting, unfocused gaze of so many of the street people, but a cold far-off seeing that weighed my presence, dismissed it, and gazed further off at something far more important.

I stood back as she rose easily to her feet. That was when I realized how graceful she was. She moved down the sidewalk as daintily as a doe, as though her bulk was filled with helium, rather than flesh, and weighed nothing. I watched her until she reached the far end of the street, turned her own corner and then, just like Ellie, was gone as well.

I ended up giving Ellie's sandwich to Johnny Rew, an old wino who's taught me a fiddle tune or two, the odd time I've run into him sober.

I started to see the Bone Woman everywhere after that day. I wasn't sure if she was just new to town, or if it was one of those cases where you see something or someone you've never noticed before and after that you see them all the time. Everybody I talked to about her seemed to know her, but no one was quite sure how long she'd been in the city, or where she lived, or even her name.

I still wasn't calling her the Bone Woman, though I knew by then that bones was all she collected. Old bones, found bones, rattling around together in her shoulder-bag until she went off at the end of the day and showed up the next morning, ready to start filling her bag again.

When she wasn't hunting bones, she spent her time with the street's worst cases—people like Ellie that no one else could talk to. She'd get them making things—little pictures or carvings or beadwork, keeping their hands busy. And talking. Someone like Ellie still made no sense to anybody else, but you could tell when she was with the Bone Woman that they were sharing a real dialogue. Which was a good thing, I suppose, but I couldn't shake the feeling that there was something more going on, something if not exactly sinister, then still strange.

It was the bones, I suppose. There were so many. How could she keep finding them the way she did? And what did she do with them?

My brother Christy collects urban legends, the way the Bone Woman collects her bones, rooting them out where you'd never think they could be. But when I told him about her, he just shrugged.

"Who knows why any of them do anything?" he said.

Christy doesn't live on the streets, for all that he haunts them. He's just an observer—always has been, ever since we were kids. To him, the street people can be pretty well evenly divided between the sad cases and the crazies. Their stories are too human for him.

"Some of these are big," I told him. "The size of a human thighbone."

"So point her out to the cops."

"And tell them what?"

A smile touched his lips with just enough superiority in it to get under my skin. He's always been able to do that. Usually, it makes me do something I regret later which I sometimes think is half his intention. It's not that he wants to see me hurt. It's just part and parcel of that air of authority that all older siblings seem to wear. You know, a raised eyebrow, a way of smiling that says "you have so much to learn, little brother."

"If you really want to know what she does with those bones," he said, "why don't you follow her home and find out?"

"Maybe I will."

It turned out that the Bone Woman had a squat on the roof of an abandoned factory building in the Tombs. She'd built herself some kind of a shed up there—just a leaning, ramshackle affair of cast-off lumber and sheet metal, but it kept out the weather and could easily be heated with a woodstove in the spring and fall. Come winter, she'd need warmer quarters, but the snows were still a month or so away.

I followed her home one afternoon, then came back the next day when she was out to finally put to rest my fear about these bones she was collecting. The thought that had stuck in my mind was that she was taking something away from the street people like Ellie, people who were already at the bottom rung and deserved to be helped, or at least just left alone. I'd gotten this weird idea that the bones were tied up with the last remnants of vitality that someone like Ellie might have, and the Bone Woman was stealing it from them.

What I found was more innocuous, and at the same time creepier, than I'd expected.

The inside of her squat was littered with bones and wire and dog-shaped skeletons that appeared to be made from the two. Bones held in place by wire, half-connected ribs and skulls and limbs. A pack of bone dogs. Some of the figures were almost complete, others were merely suggestions, but everywhere I looked, the half-finished wire-and-bone skeletons sat or stood or hung suspended from the ceiling. There had to be more than a dozen in various states of creation.

I stood in the doorway, not willing to venture any further, and just stared at them all. I don't know how long I was there, but finally I turned away and made my way back down through the abandoned building and out onto the street.

So now I knew what she did with the bones. But it didn't tell me how she could find so many of them. Surely that many stray dogs didn't die, their bones scattered the length and breadth of the city like so much autumn residue?

Amy and I had a gig opening for the Kelledys that night. It didn't take me long to set up. I just adjusted my microphone, laid out my fiddle and whistles on a small table to one side, and then kicked my heels while Amy fussed with her pipes and the complicated tangle of electronics that she used to amplify them.

I've heard it said that all Uillean pipers are a little crazy—that they have to be to play an instrument that looks more like what you'd find in the back of a plumber's truck than an instrument—but I think of them as perfectionists. Every one I've ever met spends more time fiddling with their reeds and adjusting the tuning of their various chanters, drones and regulators than would seem humanly possible.

Amy's no exception. After a while I left her there on the stage, with her red hair falling in her face as she poked and prodded at a new reed she'd made for one of her drones, and wandered into the back where the Kelledys were making their own preparations for the show, which consisted of drinking tea and looking beatific. At least that's the way I always think of the two of them. I don't think I've ever met calmer people.

Jilly likes to think of them as mysterious, attributing all kinds of fairy tale traits to them. Meran, she's convinced, with the green highlights in her nut-brown hair and her wise brown eyes, is definitely dryad material—the spirit of an oak tree come to life—while Cerin is some sort of wizard figure, a combination of adept and bard. I think the idea amuses them and they play it up to Jilly. Nothing you can put your finger on, but they seem to get a kick out of spinning a mysterious air about themselves whenever she's around.

I'm far more practical than Jilly—actually, just about anybody's more practical than Jilly, God bless her, but that's another story. I think if you find yourself using the word magic to describe the Kelledys, what you're really talking about is their musical talent. They may seem preternaturally calm off-stage, but as soon as they begin to play, that calmness is transformed into a bonfire of energy. There's enchantment then, burning on stage, but it comes from their instrumental skill.

"Geordie," Meran said after I'd paced back and forth for a few minutes. "You look a little edgy. Have some tea."

I had to smile. If the Kelledys had originated from some mysterious else-where, then I'd lean more towards them having come from a fiddle tune than Jilly's fairy tales.

"When sick is it tea you want?" I said, quoting the title of an old Irish jig that we all knew in common.

Meran returned my smile. "It can't hurt. Here," she added, rummaging around in a bag that was lying by her chair. "Let me see if I have something that'll ease your nervousness."

"I'm not nervous."

"No, of course not," Cerin put in. "Geordie just likes to pace, don't you?"

He was smiling as he spoke, but without a hint of Christy's sometimes annoying demeanor.

"No, really. It's just...."

"Just what?" Meran asked as my voice trailed off.

Well, here was the perfect opportunity to put Jilly's theories to the test, I decided. If the Kelledys were in fact as fey as she made them out to be, then they'd be able to explain this business with the bones, wouldn't they?

So I told them about the fat woman and her bones and what I'd found in her squat. They listened with far more reasonableness than I would have if someone had been telling the story to me—especially when I went on to explain the weird feeling I'd been getting from the whole business.

"It's giving me the creeps," I said, finishing up, "and I can't even say why."

"La Huesera," Cerin said when I was done.

Meran nodded. "The Bone Woman," she said, translating it for me. "It does sound like her."

"So you know her."

"No," Meran said. "It just reminds us of a story we heard when we were playing in Phoenix a few years ago. There was a young Apache man opening for us and he and I started comparing flutes. We got on to one of the Native courting flutes which used to be made from human bone and somehow from there John started telling me about a legend they have in the Southwest about this old fat woman who wanders through the mountains and arroyos, collecting bones from the desert that she brings back to her cave."

"What does she collect them for?"

"To preserve the things that are in danger of being lost to the world," Cerin said.

"I don't get it."

"I'm not sure of the exact details," Cerin went on, "but it had something to do with the spirits of endangered species."

"Giving them a new life," Meran said.

"Or a second chance."

"But there's no desert around here," I said. "What would this Bone Woman being doing up here?"

Meran smiled. "I remember John saying that she's been seen as often riding shotgun in an eighteen-wheeler as walking down a dry wash."

"And besides," Cerin added. "Any place is a desert when there's more going on underground than on the surface."

That described Newford perfectly. And who lived a more hidden life than the street people? They were right in front of us every day, but most people didn't even see them anymore. And who was more deserving of a second chance than someone like Ellie who'd never even gotten a fair first chance?

"Too many of us live desert lives," Cerin said, and I knew just what he meant.

The gig went well. I was a little bemused, but I didn't make any major mistakes. Amy complained that her regulators had sounded too buzzy in the monitors, but that was just Amy. They'd sounded great to me, their counterpointing chords giving the tunes a real punch whenever they came in.

The Kelledys' set was pure magic. Amy and I watched them from the stage wings and felt higher as they took their final bow than we had when the applause had been directed at us.

I begged off getting together with them after the show, regretfully pleading tiredness. I *was* tired, but leaving the theatre, I headed for an abandoned factory in the Tombs instead of home. When I got up on the roof of the building, the moon was full. It looked like a saucer of buttery gold, bathing everything in a warm yellow light. I heard a soft voice on the far side of the roof near the Bone Woman's squat. It wasn't exactly singing, but not chanting either. A murmuring, sliding sound that raised the hairs at the nape of my neck.

I walked a little nearer, staying in the shadows of the cornices, until I could see the Bone Woman. I paused then, laying my fiddlecase quietly on the roof and sliding down so that I was sitting with my back against the cornice.

The Bone Woman had one of her skeleton sculptures set out in front of her and she was singing over it. The dog shape was complete now, all the bones wired in place and gleaming in the moonlight. I couldn't make out the words of her song. Either there were none, or she was using a language I'd never heard before. As I watched, she stood, raising her arms up above the wired skeleton, and her voice grew louder.

The scene was peaceful—soothing, in the same way that the Kelledys' company could be—but eerie as well. The Bone Woman's voice had the cadence of one of the medicine chants I'd heard at a powwow up on the Kickaha rez—the same nasal tones and ringing quality. But that powwow hadn't prepared me for what came next.

At first I wasn't sure that I was really seeing it. The empty spaces between the skeleton's bones seemed to gather volume and fill out, as though flesh were forming on the bones. Then there was fur, highlit by the moonlight, and I couldn't deny it any more. I saw a bewhiskered muzzle lift skyward, ears twitch, a tail curl up, thick-haired and strong. The powerful chest began to move rhythmically, at first in time to the Bone Woman's song, then breathing of its own accord.

The Bone Woman hadn't been making dogs in her squat, I realized as I watched the miraculous change occur. She'd been making wolves.

The newly animated creature's eyes snapped open and it leapt up, running to the edge of the roof. There it stood with its forelegs on the cornice. Arcing its neck, the wolf pointed its nose at the moon and howled.

I sat there, already stunned, but the transformation still wasn't complete. As the wolf howled, it began to change again. Fur to human skin. Lupine shape, to that of a young woman. Howl to merry laughter. And as she turned, I recognized her features.

"Ellie," I breathed.

She still had the same horsy-features, the same skinny body, all bones and angles, but she was beautiful. She blazed with the fire of a spirit that had never been hurt, never been abused, never been degraded. She gave me a radiant smile and then leapt from the edge of the roof.

I held my breath, but she didn't fall. She walked out across the city's skyline, out across the urban desert of rooftops and chimneys, off and away, running now, laughter trailing behind her until she was swallowed by the horizon.

I stared out at the night sky long after she had disappeared, then slowly stood up and walked across the roof to where the Bone Woman was sitting outside the door of her squat. She tracked my approach, but there was neither welcome nor dismissal in those small dark eyes. It was like the first time I'd come up to her; as far as she was concerned, I wasn't there at all.

"How did you do that?" I asked.

She looked through, past me.

"Can you teach me that song? I want to help, too."

Still no response.

"Why won't you *talk* to me?"

Finally her gaze focused on me.

"You don't have their need," she said.

Her voice was thick with an accent I couldn't place. I waited for her to go on, to explain what she meant, but once again, she ignored me. The pinpoints of black that passed for eyes in that round moon face looked away into a place where I didn't belong.

Finally, I did the only thing left for me to do. I collected my fiddlecase and went on home.

Some things haven't changed. Ellie's still living on the streets and I still share my lunch with her when I'm down in her part of town. There's nothing the Bone Woman can do to change what this life has done to the Ellie Spinks of the world.

But what I saw that night gives me hope for the next turn of the wheel. I know now that no matter how downtrodden someone like Ellie might be, at least somewhere a piece of her is running free. Somewhere that wild and innocent part of her spirit is being preserved with those of the wolf and the rattlesnake and all the other creatures whose spirit-bones La Huesera collects from the desert—deserts natural, and of our own making.

Spirit-bones. Collected and preserved, nurtured in the belly of the Bone Woman's song, until we learn to welcome them upon their terms, rather than our own.

Author's note: The idea of La Huesera comes from the folklore of the American Southwest. My thanks to Clarissa Pinkola Estés for making me aware of the tale.

The Lincoln Train (1995)

MAUREEN F. McHUGH

MAUREEN McHUGH (b. 1959) began publishing short fiction in the late 1980s and published her first novel, *China Mountain Zhang*, in 1992. It won the Lambda and the James Tiptree, Jr. awards and was a finalist for both the Hugo and the Nebula. She has published three more novels—*Half the Day Is Night*, *Mission Child*, and *Nekropolis*—and two collections of short stories, *Mothers and Other Monsters* and *After the Apocalypse*. In recent years, she has been working on Alternate Reality Game projects, such as *I Love Bees*.

SOLDIERS OF THE G.A.R. stand alongside the tracks. They are General Dodge's soldiers, keeping the tracks maintained for the Lincoln Train. If I stand right, the edges of my bonnet are like blinders and I can't see the soldiers at all. It is a spring evening. At the house the lilacs are blooming. My mother wears a sprig pinned to her dress under her cameo. I can smell it, even in the crush of these people all waiting for the train. I can smell the lilac, and the smell of too many people crowded together, and a faint taste of cinders on the air. I want to go home but that house is not ours anymore. I smooth my black dress. On the train platform we are all in mourning.

The train will take us to St. Louis, from whence we will leave for the Oklahoma territories. They say we will walk, but I don't know how my mother will do that. She has been poorly since the winter of '62. I check my bag with our water and provisions.

"Julia Adelaide," my mother says, "I think we should go home."

"We've come to catch the train," I say, very sharp.

I'm Clara, my sister Julia is eleven years older than me. Julia is married and living in Tennessee. My mother blinks and touches her sprig of lilac uncertainly. If I am not sharp with her, she will keep on it.

I wait. When I was younger I used to try to school my unruly self in Christian charity. God sends us nothing we cannot bear. Now I only try to keep it from my face, try to keep my outer self disciplined. There is a feeling inside me, an anger, that I can't even speak. Something is being bent, like a bow, bending and bending and bending—

"When are we going home?" my mother says.

"Soon," I say because it is easy.

But she won't remember and in a moment she'll ask again. And again and again, through this long long train ride to St. Louis. I am trying to be a Christian daughter, and I remind myself that it is not her fault that the war turned her into an old woman, or that her mind is full of holes and everything new drains out. But it's not my fault either. I don't even try to curb my feelings and I know that they rise up to my face. The only way to be true is to be true from the inside and I am not. I am full of unchristian feelings. My mother's infirmity is her trial, and it is also mine.

I wish I were someone else.

The train comes down the track, chuffing, coming slow. It is an old, badly used thing, but I can see that once it was a model of chaste and beautiful workmanship. Under the dust it is a dark claret in color. It is said that the engine was built to be used by President Lincoln, but since the assassination attempt he is too infirm to travel. People begin to push to the edge of the platform, hauling their bags and worldly goods. I don't know how I will get our valise on. If Zeke could have come I could have at least insured that it was loaded on, but the Negroes are free now and they are not to help. The notice said no family Negroes could come to the station, although I see their faces here and there through the crowd.

The train stops outside the station to take on water.

"Is it your father?" my mother says diffidently. "Do you see him on the train?"

"No, Mother," I say. "We are taking the train."

"Are we going to see your father?" she asks.

It doesn't matter what I say to her, she'll forget it in a few minutes, but I cannot say yes to her. I cannot say that we will see my father even to give her a few moments of joy.

"Are we going to see your father?" she asks again.

"No," I say.

"Where are we going?"

I have carefully explained it all to her and she cried, every time I did. People are pushing down the platform toward the train, and I am trying to decide if I should move my valise toward the front of the platform. Why are they in such a hurry to get on the train? It is taking us all away.

"Where are we going? Julia Adelaide, you will answer me this moment," my mother says, her voice too full of quaver to quite sound like her own.

"I'm Clara," I say. "We're going to St. Louis."

"St. Louis," she says. "We don't need to go to St. Louis. We can't get through the lines, Julia, and I...I am quite indisposed. Let's go back home now, this is foolish."

We cannot go back home. General Dodge has made it clear that if we did not show up at the train platform this morning and get our names checked off the list, he would arrest every man in town, and then he would shoot every tenth man. The town knows to believe him, General Dodge was put in charge of the trains into Washington, and he did the same thing then. He arrested men and held them and every time the train was fired upon he hanged a man.

There is a shout and I can only see the crowd moving like a wave, pouring off the edge of the platform. Everyone is afraid there will not be room. I grab the valise and I grab my mother's arm and pull them both. The valise is so heavy that my fingers hurt, and the weight of our water and food is heavy on my arm. My mother is small and when I put her in bed at night she is all tiny like a child, but now she refuses to move, pulling against me and opening her mouth wide, her mouth pink inside and wet and open in a wail I can just barely hear over the shouting crowd. I don't know if I should let go of the valise to pull her, or for a moment I think of letting go of her, letting someone else get her on the train and finding her later.

A man in the crowd shoves her hard from behind. His face is twisted in wrath. What is he so angry at? My mother falls into me, and the crowd pushes us. I am trying to hold on to the valise, but my gloves are slippery, and I can only hold with my right hand, with my left I am trying to hold up my mother. The crowd is pushing all around us, trying to push us toward the edge of the platform.

The train toots as if it were moving. There is shouting all around us. My mother is fallen against me, her face pressed against my bosom, turned up toward me. She is so frightened. Her face is pressed against me in improper intimacy, as if she were my child. My mother as my child. I am filled with revulsion and horror. The pressure against us begins to lessen. I still have a hold of the valise. We'll be all right. Let the others push around, I'll wait and get the valise on somehow. They won't leave us travel without anything.

My mother's eyes close. Her wrinkled face looks up, the skin under her eyes making little pouches, as if it were a second blind eyelid. Everything is so grotesque. I am having a spell. I wish I could be somewhere where I could get away and close the windows. I have had these spells since they told us that my father was dead, where everything is full of horror and strangeness.

The person behind me is crowding into my back and I want to tell them to give way, but I cannot. People around us are crying out. I cannot see anything but the people pushed against me. People are still pushing, but now they are not pushing toward the side of the platform but toward the front, where the train will be when we are allowed to board.

Wait, I call out but there's no way for me to tell if I've really called out or not. I can't hear anything until the train whistles. The train has moved? They brought the train into the station? I can't tell, not without letting go of my mother and the valise. My mother is being pulled down into this mass. I feel her sliding against me. Her eyes are closed. She is a huge doll, limp in my arms. She is not even trying to hold herself up. She has given up to this moment.

I can't hold on to my mother and the valise. So I let go of the valise.

Oh merciful god.

I do not know how I will get through this moment.

The crowd around me is a thing that presses me and pushes me up, pulls me down. I cannot breathe for the pressure. I see specks in front of my eyes, white sparks, too bright, like metal and like light. My feet aren't under me. I am buoyed by the crowd and my feet are behind me. I am unable to stand, unable to fall. I think my mother is against me, but I can't tell, and in this mass I don't know how she can breathe.

I think I am going to die.

All the noise around me does not seem like noise anymore. It is something else, some element, like water or something, surrounding me and overpowering me.

It is like that for a long time, until finally I have my feet under me, and I'm leaning against people. I feel myself sink, but I can't stop myself. The platform is solid. My whole body feels bruised and roughly used.

My mother is not with me. My mother is a bundle of black on the ground, and I crawl to her. I wish I could say that as I crawl to her I feel concern for her condition, but at this moment I am no more than base animal nature and I crawl to her because she is mine and there is nothing else in the world I can identify as mine. Her skirt is rucked up so that her ankles and calves are showing. Her face is black. At first I think it is something about her clothes, but it is her face, so full of blood that it is black.

People are still getting on the train, but there are people on the platform around us, left behind. And other things. A surprising number of shoes, all badly used. Wraps, too. Bags. Bundles and people.

I try raising her arms above her head, to force breath into her lungs. Her arms are thin, but they don't go the way I want them to. I read in the newspaper that when President Lincoln was shot, he stopped breathing, and his personal physician started him breathing again. But maybe the newspaper was wrong, or maybe it is more complicated than I understand, or maybe it doesn't always work. She doesn't breathe.

I sit on the platform and try to think of what to do next. My head is empty of useful thoughts. Empty of prayers.

"Ma'am?"

It's a soldier of the G.A.R.

"Yes sir?" I say. It is difficult to look up at him, to look up into the sun.

He hunkers down but does not touch her. At least he doesn't touch her. "Do you have anyone staying behind?"

Like cousins or something? Someone who is not "recalcitrant" in their handling of their Negroes? "Not in town," I say.

"Did she worship?" he asks, in his northern way.

"Yes sir," I say, "she did. She was a Methodist, and you should contact the preacher. The Reverend Robert Ewald, sir."

"I'll see to it, ma'am. Now you'll have to get on the train."

"And leave her?" I say.

"Yes ma'am, the train will be leaving. I'm sorry ma'am."

"But I can't," I say.

He takes my elbow and helps me stand. And I let him.

"We are not really recalcitrant," I say. "Where were Zeke and Rachel supposed to go? Were we supposed to throw them out?"

He helps me climb onto the train. People stare at me as I get on, and I realize I must be all in disarray. I stand under all their gazes, trying to get my bonnet on straight and smoothing my dress. I do not know what to do with my eyes or hands.

There are no seats. Will I have to stand until St. Louis? I grab a seat back to hold myself up. It is suddenly warm and everything is distant and I think I am about to faint. My stomach turns. I breathe through my mouth, not even sure that I am holding on to the seat back.

But I don't fall, thank Jesus.

"It's not Lincoln," someone is saying, a man's voice, rich and baritone, and I fasten on the words as a lifeline, drawing myself back to the train car, to the world. "It's Seward. Lincoln no longer has the capacity to govern."

The train smells of bodies and warm sweaty wool. It is a smell that threatens to undo me, so I must concentrate on breathing through my mouth. I breathe in little pants, like a dog. The heat lies against my skin. It is airless.

"Of course Lincoln can no longer govern, but that damned actor made him a saint when he shot him," says a second voice. "And now no one dare oppose him. It doesn't matter if his policies make sense or not."

"You're wrong," says the first. "Seward is governing through him. Lincoln is an imbecile. He can't govern, look at the way he handled the war."

The second snorts. "He won."

"No," says the first, "we *lost*, there is a difference, sir. We lost even though the north never could find a competent general." I know the type of the first one. He's the one who thinks he is brilliant, who always knew what President Davis should have done. If they are looking for a recalcitrant southerner, they have found one.

"Grant was competent. Just not brilliant. Any military man who is not Alexander the Great is going to look inadequate in comparison with General Lee."

"Grant was a drinker," the first one says. "It was his subordinates. They'd been through years of war. They knew what to do."

It is so hot on the train. I wonder how long until the train leaves.

I wonder if the Reverend will write my sister in Tennessee and tell her about our mother. I wish the train were going east toward Tennessee instead of north and west toward St. Louis.

My valise. All I have. It is on the platform. I turn and go to the door. It is closed and I try the handle, but it is too stiff for me. I look around for help.

"It's locked," says a woman in gray. She doesn't look unkind.

"My things, I left them on the platform," I say.

"Oh, honey," she says, "they aren't going to let you back out there. They don't let anyone off the train."

I look out the window but I can't see the valise. I can see some of the soldiers, so I beat on the window. One of them glances up at me, frowning, but then he ignores me.

The train blows that it is going to leave, and I beat harder on the glass. If I could shatter that glass. They don't understand, they would help me if they understood. The train lurches and I stagger. It is out there, somewhere, on that platform. Clothes for my mother and me, blankets, things we will need. Things I will need.

The train pulls out of the station and I feel so terrible I sit down on the floor in all the dirt from people's feet and sob.

The train creeps slowly at first, but then picks up speed. The clack-clack clack-clack rocks me. It is improper, but I allow it to rock me. I am in others' hands now and there is nothing to do but be patient. I am good at that. So it has been all my life. I have tried to be dutiful, but something in me has not bent right, and I have never been able to maintain a Christian frame of mind, but like a chicken in a yard, I have always kept my eyes on the small things. I have tended to what was in front of me, first the house, then my mother. When we could not get sugar, I learned to cook with molasses and honey. Now I sit and let my mind go empty and let the train rock me.

"Child," someone says. "Child."

The woman in gray has been trying to get my attention for a while, but I have been sitting and letting myself be rocked.

"Child," she says again, "would you like some water?"

Yes, I realize, I would. She has a jar and she gives it to me to sip out of. "Thank you," I say. "We brought water, but we lost it in the crush on the platform."

"You have someone with you?" she asks.

"My mother," I say, and start crying again. "She is old, and there was such a press on the platform, and she fell and was trampled."

"What's your name," the woman says.

"Clara Corbett," I say.

"I'm Elizabeth Loudon," the woman says. "And you are welcome to travel with me." There is something about her, a simple pleasantness, that makes me trust her. She is a small woman, with a small nose and eyes as gray as her dress. She is younger than I first thought, maybe only in her thirties? "How old are you? Do you have family?" she asks.

"I am seventeen. I have a sister, Julia. But she doesn't live in Mississippi anymore."

"Where does she live?" the woman asks.

"In Beech Bluff, near Jackson, Tennessee."

She shakes her head. "I don't know it. Is it good country?"

"I think so," I say. "In her letters it sounds like good country. But I haven't seen her for seven years." Of course no one could travel during the war. She has three children in Tennessee. My sister is twenty-eight, almost as old as this woman. It is hard to imagine.

"Were you close?" she asks.

I don't know that we were close. But she is my sister. She is all I have, now. I hope that the Reverend will write her about my mother, but I don't know that he knows where she is. I will have to write her. She will think I should have taken better care.

"Are you traveling alone?"

"My companion is a few seats farther in front. He and I could not find seats together."

Her companion is a man? Not her husband, maybe her brother? But she would say her brother if that's who she meant. A woman traveling with a man. An adventuress, I think. There are stories of women traveling, hoping to find unattached girls like myself. They befriend the young girls and then deliver them to the brothels of New Orleans.

For a moment Elizabeth takes on a sinister cast. But this is a train full of recalcitrant southerners, there is no opportunity to kidnap anyone. Elizabeth is like me, a woman who has lost her home.

It takes the rest of the day and a night to get to St. Louis, and Elizabeth and I talk. It's as if we talk in ciphers, instead of talking about home we talk about gardening, and I can see the garden at home, lazy with bees. She is a quilter. I don't quilt, but I used to do petit point, so we can talk sewing and about how hard it has been to get colors. And we talk about mending and making do, we have all been making do for so long.

When it gets dark, since I have no seat, I stay where I am sitting by the door of the train. I am so tired, but in the darkness all I can think of is my mother's face in the crowd and her hopeless open mouth. I don't want to think of my mother, but I am in a delirium of fatigue, surrounded by the dark and the rumble of the train and the distant murmur of voices. I sleep sitting by the door of the train, fitful and rocked. I have dreams like fever dreams. In my dream I am in a strange house, but it is supposed to be my own house, but nothing is where it should be, and I begin to believe that I have actually entered a stranger's house, and that they'll return and find me here. When I wake up and go back to sleep, I am back in this strange house, looking through things.

I wake before dawn, only a little rested. My shoulders and hips and back all ache from the way I am leaning, but I have no energy to get up. I have no energy to do anything but endure. Elizabeth nods, sometimes awake, sometimes asleep, but neither of us speak.

Finally the train slows. We come in through a town, but the town seems to go on and on. It must be St. Louis. We stop and sit. The sun comes up and heats the car like an oven. There is no movement of the air. There are so many buildings in St. Louis, and so many of them are tall, two stories, that I wonder if they cut off the wind and that is why it's so still. But finally the train lurches and we crawl into the station.

I am one of the first off the train by virtue of my position near the door. A soldier unlocks it and shouts for all of us to disembark, but he need not have bothered for there is a rush. I am borne ahead at its beginning but I can stop at the back of the platform. I am afraid that I have lost Elizabeth, but I see her in the crowd. She is on the arm of a younger man in a bowler. There is something about his air that marks him as different—he is sprightly and apparently fresh even after the long ride.

I almost let them pass, but the prospect of being alone makes me reach out and touch her shoulder.

"There you are," she says.

We join a queue of people waiting to use a trench. The smell is appalling, ammonia acrid and eye-watering. There is a wall to separate the men from the women, but the women are all together. I crouch, trying not to notice anyone and trying to keep my skirts out of the filth. It is so awful. It's worse than anything. I feel so awful.

What if my mother were here? What would I do? I think maybe it was better, maybe it was God's hand. But that is an awful thought, too.

"Child," Elizabeth says when I come out, "what's the matter?"

"It's so awful," I say. I shouldn't cry, but I just want to be home and clean. I want to go to bed and sleep.

She offers me a biscuit.

"You should save your food," I say.

"Don't worry," Elizabeth says, "we have enough."

I shouldn't accept it, but I am so hungry. And when I have a little to eat, I feel a little better.

I try to imagine what the fort will be like where we will be going. Will we have a place to sleep, or will it be barracks? Or worse yet, tents? Although after the night I spent on the train I can't imagine anything that could be worse. I imagine if I have to stay awhile in a tent then I'll make the best of it.

"I think this being in limbo is perhaps worse than anything we can expect at the end," I say to Elizabeth. She smiles.

She introduces her companion, Michael. He is enough like her to be her brother, but I don't think that they are. I am resolved not to ask, if they want to tell me they can.

We are standing together, not saying anything, when there is some commotion farther up the platform. It is a woman, her black dress is like smoke. She is running down the platform, coming toward us. There are all of these people and yet it is as if there is no obstacle for her. "NO NO NO NO, DON'T TOUCH ME! FILTHY HANDS! DON'T LET THEM TOUCH YOU! DON'T GET ON THE TRAINS!"

People are getting out of her way. Where are the soldiers? The fabric of her dress is so threadbare it is rotten and torn at the seams. Her skirt is greasy black and matted and stained. Her face is so thin. "ANIMALS! THERE IS NOTHING OUT THERE! PEOPLE DON'T HAVE FOOD! THERE IS NOTHING THERE BUT INDIANS! THEY SENT US OUT TO SETTLE BUT THERE WAS NOTHING THERE!"

I expect she will run past me but she grabs my arm and stops and looks into my face. She has light eyes, pale eyes in her dark face. She is mad.

"WE WERE ALL STARVING, SO WE WENT TO THE FORT BUT THE FORT HAD NOTHING. YOU WILL ALL STARVE, THE WAY THEY ARE STARVING THE INDIANS! THEY WILL LET US ALL DIE! THEY DON'T CARE!" She is screaming in my face, and her spittle sprays me, warm as her breath. Her hand is all tendons and twigs, but she's so strong I can't escape.

The soldiers grab her and yank her away from me. My arm aches where she was holding it. I can't stand up.

Elizabeth pulls me upright. "Stay close to me," she says and starts to walk the other way down the platform. People are looking up following the screaming woman.

She pulls me along with her. I keep thinking of the woman's hand and wrist turned black with grime. I remember my mother's face was black when she lay on the platform. Black like something rotted.

"Here," Elizabeth says at an old door, painted green but now weathered. The door opens and we pass inside.

"What?" I say. My eyes are accustomed to the morning brightness and I can't see.

"Her name is Clara," Elizabeth says. "She has people in Tennessee."

"Come with me," says another woman. She sounds older. "Step this way. Where are her things?"

I am being kidnapped. Oh merciful God, I'll die. I let out a moan.

"Her things were lost, her mother was killed in a crush on the platform."

The woman in the dark clucks sympathetically. "Poor dear. Does Michael have his passenger yet?"

"In a moment," Elizabeth says. "We were lucky for the commotion."

I am beginning to be able to see. It is a storage room, full of abandoned things. The woman holding my arm is older. There are some broken chairs and a stool. She sits me in the chair. Is Elizabeth some kind of adventuress?

"Who are you?" I ask.

"We are friends," Elizabeth says. "We will help you get to your sister."

I don't believe them. I will end up in New Orleans. Elizabeth is some kind of adventuress.

After a moment the door opens and this time it is Michael with a young man. "This is Andrew," he says.

A man? What do they want with a man? That is what stops me from saying, "Run!" Andrew is blinded by the change in light, and I can see the astonishment working on his face, the way it must be working on mine. "What is this?" he asks.

"You are with Friends," Michael says, and maybe he has said it differently than Elizabeth, or maybe it is just that this time I have had the wit to hear it.

"Quakers?" Andrew says. "Abolitionists?"

Michael smiles, I can see his teeth white in the darkness. "Just Friends," he says.

Abolitionists. Crazy people who steal slaves to set them free. Have they come to kidnap us? We are recalcitrant southerners, I have never heard of Quakers seeking revenge, but everyone knows the Abolitionists are crazy and they are liable to do anything.

"We'll have to wait here until they begin to move people out, it will be evening before we can leave," says the older woman.

I am so frightened, I just want to be home. Maybe I should try to break free and run out to the platform, there are northern soldiers out there. Would they protect me? And then what, go to a fort in Oklahoma?

The older woman asks Michael how they could get past the guards so early and he tells her about the madwoman. A "refugee" he calls her.

"They'll just take her back," Elizabeth says, sighing.

Take her back, do they mean that she really came from Oklahoma? They talk about how bad it will be this winter. Michael says there are Wisconsin Indians re-settled down there, but they've got no food, and they've been starving on government handouts for a couple years. Now there will be more people. They're not prepared for winter.

There can't have been much handout during the war. It was hard enough to feed the armies.

They explain to Andrew and to me that we will sneak out of the train station this evening, after dark. We will spend a day with a Quaker family in St. Louis, and then they will send us on to the next family. And so we will be passed hand to hand, like a bucket in a brigade, until we get to our families.

They call it the underground railroad.

But we are slave owners.

"Wrong is wrong," says Elizabeth. "Some of us can't stand and watch people starve."

"But only two out of the whole train," Andrew says.

Michael sighs.

The old woman nods. "It isn't right."

Elizabeth picked me because my mother died. If my mother had not died, I would be out there, on my way to starve with the rest of them.

I can't help it but I start to cry. I should not profit from my mother's death. I should have kept her safe.

"Hush, now," says Elizabeth. "Hush, you'll be okay."

"It's not right," I whisper. I'm trying not to be loud, we mustn't be discovered.

"What, child?"

"You shouldn't have picked me," I say. But I am crying so hard I don't think they can understand me. Elizabeth strokes my hair and wipes my face. It may be the last time someone will do these things for me. My sister has three children of her own, and she won't need another child. I'll have to work hard to make up my keep.

There are blankets there and we lie down on the hard floor, all except Michael, who sits in a chair and sleeps. I sleep this time with fewer dreams. But when I wake up, although I can't remember what they were, I have the feeling that I have been dreaming restless dreams.

The stars are bright when we finally creep out of the station. A night full of stars. The stars will be the same in Tennessee. The platform is empty, the train and the people are gone. The Lincoln Train has gone back south while we slept, to take more people out of Mississippi.

"Will you come back and save more people?" I ask Elizabeth.

The stars are a banner behind her quiet head. "We will save what we can," she says.

It isn't fair that I was picked. "I want to help," I tell her.

She is silent for a moment. "We only work with our own," she says. There is something in her voice that has not been there before. A sharpness.

"What do you mean?" I ask.

"There are no slavers in our ranks," she says and her voice is cold.

I feel as if I have had a fever, tired, but clear of mind. I have never walked so far and not walked beyond a town. The streets of St. Louis are empty. There are few lights. Far off a woman is singing, and her voice is clear and carries easily in the night. A beautiful voice.

"Elizabeth," Michael says, "she is just a girl."

"She needs to know," Elizabeth says.

"Why did you save me then?" I ask.

"One does not fight evil with evil," Elizabeth says.

"I'm not evil!" I say.

But no one answers.

Maneki Neko (1998)

BRUCE STERLING

BRUCE STERLING (b. 1954) published his fourth novel, *Involution Ocean*, in the mid-1970s, and in the 1980s he was at the forefront of the Cyberpunk movement, both with his own fiction (including his fourth novel, *Islands in the Net*) and as an editor of the fanzine *Cheap Truth* and of the anthology *Mirrorshades*. A remarkably inventive writer, Sterling has gone on to publish eight more novels, including *The Difference Engine* (co-authored with William Gibson), *Heavy Weather*, *Holy Fire*, and *The Zenith Angle*. His inventive skills are at their playful best in "Maneki Neko," which first appeared in Japanese before *F&SF* published it in 1998.

"I CAN'T GO on," his brother said.

Tsuyoshi Shimizu looked thoughtfully into the screen of his pasokon. His older brother's face was shiny with sweat from a late-night drinking bout. "It's only a career," said Tsuyoshi, sitting up on his futon and adjusting his pajamas. "You worry too much."

"All that overtime!" his brother whined. He was making the call from a bar somewhere in Shibuya. In the background, a middle-aged office lady was singing karaoke, badly. "And the examination hells. The manager training programs. The proficiency tests. I never have time to live!"

Tsuyoshi grunted sympathetically. He didn't like these late-night videophone calls, but he felt obliged to listen. His big brother had always been a decent sort, before he had gone through the elite courses at Waseda University, joined a big corporation, and gotten professionally ambitious.

"My back hurts," his brother groused. "I have an ulcer. My hair is going gray. And I know they'll fire me. No matter how loyal you are to the big companies, they have no loyalty to their employees anymore. It's no wonder that I drink."

"You should get married," Tsuyoshi offered.

"I can't find the right girl. Women never understand me." He shuddered. "Tsuyoshi, I'm truly desperate. The market pressures are crushing me. I can't breathe. My life has got to change. I'm thinking of taking the vows. I'm serious! I want to renounce this whole modern world."

Tsuyoshi was alarmed. "You're very drunk, right?"

His brother leaned closer to the screen. "Life in a monastery sounds truly good to me. It's so quiet there. You recite the sutras. You consider your existence. There are rules to follow, and rewards that make sense. It's just the way that Japanese business used to be, back in the good old days."

Tsuyoshi grunted skeptically.

"Last week I went out to a special place in the mountains...Mount Aso," his brother confided. "The monks there, they know about people in trouble, people who are burned out by modern life. The monks protect you from the world. No computers, no phones, no faxes, no e-mail, no overtime, no commuting, nothing at all. It's beautiful, and it's peaceful, and nothing ever happens there. Really, it's like paradise."

"Listen, older brother," Tsuyoshi said, "you're not a religious man by nature. You're a section chief for a big import-export company."

"Well...maybe religion won't work for me. I did think of running away to America. Nothing much ever happens there, either."

Tsuyoshi smiled. "That sounds much better! America is a good vacation spot. A long vacation is just what you need! Besides, the Americans are real friendly since they gave up their handguns."

"But I can't go through with it," his brother wailed. "I just don't dare. I can't just wander away from everything that I know, and trust to the kindness of strangers."

"That always works for me," Tsuyoshi said. "Maybe you should try it."

Tsuyoshi's wife stirred uneasily on the futon. Tsuyoshi lowered his voice. "Sorry, but I have to hang up now. Call me before you do anything rash."

"Don't tell Dad," Tsuyoshi's brother said. "He worries so."

"I won't tell Dad." Tsuyoshi cut the connection and the screen went dark.

Tsuyoshi's wife rolled over, heavily. She was seven months pregnant. She stared at the ceiling, puffing for breath. "Was that another call from your brother?" she said.

"Yeah. The company just gave him another promotion. More responsibilities. He's celebrating."

"That sounds nice," his wife said tactfully.

Next morning, Tsuyoshi slept late. He was self-employed, so he kept his own hours. Tsuyoshi was a video format upgrader by trade. He transferred old videos from obsolete formats into the new high-grade storage media. Doing this properly took a craftsman's eye. Word of Tsuyoshi's skills had gotten out on the network, so he had as much work as he could handle.

At ten a.m., the mailman arrived. Tsuyoshi abandoned his breakfast of raw egg and miso soup, and signed for a shipment of flaking, twentieth-century analog television tapes. The mail also brought a fresh overnight shipment of strawberries, and a homemade jar of pickles.

"Pickles!" his wife enthused. "People are so nice to you when you're pregnant."

"Any idea who sent us that?"

"Just someone on the network."

"Great."

Tsuyoshi booted his mediator, cleaned his superconducting heads and examined the old tapes. Home videos from the 1980s. Someone's grandmother as a child, presumably. There had been a lot of flaking and loss of polarity in the old recording medium.

Tsuyoshi got to work with his desktop fractal detail generator, the image stabilizer, and the interlace algorithms. When he was done, Tsuyoshi's new digital copies would look much sharper, cleaner, and better composed than the original primitive videotape.

Tsuyoshi enjoyed his work. Quite often he came across bits and pieces of videotape that were of archival interest. He would pass the images on to the net. The really big network databases, with their armies of search engines, indexers, and catalogues, had some very arcane interests. The net machines would never pay for data, because the global information networks were noncommercial. But the net machines were very polite, and had excellent net etiquette. They returned a favor for a favor, and since they were machines with excellent, enormous memories, they never forgot a good deed.

Tsuyoshi and his wife had a lunch of ramen with naruto, and she left to go shopping. A shipment arrived by overseas package service. Cute baby clothes from Darwin, Australia. They were in his wife's favorite color, sunshine yellow.

Tsuyoshi finished transferring the first tape to a new crystal disk. Time for a break. He left his apartment, took the elevator and went out to the corner coffeeshop. He ordered a double iced mocha cappuccino and paid with a chargecard.

His pokkecon rang. Tsuyoshi took it from his belt and answered it. "Get one to go," the machine told him.

"Okay," said Tsuyoshi, and hung up. He bought a second coffee, put a lid on it and left the shop.

A man in a business suit was sitting on a park bench near the entrance of Tsuyoshi's building. The man's suit was good, but it looked as if he'd slept in it. He was holding his head in his hands and rocking gently back and forth. He was unshaven and his eyes were red-rimmed.

The pokkecon rang again. "The coffee's for him?" Tsuyoshi said.

"Yes," said the pokkecon. "He needs it."

Tsuyoshi walked up to the lost businessman. The man looked up, flinching warily, as if he were about to be kicked. "What is it?" he said.

"Here," Tsuyoshi said, handing him the cup. "Double iced mocha cappuccino."

The man opened the cup, and smelled it. He looked up in disbelief. "This is my favorite kind of coffee.... Who are you?"

Tsuyoshi lifted his arm and offered a hand signal, his fingers clenched like a cat's paw. The man showed no recognition of the gesture. Tsuyoshi shrugged, and smiled. "It doesn't matter. Sometimes a man really needs a coffee. Now you have a coffee. That's all."

"Well...." The man cautiously sipped his cup, and suddenly smiled. "It's really great. Thanks!"

"You're welcome." Tsuyoshi went home.

His wife arrived from shopping. She had bought new shoes. The pregnancy was making her feet swell. She sat carefully on the couch and sighed.

"Orthopedic shoes are expensive," she said, looking at the yellow pumps. "I hope you don't think they look ugly."

"On you, they look really cute," Tsuyoshi said wisely. He had first met his wife at a video store. She had just used her credit card to buy a disk of primitive black-and-white American anime of the 1950s. The pokkecon had urged him to go up and speak to her on the subject of Felix the Cat. Felix was an early television cartoon star and one of Tsuyoshi's personal favorites.

Tsuyoshi would have been too shy to approach an attractive woman on his own, but no one was a stranger to the net. This fact gave him the confidence to speak to her. Tsuyoshi had soon discovered that the girl was delighted to discuss her deep fondness for cute, antique, animated cats. They'd had lunch together. They'd had a date the next week. They had spent Christmas Eve together in a love hotel. They had a lot in common.

She had come into his life through a little act of grace, a little gift from Felix the Cat's magic bag of tricks. Tsuyoshi had never gotten over feeling grateful for this. Now that he was married and becoming a father, Tsuyoshi Shimizu could feel himself becoming solidly fixed in life. He had a man's role to play now. He knew who he was, and he knew where he stood. Life was good to him.

"You need a haircut, dear," his wife told him.

"Sure."

His wife pulled a gift box out of her shopping bag. "Can you go to the Hotel Daruma, and get your hair cut, and deliver this box for me?"

"What is it?" Tsuyoshi said.

Tsuyoshi's wife opened the little wooden gift box. A maneki neko was nestled inside white foam padding. The smiling ceramic cat held one paw upraised, beckoning for good fortune.

"Don't you have enough of those yet?" he said. "You even have maneki neko underwear."

"It's not for my collection. It's a gift for someone at the Hotel Daruma."

"Oh."

"Some foreign woman gave me this box at the shoestore. She looked American. She couldn't speak Japanese. She had really nice shoes, though...."

"If the network gave you that little cat, then you're the one who should take care of that obligation, dear."

"But dear," she sighed, "my feet hurt so much, and you could do with a haircut anyway, and I have to cook supper, and besides, it's not really a nice maneki neko, it's just cheap tourist souvenir junk. Can't you do it?"

"Oh, all right," Tsuyoshi told her. "Just forward your pokkecon prompts onto my machine, and I'll see what I can do for us."

She smiled. "I knew you would do it. You're really so good to me."

Tsuyoshi left with the little box. He wasn't unhappy to do the errand, as it wasn't always easy to manage his pregnant wife's volatile moods in their small six-tatami apartment. The local neighborhood was good, but he was hoping to find bigger accommodations before the child was born. Maybe a place with a little studio, where he could expand the scope of his work. It was very hard to find decent housing in Tokyo, but word was out on the net. Friends he didn't even know were working every day to help him. If he kept up with the net's obligations, he had every confidence that some day something nice would turn up.

Tsuyoshi went into the local pachinko parlor, where he won half a liter of beer and a train chargecard. He drank the beer, took the new train card and wedged himself into the train. He got out at the Ebisu station, and turned on his pokkecon Tokyo street map to guide his steps. He walked past places called Chocolate Soup, and Freshness Physique, and The Aladdin Mai-Tai Panico Trattoria.

He entered the Hotel Daruma and went to the hotel barber shop, which was called the Daruma Planet Look. "May I help you?" said the receptionist.

"I'm thinking, a shave and a trim," Tsuyoshi said.

"Do you have an appointment with us?"

"Sorry, no." Tsuyoshi offered a hand gesture.

The woman gestured back, a jerky series of cryptic finger movements. Tsuyoshi didn't recognize any of the gestures. She wasn't from his part of the network.

"Oh well, never mind," the receptionist said kindly. "I'll get Nahoko to look after you."

Nahoko was carefully shaving the fine hair from Tsuyoshi's forehead when the pokkecon rang. Tsuyoshi answered it.

"Go to the ladies' room on the fourth floor," the pokkecon told him.

"Sorry, I can't do that. This is Tsuyoshi Shimizu, not Ai Shimizu. Besides, I'm having my hair cut right now."

"Oh, I see," said the machine. "Recalibrating." It hung up.

Nahoko finished his hair. She had done a good job. He looked much better. A man who worked at home had to take special trouble to keep up appearances. The pokkecon rang again.

"Yes?" said Tsuyoshi.

"Buy bay rum aftershave. Take it outside."

"Right." He hung up. "Nahoko, do you have bay rum?"

"Odd you should ask that," said Nahoko. "Hardly anyone asks for bay rum anymore, but our shop happens to keep it in stock."

Tsuyoshi bought the aftershave, then stepped outside the barbershop.

Nothing happened, so he bought a manga comic and waited. Finally a hairy, blond stranger in shorts, a tropical shirt, and sandals approached him. The foreigner was carrying a camera bag and an old-fashioned pokkecon. He looked about sixty years old, and he was very tall.

The man spoke to his pokkecon in English. "Excuse me," said the pokkecon, translating the man's speech into Japanese. "Do you have a bottle of bay rum aftershave?"

"Yes I do." Tsuyoshi handed the bottle over. "Here."

"Thank goodness!" said the man, his words relayed through his machine. "I've asked everyone else in the lobby. Sorry I was late."

"No problem," said Tsuyoshi. "That's a nice pokkecon you have there."

"Well," the man said, "I know it's old and out of style. But I plan to buy a new pokkecon here in Tokyo. I'm told that they sell pokkecons by the basketful in Akihabara electronics market."

"That's right. What kind of translator program are you running? Your translator talks like someone from Osaka."

"Does it sound funny?" the tourist asked anxiously.

"Well, I don't want to complain, but...." Tsuyoshi smiled. "Here, let's trade meishi. I can give you a copy of a brand-new freeware translator."

"That would be wonderful." They pressed buttons and squirted copies of their business cards across the network link.

Tsuyoshi examined his copy of the man's electronic card and saw that his name was Zimmerman. Mr. Zimmerman was from New Zealand. Tsuyoshi activated a transfer program. His modern pokkecon began transferring a new translator onto Zimmerman's machine.

A large American man in a padded suit entered the lobby of the Daruma. The man wore sunglasses, and was sweating visibly in the summer heat. The American looked huge, as if he lifted a lot of weights. Then a Japanese woman followed him. The woman was sharply dressed, with a dark blue dress suit, hat, sunglasses, and an attaché case. She had a haunted look.

Her escort turned and carefully watched the bellhops, who were bringing in a series of bags. The woman walked crisply to the reception desk and began making anxious demands of the clerk.

"I'm a great believer in machine translation," Tsuyoshi said to the tall man from New Zealand. "I really believe that computers help human beings to relate in a much more human way."

"I couldn't agree with you more," said Mr. Zimmerman, through his machine. "I can remember the first time I came to your country, many years ago. I had no portable translator. In fact, I had nothing but a printed phrasebook. I happened to go into a bar, and..."

Zimmerman stopped and gazed alertly at his pokkecon. "Oh dear, I'm getting a screen prompt. I have to go up to my room right away."

"Then I'll come along with you till this software transfer is done," Tsuyoshi said.

"That's very kind of you." They got into the elevator together. Zimmerman punched for the fourth floor. "Anyway, as I was saying, I went into this bar in Roppongi late at night, because I was jetlagged and hoping for something to eat..."

"Yes?"

"And this woman...well, let's just say this woman was hanging out in a foreigner's bar in Roppongi late at night, and she wasn't wearing a whole lot of clothes, and she didn't look like she was any better than she ought to be...."

"Yes, I think I understand you."

"Anyway, this menu they gave me was full of kanji, or katakana, or romanji, or whatever they call those, so I had my phrasebook out, and I was trying very hard to puzzle out these pesky ideograms..." The elevator opened and they stepped into the carpeted hall of the hotel's fourth floor. "So I opened the menu and I pointed to an entree, and I told this girl...." Zimmerman stopped suddenly, and stared at his screen. "Oh dear, something's happening. Just a moment."

Zimmerman carefully studied the instructions on his pokkecon. Then he pulled the bottle of bay rum from the baggy pocket of his shorts, and unscrewed the cap. He stood on tiptoe, stretching to his full height, and carefully poured the contents of the bottle through the iron louvers of a ventilation grate, set high in the top of the wall.

Zimmerman screwed the cap back on neatly, and slipped the empty bottle back in his pocket. Then he examined his pokkecon again. He frowned, and shook it. The screen had frozen. Apparently Tsuyoshi's new translation program had overloaded Zimmerman's old-fashioned operating system. His pokkecon had crashed.

Zimmerman spoke a few defeated sentences in English. Then he smiled, and spread his hands apologetically. He bowed, and went into his room, and shut the door.

The Japanese woman and her burly American escort entered the hall. The man gave Tsuyoshi a hard stare. The woman opened the door with a passcard. Her hands were shaking.

Tsuyoshi's pokkecon rang. "Leave the hall," it told him. "Go downstairs. Get into the elevator with the bellboy."

Tsuyoshi followed instructions.

The bellboy was just entering the elevator with a cart full of the woman's baggage. Tsuyoshi got into the elevator, stepping carefully behind the wheeled metal cart. "What floor, sir?" said the bellboy.

"Eight," Tsuyoshi said, ad-libbing. The bellboy turned and pushed the buttons. He faced forward attentively, his gloved hands folded.

The pokkecon flashed a silent line of text to the screen. "Put the gift box inside her flight bag," it read.

Tsuyoshi located the zippered blue bag at the back of the cart. It was a matter of instants to zip it open, put in the box with the maneki neko, and zip the bag shut again. The bellboy noticed nothing. He left, tugging his cart.

Tsuyoshi got out on the eighth floor, feeling slightly foolish. He wandered down the hall, found a quiet nook by an ice machine and called his wife. "What's going on?" he said.

"Oh, nothing." She smiled. "Your haircut looks nice! Show me the back of your head."

Tsuyoshi held the pokkecon screen behind the nape of his neck.

"They do good work," his wife said with satisfaction. "I hope it didn't cost too much. Are you coming home now?"

"Things are getting a little odd here at the hotel," Tsuyoshi told her. "I may be some time."

His wife frowned. "Well, don't miss supper. We're having bonito."

Tsuyoshi took the elevator back down. It stopped at the fourth floor. The woman's American companion stepped onto the elevator. His nose was running and his eyes were streaming with tears.

"Are you all right?" Tsuyoshi said.

"I don't understand Japanese," the man growled. The elevator doors shut.

The man's cellular phone crackled into life. It emitted a scream of anguish and a burst of agitated female English. The man swore and slammed his hairy fist against the elevator's emergency button. The elevator stopped with a lurch. An alarm bell began ringing.

The man pried the doors open with his large hairy fingers and clambered out into the fourth floor. He then ran headlong down the hall.

The elevator began buzzing in protest, its doors shuddering as if broken. Tsuyoshi climbed hastily from the damaged elevator, and stood there in the hallway. He hesitated a moment. Then he produced his pokkecon and loaded his Japanese-to-English translator. He walked cautiously after the American man.

The door to their suite was open. Tsuyoshi spoke aloud into his pokkecon. "Hello?" he said experimentally. "May I be of help?"

The woman was sitting on the bed. She had just discovered the maneki neko box in her flight bag. She was staring at the little cat in horror.

"Who are you?" she said, in bad Japanese.

Tsuyoshi realized suddenly that she was a Japanese American. Tsuyoshi had met a few Japanese Americans before. They always troubled him. They looked fairly normal from the outside, but their behavior was always bizarre. "I'm just a passing friend," he said. "Something I can do?"

"Grab him, Mitch!" said the woman in English. The American man rushed into the hall and grabbed Tsuyoshi by the arm. His hands were like steel bands.

Tsuyoshi pressed the distress button on his pokkecon.

"Take that computer away from him," the woman ordered in English. Mitch quickly took Tsuyoshi's pokkecon away, and threw it on the bed. He deftly patted Tsuyoshi's clothing, searching for weapons. Then he shoved Tsuyoshi into a chair.

The woman switched back to Japanese. "Sit right there, you. Don't you dare move." She began examining the contents of Tsuyoshi's wallet.

"I beg your pardon?" Tsuyoshi said. His pokkecon was lying on the bed. Lines of red text scrolled up its little screen as it silently issued a series of emergency net alerts.

The woman spoke to her companion in English. Tsuyoshi's pokkecon was still translating faithfully. "Mitch, go call the local police."

Mitch sneezed uncontrollably. Tsuyoshi noticed that the room smelled strongly of bay rum. "I can't talk to the local cops. I can't speak Japanese." Mitch sneezed again.

"Okay, then I'll call the cops. You handcuff this guy. Then go down to the infirmary and get yourself some antihistamines, for Christ's sake."

Mitch pulled a length of plastic whipcord cuff from his coat pocket, and attached Tsuyoshi's right wrist to the head of the bed. He mopped his streaming eyes with a tissue. "I'd better stay with you. If there's a cat in your luggage, then the criminal network already knows we're in Japan. You're in danger."

"Mitch, you may be my bodyguard, but you're breaking out in hives."

"This just isn't supposed to happen," Mitch complained, scratching his neck. "My allergies never interfered with my job before."

"Just leave me here and lock the door," the woman told him. "I'll put a chair against the knob. I'll be all right. You need to look after yourself."

Mitch left the room.

The woman barricaded the door with a chair. Then she called the front desk on the hotel's bedside pasokon. "This is Louise Hashimoto in room 434. I have a gangster in my room. He's an information criminal. Would you call the Tokyo police, please? Tell them to send the organized crime unit. Yes, that's right. Do it. And you should put your hotel security people on full alert. There may be big trouble here. You'd better hurry." She hung up.

Tsuyoshi stared at her in astonishment. "Why are you doing this? What's all this about?"

"So you call yourself Tsuyoshi Shimizu," said the woman, examining his credit cards. She sat on the foot of the bed and stared at him. "You're yakuza of some kind, right?"

"I think you've made a big mistake," Tsuyoshi said.

Louise scowled. "Look, Mr. Shimizu, you're not dealing with some Yankee tourist here. My name is Louise Hashimoto and I'm an assistant federal prosecutor from Providence, Rhode Island, USA." She showed him a magnetic ID card with a gold official seal.

"It's nice to meet someone from the American government," said Tsuyoshi, bowing a bit in his chair. "I'd shake your hand, but it's tied to the bed."

"You can stop with the innocent act right now. I spotted you out in the hall earlier, and in the lobby, too, casing the hotel. How did you know my bodyguard is violently allergic to bay rum? You must have read his medical records."

"Who, me? Never!"

"Ever since I discovered you network people, it's been one big pattern," said Louise. "It's the biggest criminal conspiracy I ever saw. I busted this software pirate in Providence. He had a massive network server and a whole bunch of

AI freeware search engines. We took him in custody, we bagged all his search engines, and catalogs, and indexers…. Later that very same day, these *cats* start showing up."

"Cats?"

Louise lifted the maneki neko, handling it as if it were a live eel. "These little Japanese voodoo cats. Maneki neko, right? They started showing up everywhere I went. There's a china cat in my handbag. There's three china cats at the office. Suddenly they're on display in the windows of every antique store in Providence. My car radio starts making meowing noises at me."

"You *broke* part of the network?" Tsuyoshi said, scandalized. "You took someone's machines away? That's terrible! How could you do such an inhuman thing?"

"You've got a real nerve complaining about that. What about *my* machinery?" Louise held up her fat, eerie-looking American pokkecon. "As soon as I stepped off the airplane at Narita, my PDA was attacked. Thousands and thousands of e-mail messages. All of them pictures of cats. A denial-of-service attack! I can't even communicate with the home office! My PDA's useless!"

"What's a PDA?"

"It's a PDA, my Personal Digital Assistant! Manufactured in Silicon Valley!"

"Well, with a goofy name like that, no wonder our pokkecons won't talk to it."

Louise frowned grimly. "That's right, wise guy. Make jokes about it. You're involved in a malicious software attack on a legal officer of the United States Government. You'll see." She paused, looking him over. "You know, Shimizu, you don't look much like the Italian mafia gangsters I have to deal with, back in Providence."

"I'm not a gangster at all. I never do anyone any harm."

"Oh no?" Louise glowered at him. "Listen, pal, I know a lot more about your set-up, and your kind of people, than you think I do. I've been studying your outfit for a long time now. We computer cops have names for your kind of people. Digital panarchies. Segmented, polycephalous, integrated influence networks. What about all these *free goods and services* you're getting all this time?"

She pointed a finger at him. "Ha! Do you ever pay *taxes* on those? Do you ever *declare* that income and those benefits? All the free shipments from other countries! The little homemade cookies, and the free pens and pencils and bumper stickers, and the used bicycles, and the helpful news about fire sales.... You're a tax evader! You're living through kickbacks! And bribes! And influence peddling! And all kinds of corrupt off-the-books transactions!"

Tsuyoshi blinked. "Look, I don't know anything about all that. I'm just living my life."

"Well, your network gift economy is undermining the lawful, government approved, regulated economy!"

"Well," Tsuyoshi said gently, "maybe my economy is better than your economy."

"Says who?" she scoffed. "Why would anyone think that?"

"It's better because we're *happier* than you are. What's wrong with acts of kindness? Everyone likes gifts. Midsummer gifts. New Years Day gifts. Year-end presents. Wedding presents. Everybody likes those."

"Not the way you Japanese like them. You're totally crazy for gifts."

"What kind of society has no gifts? It's barbaric to have no regard for common human feelings."

Louise bristled. "You're saying I'm barbaric?"

"I don't mean to complain," Tsuyoshi said politely, "but you do have me tied up to your bed."

Louise crossed her arms. "You might as well stop complaining. You'll be in much worse trouble when the local police arrive."

"Then we'll probably be waiting here for quite a while," Tsuyoshi said. "The police move rather slowly, here in Japan. I'm sorry, but we don't have as much crime as you Americans, so our police are not very alert."

The pasokon rang at the side of the bed. Louise answered it. It was Tsuyoshi's wife.

"Could I speak to Tsuyoshi Shimizu please?"

"I'm over here, dear," Tsuyoshi called quickly. "She's kidnapped me! She tied me to the bed!"

"Tied to her *bed*?" His wife's eyes grew wide. "That does it! I'm calling the police!"

Louise quickly hung up the pasokon. "I haven't kidnapped you! I'm only detaining you here until the local authorities can come and arrest you."

"Arrest me for what, exactly?"

Louise thought quickly. "Well, for poisoning my bodyguard by pouring bay rum into the ventilator."

"But I never did that. Anyway, that's not illegal, is it?"

The pasokon rang again. A shining white cat appeared on the screen. It had large, staring, unearthly eyes.

"Let him go," the cat commanded in English.

Louise shrieked and yanked the pasokon's plug from the wall.

Suddenly the lights went out. "Infrastructure attack!" Louise squalled. She rolled quickly under the bed.

The room went gloomy and quiet. The air conditioner had shut off. "I think you can come out," Tsuyoshi said at last, his voice loud in the still room. "It's just a power failure."

"No it isn't," Louise said. She crawled slowly from beneath the bed, and sat on the mattress. Somehow, the darkness had made them more intimate. "I know very well what this is. I'm under attack. I haven't had a moment's peace since I broke that network. Stuff just happens to me now. Bad stuff. Swarms of it. It's never anything you can touch, though. Nothing you can prove in a court of law."

She sighed. "I sit in chairs, and somebody's left a piece of gum there. I get free pizzas, but they're not the kind of pizzas I like. Little kids spit on my sidewalk. Old women in walkers get in front of me whenever I need to hurry."

The shower came on, all by itself. Louise shuddered, but said nothing. Slowly, the darkened, stuffy room began to fill with hot steam.

"My toilets don't flush," Louise said. "My letters get lost in the mail. When I walk by cars, their theft alarms go off. And strangers stare at me. It's always little things. Lots of little tiny things, but they never, ever stop. I'm up against something that is very very big, and very very patient. And it knows all about me. And it's got a million arms and legs. And all those arms and legs are people."

There was the noise of scuffling in the hall. Distant voices, confused shouting.

Suddenly the chair broke under the doorknob. The door burst open violently. Mitch tumbled through, the sunglasses flying from his head. Two hotel security guards were trying to grab him. Shouting incoherently in English, Mitch fell headlong to the floor, kicking and thrashing. The guards lost their hats in the struggle. One tackled Mitch's legs with both his arms, and the other whacked and jabbed him with a baton.

Puffing and grunting with effort, they hauled Mitch out of the room. The darkened room was so full of steam that the harried guards hadn't even noticed Tsuyoshi and Louise.

Louise stared at the broken door. "Why did they do that to him?"

Tsuyoshi scratched his head in embarrassment. "Probably a failure of communication."

"Poor Mitch! They took his gun away at the airport. He had all kinds of technical problems with his passport.... Poor guy, he's never had any luck since he met me."

There was a loud tapping at the window. Louise shrank back in fear. Finally she gathered her courage, and opened the curtains. Daylight flooded the room.

A window-washing rig had been lowered from the roof of the hotel, on cables and pulleys. There were two window-washers in crisp gray uniforms. They waved cheerfully, making little catpaw gestures.

There was a third man with them. It was Tsuyoshi's brother.

One of the washers opened the window with a utility key. Tsuyoshi's brother squirmed into the room. He stood up and carefully adjusted his coat and tie.

"This is my brother," Tsuyoshi explained.

"What are you doing here?" Louise said.

"They always bring in the relatives when there's a hostage situation," Tsuyoshi's brother said. "The police just flew me in by helicopter and landed me on the roof." He looked Louise up and down. "Miss Hashimoto, you just have time to escape."

"What?" she said.

"Look down at the streets," he told her. "See that? You hear them? Crowds are pouring in from all over the city. All kinds of people, everyone with wheels. Street noodle salesmen. Bicycle messengers. Skateboard kids. Takeout delivery guys."

Louise gazed out the window into the streets, and shrieked aloud. "Oh no! A giant swarming mob! They're surrounding me! I'm doomed!"

"You are not doomed," Tsuyoshi's brother told her intently. "Come out the window. Get onto the platform with us. You've got one chance, Louise. It's a place I know, a sacred place in the mountains. No computers there, no phones, nothing." He paused. "It's a sanctuary for people like us. And I know the way."

She gripped his suited arm. "Can I trust you?"

"Look in my eyes," he told her. "Don't you see? Yes, of course you can trust me. We have everything in common."

Louise stepped out the window. She clutched his arm, the wind whipping at her hair. The platform creaked rapidly up and out of sight.

Tsuyoshi stood up from the chair. When he stretched out, tugging at his handcuffed wrist, he was just able to reach his pokkecon with his fingertips. He drew it in, and clutched it to his chest. Then he sat down again, and waited patiently for someone to come and give him freedom.

Winemaster (1999)

Robert Reed

Robert Reed's (b. 1956) novels include *The Leeshore*, *Black Milk*, *Down the Bright Way*, and *An Exaltation of Larks*. His short-fiction output is prodigious; very few writers can rival the number of science-fiction short stories he has published in the past twenty-five years. His stories are often inventive, compelling, and far-reaching, as "Winemaster" demonstrates.

T HE STRANGER PULLED into the Quik Shop outside St. Joe. Nothing was remarkable about him, which was why he caught Blaine's eye. Taller than average, but not much, he was thin in an unfit way, with black hair and a handsome, almost pretty face, fine bones floating beneath skin that didn't often get into the sun. Which meant nothing, of course. A lot of people were staying indoors lately. Blaine watched him climb out of an enormous Buick—a satin black '17 Gibraltar that had seen better days—and after a lazy long stretch, he passed his e-card through the proper slot and inserted the nozzle, filling the Buick's cavernous tank with ten cold gallons of gasoline and corn alcohol.

By then, Blaine had run his plates.

The Buick was registered to a Julian Winemaster from Wichita, Kansas; twenty-nine accompanying photographs showed pretty much the same fellow who stood sixty feet away.

His entire bio was artfully bland, rigorously seamless. Winemaster was an accountant, divorced and forty-four years old, with O negative blood and five neo-enamel fillings imbedded in otherwise perfect teeth, plus a small pink birthmark somewhere on his right buttock. Useless details, Blaine reminded himself, and with that he lifted his gaze, watching the traveler remove the dripping nozzle, then cradling it on the pump with the overdone delicacy of a man ill-at-ease with machinery.

Behind thick fingers, Blaine was smiling.

Winemaster moved with a stiff, road-weary gait, walking into the convenience store and asking, "Ma'am? Where's your restroom, please?"

The clerk ignored him.

It was the men's room that called out, "Over here, sir."

Sitting in one of the hard plastic booths, Blaine had a good view of everything. A pair of militia boys in their brown uniforms were the only others in the store. They'd been gawking at dirty comic books, minding their own business until they heard Winemaster's voice. Politeness had lately become a suspicious behavior. Blaine watched the boys look up and elbow each other, putting their sights on the stranger. And he watched Winemaster's walk, the expression on his pretty frail face, and a myriad of subtleties, trying to decide what he should do, and when, and what he should avoid at all costs.

It was a bright warm summer morning, but there hadn't been twenty cars in the last hour, most of them sporting local plates.

The militia boys blanked their comics and put them on the wrong shelves, then walked out the front door, one saying, "Bye now," as he passed the clerk.

"Sure," the old woman growled, never taking her eyes off a tiny television screen.

The boys might simply be doing their job, which meant they were harmless. But the state militias were full of bullies who'd found a career in the last couple years. There was no sweeter sport than terrorizing the innocent traveler, because of course the genuine refugee was too rare of a prospect to hope for.

Winemaster vanished into the men's room.

The boys approached the black Buick, doing a little dance and showing each other their malicious smiles. Thugs, Blaine decided. Which meant that he had to do something now. Before Winemaster, or whoever he was, came walking out of the toilet.

Blaine climbed out of the tiny booth.

He didn't waste breath on the clerk.

Crossing the greasy pavement, he watched the boys using a police-issue lock pick. The front passenger door opened, and both of them stepped back, trying to keep a safe distance. With equipment that went out of date last spring, one boy probed the interior air, the cultured leather seats, the dashboard and floorboard and even an empty pop can standing in its cradle. "Naw, it's okay," he was saying. "Get on in there."

His partner had a knife. The curled blade was intended for upholstery. Nothing could be learned by ripping apart the seats, but it was a fun game nonetheless.

"Get in there," the first boy repeated.

The second one started to say, "I'm getting in—" But he happened to glance over his shoulder, seeing Blaine coming, and he turned fast, lifting the knife, seriously thinking about slashing the interloper.

Blaine was bigger than some pairs of men.

He was fat, but in a powerful, focused way. And he was quick, grabbing the knife hand and giving a hard squeeze, then flinging the boy against the car's composite body, the knife dropping and Blaine kicking it out of reach, then giving the boy a second shove, harder this time, telling both of them, "That's enough, gentlemen."

"Who the fuck are you—?" they sputtered, in a chorus.

Blaine produced a badge and ID bracelet. "Read these," he suggested coldly. Then he told them, "You're welcome to check me out. But we do that somewhere else. Right now, this man's door is closed and locked, and the three of us are hiding. Understand?"

The boy with the surveillance equipment said, "We're within our rights."

Blaine shut and locked the door for them, saying, "This way. Stay with me."

"One of their nests got hit last night," said the other boy, walking. "We've been checking people all morning!"

"Find any?"

"Not yet—"

"With that old gear, you won't."

"We've caught them before," said the first boy, defending his equipment. His status. "A couple, three different carloads..."

Maybe they did, but that was months ago. Generations ago.

"Is that yours?" asked Blaine. He pointed to a battered Python, saying, "It better be. We're getting inside."

The boys climbed in front. Blaine filled the back seat, sweating from exertion and the car's brutal heat.

"What are we doing?" one of them asked.

"We're waiting. Is that all right with you?"

"I guess."

But his partner couldn't just sit. He turned and glared at Blaine, saying, "You'd better be Federal."

"And if not?" Blaine inquired, without interest.

No appropriate threat came to mind. So the boy simply growled and repeated himself. "You'd just better be. That's all I'm saying."

A moment later, Winemaster strolled out of the store. Nothing in his stance or pace implied worry. He was carrying a can of pop and a red bag of corn nuts. Resting his purchases on the roof, he punched in his code to unlock the driver's door, then gave the area a quick glance. It was the glance of someone who never intended to return here, even for gasoline—a dismissive expression coupled with a tangible sense of relief.

That's when Blaine knew.

When he was suddenly and perfectly sure.

The boys saw nothing incriminating. But the one who'd held the knife was quick to say the obvious: A man with Blaine's credentials could get his hands on the best EM sniffers in the world. "Get them," he said, "and we'll find out what he is!"

But Blaine already felt sure.

"He's going," the other one sputtered. "Look, he's gone—!"

The black car was being driven by a cautious man. Winemaster braked and looked both ways twice before he pulled out onto the access road, accelerating gradually toward I-29, taking no chances even though there was precious little traffic to avoid as he drove north.

"Fuck," said the boys, in one voice.

Using a calm-stick, Blaine touched one of the thick necks; without fuss, the boy slumped forward.

"Hey!" snapped his partner. "What are you doing—?"

"What's best," Blaine whispered afterward. Then he lowered the Python's windows and destroyed its ignition system, leaving the pair asleep in the front seats. And because the moment required justice, he took one of their hands each, shoving them inside the other's pants, then he laid their heads together, in the pose of lovers.

⌐

The other refugees pampered Julian: His cabin wasn't only larger than almost anyone else's, it wore extra shielding to help protect him from malicious high-energy particles. Power and shaping rations didn't apply to him, although he rarely indulged himself, and a platoon of autodocs did nothing but watch over his health. In public, strangers applauded him. In private, he could select almost any woman as a lover. And in bed, in the afterglow of whatever passed for sex at that particular moment, Julian could tell his stories, and his lovers would listen as if enraptured, even if they already knew each story by heart.

No one on board was more ancient than Julian. Even before the attack, he was one of the few residents of the Shawnee Nest who could honestly claim to be DNA-made, his life beginning as a single wet cell inside a cavernous womb, a bloody birth followed by sloppy growth that culminated in a vast and slow and decidedly old-fashioned human being.

Julian was nearly forty when Transmutations became an expensive possibility.

Thrill seekers and the terminally ill were among the first to undergo the process, their primitive bodies and bloated minds consumed by the microchines, the sum total of their selves compressed into tiny robotic bodies meant to duplicate every normal human function.

Being pioneers, they endured heavy losses. Modest errors during the Transmutation meant instant death. Tiny errors meant a pathetic and incurable insanity. The fledging Nests were exposed to heavy nuclei and subtle EM effects, all potentially disastrous. And of course there were the early terrorist attacks, crude and disorganized, but extracting a horrible toll nonetheless.

The survivors were tiny and swift, and wiser, and they were able to streamline the Transmutation, making it more accurate and affordable, and to a degree, routine.

"I was forty-three when I left the other world." Julian told his lover of the moment. He always used those words, framing them with defiance and a hint of bittersweet longing. "It was three days and two hours before the President signed the McGrugger Bill."

That's when Transmutation became illegal in the United States.

His lover did her math, then with a genuine awe said, "That was five hundred and twelve days ago."

A day was worth years inside a Nest.

"Tell me," she whispered. "Why did you do it? Were you bored? Or sick?"

"Don't you know why?" he inquired.

"No," she squeaked.

Julian was famous, but sometimes his life wasn't. And why should the youngsters know his biography by heart?

"I don't want to force you," the woman told him. "If you'd rather not talk about it, I'll understand."

Julian didn't answer immediately.

Instead, he climbed from his bed and crossed the cabin. His kitchenette had created a drink—hydrocarbons mixed with nanochines that were nutritious, appetizing, and pleasantly narcotic. Food and drink were not necessities, but habits, and they were enjoying a renewed popularity. Like any credible Methuselah, Julian was often the model on how best to do archaic oddities.

The woman lay on top of the bed. Her current body was a hologram laid over her mechanical core. It was a traditional body, probably worn for his pleasure; no wings or fins or even more bizarre adornments. As it happened, she had selected a build and complexion not very different from Julian's first wife. A coincidence? Or had she actually done research, and she already knew the answers to her prying questions?

"Sip," he advised, handing her the drink.

Their hands brushed against one another, shaped light touching its equivalent. What each felt was a synthetically generated sensation, basically human, intended to feel like warm, water-filled skin.

The girl obeyed, smiling as she sipped, an audible slurp amusing both of them.

"Here," she said, handing back the glass. "Your turn."

Julian glanced at the far wall. A universal window gave them a live view of the Quik Shop, the image supplied by one of the multitude of cameras hidden on the Buick's exterior. What held his interest was the old muscle car, a Python with smoked glass windows. When he first saw that car, three heads were visible. Now two of the heads had gradually dropped out of sight, with the remaining man still sitting in back, big eyes opened wide, making no attempt to hide his interest in the Buick's driver.

No one knew who the fat man was, or what he knew, much less what his intentions might be. His presence had been a complete surprise, and what he had done with those militia members, pulling them back as he did as well as the rest of it, had left the refugees more startled than grateful, and more scared than any time since leaving the Nest.

Julian had gone to that store with the intent of suffering a clumsy, even violent interrogation. A militia encounter was meant to give them authenticity. And more importantly, to give Julian experience—precious and sobering firsthand experience with the much-changed world around them.

A world that he hadn't visited for more than a millennium, Nest-time.

Since he last looked, nothing of substance had changed at that ugly store. And probably nothing would change for a long while. One lesson that no refugee needed, much less craved, was that when dealing with that other realm, nothing helped as much as patience.

Taking a long, slow sip of their drink, he looked back at the woman— twenty days old; a virtual child—and without a shred of patience, she said, "You were sick, weren't you? I heard someone saying that's why you agreed to be Transmutated...five hundred and twelve days ago..."

"No." He offered a shy smile. "And it wasn't because I wanted to live this way, either. To be honest, I've always been conservative. In that world, and this one, too."

She nodded amiably, waiting.

"It was my daughter," he explained. "She was sick. An incurable leukemia." Again he offered the shy smile, adding, "She was nine years old, and terrified. I could save her life by agreeing to her Transmutation, but I couldn't just abandon her to life in the Nest...making her into an orphan, basically..."

"I see," his lover whispered.

Then after a respectful silence, she asked, "Where's your daughter now?"

"Dead."

"Of course..." Not many people were lucky enough to live five hundred days in a Nest; despite shields, a single heavy nucleus could still find you, ravaging your mind, extinguishing your very delicate soul. "How long ago...did it happen...?"

"This morning," he replied. "In the attack."

"Oh...I'm very sorry..."

With the illusion of shoulders, Julian shrugged. Then with his bittersweet voice, he admitted, "It already seems long ago."

Winemaster headed north into Iowa, then did the unexpected, making the sudden turn east when he reached the new Tollway.

Blaine shadowed him. He liked to keep two minutes between the Buick and his little Tokamak, using the FBI's recon network to help monitor the situation. But the network had been compromised in the past, probably more often than anyone knew, which meant that he had to occasionally pay the Tollway a little extra to boost his speed, the gap closing to less than fifteen seconds. Then with the optics in his windshield, he would get a good look at what might or might not be Julian Winemaster—a stiffly erect gentleman who kept one hand on the wheel, even when the AI-managed road was controlling every vehicle's speed and direction, and doing a better job of driving than any human could do.

Iowa was half-beautiful, half-bleak. Some fields looked tended, genetically tailored crops planted in fractal patterns and the occasional robot working carefully, pulling weeds and killing pests as it spider-walked back and forth. But there were long stretches where the farms had been abandoned, wild grasses and the spawn of last year's crops coming up in ragged green masses. Entire neighborhoods had pulled up and gone elsewhere. How many farmers had accepted the Transmutation, in other countries or illegally? Probably only a fraction of them, Blaine knew. Habit-bound and suspicious by nature, they'd never agree to the dismantlement of their bodies, the transplantation of their crusty souls. No, what happened was that farms were simply falling out of production, particularly where the soil was marginal. Yields were still improving in a world where the old-style population was tumbling. If patterns held, most of the arable land would soon return to prairie and forest. And eventually, the entire human species wouldn't fill so much as one of these abandoned farms…leaving the old world entirely empty…if those patterns were allowed to hold, naturally…

Unlike Winemaster, Blaine kept neither hand on the wheel, trusting the AIs to look after him. He spent most of his time watching the news networks, keeping tabs on moods more than facts. What had happened in Kansas was still the big story. By noon, more than twenty groups and individuals had claimed responsibility for the attack. Officially, the Emergency Federal Council deplored any senseless violence—a cliché which implied that sensible violence was an entirely different question. When asked about the government's response, the President's press secretary looked at the world with a stony face, saying, "We're investigating the regrettable incident. But the fact remains, it happened outside our borders. We are observers here. The Shawnee Nest was responsible for its own security, just as every other Nest is responsible…"

Questions came in a flurry. The press secretary pointed to a small, severe-looking man in the front row—a reporter for the Christian Promise organization. "Are we taking any precautions against counterattacks?" the reporter inquired. Then, not waiting for an answer, he added, "There have been reports of activity in the other Nests, inside the United States and elsewhere."

A tense smile was the first reply.

Then the stony face told everyone, "The President and the Council have taken every appropriate precaution. As for any activity in any Nest, I can only say: We have everything perfectly well in hand."

"Is anything left of the Shawnee Nest?" asked a second reporter.

"No." The press secretary was neither sad nor pleased. "Initial evidence is that the entire facility has been sterilized."

A tenacious gray-haired woman—the perpetual symbol of the Canadian Newsweb—called out, "Mr. Secretary…Lennie—!"

"Yes, Cora…"

"How many were killed?"

"I wouldn't know how to answer that question, Cora…"

"Your government estimates an excess of one hundred million. If the entire Nest was sterilized, as you say, then we're talking about more than two-thirds of the current U.S. population."

"Legally," he replied, "we are talking about machines."

"Some of those machines were once your citizens," she mentioned.

The reporter from Christian Promise was standing nearby. He grimaced, then muttered bits of relevant Scripture.

"I don't think this is the time or place to debate what life is or isn't," said the press secretary, juggling things badly.

Cora persisted. "Are you aware of the Canadian position on this tragedy?"

"Like us, they're saddened."

"They've offered sanctuary to any survivors of the blast—"

"Except there are none," he replied, his face pink as granite.

"But if there were? Would you let them move to another Nest in the United States, or perhaps to Canada…?"

There was a pause, brief and electric.

Then with a flat cool voice, the press secretary reported, "The McGrugger Bill is very specific. Nests may exist only in sealed containment facilities, monitored at all times. And should any of the microchines escape, they will be treated as what they are…grave hazards to normal life…and this government will not let them roam at will…!"

Set inside an abandoned salt mine near Kansas City, the Shawnee Nest had been one of the most secure facilities of its kind ever built. Its power came from clean geothermal sources. Lead plates and intricate defense systems stood against natural hazards as well as more human threats. Thousands of government-loyal AIs, positioned in the surrounding salt, did nothing but watch its borders, making certain that none of the microchines could escape. That was why the thought that local terrorists could launch any attack was so ludicrous. To have that attack succeed was simply preposterous. Whoever was responsible for the bomb, it was done with the abeyance of the highest authorities. No sensible soul doubted it. That dirty little nuke had Federal fingerprints on it, and the attack was planned carefully, and its goals were instantly apparent to people large and small.

Julian had no doubts. He had enemies, vast and malicious, and nobody was more entitled to his paranoias.

Just short of Illinois, the Buick made a long-scheduled stop.

Julian took possession of his clone at the last moment. The process was supposed to be routine—a simple matter of slowing his thoughts a thousandfold, then integrating them with his body—but there were always phantom pains and a sick falling sensation. Becoming a bloated watery bag wasn't the strangest part of it. After all, the Nest was designed to mimic this kind of existence. What gnawed at Julian was the gargantuan sense of Time: A half an hour in this realm was nearly a month in his realm. No matter how brief the stop, Julian would feel a little lost when he returned, a step behind the others, and far more emotionally drained than he would ever admit.

By the time the car had stopped, Julian was in full control of the body. His body, he reminded himself. Climbing out into the heat and brilliant sunshine, he felt a purposeful stiffness in his back and the familiar ache running down his right leg. In his past life, he was plagued by sciatica pains. It was one of many ailments that he hadn't missed after his Transmutation. And it was just another detail that someone had thought to include, forcing him to wince and stretch, showing the watching world that he was their flavor of mortal.

Suddenly another old pain began to call to Julian.

Hunger.

His duty was to fill the tank, then do everything expected of a road-weary driver. The rest area was surrounded by the Tollway, gas pumps surrounding a fast food/playground complex. Built to handle tens of thousands of people daily, the facility had suffered with the civil chaos, the militias and the plummeting populations. A few dozen travelers went about their business in near-solitude, and presumably a team of state or Federal agents were lurking nearby, using sensors to scan for those who weren't what they seemed to be.

Without incident, Julian managed the first part of his mission. Then he drove a tiny distance and parked, repeating his stiff climb out of the car, entering the restaurant and steering straight for the restroom.

He was alone, thankfully.

The diagnostic urinal gently warned him to drink more fluids, then wished him a lovely day.

Taking the advice to heart, Julian ordered a bucket-sized ice tea along with a cultured guinea hen sandwich.

"For here or to go?" asked the automated clerk.

"I'm staying," he replied, believing it would look best.

"Thank you, sir. Have a lovely day."

Julian sat in the back booth, eating slowly and mannerly, scanning the pages of someone's forgotten e-paper. He made a point of lingering over the trite and trivial, concentrating on the comics with their humanized cats and cartoonish people, everyone playing out the same jokes that must have amused him in the very remote past.

"How's it going?"

The voice was slow and wet. Julian blanked the page, looking over his shoulder, betraying nothing as his eyes settled on the familiar wide face. "Fine," he replied, his own voice polite but distant. "Thank you."

"Is it me? Or is it just too damned hot to live out there…?"

"It is hot," Julian conceded.

"Particularly for the likes of me." The man settled onto a plastic chair bolted into the floor with clown heads. His lunch buried his little table: Three sandwiches, a greasy sack of fried cucumbers, and a tall chocolate shake. "It's murder when you're fat. Let me tell you…I've got to be careful in this weather. I don't move fast. I talk softly. I even have to ration my thinking. I mean it! Too many thoughts, and I break out in a killing sweat!"

Julian had prepared for this moment. Yet nothing was happening quite like he or anyone else had expected.

Saying nothing, Julian took a shy bite out of his sandwich.

"You look like a smart guy," said his companion. "Tell me. If the world's getting emptier, like everyone says, why am I still getting poorer?"

"Excuse me?"

"That's the way it feels, at least." The man was truly fat, his face smooth and youthful, every feature pressed outward by the remnants of countless lunches. "You'd think that with all the smart ones leaving for the Nests...you'd think guys like you and me would do pretty well for ourselves. You know?"

Using every resource, the refugees had found three identities for this man: He was a salesman from St. Joseph, Missouri. Or he was a Federal agent working for the Department of Technology, in its Enforcement division, and his salesman identity was a cover. Or he was a charter member of the Christian Promise organization, using that group's political connections to accomplish its murderous goals.

What does he want? Julian asked himself.

He took another shy bite, wiped his mouth with a napkin, then offered his own question. "Why do you say that...that it's the smart people who are leaving...?"

"That's what studies show," said a booming, unashamed voice. "Half our people are gone, but we've lost ninety percent of our scientists. Eighty percent of our doctors. And almost every last member of Mensa...which between you and me is a good thing, I think...!"

Another bite, and wipe. Then with a genuine firmness, Julian told him, "I don't think we should be talking. We don't know each other."

A huge cackling laugh ended with an abrupt statement:

"That's why we should talk. We're strangers, so where's the harm?"

Suddenly the guinea hen sandwich appeared huge and inedible. Julian set it down and took a gulp of tea.

His companion watched him, apparently captivated.

Julian swallowed, then asked, "What do you do for a living?"

"What I'm good at." He unwrapped a hamburger, then took an enormous bite, leaving a crescent-shaped sandwich and a fine glistening stain around his smile. "Put it this way, Mr. Winemaster. I'm like anyone. I do what I hope is best."

"How do you—?"

"Your name? The same way I know your address, and your social registration number, and your bank balance, too." He took a moment to consume half of the remaining crescent, then while chewing, he choked out the words, "Blaine. My name is. If you'd like to use it."

Each of the man's possible identities used Blaine, either as a first or last name.

Julian wrapped the rest of his sandwich in its insulated paper, watching his hands begin to tremble. He had a pianist's hands in his first life but absolutely no talent for music. When he went through the Transmutation, he'd asked for a better ear and more coordination—both of which were given to him with minimal fuss. Yet he'd never learned how to play, not even after five hundred days. It suddenly seemed like a tragic waste of talent, and with a secret voice, he promised himself to take lessons, starting immediately.

"So, Mr. Winemaster…where are you heading…?"

Julian managed another sip of tea, grimacing at the bitter taste.

"Someplace east, judging by what I can see…"

"Yes," he allowed. Then he added, "Which is none of your business."

Blaine gave a hearty laugh, shoving the last of the burger deep into his gaping mouth. Then he spoke, showing off the masticated meat and tomatoes, telling his new friend, "Maybe you'll need help somewhere up ahead. Just maybe. And if that happens, I want you to think of me."

"You'll help me, will you?"

The food-stuffed grin was practically radiant. "Think of me," he repeated happily. "That's all I'm saying."

For a long while, the refugees spoke and dreamed of nothing but the mysterious Blaine. Which side did he represent? Should they trust him? Or move against him? And if they tried to stop the man, which way was best? Sabotage his car? Drug his next meal? Or would they have to do something genuinely horrible?

But there were no answers, much less a consensus. Blaine continued shadowing them, at a respectful distance; nothing substantial was learned about him; and despite the enormous stakes, the refugees found themselves gradually drifting back into the moment-by-moment business of ordinary life.

Couples and amalgamations of couples were beginning to make babies.

There was a logic: Refugees were dying every few minutes, usually from radiation exposure. The losses weren't critical, but when they reached their new home—the deep cold rock of the Canadian Shield—they would need numbers, a real demographic momentum. And logic always dances with emotion. Babies served as a tonic to the adults. They didn't demand too many resources, and they forced their parents to focus on more managable problems, like building tiny bodies and caring for needy souls.

Even Julian was swayed by fashion.

With one of his oldest women friends, he found himself hovering over a crystalline womb, watching nanochines sculpt their son out of single atoms and tiny electric breaths.

It was only Julian's second child.

As long as his daughter had been alive, he hadn't seen the point in having another. The truth was that it had always disgusted him to know that the children in the Nest were manufactured—there was no other word for it—and he didn't relish being reminded that he was nothing, more or less, than a fancy machine among millions of similar machines.

Julian often dreamed of his dead daughter. Usually she was on board their strange ark, and he would find a note from her, and a cabin number, and he would wake up smiling, feeling certain that he would find her today. Then he would suddenly remember the bomb, and he would start to cry, suffering through the wrenching, damning loss all over again.

Which was ironic, in a fashion.

During the last nineteen months, father and daughter had gradually and inexorably drifted apart. She was very much a child when they came to the Nest, as flexible as her father wasn't, and how many times had Julian lain awake in bed, wondering why he had ever bothered being Transmutated. His daughter didn't need him, plainly. He could have remained behind. Which always led to the same questions: When he was a normal human being, was he genuinely happy? Or was his daughter's illness simply an excuse…a spicy bit of good fortune that offered an escape route…?

When the Nest was destroyed, Julian survived only through more good fortune. He was as far from the epicenter as possible, shielded by the Nest's interior walls and emergency barricades. Yet even then, most of the people near him were killed, an invisible neutron rain scrambling their minds. That same rain had knocked him unconscious just before the firestorm arrived, and if an autodoc hadn't found his limp body, then dragged him into a shelter, he would have been cremated. And of course if the Nest hadn't devised its elaborate escape plan, stockpiling the Buick and cloning equipment outside the Nest, Julian would have had no choice but to remain in the rubble, fighting to survive the next moment, and the next.

But those coincidences happened, making his present life feel like the culmination of some glorious Fate.

The secret truth was that Julian relished his new importance, and he enjoyed the pressures that came with each bathroom break and every stop for gas. If he died now, between missions, others could take his place, leading Winemaster's cloned body through the needed motions…but they wouldn't do as well, Julian could tell himself…a secret part of him wishing that this bizarre, slow-motion chase would never come to an end…

The Buick stayed on the Tollway through northern Illinois, slipping beneath Chicago before skipping across a sliver of Indiana. Julian was integrated with his larger self several times, going through the motions of the stiff, tired, and hungry traveler. Blaine always arrived several minutes later, never approaching his quarry, always finding gas at different pumps, standing outside the restrooms, waiting to show Julian a big smile but never uttering so much as a word in passing.

A little after midnight, the Buick's driver took his hand off the wheel, lay back and fell asleep. Trusting the Tollway's driving was out of character, but with Blaine trailing them and the border approaching, no one was eager to waste time in a motel bed.

At two in the morning, Julian was also asleep, dipping in and out of dreams. Suddenly a hand took him by the shoulder, shaking him, and several voices, urgent and close, said, "We need you, Julian. Now."

In his dreams, a thousand admiring faces were saying, "We need you."

Julian awoke.

His cabin was full of people. His mate had been ushered away, but his unborn child, nearly complete now, floated in his bubble of blackened crystal, oblivious to the nervous air and the tight, crisp voices.

"What's wrong?" Julian asked.

"Everything," they assured.

His universal window showed a live feed from a security camera on the North Dakota-Manitoba border. Department of Technology investigators, backed up by a platoon of heavily armed Marines, were dismantling a Toyota Sunrise. Even at those syrupy speeds, the lasers moved quickly, leaving the vehicle in tiny pieces that were photographed, analyzed, then fed into a state-of-the-art decontamination unit.

"What is this?" Julian sputtered.

But he already knew the answer.

"There was a second group of refugees," said the President, kneeling beside his bed. She was wearing an oversized face—a common fashion, of late—and with a very calm, very grim voice, she admitted, "We weren't the only survivors."

They had kept it a secret, at least from Julian. Which was perfectly reasonable, he reminded himself. What if he had been captured? Under torture, he could have doomed that second lifeboat, and everyone inside it...

"Is my daughter there?" he blurted, uncertain what to hope for.

The President shook her head. "No, Julian."

Yet if two arks existed, couldn't there be a third? And wouldn't the President keep its existence secret from him, too?

"We've been monitoring events," she continued. "It's tragic, what's happening to our friends...but we'll be able to adjust our methods...for when we cross the border..."

He looked at the other oversized faces. "But why do you need me? We won't reach Detroit for hours."

The President looked over her shoulder. "Play the recording."

Suddenly Julian was looking back in time. He saw the Sunrise pull up to the border post, waiting in line to be searched. A pickup truck with Wyoming plates pulled up behind it, and out stepped a preposterously tall man brandishing a badge and a handgun. With an eerie sense of purpose, he strode up to the little car, took aim and fired his full clip through the driver's window. The body behind the wheel jerked and kicked as it was ripped apart. Then the murderer reached in and pulled the corpse out through the shattered glass, shouting at the Tech investigators:

"I've got them! Here! For Christ's sake, help me!"

The image dissolved, the window returning to the real-time, real-speed scene.

To himself, Julian whispered, "No, it can't be..."

The President took his hands in hers, their warmth a comfortable fiction. "We would have shown you this as it was happening, but we weren't sure what it meant."

"But you're sure now?"

"That man followed our people. All the way from Nebraska." She shook her head, admitting, "We don't know everything, no. For security reasons, we rarely spoke with those other survivors—"

"What are we going to do?" Julian growled.

"The only reasonable thing left for us." She smiled in a sad fashion, then warned him, "We're pulling off the Tollway now. You still have a little while to get ready…"

He closed his eyes, saying nothing.

"Not as long as you'd like, I'm sure…but with this sort of thing, maybe it's best to hurry…"

There were no gas pumps or restaurants in the rest area. A small divided parking lot was surrounded by trees and fake log cabin lavatories that in turn were sandwiched between broad lanes of moonlit pavement. The parking lot was empty. The only traffic was a single truck in the westbound freighter lane, half a dozen trailers towed along in its wake. Julian watched the truck pass, then walked into the darkest shadows, and kneeled.

The security cameras were being fed false images—images that were hopefully more convincing than the ludicrous log cabins. Yet even when he knew that he was safe, Julian felt exposed. Vulnerable. The feeling worsened by the moment, becoming a black dread, and by the time the Tokamak pulled to stop, his newborn heart was racing, and his quick damp breath tasted foul.

Blaine parked two slots away from the sleeping Buick. He didn't bother looking through the windows. Instead, guided by intuition or hidden sensor, he strolled toward the men's room, hesitated, then took a few half-steps toward Julian, passing into a patch of moonlight.

Using both hands, Julian lifted his weapon, letting it aim itself at the smooth broad forehead.

"Well," said Blaine, "I see you're thinking about me."

"What do you want?" Julian whispered. Then with a certain clumsiness, he added, "With me."

The man remained silent for a moment, a smile building.

"Who am I?" he asked suddenly. "Ideas? Do you have any?"

Julian gulped a breath, then said, "You work for the government." His voice was testy, pained. "And I don't know why you're following me!"

Blaine didn't offer answers. Instead he warned his audience, "The border is a lot harder to pierce than you think."

"Is it?"

"Humans aren't fools," Blaine reminded him. "After all, they designed the technologies used by the Nests, and they've had just as long as you to improve on old tricks."

"People in the world are getting dumber," said Julian. "You told me that."

"And those same people are very scared, very focused," his opponent countered. "Their borders are a priority to them. You are their top priority. And even if your thought processes are accelerated a thousandfold, they've got AIs who can blister you in any race of intellect. At least for the time being, they can."

Shoot him, an inner voice urged.

Yet Julian did nothing, waiting silently, hoping to be saved from this onerous chore.

"You can't cross into Canada without me," Blaine told him.

"I know what happened..." Julian felt the gun's barrel adjusting itself as his hands grew tired and dropped slightly. "Up in North Dakota...we know all about it..."

It was Blaine's turn to keep silent.

Again, Julian asked, "Who are you? Just tell me that much."

"You haven't guessed it, have you?" The round face seemed genuinely disappointed. "Not even in your wildest dreams..."

"And why help us?" Julian muttered, saying too much.

"Because in the long run, helping you helps me."

"How?"

Silence.

"We don't have any wealth," Julian roared. "Our homes were destroyed. By you, for all I know—"

The man laughed loudly, smirking as he began to turn away. "You've got some time left. Think about the possibilities, and we'll talk again."

Julian tugged on the trigger. Just once.

Eighteen shells pierced the back of Blaine's head, then worked down the wide back, devastating every organ even as the lifeless body crumpled. Even a huge man falls fast, Julian observed. Then he rose, walking on weak legs, and with his own aim, he emptied the rest of his clip into the gore.

It was easy, pumping in those final shots.

What's more, shooting the dead carried an odd, unexpected satisfaction— which was probably the same satisfaction that the terrorists had felt when their tiny bomb destroyed a hundred million soulless machines.

With every refugee watching, Julian cut open the womb with laser shears.

Julian Jr. was born a few seconds after two-thirty a.m., and the audience, desperate for a good celebration, nearly buried the baby with gifts and sweet words. Yet nobody could spoil him like his father could. For the next few hours, Julian pestered his first son with love and praise, working with a manic energy to fill every need, every whim. And his quest to be a perfect father only grew worse. The sun was beginning to show itself; Canada was waiting over the horizon; but Julian was oblivious, hunched over the toddler with sparkling toys in both hands, his never-pretty voice trying to sing a child's song, nothing half as important in this world as making his son giggle and smile…!

They weren't getting past the border. Their enemies were too clever, and too paranoid. Julian could smell the inevitable, but because he didn't know what else to do, he went through the motions of smiling for the President and the public, saying the usual brave words whenever it was demanded of him.

Sometimes Julian took his boy for long rides around the lifeboat.

During one journey, a woman knelt and happily teased the baby, then looked up at the famous man, mentioning in an off-handed way, "We'll get to our new home just in time for him to grow into it."

Those words gnawed at Julian, although he was helpless to explain why.

By then the sun had risen, its brilliant light sweeping across a sleepy border town. Instead of crossing at Detroit, the refugees had abandoned the Tollway, taking an old highway north to Port Huron. It would be easier here, was the logic. The prayer. Gazing out the universal window, Julian looked at the boarded up homes and abandoned businesses, cars parked and forgotten, weeds growing in every yard, every crack. The border cities had lost most of their people in the last year-plus, he recalled. It was too easy and too accepted, this business of crossing into a land where it was still legal to be remade. In another year, most of the United States would look this way, unless the government took more drastic measures such as closing its borders, or worse, invading its wrong-minded neighbors…!

Julian felt a deep chill, shuddering.

That's when he suddenly understood. Everything. And in the next few seconds, after much thought, he knew precisely what he had to do.

Assuming there was still time…

A dozen cars were lined up in front of the customs station. The Buick had slipped in behind a couple on a motorcycle. Only one examination station was open, and every traveler was required to first declare his intentions, then permanently give up his citizenship. It would be a long wait. The driver turned the engine off, watching the Marines and Tech officials at work, everything about them relentlessly professional. Three more cars pulled up behind him, including a Tokamak, and he happened to glance at the rearview screen when Blaine climbed out, walking with a genuine bounce, approaching on the right and rapping on the passenger window with one fat knuckle, then stooping down and smiling through the glass, proving that he had made a remarkable recovery since being murdered.

Julian unlocked the door for him.

With a heavy grunt, Blaine pulled himself in and shut the door, then gave his companion a quick wink.

Julian wasn't surprised. If anything, he was relieved, telling his companion, "I think I know what you are."

"Good," said Blaine. "And what do your friends think?"

"I don't know. I never told them." Julian took the steering wheel in both hands. "I was afraid that if I did, they wouldn't believe me. They'd think I was crazy, and dangerous. And they wouldn't let me come here."

The line was moving, jerking forward one car-length. Julian started the Buick and crept forward, then turned it off again.

With a genuine fondness, Blaine touched him on a shoulder, commenting, "Your friends might pull you back into their world now. Have you thought of that?"

"Sure," said Julian. "But for the next few seconds, they'll be too confused to make any big decisions."

Lake Huron lay on Blaine's left, vast and deeply blue, and he studied the picket boats that dotted the water, bristling with lasers that did nothing but flip back and forth, back and forth, incinerating any flying object that appeared even remotely suspicious.

"So tell me," he asked his companion, "why do you think I'm here?"

Julian turned his body, the cultured leather squeaking beneath him. Gesturing at Port Huron, he said, "If these trends continue, everything's going to look that way soon. Empty. Abandoned. Humans will have almost vanished from this world, which means that perhaps someone else could move in without too much trouble. They'll find houses, and good roads to drive on, and a communication system already in place. Ready-made lives, and practically free for the taking."

"What sort of someone?"

"That's what suddenly occurred to me." Julian took a deep breath, then said, "Humans are making themselves smaller, and faster. But what if something other than humans is doing the same thing? What if there's something in the universe that's huge, and very slow by human standards, but intelligent nonetheless. Maybe it lives in cold places between the stars. Maybe somewhere else. The point is, this other species is undergoing a similar kind of transformation. It's making itself a thousand times smaller, and a thousand times quicker, which puts it roughly equal to this." The frail face was smiling, and he lifted his hands from the wheel. "Flesh and blood, and bone…these are the high-technology materials that build your version of microchines!"

Blaine winked again, saying, "You're probably right. If you'd explained it that way, your little friends would have labeled you insane."

"But am I right?"

There was no reason to answer him directly. "What about me, Mr. Winemaster? How do you look at me?"

"You want to help us." Julian suddenly winced, then shuddered. But he didn't mention it, saying, "I assume that you have different abilities than we do…that you can get us past their sensors—"

"Is something wrong, Mr. Winemaster?"

"My friends…they're trying to take control of this body…"

"Can you deal with them?"

"For another minute. I changed all the control codes." Again, he winced. "You don't want the government aware of you, right? And you're trying to help steer us and them away from war…during this period of transition—"

"The way we see it," Blaine confessed, "the chance of a worldwide cataclysm is just about one in three, and worsening."

Julian nodded, his face contorting in agony. "If I accept your help…?"

"Then I'll need yours." He set a broad hand on Julian's neck. "You've done a remarkable job hiding yourselves. You and your friends are in this car, but my tools can't tell me where. Not without more time, at least. And that's time we don't have…"

Julian stiffened, his clothes instantly soaked with perspiration.

Quietly, quickly, he said, "But if you're really a government agent…here to fool me into telling you…everything…?"

"I'm not," Blaine promised.

A second examination station had just opened; people were maneuvering for position, leaving a gap in front of them.

Julian started his car, pulling forward. "If I do tell you…where we are… they'll think that I've betrayed them…!"

The Buick's anticollision system engaged, bringing them to an abrupt stop.

"Listen," said Blaine. "You've got only a few seconds to decide—"

"I know…"

"Where, Mr. Winemaster? Where?"

"Julian," he said, wincing again. "Julian."

A glint of pride showed in the eyes. "We're not…in the car…" Then the eyes grew enormous, and Julian tried shouting the answer…his mind suddenly losing its grip on that tiny, lovely mouth…

Blaine swung with his right fist, shattering a cheekbone with his first blow, killing the body before the last blow.

By the time the Marines had surrounded the car, its interior was painted with gore, and in horror, the soldiers watched as the madman—he couldn't be anything but insane—calmly rolled down his window and smiled with a blood-rimmed mouth, telling his audience, "I had to kill him. He's Satan."

A hardened lieutenant looked in at the victim, torn open like a sack, and she shivered, moaning aloud for the poor man.

With perfect calm, Blaine declared, "I had to eat his heart. That's how you kill Satan. Don't you know?"

For disobeying orders, the President declared Julian a traitor, and she oversaw his trial and conviction. The entire process took less than a minute. His quarters were remodeled to serve as his prison cell. In the next ten minutes, three separate attempts were made on his life. Not everyone agreed with the court's sentence, it seemed. Which was understandable. Contact with the outside world had been lost the instant Winemaster died. The refugees and their lifeboat were lost in every kind of darkness. At any moment, the Tech specialists would throw them into a decontamination unit, and they would evaporate without warning. And all because they'd entrusted themselves to an old DNA-born human who never really wanted to be Transmuted in the first place, according to at least one of his former lovers…

Ostensibly for security reasons, Julian wasn't permitted visitors.

Not even his young son could be brought to him, nor was he allowed to see so much as a picture of the boy.

Julian spent his waking moments pacing back and forth in the dim light, trying to exhaust himself, then falling into a hard sleep, too tired to dream at all, if he was lucky…

Before the first hour was finished, he had lost all track of time.

After nine full days of relentless isolation, the universe had shriveled until nothing existed but his cell, and him, his memories indistinguishable from fantasies.

On the tenth day, the cell door opened.

A young man stepped in, and with a stranger's voice, he said, "Father."

"Who are you?" asked Julian.

His son didn't answer, giving him the urgent news instead. "Mr. Blaine finally made contact with us, explaining what he is and what's happened so far, and what will happen…!"

Confusion wrestled with a fledging sense of relief.

"He's from between the stars, just like you guessed, Father. And he's been found insane for your murder. Though of course you're not dead. But the government believes there was a Julian Winemaster, and it's holding Blaine in a Detroit hospital, and he's holding us. His metabolism is augmenting our energy production, and when nobody's watching, he'll connect us with the outside world."

Julian couldn't imagine such a wild story: It had to be true!

"When the world is safe, in a year or two, he'll act cured or he'll escape—whatever is necessary—and he'll carry us wherever we want to go."

The old man sat on his bed, suddenly exhausted.

"Where would you like to go, Father?"

"Out that door," Julian managed. Then a wondrous thought took him by surprise, and he grinned, saying, "No, I want to be like Blaine was. I want to live between the stars, to be huge and cold, and slow…

"Not today, maybe…

"But soon…definitely soon…!"

Suicide Coast (1999)

M. JOHN HARRISON

At the start of his career, M. JOHN HARRISON (b. 1945) was part of the New Wave movement in science fiction, and he served in London as the literary editor for *New Worlds* magazine for eight years. Over the course of the next four decades, he published more than a dozen novels, including high-fantasy novels (the long-running Viriconium series); science-fiction novels, such as *The Centauri Device* and *Light*; *Climbers*, a mainstream novel about rock climbers; literary fantasy novels, such as *Signs of Life* and *The Course of the Heart*; and a series of cat-fantasy novels co-written with Jane Johnson under the pen name Gabriel King.

In a recent interview, Harrison says that every genre needs contrarians: "It needs constantly reminding that it isn't the centre of the world." In "Suicide Coast," he takes on the subgenre of Virtual Reality and pushes it to its limits.

FOUR-THIRTY IN the afternoon in a converted warehouse near Mile End underground station. Heavy, persistent summer rain was falling on the roof. Inside, the air was still and humid, dark despite the fluorescent lights. It smelled of sweat, dust, gymnasts' chalk. Twenty-five feet above the thick blue crash-mats, a boy with dreadlocks and baggy knee-length shorts was supporting his entire weight on two fingers of his right hand. The muscles of his upper back, black and shiny with sweat, fanned out exotically with the effort, like the hood of a cobra or the shell of a crab. One leg trailed behind him for balance. He had raised the other so that the knee was almost touching his chin. For two or three minutes he had been trying to get the ball of his foot in the same place as his fingers. Each time he moved, his center of gravity shifted and he had to go back to a resting position. Eventually he said quietly:

"I'm coming off."

We all looked up. It was a slow afternoon in Mile End. Nobody bothers much with training in the middle of summer. Some teenagers were in from the local schools and colleges. A couple of men in their late thirties had sneaked out of a civil engineering contract near Cannon Street. Everyone was tired. Humidity had made the handholds slippery. Despite that, a serious atmosphere prevailed.

"Go on," we encouraged him. "You can do it."

We didn't know him, or one another, from Adam.

"Go on!"

The boy on the wall laughed. He was good but not that good. He didn't want to fall off in front of everyone. An intention tremor moved through his bent leg. Losing patience with himself, he scraped at the foothold with the toe of his boot. He lunged upward. His body pivoted away from the wall and dropped onto the mats, which, absorbing the energy of the fall, made a sound like a badly winded heavyweight boxer. Chalk and dust billowed up. He got to his feet, laughing and shaking his dreadlocks.

"I can never do that."

"You'll get it in the end," I told him. "Me, I'm going to fall off this roof once more then fuck off home. It's too hot in here."

"See you, man."

I had spent most of that winter in London, assembling copy for MAX, a web site that fronted the adventure sports software industry. They were always interested in stuff about cave diving, BASE jumping, snowboarding, hang-gliding, ATB and so on: but they didn't want to know about rock climbing.

"Not enough to buy," my editor said succinctly. "And too obviously skill-based." He leafed through my samples. "The punter needs equipment to invest in. It strengthens his self-image. With the machine parked in his hall, he believes he could disconnect from the software and still do the sport." He tapped a shot of Isobelle Patissier seven hundred feet up some knife-edge arête in Colorado. "Where's the hardware? These are just bodies."

"The boots are pretty high tech."

"Yeah? And how much a pair? Fifty, a hundred and fifty? Mick, we can get them to lay out three grand for the *frame* of an ATB."

He thought for a moment. Then he said: "We might do something with the women."

"The good ones are French."

"Even better."

I gathered the stuff together and put it away.

"I'm off then," I said.

"You still got the 190?"

I nodded.

"Take care in that thing," he said.

"I will."

"Focke-Wulf 190," he said. "Hey."

"It's a Mercedes," I said.

He laughed. He shook his head.

"Focke-Wulf, Mercedes, no one drives themselves anymore," he said. "You mad fucker."

He looked round his office—a dusty metal desk, a couple of posters with the MAX logo, a couple of PCs. He said: "No one comes in here in person anymore. You ever hear of the modem?"

"Once or twice," I said.

"Well they've invented it now."

I looked around too.

"One day," I said, "the poor wankers are going to want back what you stole from them."

"Come on. They pissed it all away long before we arrived."

As I left the office he advised:

"Keep walking the walk, Mick."

I looked at my watch. It was late and the MAX premises were in EC1. But I thought that if I got a move on and cut up through Tottenham, I could go and see a friend of mine. His name was Ed and I had known him since the 1980s.

Back then, I was trying to write a book about people like him. Ed Johnson sounded interesting. He had done everything from roped-access engineering in Telford to harvesting birds' nests for soup in Southeast Asia. But he was hard to pin down. If I was in Birmingham, he was in Exeter. If we were both in London, he had something else to do. In the end it was Moscow Davis who made the introduction.

Moscow was a short, hard, cheerful girl with big feet and bedraggled hair. She was barely out of her teens. She had come from Oldham, I think, originally, and she had an indescribable snuffling accent. She and Ed had worked as steeplejacks together before they both moved down from the north in search of work. They had once been around a lot together. She thought Johnson would enjoy talking to me if I was still interested. I was. The arrangement we made was to be on the lookout for him in one of the Suicide Coast pubs, the Harbour Lights, that Sunday afternoon.

"Sunday afternoons are quiet, so we can have a chat," said Moscow. "Everyone's eating their dinner then."

We had been in the pub for half an hour when Johnson arrived, wearing patched 501s and a dirty T-shirt with a picture of a mole on the front of it. He came over to our table and began kicking morosely at the legs of Moscow's chair. The little finger of his left hand was splinted and wrapped in a wad of bandage.

"This is Ed," Moscow told me, not looking at him.

"Fuck off, Moscow," Ed told her, not looking at me. He scratched his armpit and stared vaguely into the air above Moscow's head. "I want my money back," he said. Neither of them could think of anything to add to this, and after a pause he wandered off.

"He's always like that," Moscow said. "You don't want to pay any attention." Later in the afternoon she said: "You'll get on well with Ed, though. You'll like him. He's a mad bastard."

"You say that about all the boys," I said.

In this case Moscow was right, because I had heard it not just from her, and later I would get proof of it anyway—if you can ever get proof of anything. Everyone said that Ed should be in a straightjacket. In the end, nothing could be arranged. Johnson was in a bad mood, and Moscow had to be up the Coast that week, on Canvey Island, to do some work on one of the cracking-plants there. There was always a lot of that kind of work, oil work, chemical work, on Canvey Island. "I haven't time for him," Moscow explained as she got up to go. "I'll see you later, anyway," she promised.

As soon as she was gone, Ed Johnson came back and sat down in front of me. He grinned. "Ever done anything worth doing in your whole life?" he asked me. "Anything real?"

The MAX editor was right: since coring got popular, the roads had been deserted. I left EC1 and whacked the 190 up through Hackney until I got the Lea Valley reservoirs on my right like a splatter of moonlit verglas. On empty roads the only mistakes that need concern you are your own; every bend becomes a dreamy interrogation of your own technique. Life should be more like that. I made good time. Ed lived just back from Montagu Road, in a quiet street behind the Jewish Cemetery. He shared his flat with a woman in her early thirties whose name was Caitlin. Caitlin had black hair and soft, honest brown eyes. She and I were old friends. We hugged briefly on the doorstep. She looked up and down the street and shivered.

"Come in," she said. "It's cold."

"You should wear a jumper."

"I'll tell him you're here," she said. "Do you want some coffee?"

Caitlin had softened the edges of Ed's life, but less perhaps than either of them had hoped. His taste was still very minimal—white paint, ash floors, one or two items of furniture from Heals. And there was still a competition Klein mounted on the living room wall, its polished aerospace alloys glittering in the halogen lights.

"Espresso," I said.

"I'm not giving you espresso at this time of night. You'll explode."

"It was worth a try."

"Ed!" she called. "Ed! Mick's here!"

He didn't answer.

She shrugged at me, as if to say, "What can I do?" and went into the back room. I heard their voices but not what they were saying. After that she went upstairs. "Go in and see him," she suggested when she came down again three or four minutes later. "I told him you were here." She had pulled a Jigsaw sweater on over her Racing Green shirt and Levi's; and fastened her hair back hastily with a dark brown velvet scrunchy.

"That looks nice," I said. "Do you want me to fetch him out?"

"I doubt he'll come."

The back room was down a narrow corridor. Ed had turned it into a bleak combination of office and storage. The walls were done with one coat of what builders call "obliterating emulsion" and covered with metal shelves. Chipped diving tanks hollow with the ghosts of exotic gases were stacked by the filing cabinet. His BASE chute spilled half out of its pack, yards of cold nylon a vile but exciting rose color—a color which made you want to be hurtling downward face-first screaming with fear until you heard the canopy bang out behind you and you knew you weren't going to die that day (although you might still break both legs). The cheap beige carpet was strewn with high-access mess—hanks of graying static rope; a yellow bucket stuffed with tools; Ed's Petzl stop, harness and knocked-about CPTs. Everything was layered with dust. The radiators were turned off. There was a bed made up in one corner.

Deep in the clutter on the cheap white desk stood a 5-gig Mac with a screen to design-industry specs. It was spraying Ed's face with icy blue light.

"Hi, Ed."

"Hi, Mick."

There was a long silence after that. Ed stared at the screen. I stared at his back. Just when I thought he had forgotten I was there, he said:

"Fuck off and talk to Caitlin a moment."

"I brought us some beer."

"That's great."

"What are you running here?"

"It's a game. I'm running a game, Mick."

Ed had lost weight since I last saw him. Though they retained their distinctive cabled structure, his forearms were a lot thinner. Without releasing him from anything it represented, the yoke of muscle had lifted from his shoulders. I had expected that. But I was surprised by how much flesh had melted off his face, leaving long vertical lines of sinew, fins of bone above the cheeks and at the corners of the jaw. His eyes were a long way back in his head. In a way it suited him. He would have seemed okay—a little tired perhaps; a little burned down, like someone who was working too hard—if it hadn't been for the light from the display. Hunched in his chair with that splashing off him, he looked like a vampire. He looked like a junkie.

I peered over his shoulder.

"You were never into this shit," I said.

He grinned.

"Everyone's into it now. Why not me? Wanking away and pretending it's sex."

"Oh, come on."

He looked down at himself.

"It's better than living," he said.

There was no answer to that.

I went and asked Caitlin, "Has he been doing this long?"

"Not long," she said. "Have some coffee."

We sat in the L-shaped living area drinking decaffeinated Java. The sofa was big enough for Caitlin to curl up in a corner of it like a cat. She had turned the overhead lights off, tucked her bare feet up under her. She was smoking a cigarette. "It's been a bloody awful day," she warned me. "So don't say a word."

She grinned wryly, then we both looked up at the Klein for a minute or two. Some kind of ambient music was issuing faintly from the stereo speakers, full of South American bird calls and bouts of muted drumming. "Is he winning?" she asked.

"He didn't tell me."

"You're lucky. It's all he ever tells me."

"Aren't you worried?" I said.

She smiled.

"He's still using a screen," she said. "He's not plugging in."

"Yet," I said.

"Yet," she agreed equably. "Want more coffee? Or will you do me a favor?"

I put my empty cup on the floor.

"Do you a favor," I said.

"Cut my hair."

I got up and went to her end of the sofa. She turned away from me so I could release her hair from the scrunchy. "Shake it," I said. She shook it. She ran her hands through it. Perfume came up; something I didn't recognize. "It doesn't need much," I said. I switched the overhead light back on and fetched a kitchen chair. "Sit here. No, right in the light. You'll have to take your jumper off."

"The good scissors are in the bathroom," she said.

Cut my hair. She had asked me that before, two or three days after she decided we should split up. I remembered the calm that came over me at the gentle, careful sound of the scissors, the way her hair felt as I lifted it away from the nape of her neck, the tenderness and fear because everything was changing around the two of us forever and somehow this quiet action signaled and blessed that. The shock of these memories made me ask:

"How are you two getting on?"

She lowered her head to help me cut. I felt her smile.

"You and Ed always liked the same kind of girls," she said.

"Yes," I said.

I finished the cut, then lightly kissed the nape of her neck. "There," I said. Beneath the perfume she smelled faintly of hypoallergenic soap and unscented deodorants. "No, Mick," she said softly. "Please." I adjusted the collar of her shirt, let her hair fall back round it. My hand was still on her shoulder. She had to turn her head at an awkward angle to look up at me. Her eyes were wide and full of pain. "Mick." I kissed her mouth and brushed the side of her face with my fingertips. Her arms went round my neck, I felt her settle in the chair. I touched her breasts. They were warm, the cotton shirt was clean and cool. She made a small noise and pulled me closer. Just then, in the back room among the dusty air tanks and disused parachutes, Ed Johnson fell out of his chair and began to thrash about, the back of his head thudding rhythmically on the floor.

Caitlin pushed me away.

"Ed?" she called, from the passage door.

"Help!" cried Ed.

"I'll go," I said.

Caitlin put her arm across the doorway and stared up at me calmly.

"No," she said.

"How can you lift him on your own?"

"This is me and Ed," she said.

"For God's sake!"

"It's late, Mick. I'll let you out, then I'll go and help him."

At the front door I said:

"I think you're mad. Is this happening a lot? You're a fool to let him do this."

"It's his life."

I looked at her. She shrugged.

"Will you be all right?" I said.

When I offered to kiss her goodbye, she turned her face away.

"Fuck off then, both of you," I said.

I knew which game Ed was playing, because I had seen the software wrapper discarded on the desk near his Mac. Its visuals were cheap and schematic, its values self-consciously retro. It was nothing like the stuff we sold off the MAX site, which was quite literally the experience itself, stripped of its consequences. You had to plug in for that: you had to be cored. This was just a game; less a game, even, than a trip. You flew a silvery V-shaped graphic down an endless V-shaped corridor, a notional perspective sometimes bounded by lines of objects, sometimes just by lines, sometimes bounded only by your memory of boundaries. Sometimes the graphic floated and mushed like a moth. Sometimes it traveled in flat vicious arcs at an apparent Mach 5. There were no guns, no opponent. There was no competition. You flew. Sometimes the horizon tilted one way, sometimes the other. You could choose your own music. It was a bleakly minimal experience. But after a minute or two, five at the most, you felt as if you could fly your icon down the perspective forever, to the soundtrack of your own life.

It was quite popular.

It was called *Out There*.

"Rock climbing is theater," I once wrote.

It had all the qualities of theater, I went on, but a theater-in-reverse:

"In obedience to some devious vanished script, the actors abandon the stage and begin to scale the seating arrangements, the balconies and hanging boxes now occupied only by cleaning-women."

"Oh, very deep," said Ed Johnson when he read this. "Shall I tell you what's wrong here? Eh? Shall I tell you?"

"Piss off, Ed."

"If you fall on your face from a hundred feet up, it comes off the front of your head *and you don't get a second go*. Next to that, theater is wank. Theater is flat. Theater is *Suicide Coast*."

Ed hated anywhere flat. "Welcome to the Suicide Coast," he used to say when I first knew him. To start with, that had been because he lived in Canterbury. But it had quickly become his way of describing most places, most experiences. You didn't actually have to be near the sea. Suicide Coast syndrome had caused Ed to do some stupid things in his time. One day, when he and Moscow still worked in roped-access engineering together, they were going up in the lift to the top of some shitty council highrise in Birmingham or Bristol, when suddenly Ed said:

"Do you bet me I can keep the doors open with my head?"

"What?"

"Next floor! When the doors start to close, do you bet me I can stop them with my head?"

It was Monday morning. The lift smelled of piss. They had been hand-ripping mastic out of expansion joints for two weeks, using Stanley knives. Moscow was tired, hung over, weighed down by a collection of CPTs, mastic guns and hundred-foot coils of rope. Her right arm was numb from repeating the same action hour after hour, day after day.

"Fuck off, Ed," she said.

But she knew Ed would do it whether she took the bet or not.

Two or three days after she first introduced me to Ed, Moscow telephoned me. She had got herself a couple of weeks cutting out on Thamesmead Estate. "They don't half work hard, these fuckers," she said. We talked about that for a minute or two, then she asked:

"Well?"

"Well what, Moscow?"

"Ed. Was he what you were looking for, then? Or what?"

I said that though I was impressed I didn't think I would be able to write anything about Ed.

"He's a mad fucker, though, isn't he?"

"Oh he is," I said. "He certainly is."

The way Moscow said "isn't he" made it sound like "innie."

Another thing I once wrote:

"Climbing takes place in a special kind of space, the rules of which are simple. You must be able to see immediately what you have to lose; and you must choose the risk you take."

What do I know?

I know that a life without consequences isn't a life at all. Also, if you want to do something difficult, something real, you can't shirk the pain. What I learned in the old days, from Ed and Moscow, from Gabe King, Justine Townsend and all the others who taught me to climb rock or jump off buildings or stay the right way up in a tube of pitch-dark water two degrees off freezing and two hundred feet under the ground, was that you can't just plug in and be a star: you have to practice. You have to keep loading your fingers until the tendons swell.

So it's back to the Mile End wall, with its few thousand square feet of board and bolt-on holds, its few thousand cubic meters of emphysemic air through which one very bright ray of sun sometimes falls in the middle of the afternoon, illuminating nothing much at all. Back to the sound of the fan heater, the dust-filled Akai radio playing some mournful aggressive thing, and every so often a boy's voice saying softly, "Oh shit," as some sequence or other fails to work out. You go back there, and if you have to fall off the same ceiling move thirty times in an afternoon, that's what you do. The mats give their gusty wheeze, chalk dust flies up, the fan heater above the Monkey House door rattles and chokes and flatlines briefly before puttering on.

"Jesus Christ. I don't know why I do this."

Caitlin telephoned me.

"Come to supper," she said.

"No," I said.

"Mick, why?"

"Because I'm sick of it."

"Sick of what?"

"You. Me. Him. Everything."

"Look," she said, "he's sorry about what happened last time."

"Oh, *he's* sorry."

"We're both sorry, Mick."

"All right, then: I'm sorry, too."

There was a gentle laugh at the other end.

"So you should be."

I went along all the deserted roads and got there at about eight, to find a brand-new motorcycle parked on the pavement outside the house. It was a Kawasaki *Ninja*. Its fairing had been removed, to give it the look of a '60s café racer, but no one was fooled. Even at a glance it appeared too hunched, too short-coupled: too knowing. The remaining plastics shone with their own harsh inner light.

Caitlin met me on the doorstep. She put her hands on my shoulders and kissed me. "Mm," she said. She was wearing white tennis shorts and a soft dark blue sweatshirt.

"We've got to stop meeting like this," I said.

She smiled and pushed me away.

"My hands smell of garlic," she said.

Just as we were going inside, she turned back and nodded at the Kawa.

"That thing," she said.

"It's a motorcycle, Caitlin."

"It's his."

I stared at her.

"Be enthusiastic," she said. "Please."

"But—"

"Please?"

The main course was penne with mushrooms in an olive and tomato sauce. Ed had cooked it, Caitlin said, but she served. Ed pushed his chair over to the table and rubbed his hands. He picked his plate up and passed it under his nose. "Wow!" he said. As we ate, we talked about this and that. The Kawa was behind everything we said, but Ed wouldn't mention it until I did. Caitlin smiled at us both. She shook her head as if to say: "Children! You children!" It was like Christmas, and she was the parent. The three of us could feel Ed's excitement and impatience. He grinned secretively. He glanced up from his food at one or both of us; quickly back down again. Finally, he couldn't hold back any longer.

"What do you think, then?" he said. "What do you think, Mick?"

"I think this is good pasta," I said. "For a cripple."

He grinned and wiped his mouth.

"It's not bad," he said, "is it?"

"I think what I like best is the way you've let the mushrooms take up a touch of sesame oil."

"Have some more. There's plenty."

"That's new to me in Italian food," I said. "Sesame oil."

Ed drank some more beer.

"It was just an idea," he said.

"You children," said Caitlin. She shook her head. She got up and took the plates away. "There's ice cream for pudding," she said over her shoulder just before she disappeared. When I was sure she was occupied in the kitchen I said:

"Nice idea, Ed: a *motor*cycle. What are you going to do with it? Hang it on the wall with the Klein?"

He drank the rest of his beer, opened a new one and poured it thoughtfully into his glass. He watched the bubbles rising through it, then grinned at me as if he had made a decision. He had. In that moment I saw that he was lost, but not what I could do about it.

"Isn't it brilliant? Isn't it just a *fucker*, that bike? I haven't had a bike since I was seventeen. There's a story attached to that."

"Ed—"

"Do you want to hear it or not?"

Caitlin came back in with the ice cream and served it out to us and sat down.

"Tell us, Ed," she said tiredly. "Tell us the story about that."

Ed held onto his glass hard with both hands and stared into it for a long time as if he was trying to see the past there. "I had some ace times on bikes when I was a kid," he said finally: "but they were always someone else's. My old dear—She really hated bikes, my old dear. You know: they were dirty, they were dangerous, she wasn't going to have one in the house. Did that stop me? It did not. I bought one of the first good Ducati 125s in Britain, *but I had to keep it in a coal cellar down the road.*"

"That's really funny, Ed."

"Fuck off, Mick. I'm seventeen, I'm still at school, and I've got this fucking *projectile* stashed in someone's coal cellar. The whole time I had it, the old dear never knew. I'm walking three miles in the piss wet rain every night, dressed to go to the library, then unlocking this thing and *stuffing* it round the back lanes with my best white shortie raincoat ballooning up like a fucking tent."

He looked puzzledly down at his plate.

"What's this? Oh. Ice cream. Ever ridden a bike in a raincoat?" he asked Caitlin.

Caitlin shook her head. She was staring at him with a hypnotized expression; she was breaking wafers into her ice cream.

"Well they were all the rage then," he said.

He added: "The drag's enormous."

"Eat your pudding, Ed," I said. "And stop boasting. How fast would a 125 go in those days? Eighty miles an hour? Eighty-five?"

"They went faster if you ground your teeth, Mick," Ed said. "Do you want to hear the rest?"

"Of course I want to hear it, Ed."

"Walk three miles in the piss-wet rain," said Ed, "to go for a ride on a motorbike, what a joke. But the real joke is this: the fucker had an alloy crank-case. That was a big deal in those days, an alloy crank-case. The first time I dropped it on a bend, it cracked. Oil everywhere. I pushed it back to the coal-house and left it there. You couldn't weld an alloy crank-case worth shit in those days. I had three years' payments left to make on a bunch of scrap."

He grinned at us triumphantly.

"Ask me how long I'd had it," he ordered.

"How long, Mick?"

"Three weeks. I'd had the fucker three weeks."

He began to laugh. Suddenly, his face went so white it looked green. He looked rapidly from side to side, like someone who can't understand where he is. At the same time, he pushed himself up out of the wheelchair until his arms wouldn't straighten any further and he was almost standing up. He tilted his head back until the tendons in his neck stood out. He shouted, "I want to get out of here! Caitlin, I want to get out!" Then his arms buckled and he let his weight go onto his feet and his legs folded up like putty and he fell forward with a gasp, his face in the ice cream and his hands smashing and clutching and scraping at anything they touched on the dinner table until he had bunched the cloth up under him and everything was a sodden mess of food and broken dishes, and he had slipped out of the chair and on to the floor. Then he let himself slump and go quite still.

"Help me," said Caitlin.

We couldn't get him back into the chair. As we tried, his head flopped forward, and I could see quite clearly the bruises and deep, half-healed scabs at the base of his skull, where they had cored his cervical spine for the computer connection. When he initialized *Out There* now, the graphics came up live in his head. No more screen. Only the endless V of the perspective. The endless, effortless dip-and-bank of the viewpoint. What did he see out there? Did he see himself, hunched up on the Kawasaki *Ninja*? Did he see highways, bridges, tunnels, weird motorcycle flights through endless space?

Halfway along the passage, he woke up.

"Caitlin!" he shouted.

"I'm here."

"Caitlin!"

"I'm here, Ed."

"Caitlin, I never did any of that."

"Hush, Ed. Let's get you to bed."

"Listen!" he shouted. "*Listen.*"

He started to thrash about and we had to lay him down where he was. The passage was so narrow his head hit one wall, then the other, with a solid noise. He stared desperately at Caitlin, his face smeared with Ben & Jerry's. "I never could ride a bike," he admitted. "I made all that up."

She bent down and put her arms round his neck.

"I know," she said.

"I made all that up!" he shouted.

"It's all right. It's all right."

We got him into bed in the back room. She wiped the ice cream off his face with a Kleenex. He stared over her shoulder at the wall, rigid with fear and self-loathing. "Hush," she said. "You're all right." That made him cry; him crying made her cry. I didn't know whether to cry or laugh. I sat down and watched them for a moment, then got to my feet. I felt tired.

"It's late," I said. "I think I'll go."

Caitlin followed me out onto the doorstep. It was another cold night. Condensation had beaded on the fuel tank of the Kawasaki, so that it looked like some sort of frosted confection in the streetlight.

"Look," she said, "can you do anything with that?"

I shrugged.

"It's still brand new," I said. I drew a line in the condensation, along the curve of the tank; then another, at an angle to it.

"I could see if the dealer would take it back."

"Thanks."

I laughed.

"Go in now," I advised her. "It's cold."

"Thanks, Mick. Really."

"That's what you always say."

The way Ed got his paraplegia was this. It was a miserable January about four months after Caitlin left me to go and live with him. He was working over in mid-Wales with Moscow Davis. They had landed the inspection contract for three point-blocks owned by the local council; penalty clauses meant they had to complete that month. They lived in a bed-and-breakfast place a mile from the job, coming back so tired in the evening that they just about had time to eat fish and chips and watch *Coronation Street* before they fell asleep with their mouths open. "We were too fucked even to take drugs," Ed admitted afterward, in a kind of wonder. "Can you imagine that?" Their hands were bashed and bleeding from hitting themselves with sample hammers in the freezing rain. At the end of every afternoon the sunset light caught a thin, delicate layer of water-ice that had welded Moscow's hair to her cheek. Ed wasn't just tired, he was missing Caitlin. One Friday he said, "I'm fucked off with this, let's have a weekend at home."

"We agreed we'd have to work weekends," Moscow reminded him. She watched a long string of snot leave her nose, stretch out like spider-silk, then snap and vanish on the wind. "To finish in time," she said.

"Come on, you wanker," Ed said. "Do something real in your life."

"I never wank," said Moscow. "I can't fancy myself."

They got in her 1984 320i with the M-Technic pack, Garrett turbo and extra wide wheels, and while the light died out of a bad afternoon she pushed it eastward through the Cambrians, letting the rear end hang out on corners. She had Lou Reed *Retro* on the CD and her plan was to draw a line straight across the map and connect with the M4 at the Severn Bridge. It was ghostly and fog all the way out of Wales that night, lost sheep coming at you from groups of wet trees and folds in the hills. "Tregaron to Abergwesyn. One of the great back roads!" Moscow shouted over the music, as they passed a single lonely house in the rain, miles away from anywhere, facing south into the rolling moors of mid-Wales.

Ed shouted back: "They can go faster than this, these 320s." So on the next bend she let the rear end hang out an inch too far and they surfed five hundred feet into a ravine below Cefn Coch, with the BMW crumpled up round them like a chocolate wrapper. Just before they went over, the tape had got to "Sweet Jane"—the live version with the applause welling up across the opening chords as if God himself was stepping out on stage. In the bottom of the ravine a shallow stream ran through pressure-metamorphosed Ordovician shale. Ed sat until daylight the next morning, conscious but unable to move, watching the water hurry toward him and listening to Moscow die of a punctured lung in the heavy smell of fuel. It was a long wait. Once or twice she regained consciousness and said: "I'm sorry, Ed."

Once or twice he heard himself reassure her, "No, it was my fault."

At Southwestern Orthopaedic a consultant told him that key motor nerves had been ripped out of his spine.

"Stuff the fuckers back in again then!" he said, in an attempt to impress her.

She smiled.

"That's exactly what we're going to try," she replied. "We'll do a tuck-and-glue and encourage the spinal cord to send new filaments into the old cable channel."

She thought for a moment.

"We'll be working very close to the cord itself," she warned him.

Ed stared at her.

"It was a joke," he said.

For a while it seemed to work. Two months later he could flex the muscles in his upper legs. But nothing more happened; and, worried that a second try would only make the damage worse, they had to leave it.

Mile End Monkey House. Hanging upside down from a painful foot-hook, you chalk your hands meditatively, staring at the sweaty triangular mark your back left on the blue plastic cover of the mat last time you fell on it. Then, reluctantly, feeling your stomach muscles grind as they curl you upright again, you clutch the starting holds and go for the move: reach up: lock out on two fingers: let your left leg swing out to rebalance: strain upward with your right fingertips, and just as you brush the crucial hold, fall off again.

"Jesus Christ. I don't know why I come here."

You come so that next weekend you can get into a Cosworth-engined Merc 190E and drive very fast down the M4 ("No one drives themselves anymore!") to a limestone outcrop high above the Wye Valley. Let go here and you will not land on a blue safety mat in a puff of chalk dust. Instead you will plummet eighty feet straight down until you hit a small ledge, catapult out into the trees, and land a little later face-first among moss-grown boulders flecked with sunshine. Now all the practice is over. Now you are on the route. Your friends look up, shading their eyes against the white glare of the rock. They are wondering if you can make the move. So are you. The only exit from shit creek is to put two fingers of your left hand into a razor-sharp solution pocket, lean away from it to the full extent of your arm, run your feet up in front of you, and, just as you are about to fall off, lunge with your right hand for the good hold above.

At the top of the cliff grows a large yew tree. You can see it very clearly. It has a short horizontal trunk, and contorted limbs perhaps eighteen inches thick curving out over the drop as if they had just that moment stopped moving. When you reach it you will be safe. But at this stage on a climb, the top of anything is an empty hypothesis. You look up: it might as well be the other side of the Atlantic. All that air is burning away below you like a fuse. Suddenly you're moving anyway. Excitement has short-circuited the normal connections between intention and action. Where you look, you go. No effort seems to be involved. It's like falling upward. It's like that moment when you first understood how to swim, or ride a bike. Height and fear have returned you to your childhood. Just as it was then, your duty is only to yourself. Until you get safely down again, contracts, business meetings, household bills, emotional problems will mean nothing.

When you finally reach that yew tree at the top of the climb, you find it full of grown men and women wearing faded shorts and T-shirts. They are all in their forties and fifties. They have all escaped. With their bare brown arms, their hair bleached out by weeks of sunshine, they sit at every fork or junction, legs dangling in the dusty air, like child-pirates out of some storybook of the 1920s: an investment banker from Greenwich, an AIDS counselor from Bow; a designer of French Connection clothes; a publisher's editor. There is a comfortable silence broken by the odd friendly murmur as you arrive, but their eyes are inturned and they would prefer to be alone, staring dreamily out over the valley, the curve of the river, the woods which seem to stretch away to Tintern Abbey and then Wales. This is the other side of excitement, the other pleasure of height: the space without anxiety. The space without anxiety. The space without anxiety. The space without anxiety. The space without anxiety. The space without anxiety. The space without anxiety. The space with—

You are left with this familiar glitch or loop in the MAXware. *Suicide Coast* won't play any farther. Reluctantly, you abandon Mick to his world of sad acts, his faith that reality can be relied upon to scaffold his perceptions. To run him again from the beginning would only make the frailty of that faith more obvious. So you wait until everything has gone black, unplug yourself from the machine, and walk away, unconsciously rolling your shoulders to ease the stiffness, massaging the sore place at the back of your neck. What will you do next? Everything is flat out here. No one drives themselves anymore.

Have Not Have (2001)

GEOFF RYMAN

GEOFF RYMAN (b. 1951) grew up in North America and moved to England in 1973, and most of his fiction is conscious of its setting and its place in the world. His novel *Was* focuses on America (particularly its heartland), while his science-fiction novel *The Child Garden* is set in a semitropical England, and his novel *The King's Last Song* is set in Cambodia, a region that also influenced his novel *The Unconquered Country*.

"Have Not Have" uses a remote area of central Asia as the setting for a conflict between technological change and traditional lifestyles. The story was later incorporated into Ryman's award-winning novel *Air*.

MAE LIVED IN the last village in the world to go on line. After that, everyone else went on Air.

Mae was the village's fashion expert. She advised on makeup, sold cosmetics, and provided good dresses. Every farmer's wife needed at least one good dress. The richer wives, like Mr. Wing's wife Kwan, wanted more than one.

Mae would sketch what was being worn in the capital. She would always add a special touch: a lime green scarf with sequins; or a lacy ruffle with colorful embroidery. A good dress was for display. "We are a happier people and we can wear these gay colors," Mae would advise.

"Yes, that is true," her customer might reply, entranced that fashion expressed their happy culture. "In the photographs, the Japanese women all look so solemn."

"So full of themselves," said Mae, and lowered her head and scowled, and she and her customer would laugh, feeling as sophisticated as anyone in the world.

Mae got her ideas as well as her mascara and lipsticks from her trips to the town. Even in those days, she was aware that she was really a dealer in information. Mae had a mobile phone. The mobile phone was necessary, for the village had only one line telephone, in the tea room. She needed to talk to her suppliers in private, because information shared aloud in the tea room was information that could no longer be sold.

It was a delicate balance. To get into town, she needed to be driven, often by a client. The art then was to screen the client from her real sources.

So Mae took risks. She would take rides by herself with the men, already boozy after the harvest, going down the hill for fun. Sometimes she needed to speak sharply to them, to remind them who she was.

The safest ride was with the village's schoolteacher, Mr. Shen. Teacher Shen only had a pony and trap, so the trip, even with an early rise, took one whole day down and one whole day back. But there was no danger of fashion secrets escaping with Teacher Shen. His interests lay in poetry and the science curriculum. In town, they would visit the ice cream parlor, with its clean tiles, and he would lick his bowl, guiltily, like a child. He was a kindly man, one of their own, whose education was a source of pride for the whole village. He and Mae had known each other longer than they could remember.

Sometimes, however, the ride had to be with someone who was not exactly a friend.

In the April before everything changed there was to be an important wedding.

Seker, whose name meant Sugar, was the daughter of the village's pilgrim to Mecca, their Haj. Seker was marrying into the Atakoloo family, and the wedding was a big event. Mae was to make her dress.

One of Mae's secrets was that she was a very bad seamstress. The wedding dress was being made professionally, and Mae had to get into town and collect it. When Sunni Haseem offered to drive her down in exchange for a fashion expedition, Mae had to agree.

Sunni herself was from an old village family, but her husband Faysal Haseem was from further down the hill. Mr. Haseem was a beefy brute whom even his wife did not like except for his suits and money. He puffed on cigarettes and his tanned fingers were as thick and weathered as the necks of turtles. In the back seat with Mae, Sunni giggled and prodded and gleamed with the thought of visiting town with her friend and confidant who was going to unleash her beauty secrets.

Mae smiled and whispered, promising much. "I hope my source will be present today," she said. "She brings me my special colors, you cannot get them anywhere else. I don't ask where she gets them." Mae lowered her eyes and her voice. "I think her husband...."

A dubious gesture, meaning, that perhaps the goods were stolen, stolen from—who knows?—supplies meant for foreign diplomats? The tips of Mae's fingers rattled once, in provocation, across her client's arm.

The town was called Yeshibozkay, which meant Green Valley. It was now approached through corridors of raw apartment blocks set on beige desert soil. It had a new jail and discos with mirror balls, billboards, illuminated shop signs and Toyota jeeps that belched out blue smoke.

But the town center was as Mae remembered it from childhood. Traditional wooden houses crowded crookedly together, flat-roofed with shutters, shingle-covered gables and tiny fading shop signs. The old market square was still full of peasants selling vegetables laid out on mats. Middle-aged men still played chess outside tiny cafes; youths still prowled in packs.

There was still the public address system. The address system barked out news and music from the top of the electricity poles. Its sounds drifted over the city, announcing public events or new initiatives against drug dealers. It told of progress on the new highway, and boasted of the well-known entertainers who were visiting the town.

Mr. Haseem parked near the market, and the address system seemed to enter Mae's lungs, like cigarette smoke, perfume, or hair spray. She stepped out of the van and breathed it in. The excitement of being in the city trembled in her belly. As much as the bellowing of shoppers, farmers and donkeys; as much as the smell of raw petrol and cut greenery and drains, the address system made her spirits rise. She and her middle-aged client looked on each other and gasped and giggled at themselves.

"Now," Mae said, stroking Sunni's hair, her cheek. "It is time for a complete makeover. Let's really do you up. I cannot do as good work up in the hills."

Mae took her client to Halat's, the same hairdresser as Sunni might have gone to anyway. But Mae was greeted by Halat with cries and smiles and kisses on the cheek. That implied a promise that Mae's client would get special treatment. There was a pretense of consultancy. Mae offered advice, comments, cautions. Careful! she has such delicate skin! Hmm, the hair could use more shaping there. And Halat hummed as if perceiving what had been hidden before and then agreed to give the client what she would otherwise have given. But Sunni's nails were soaking, and she sat back in the center of attention, like a queen.

All of this allowed the hairdresser to charge more. Mae had never pressed her luck and asked for a cut. Something beady in Halat's eyes told her there would be no point. What Mae got out of it was standing, and that would lead to more work later.

With cucumbers over her eyes, Sunni was safely trapped. Mae announced, "I just have a few errands to run. You relax and let all cares fall away." She disappeared before Sunni could protest.

Mae ran to collect the dress. A disabled girl, a very good seamstress called Miss Soo, had opened up a tiny shop of her own.

Miss Soo was grateful for any business, poor thing, skinny as a rail and twisted. After the usual greetings, Miss Soo shifted round and hobbled and dragged her way to the back of the shop to fetch the dress. Her feet hissed sideways across the uneven concrete floor. Poor little thing, Mae thought. How can she sew?

Yet Miss Soo had a boyfriend in the fashion business. Genuinely in the fashion business, far away in the capital city, Balshang. The girl often showed Mae his photograph. It was like a magazine photograph. The boy was very handsome, with a shiny shirt and coiffed-up hair. She kept saying she was saving up money to join him. It was a mystery to Mae what such a boy was doing with a cripple for a girlfriend. Why did he keep contact with her? Publicly Mae would say to friends of the girl: it is the miracle of love, what a good heart he must have. Otherwise she kept her own counsel which was this: you would be very wise not to visit him in Balshang.

The boyfriend sent Miss Soo the patterns of dresses, photographs, magazines, or even whole catalogs. There was one particularly treasured thing; a showcase publication. The cover was like the lid of a box, and it showed in full color the best of the nation's fashion design.

Models so rich and thin they looked like ghosts. They looked half asleep, as if the only place they carried the weight of their wealth was on their eyelids. It was like looking at Western or Japanese women, and yet not. These were their own people, so long-legged, so modern, so ethereal, as if they were made of air.

Mae hated the clothes. They looked like washing-up towels. Oatmeal or gray in one color and without a trace of adornment.

Mae sighed with lament. "Why do these rich women go about in their underwear?"

The girl shuffled back with the dress, past piles of unsold oatmeal cloth.

Miss Soo had a skinny face full of teeth, and she always looked like she was staring ahead in fear. "If you are rich you have no need to try to look rich." Her voice was soft. She made Mae feel like a peasant without meaning to. She made Mae yearn to escape herself, to be someone else, for the child was effortlessly talented, somehow effortlessly in touch with the outside world.

"Ah yes," Mae sighed. "But my clients, you know, they live in the hills." She shared a conspiratorial smile with the girl. "Their taste! Speaking of which, let's have a look at my wedding cake of a dress."

The dress was actually meant to look like a cake, all pink and white sugar icing, except that it kept moving all by itself. White wires with Styrofoam bobbles on the ends were surrounded with clouds of white netting.

"Does it need to be quite so busy?" the girl asked, doubtfully, encouraged too much by Mae's smile.

"I know my clients," replied Mae coolly. This is at least, she thought, a dress that makes some effort. She inspected the work. The needlework was delicious, as if the white cloth were cream that had flowed together. The poor creature could certainly sew, even when she hated the dress.

"That will be fine," said Mae, and made move toward her purse.

"You are so kind!" murmured Miss Soo, bowing slightly.

Like Mae, Miss Soo was of Chinese extraction. That was meant not to make any difference, but somehow it did. Mae and Miss Soo knew what to expect of each other.

"Some tea?" the girl asked. It would be pale, fresh-brewed, not the liquid tar that the native Karsistanis poured from continually boiling kettles.

"It would be delightful, but I do have a customer waiting," explained Mae.

The dress was packed in brown paper and carefully tied so it would not crease. There were farewells, and Mae scurried back to the hairdresser's. Sunni was only just finished, hair spray and scent rising off her like steam.

"This is the dress," said Mae and peeled back part of the paper, to give Halat and Sunni a glimpse of the tulle and Styrofoam.

"Oh!" the women said, as if all that white were clouds, in dreams.

And Halat was paid. There were smiles and nods and compliments and then they left.

Outside the shop, Mae breathed out as though she could now finally speak her mind. "Oh! She is good, that little viper, but you have to watch her, you have to make her work. Did she give you proper attention?"

"Oh, yes, very special attention. I am lucky to have you for a friend," said Sunni. "Let me pay you something for your trouble."

Mae hissed through her teeth. "No, no, I did nothing, I will not hear of it." It was a kind of ritual.

There was no dream in finding Sunni's surly husband. Mr. Haseem was red-faced, half-drunk in a club with unvarnished walls and a television.

"You spend my money," he declared. His eyes were on Mae.

"My friend Mae makes no charges," snapped Sunni.

"She takes something from what they charge you." Mr. Haseem glowered like a thunderstorm.

"She makes them charge me less, not more," replied Sunni, her face going like stone.

The two women exchanged glances. Mae's eyes could say: How can you bear it, a woman of culture like you?

It is my tragedy, came the reply, aching out of the ashamed eyes. So they sat while the husband sobered up and watched television. Mae contemplated the husband's hostility to her, and what might lie behind it. On the screen, the local female newsreader talked: Talents, such people were called. She wore a red dress with a large gold broach. Something had been done to her hair to make it stand up in a sweep before falling away. She was as smoothly groomed as ice. She chattered in a high voice, perky through a battery of tiger's teeth. "She goes to Halat's as well," Mae whispered to Sunni. Weather, maps, shots of the honored President and the full cabinet one by one, making big decisions.

The men in the club chose what movie they wanted. Since the Net, they could do that. It had ruined visits to the town. Before, it used to be that the men were made to sit through something the children or families might also like, so you got everyone together for the watching of the television. The clubs had to be more polite. Now, because of the Net, women hardly saw TV at all and the clubs were full of drinking. The men chose another kung-fu movie. Mae and Sunni endured it, sipping Coca-Cola. It became apparent that Mr. Haseem would not buy them dinner.

Finally, late in the evening, Mr. Haseem loaded himself into the van. Enduring, unstoppable, and quite dangerous, he drove them back up into the mountains, weaving across the middle of the road.

"You make a lot of money out of all this," Mr. Haseem said to Mae.

"I…I make a little something. I try to maintain the standards of the village. I do not want people to see us as peasants. Just because we live on the high road."

Sunni's husband barked out a laugh. "We are peasants!" Then he added, "You do it for the money."

Sunni sighed in embarrassment. And Mae smiled a hard smile to herself in the darkness. You give yourself away, Sunni's-man. You want my husband's land. You want him to be your dependent. And you don't like your wife's money coming to me to prevent it. You want to make both me and my husband your slaves.

It is a strange thing to spend four hours in the dark listening to an engine roar with a man who seeks to destroy you.

In late May, school ended.

There were no fewer than six girls graduating and each one of them needed a new dress. Miss Soo was making two of them; Mae would have to do the others, but she needed to buy the cloth. She needed another trip to Yeshibozkay.

Mr. Wing was going to town to collect a new television set for the village. It was going to be connected to the Net. There was high excitement: graduation, a new television set. Some of the children lined up to wave good-bye to them.

Their village, Kizuldah, was surrounded by high, terraced mountains. The rice fields went up in steps, like a staircase into clouds. There was snow on the very tops year round.

It was a beautiful day, cloudless, but still relatively cool. Kwan, Mr. Wing's wife, was one of Mae's favorite women; she was intelligent, sensible; there was less dissembling with her. Mae enjoyed the drive.

Mr. Wing parked the van in the market square. As Mae reached into the back for her hat, she heard the public address system. The voice of the Talent was squawking.

"…a tremendous advance for culture," the Talent said. "Now the Green Valley is no farther from the center of the world than Paris, Singapore, or Tokyo."

Mae sniffed. "Hmm. Another choice on this fishing net of theirs."

Wing stood outside the van, ramrod straight in his brown and tan town shirt. "I want to hear this," he said, smiling slightly, taking nips of smoke from his cigarette.

Kwan fanned the air. "Your modern wires say that smoking is dangerous. I wish you would follow all this news you hear."

"Ssh!" he insisted.

The bright female voice still enthused. "Previously all such advances left the Valley far behind because of wiring. This advance will be in the air we breathe. Previously all such advances left the Valley behind because of the cost of the new devices needed to receive messages. This new thing will be like Net TV in your head. All you need is the wires in the human mind."

Kwan gathered up her things. "Some nonsense or another," she murmured.

"Next Sunday, there will be a test. The test will happen in Tokyo and Singapore but also here in the Valley at the same time. What Tokyo sees and hears, we will see and hear. Tell everyone you know, next Sunday, there will be a test. There is no need for fear, alarm, or panic."

Mae listened then. There would certainly be a need for fear and panic if the address system said there was none.

"What test, what kind of test? What? What?" the women demanded of the husband.

Mr. Wing played the relaxed, superior male. He chuckled. "Ho-ho, now you are interested, yes?"

Another man looked up and grinned. "You should watch more TV," he called. He was selling radishes and shook them at the women.

Kwan demanded, "What are they talking about?"

"They will be able to put TV in our heads," said the husband, smiling. He looked down, thinking perhaps wistfully of his own new venture. "Tut. There has been talk of nothing else on the TV for the last year. But I didn't think it would happen."

All the old market was buzzing like flies on carrion, as if it were still news to them. Two youths in strange puffy clothes spun on their heels and slapped each other' s palms, in a gesture that Mae had seen only once or twice before. An old granny waved it all away and kept on accusing a dealer of short measures.

Mae felt grave doubt. "TV in our heads. I don't want TV in my head." She thought of viper newsreaders and kung fu.

Wing said, "It's not just TV. It is more than TV. It is the whole world."

"What does that mean?"

"It will be the Net. Only, in your head. The fools and drunks in these parts just use it to watch movies from Hong Kong. The Net is all things." He began to falter.

"Explain! How can one thing be all things?"

There was a crowd of people gathering to listen.

"Everything is on it. You will see on our new TV." Kwan's husband did not really know either.

The routine was soured. Halat the hairdresser was in a very strange mood, giggly, chattery, her teeth clicking together as if it were cold.

"Oh, nonsense," she said when Mae went into her usual performance. "Is this for a wedding? For a feast?"

"No," said Mae. "It is for my special friend."

The little hussy put both hands to either side of her mouth as if in awe. "Oh! Uh!"

"Are you going to do a special job for her or not?" demanded Mae. Her eyes were able to say: I see no one else in your shop.

Oh, how the girl would have loved to say: I am very busy—if you need something special come back tomorrow. But money spoke. Halat slightly amended her tone. "Of course. For you."

"I bring my friends to you regularly because you do such good work for them."

"Of course," the child said. "It is all this news, it makes me forget myself."

Mae drew herself up, and looked fierce, forbidding, in a word, older. Her entire body said: do not forget yourself again. The way the child dug away at Kwan's hair with the long comb handle said back: peasants.

The rest of the day did not go well. Mae felt tired, distracted. She made a terrible mistake and, with nothing else to do, accidentally took Kwan to the place where she bought her lipsticks.

"Oh! It is a treasure trove!" exclaimed Kwan.

Idiot, thought Mae to herself. Kwan was good-natured and would not take advantage. But if she talked! There would be clients who would not take such a good-natured attitude, not to have been shown this themselves.

"I do not take everyone here," whispered Mae. "Hmm? This is for special friends only."

Kwan was good-natured, but very far from stupid. Mae remembered, in school Kwan had always been best at letters, best at maths. Kwan was pasting on false eyelashes in a mirror and said, very simply and quickly, "Don't worry, I won't tell anyone."

And that was far too simple and direct. As if Kwan were saying: fashion expert, we all know you. She even looked around and smiled at Mae, and batted her now huge eyes, as if mocking fashion itself.

"Not for you," said Mae. "The false eyelashes. You don't need them."

The dealer wanted a sale. "Why listen to her?" she asked Kwan.

Because, thought Mae, I buy fifty riels' worth of cosmetics from you a year.

"My friend is right," said Kwan, to the dealer. The sad fact was that Kwan was almost magazine-beautiful anyway, except for her teeth and gums. "Thank you for showing me this," said Kwan, and touched Mae's arm. "Thank you," she said to the dealer, having bought one lowly lipstick.

Mae and the dealer glared at each other, briefly. I go somewhere else next time, Mae promised herself.

There were flies in the ice cream shop, which was usually so frosted and clean. The old man was satisfyingly apologetic, swiping at the flies with a towel. "I am so sorry, so distressing for ladies," he said, as sincerely as possible knowing that he was addressing farm wives from the hills. "The boys have all gone mad, they are not here to help."

Three old Karz grannies in layers of flower-patterned cotton thumped the linoleum floor with sticks. "It is this new madness. I tell you madness is what it is. Do they think people are incomplete? Do they think that Emel here or Fatima need to have TV all the time? In their heads?"

"We have memories," said another old granny, head bobbing.

"We knew a happier world. Oh so polite!"

Kwan murmured to Mae, "Yes. A world in which babies died overnight and the Red Guards would come and take all the harvest."

"What is happening, Kwan?" Mae asked, suddenly forlorn.

"The truth?" said Kwan. "Nobody knows. Not even the big people who make this test. That is why there will be a test." She went very calm and quiet. "No one knows," she said again.

The worst came last. Kwan's ramrod husband was not a man for drinking. He was in the promised cafe at the promised time, sipping tea, having had a haircut and a professional shave. He brandished a set of extension plugs and a coil of thin silky cable rolled around a drum. He lit his cigarette lighter near one end, and the light gleamed like a star at the other.

"Fye buh Ho buh tih kuh," Wing explained. "Light river rope." He shook his head in wonder.

A young man called Sloop, a tribesman, was with him. Sloop was a telephone engineer and thus a member of the aristocracy as far as Mae was concerned. He was going to wire up their new TV. Sloop said with a woman's voice, "The rope was cheap. Where they already have wires, they use DSL." He might as well have been talking English for all Mae understood him.

Wing seemed cheerful. "Come," he said to the ladies. "I will show you what this is all about."

He went to the communal TV and turned it on with an expert's flourish. Up came not a movie or the local news, but a screen full of other buttons.

"You see? You can choose what you want. You can choose anything." And he touched the screen.

Up came the local Talent, still baring her perfect teeth. She piped in a high, enthusiastic voice that was meant to appeal to men and bright young things.

"Hello. Welcome to the Airnet Information Service. For too long the world has been divided into information haves and have-nots." She held up one hand toward the Heavens of information and the other out toward the citizens of the Valley, inviting them to consider themselves as have-nots.

"Those in the developed world can use their TVs to find any information they need at any time. They do this through the Net."

Incomprehension followed. There were circles and squares linked by wires in diagrams. Then they jumped up into the sky, into the air, only the air was full of arching lines. The field, they called it, but it was nothing like a field. In Karsistani, it was called the Lightning-flow, Compass-point Yearning Field. "Everywhere in the world." Then the lightning flow was shown striking people's heads. "There have been many medical tests to show this is safe."

"Hitting people with lightning?" Kwan asked in crooked amusement. "That does sound so safe."

"Umm," said Wing, trying to think how best to advocate the new world. "Thought is electrical messages. In our heads. So, this thing, it works in the head like thought."

"That's only the Format," said Sloop. "Once we're formatted, we can use Air, and Air happens in other dimensions."

What?

"There are eleven dimensions," he began, and began to see the hopelessness of it. "They were left over after the Big Bang."

"I know what will interest you ladies," said her husband. And with another flourish, he touched the screen. "You'll be able to have this in your heads, whenever you want." Suddenly the screen was full of cream color. One of the capital's ladies spun on her high heel. She was wearing the best of the nation's fashion design. She was one of the ladies in Mae's secret treasure book.

"Oh!" breathed out Kwan. "Oh, Mae, look, isn't she lovely!"

"This address shows nothing but fashion," said her husband.

"All the time?" Kwan exclaimed and looked back at Mae in wonder. For a moment, she stared up at the screen, her own face reflected over those of the models. Then, thankfully, she became Kwan again. "Doesn't that get boring?"

Her husband chuckled. "You can choose something else. Anything else."

It was happening very quickly and Mae's guts churned faster than her brain to certain knowledge: Kwan and her husband would be fine with all this.

"Look," he said. "You can even buy the dress."

Kwan shook her head in amazement. Then a voice said the price and Kwan gasped again. "Oh, yes, all I have to do is sell one of our four farms, and I can have a dress like that."

"I saw all that two years ago," said Mae. "It is too plain for the likes of us. We want people to see everything."

Kwan's face went sad. "That is because we are poor, back in the hills." It was the common yearning, the common forlorn knowledge. Sometimes it had to cease, all the business-making, you had to draw a breath, because after all, you had known your people for as long as you had lived.

Mae said, "None of them are as beautiful as you are, Kwan." It was true, except for her teeth.

"Flattery talk from a fashion expert," said Kwan lightly. But she took Mae's hand. Her eyes yearned up at the screen, as secret after secret was spilled like blood.

"With all this in our heads," said Kwan to her husband. "We won't need your TV."

It was a busy week.

It was not only the six dresses. For some reason, there was much extra business.

On Wednesday, Mae had a discreet morning call to make on Tsang Muhammad. She liked Tsang, she was like a peach that was overripe, round and soft to the touch and very slightly wrinkled. Tsang loved to lie back and be pampered, but only did it when she had an assignation. Everything about Tsang was off-kilter. She was Chinese with a religious Karz husband, who was ten years her senior. He was a Muslim who allowed, or perhaps could not prevent, his Chinese wife from keeping a family pig.

The family pig was in the front room being fattened. Half of the room was full of old shucks. The beast looked lordly and pleased with itself. Tsang's four-year-old son sat tamely beside it, feeding it the greener leaves, as if the animal could not find them for itself.

"Is it all right to talk?" Mae whispered, her eyes going sideways toward the boy.

Tsang, all plump smiles, nodded very quickly yes.

"Who is it?" Mae mouthed.

Tsang simply waggled a finger.

So it was someone they knew. Mae suspected it was Kwan's oldest boy, Luk. Luk was sixteen but fully grown, kept in pressed white shirt and shorts like a baby, but the shorts only showed he had hair on his football-player calves. His face was still round and soft and babylike but lately had been full of a new and different confusion.

"Tsang. Oh!" gasped Mae.

"Sssh," giggled Tsang, who was red as a radish. As if either of them could be certain what the other one meant. "I need a repair job!" So it was someone younger.

Almost certainly Kwan's handsome son.

"Well, they have to be taught by someone," whispered Mae.

Tsang simply dissolved into giggles. She could hardly stop laughing.

"I can do nothing for you. You certainly don't need redder cheeks," said Mae.

Tsang uttered a squawk of laughter.

"There is nothing like it for a woman's complexion." Mae pretended to put away the tools of her trade. "No, I can affect no improvement. Certainly I cannot compete with the effects of a certain young man."

"Nothing…nothing," gasped Tsang. "Nothing like a good prick."

Mae howled in mock outrage, and Tsang squealed and both squealed and pressed down their cheeks, and shushed each other. Mae noted exactly which part of the cheeks were blushing so she would know where the color should go later.

As Mae painted, Tsang explained how she escaped her husband's view. "I tell him that I have to get fresh garbage for the pig," whispered Tsang. "So I go out with the empty bucket.…"

"And come back with a full bucket," said Mae airily.

"Oh!" Tsang pretended to hit her. "You are as bad as me!"

"What do you think I get up to in the City?" asked Mae, arched eyebrow, lying.

Love, she realized later, walking back down the track and clutching her cloth bag of secrets, love is not mine. She thought of the boy's naked calves.

On Thursday, Kwan wanted her teeth to be flossed. This was new; Kwan had never been vain before. This touched Mae, because it meant her friend was getting older. Or was it because she had seen the TV models with their impossible teeth? How were real people supposed to have teeth like that?

Kwan's handsome son ducked as he entered, wearing his shorts, showing smooth full thighs, and a secret swelling about his groin. He ducked as he went out again. Guilty, Mae thought. For certain it is him.

She laid Kwan's head back over a pillow with a towel under her.

Should she not warn her friend to keep watch on her son? Which friend should she betray? To herself, she shook her head; there was no possibility of choosing between them. She could only keep silent. "Just say if I hit a nerve," Mae said.

Kwan had teeth like an old horse, worn, brown, black. Her gums were scarred from a childhood disease, and her teeth felt loose as Mae rubbed the floss between them. She had a neat little bag into which she flipped each strand after it was used.

It was Mae's job to talk: Kwan could not. Mae said she did not know how she would finish the dresses in time. The girls' mothers were never satisfied, each wanted her daughter to have the best. Well, the richest would have the best in the end because they bought the best cloth. Oh! Some of them had asked to pay for the fabric later! As if Mae could afford to buy cloth for six dresses without being paid!

"They all think their fashion expert is a woman of wealth." Mae sometimes found the whole pretense funny. Kwan's eyes crinkled into a smile. But they were also moist from pain.

It was hurting. "You should have told me your teeth were sore," said Mae, and inspected the gums. In the back, they were raw.

If you were rich, Kwan, you would have good teeth, rich people keep their teeth, and somehow keep them white, not brown. Mae pulled stray hair out of Kwan's face.

"I will have to pull some of them," Mae said quietly. "Not today, but soon."

Kwan closed her mouth and swallowed. "I will be an old lady," she said and managed a smile.

"A granny with a thumping stick."

"Who always hides her mouth when she laughs."

Both of them chuckled. "And thick glasses that make your eyes look like a fish."

Kwan rested her hand on her friend's arm. "Do you remember, years ago? We would all get together and make little boats, out of paper, or shells. And we would put candles in them, and send them out on the ditches."

"Yes!" Mae sat forward. "We don't do that anymore."

"We don't wear pillows and a cummerbund anymore either."

There had once been a festival of wishes every year, and the canals would be full of little glowing candles, that floated for a while and then sank with a hiss. "We would always wish for love," said Mae, remembering.

Next morning, Mae mentioned the candles to her neighbor Old Mrs. Tung. Mae visited her nearly every day. Mrs. Tung had been her teacher, during the flurry of what passed for Mae's schooling. She was ninety years old, and spent her days turned toward the tiny loft window that looked out over the valley. She was blind, her eyes pale and unfocused. She could see nothing through the window. Perhaps she breathed in the smell of the fields.

"There you are." Mrs. Tung would smile underneath the huge spectacles that did so little to improve her vision. She remembered the candles. "And we would roast pumpkin seeds. And the ones we didn't eat, we would turn into jewelry. Do you remember that?"

Mrs. Tung was still beautiful, at least in Mae's eyes. Mrs. Tung's face had grown even more delicate in extreme old age, like the skeleton of a cat, small and fine. She gave an impression of great merriment, by continually laughing at not very much. She repeated herself.

"I remember the day you first came to me," she said. Before Shen's village school, Mrs. Tung kept a nursery, there in their courtyard. "I thought: is that the girl whose father has been killed? She is so pretty. I remember you looking at all my dresses hanging on the line."

"And you asked me which one I liked best."

Mrs. Tung giggled. "Oh yes, and you said the butterflies."

Blindness meant that she could only see the past.

"We had tennis courts, you know. Here in Kizuldah."

"Did we?" Mae pretended she had not heard that before.

"Oh yes, oh yes. When the Chinese were here, just before the Communists came. Part of the Chinese army was here, and they built them. We all played tennis, in our school uniforms."

The Chinese officers had supplied the tennis rackets. The traces of the courts were broken and grassy, where Mr. Pin now ran his car repair business.

"Oh! They were all so handsome, all the village girls were so in love." Mrs. Tung chuckled. "I remember, I couldn't have been more than ten years old, and one of them adopted me, because he said I looked like his daughter. He sent me a teddy bear after the war." She chuckled and shook her head. "I was too old for teddy bears by then. But I told everyone it meant we were getting married. Oh!" Mrs. Tung shook her head at foolishness. "I wish I had married him," she confided, feeling naughty. She always said that.

Mrs. Tung even now had the power to make Mae feel calm and protected. Mrs. Tung had come from a family of educated people and once had a house full of books. The books had all been lost in a flood many years ago, but Mrs. Tung could still recite to Mae the poems of the Turks, the Karz, the Chinese. She had sat the child Mae on her lap, and rocked her. She could still recite now, the same poems.

"Listen to the reed flute," she began now, *"How it tells a tale!"* Her old blind face swayed with the words, the beginning of *The Mathnawi. "This noise of the reed is fire, it is not the wind."*

Mae yearned. "Oh. I wish I remembered all those poems!" When she saw Mrs. Tung, she could visit the best of her childhood.

On Friday, Mae saw the Ozdemirs.

The mother was called Hatijah, and her daughter was Sezen. Hatijah was a shy, flighty little thing, terrified of being overcharged by Mae, and of being under-served. Hatijah's low, old stone house was tangy with the smells of burning charcoal, sweat, dung, and the constantly stewing tea. From behind the house came a continual, agonized lowing: the family cow, neglected, needed milking. The poor animal's voice was going raw and harsh. Hatijah seemed not to hear it. She ushered Mae in and fluttered around her, touching the fabric.

"This is such good fabric," Hatijah said, too frightened of Mae to challenge her. It was not good fabric, but good fabric cost real money. Hatijah had five children, and a skinny shiftless husband who probably had worms. Half of the main room was heaped up with corn cobs. The youngest of her babes wore only shirts and sat with their dirty naked bottoms on the corn.

Oh, this was a filthy house. Perhaps Hatijah was a bit simple. She offered Mae roasted corn. Not with your child's wet shit on it, thought Mae, but managed to be polite. The daughter, Sezen, stomped in barefoot for her fitting. Sezen was a tough, raunchy brute of girl and kept rolling her eyes at everything: at her nervous mother, at Mae's efforts to make the yellow and red dress hang properly, at anything either one of the adults said.

"Does…will…on the day…," Sezen's mother tried to begin.

Yes, thought Mae with some bitterness, on the day Sezen will finally have to wash. Sezen's bare feet were slashed with infected cuts.

"What my mother means is," Sezen said. "Will you make up my face Saturday?" Sezen blinked, her unkempt hair making her eyes itch.

"Yes, of course," said Mae, curtly to a younger person who was forward.

"What, with all those other girls on the same day? For someone as lowly as us?"

The girl's eyes were angry. Mae pulled in a breath.

"No one can make you feel inferior without you agreeing with them first," said Mae. It was something Old Mrs. Tung had once told Mae when she herself was poor, hungry, and famished for magic.

"Take off the dress," Mae said. "I'll have to take it back for finishing."

Sezen stepped out of it, right there, naked on the dirt floor. Hatijah did not chastise her, but offered Mae tea. Because she had refused the corn, Mae had to accept the tea. At least that would be boiled.

Hatijah scuttled off to the black kettle and her daughter leaned back in full insolence, her supposedly virgin pubes plucked as bare as the baby's bottom.

Mae fussed with the dress, folding it, so she would have somewhere else to look. The daughter just stared. Mae could take no more. "Do you want people to see you? Go put something on!"

"I don't have anything else," said Sezen.

Her other sisters had gone shopping in the town for graduation gifts. They would have taken all the family's good dresses.

"You mean you have nothing else you will deign to put on." Mae glanced at Hatijah: she really should not be having to do this woman's work for her. "You have other clothes, old clothes. Put them on."

The girl stared at her in even greater insolence.

Mae lost her temper. "I do not work for pigs. You have paid nothing so far for this dress. If you stand there like that I will leave, now, and the dress will not be yours. Wear what you like to the graduation. Come to it naked like a whore for all I care."

Sezen turned and slowly walked toward the side room.

Hatijah the mother still squatted over the kettle, boiling more water to dilute the stew of leaves. She lived on tea and burnt corn that was more usually fed to cattle. Her cow's eyes were averted. Untended, the family cow was still bellowing.

Mae sat and blew out air from stress. This week! She looked at Hatijah's dress. It was a patchwork assembly of her husband's old shirts, beautifully stitched. Hatijah could sew. Mae could not. Hatijah would know that; it was one of the things that made the woman nervous. With all these changes, Mae was going to have to find something else to do beside sketch photographs of dresses. She had a sudden thought.

"Would you be interested in working for me?" Mae asked. Hatijah looked fearful and pleased and said she would have to ask her husband.

Everything is going to have to change, thought Mae, as if to convince herself.

That night Mae worked nearly to dawn on the other three dresses. Her racketing sewing machine sat silent in the corner. It was fine for rough work, but not for finishing, not for graduation dresses.

The bare electric light glared down at her like a headache, as Mae's husband Joe snored. Above them in the loft, his brother and father snored too, as they had done for twenty years.

Mae looked into Joe's open mouth like a mystery. When he was sixteen Joe had been handsome, in the context of the village, wild, and clever. They'd been married a year when she first went to Yeshibozkay with him, where he worked between harvests building a house. She saw the clever city man, an acupuncturist who had money. She saw her husband bullied, made to look foolish, asked questions for which he had no answer. The acupuncturist made Joe do the work again. In Yeshibozkay, her handsome husband was a dolt.

Here they were, both of them now middle-aged. Their son Vikram was a major in the Army. They had sent him to Balshang. He mailed them parcels of orange skins for potpourri; he sent cards and matches in picture boxes. He had met some city girl. Vik would not be back. Their daughter Lily lived on the other side of Yeshibozkay, in a bungalow with a toilet. Life pulled everything away.

At this hour of the morning, she could hear their little river, rushing down the steep slope to the valley. Then a door slammed in the North End. Mae knew who it would be: their Muerain, Mr. Shenyalar. He would be walking across the village to the mosque. A dog started to bark at him; Mrs. Doh's, by the bridge.

Mae knew that Kwan would be cradled in her husband's arms and that Kwan was beautiful because she was an Eloi tribeswoman. All the Eloi had fine features. Her husband Wing did not mind and no one now mentioned it. But Mae could see Kwan shiver now in her sleep. Kwan had dreams, visions, she had tribal blood and it made her shift at night as if she had another, tribal life.

Mae knew that Kwan's clean and noble athlete son would be breathing like a moist baby in his bed, cradling his younger brother.

Without seeing them, Mae could imagine the moon and clouds over their village. The moon would be reflected shimmering on the water of the irrigation canals which had once borne their paper boats of wishes. There would be old candles, deep in the mud.

Then, the slow, sad voice of their Muerain began to sing. Even amplified, his voice was deep and soft, like pillows that allowed the unfaithful to sleep. In the byres, the lonely cows would be stirring. The beasts would walk themselves to the town square, for a lick of salt, and then wait to be herded to pastures. In the evening, they would walk themselves home. Mae heard the first clanking of a cowbell.

At that moment something came into the room, something she did not want to see, something dark and whole like a black dog with froth around its mouth that sat in her corner and would not go away, nameless yet.

Mae started sewing faster.

The dresses were finished on time, all six, each a different color.

Mae ran barefoot in her shift to deliver them. The mothers bowed sleepily in greeting. The daughters were hopping with anxiety like water on a skillet.

It all went well. Under banners the children stood together, including Kwan's son Luk, Sezen, all ten children of the village, all smiles, all for a moment looking like an official poster of the future, brave, red-cheeked with perfect teeth.

Teacher Shen read out each of their achievements. Sezen had none, except in animal husbandry, but she still collected her certificate to applause. And then Mae's friend Shen did something special.

He began to talk about a friend to all of the village, who had spent more time on this ceremony than anyone else, whose only aim was to bring a breath of beauty into this tiny village, the seamstress who worked only to adorn other people....

He was talking about her.

...one was devoted to the daughters and mothers of rich and poor alike and who spread kindness and good will.

The whole village was applauding her, under the white clouds, the blue sky. All were smiling at her. Someone, Kwan perhaps, gave her a push from behind and she stumbled forward.

And her friend Shen was holding out a certificate for her.

"In our day, Lady Chung," he said, "there were no schools for the likes of us, not after early childhood. So. This is a graduation certificate for you. From all your friends. It is in Fashion Studies."

There was applause. Mae tried to speak and found only fluttering sounds came out, and she saw the faces, ranged all in smiles, friends and enemies, cousins and no kin alike.

"This is unexpected," she finally said, and they all chuckled. She looked at the high-school certificate, surprised by the power it had, surprised that she still cared about her lack of education. She couldn't read it. "I do not do fashion as a student, you know."

They knew well enough that she did it for money and how precariously she balanced things.

Something stirred, like the wind in the clouds.

"After tomorrow, you may not need a fashion expert. After tomorrow, everything changes. They will give us TV in our heads, all the knowledge we want. We can talk to the President. We can pretend to order cars from Tokyo. We'll all be experts." She looked at her certificate, hand-lettered, so small.

Mae found she was angry, and her voice seemed to come from her belly, an octave lower.

"I'm sure that it is a good thing. I am sure the people who do this think they do a good thing. They worry about us, like we were children." Her eyes were like two hearts, pumping furiously. "We don't have time for TV or computers. We face sun, rain, wind, sickness, and each other. It is good that they want to help us." She wanted to shake her certificate, she wished it was one of them, who had upended everything. "But how dare they? How dare they call us have-nots?"

The People of Sand and Slag (2004)

PAOLO BACIGALUPI

PAOLO BACIGALUPI's (b. 1972) novels include *The Windup Girl, Ship Breaker,* and *The Drowned Cities*. A new novel entitled *The Water Knife* is currently in the works. His short fiction—much of which has been collected in *Pump Six and Other Stories*—often takes a dark, imaginative, and uncompromising view of the future. These characteristics are most definitely on display in "The People of Sand and Slag."

"HOSTILE MOVEMENT! WELL inside the perimeter! Well inside!" I stripped off my Immersive Response goggles as adrenaline surged through me. The virtual cityscape I'd been about to raze disappeared, replaced by our monitoring room's many views of SesCo's mining operations. On one screen, the red phosphorescent tracery of an intruder skated across a terrain map, a hot blip like blood spattering its way toward Pit 8.

Jaak was already out of the monitoring room. I ran for my gear.

I caught up with Jaak in the equipment room as he grabbed a TS-101 and slashbangs and dragged his impact exoskeleton over his tattooed body. He draped bandoleers of surgepacks over his massive shoulders and ran for the outer locks. I strapped on my own exoskeleton, pulled my 101 from its rack, checked its charge, and followed.

Lisa was already in the HEV, its turbofans screaming like banshees when the hatch dilated. Sentry centaurs leveled their 101s at me, then relaxed as friend/foe data spilled into their heads-up displays. I bolted across the tarmac, my skin pricking under blasts of icy Montana wind and the jet wash of Hentasa Mark V engines. Overhead, the clouds glowed orange with light from SesCo's mining bots.

"Come on, Chen! Move! Move! Move!"

I dove into the hunter. The ship leaped into the sky. It banked, throwing me against a bulkhead, then the Hentasas cycled wide and the hunter punched forward. The HEV's hatch slid shut. The wind howl muted.

I struggled forward to the flight cocoon and peered over Jaak's and Lisa's shoulders to the landscape beyond.

"Have a good game?" Lisa asked.

I scowled. "I was about to win. I made it to Paris."

We cut through the mists over the catchment lakes, skimming inches above the water, and then we hit the far shore. The hunter lurched as its anti-collision software jerked us away from the roughening terrain. Lisa overrode the computers and forced the ship back down against the soil, driving us so low I could have reached out and dragged my hands through the broken scree as we screamed over it.

Alarms yowled. Jaak shut them off as Lisa pushed the hunter lower. Ahead, a tailings ridge loomed. We ripped up its face and dropped sickeningly into the next valley. The Hentasas shuddered as Lisa forced them to the edge of their design buffer. We hurtled up and over another ridge. Ahead, the ragged cutscape of mined mountains stretched to the horizon. We dipped again into mist and skimmed low over another catchment lake, leaving choppy wake in the thick golden waters.

Jaak studied the hunter's scanners. "I've got it." He grinned. "It's moving, but slow."

"Contact in one minute," Lisa said. "He hasn't launched any countermeasures."

I watched the intruder on the tracking screens as they displayed real-time data fed to us from SesCo's satellites. "It's not even a masked target. We could have dropped a mini on it from base if we'd known he wasn't going to play hide-and-seek."

"Could have finished your game," Lisa said.

"We could still nuke him." Jaak suggested.

I shook my head. "No, let's take a look. Vaporizing him won't leave us anything and Bunbaum will want to know what we used the hunter for."

"Thirty seconds."

"He wouldn't care if someone had taken the hunter on a joyride to Cancun."

Lisa shrugged. "I wanted to swim. It was either that, or rip off your kneecaps."

The hunter lunged over another series of ridges.

Jaak studied his monitor. "Target's moving away. He's still slow. We'll get him."

"Fifteen seconds to drop," Lisa said. She unstrapped and switched the hunter to software. We all ran for the hatch as the HEV yanked itself skyward, its auto pilot desperate to tear away from the screaming hazard of the rocks beneath its belly.

We plunged out the hatch, one, two, three, falling like Icarus. We slammed into the ground at hundreds of kilometers per hour. Our exoskeletons shattered like glass, flinging leaves into the sky. The shards fluttered down around us, black metallic petals absorbing our enemy's radar and heat detection while we rolled to jarred vulnerable stops in muddy scree.

The hunter blew over the ridge, Hentasas shrieking, a blazing target. I dragged myself upright and ran for the ridge, my feet churning through yellow tailings mud and rags of jaundiced snow. Behind me, Jaak was down with smashed arms. The leaves of his exoskeleton marked his roll path, a long trail of black shimmering metal. Lisa lay a hundred yards away, her femur rammed through her thigh like a bright white exclamation mark.

I reached the top of the ridge and stared down into the valley.

Nothing.

I dialed up the magnification of my helmet. The monotonous slopes of more tailings rubble spread out below me. Boulders, some as large as our HEV, some cracked and shattered by high explosives, shared the slopes with the un-stable yellow shale and fine grit of waste materials from SesCo's operations.

Jaak slipped up beside me, followed a moment later by Lisa, her flight suit's leg torn and bloodied. She wiped yellow mud off her face and ate it as she studied the valley below. "Anything?"

I shook my head. "Nothing yet. You okay?"

"Clean break."

Jaak pointed. "There!"

Down in the valley, something was running, flushed by the hunter. It slipped along a shallow creek, viscous with tailings acid. The ship herded it toward us. Nothing. No missile fire. No slag. Just the running creature. A mass of tangled hair. Quadrupedal. Splattered with mud.

"Some kind of bio-job?" I wondered.

"It doesn't have any hands," Lisa murmured.

"No equipment either."

Jaak muttered. "What kind of sick bastard makes a bio-job without hands?"

I searched the nearby ridgelines. "Decoy, maybe?"

Jaak checked his scanner data, piped in from the hunter's more aggressive instruments. "I don't think so. Can we put the hunter up higher? I want to look around."

At Lisa's command, the hunter rose, allowing its sensors a fuller reach. The howl of its turbofans became muted as it gained altitude.

Jaak waited as more data spat into his heads-up display. "Nope, nothing. And no new alerts from any of the perimeter stations, either. We're alone."

Lisa shook her head. "We should have just dropped a mini on it from base."

Down in the valley, the bio-job's headlong run slowed to a trot. It seemed unaware of us. Closer now, we could make out its shape: A shaggy quadruped with a tail. Dreadlocked hair dangled from its shanks like ornaments, tagged with tailings mud clods. It was stained around its legs from the acids of the catchment ponds, as though it had forded streams of urine.

"That's one ugly bio-job," I said.

Lisa shouldered her 101. "Bio-melt when I'm done with it."

"Wait!" Jaak said. "Don't slag it!"

Lisa glanced over at him, irritated. "What now?"

"That's not a bio-job at all." Jaak whispered. "That's a dog."

He stood suddenly and jumped over the hillside, running headlong down the scree toward the animal.

"Wait!" Lisa called, but Jaak was already fully exposed and blurring to his top speed.

The animal took one look at Jaak, whooping and hollering as he came roaring down the slope, then turned and ran. It was no match for Jaak. Half a minute later he overtook the animal.

Lisa and I exchanged glances. "Well," she said, "it's awfully slow if it's a bio-job. I've seen centaurs walk faster."

By the time we caught up with Jaak and the animal, Jaak had it cornered in a dull gully. The animal stood in the center of a trickling ditch of sludgy water, shaking and growling and baring its teeth at us as we surrounded it. It tried to break around us, but Jaak kept it corralled easily.

Up close, the animal seemed even more pathetic than from a distance, a good thirty kilos of snarling mange. Its paws were slashed and bloody and patches of fur were torn away, revealing festering chemical burns underneath.

"I'll be damned," I breathed, staring at the animal. "It really looks like a dog."

Jaak grinned. "It's like finding a goddamn dinosaur."

"How could it live out here?" Lisa's arm swept the horizon. "There's nothing to live on. It's got to be modified." She studied it closely, then glanced at Jaak. "Are you sure nothing's coming in on the perimeter? This isn't some kind of decoy?"

Jaak shook his head. "Nothing. Not even a peep."

I leaned in toward the creature. It bared its teeth in a rictus of hatred. "It's pretty beat up. Maybe it's the real thing."

Jaak said, "Oh yeah, it's the real thing all right. I saw a dog in a zoo once. I'm telling you, this is a dog."

Lisa shook her head. "It can't be. It would be dead, if it were a real dog."

Jaak just grinned and shook his head. "No way. Look at it." He reached out to push the hair out of the animal's face so that we could see its muzzle.

The animal lunged and its teeth sank into Jaak's arm. It shook his arm violently, growling as Jaak stared down at the creature latched onto his flesh. It yanked its head back and forth, trying to tear Jaak's arm off. Blood spurted around its muzzle as its teeth found Jaak's arteries.

Jaak laughed. His bleeding stopped. "Damn. Check that out." He lifted his arm until the animal dangled fully out of the stream, dripping. "I got me a pet."

The dog swung from the thick bough of Jaak's arm. It tried to shake his arm once again, but its movements were ineffectual now that it hung off the ground. Even Lisa smiled.

"Must be a bummer to wake up and find out you're at the end of your evolutionary curve."

The dog growled, determined to hang on.

Jaak laughed and drew his monomol knife. "Here you go, doggy." He sliced his arm off, leaving it in the bewildered animal's mouth.

Lisa cocked her head. "You think we could make some kind of money on it?"

Jaak watched as the dog devoured his severed arm. "I read somewhere that they used to eat dogs. I wonder what they taste like."

I checked the time in my heads-up display. We'd already killed an hour on an exercise that wasn't giving any bonuses. "Get your dog, Jaak, and get it on the hunter. We aren't going to eat it before we call Bunbaum."

"He'll probably call it company property," Jaak groused.

"Yeah, that's the way it always goes. But we still have to report. Might as well keep the evidence, since we didn't nuke it."

We ate sand for dinner. Outside the security bunker, the mining robots rumbled back and forth, ripping deeper into the earth, turning it into a mush of tailings and rock acid that they left in exposed ponds when they hit the water table, or piled into thousand-foot mountainscapes of waste soil. It was comforting to hear those machines cruising back and forth all day. Just you and the bots and the profits, and if nothing got bombed while you were on duty, there was always a nice bonus.

After dinner we sat around and sharpened Lisa's skin, implanting blades along her limbs so that she was like a razor from all directions. She'd considered mono-mol blades, but it was too easy to take a limb off accidentally, and we lost enough body parts as it was without adding to the mayhem. That kind of garbage was for people who didn't have to work: aesthetes from New York City and California.

Lisa had a DermDecora kit for the sharpening. She'd bought it last time we'd gone on vacation and spent extra to get it, instead of getting one of the cheap knock-offs that were cropping up. We worked on cutting her skin down to the bone and setting the blades. A friend of ours in L.A said that he just held DermDecora parties so everyone could do their modifications and help out with the hard-to-reach places.

Lisa had done my glowspine, a sweet tracery of lime landing lights that ran from my tailbone to the base of my skull, so I didn't mind helping her out, but Jaak, who did all of his modification with an old-time scar and tattoo shop in Hawaii, wasn't so pleased. It was a little frustrating because her flesh kept try-ing to close before we had the blades set, but eventually we got the hang of it, and an hour later, she started looking good.

Once we finished with Lisa's front settings, we sat around and fed her. I had a bowl of tailings mud that I drizzled into her mouth to speed her integration process. When we weren't feeding her, we watched the dog. Jaak had shoved it into a makeshift cage in one corner of our common room. It lay there like it was dead.

Lisa said, "I ran its DNA. It really is a dog."

"Bunbaum believe you?"

She gave me a dirty look. "What do you think?"

I laughed. At SesCo, tactical defense responders were expected to be fast, flexible, and deadly, but the reality was our SOP was always the same: drop nukes on intruders, slag the leftovers to melt so they couldn't regrow, hit the beaches for vacation. We were independent and trusted as far as tactical decisions went, but there was no way SesCo was going to believe its slag soldiers had found a dog in their tailings mountains.

Lisa nodded. "He wanted to know how the hell a dog could live out here. Then he wanted to know why we didn't catch it sooner. Wanted to know what he pays us for." She pushed her short blond hair off her face and eyed the animal. "I should have slagged it."

"What's he want us to do?"

"It's not in the manual. He's calling back."

I studied the limp animal. "I want to know how it was surviving. Dogs are meat eaters, right?"

"Maybe some of the engineers were giving it meat. Like Jaak did."

Jaak shook his head. "I don't think so. The sucker threw up my arm almost right after he ate it." He wiggled his new stump where it was rapidly regrowing. "I don't think we're compatible for it."

I asked, "But we could eat it, right?"

Lisa laughed and took a spoonful of tailings. "We can eat anything. We're the top of the food chain."

"Weird how it can't eat us."

"You've probably got more mercury and lead running through your blood than any pre-weeviltech animal ever could have had."

"That's bad?"

"Used to be poison."

"Weird."

Jaak said, "I think I might have broken it when I put it in the cage." He studied it seriously. "It's not moving like it was before. And I heard something snap when I stuffed it in."

"So?"

Jaak shrugged. "I don't think it's healing."

The dog did look kind of beat up. It just lay there, its sides going up and down like a bellows. Its eyes were half-open, but didn't seem to be focused on any of us. When Jaak made a sudden movement, it twitched for a second, but it didn't get up. It didn't even growl.

Jaak said, "I never thought an animal could be so fragile."

"You're fragile, too. That's not such a big surprise."

"Yeah, but I only broke a couple bones on it, and now look at it. It just lies there and pants."

Lisa frowned thoughtfully. "It doesn't heal." She climbed awkwardly to her feet and went to peer into the cage. Her voice was excited. "It really is a dog. Just like we used to be. It could take weeks for it to heal. One broken bone, and it's done for."

She reached a razored hand into the cage and sliced a thin wound into its shank. Blood oozed out, and kept oozing. It took minutes for it to begin clotting. The dog lay still and panted, clearly wasted.

She laughed. "It's hard to believe we ever lived long enough to evolve out of that. If you chop off its legs, they won't regrow." She cocked her head, fascinated. "It's as delicate as rock. You break it, and it never comes back together." She reached out to stroke the matted fur of the animal. "It's as easy to kill as the hunter."

The comm buzzed. Jaak went to answer.

Lisa and I stared at the dog, our own little window into pre-history.

Jaak came back into the room. "Bunbaum's flying out a biologist to take a look at it."

"You mean a bio-engineer," I corrected him.

"Nope. Biologist. Bunbaum said they study animals."

Lisa sat down. I checked her blades to see if she'd knocked anything loose. "There's a dead-end job."

"I guess they grow them out of DNA. Study what they do. Behavior, shit like that."

"Who hires them?"

Jaak shrugged. "Pau Foundation has three of them on staff. Origin of life guys. That's who's sending out this one. Mushi-something. Didn't get his name."

"Origin of life?"

"Sure, you know, what makes us tick. What makes us alive. Stuff like that."

I poured a handful of tailings mud into Lisa's mouth. She gobbled it gratefully. "Mud makes us tick," I said.

Jaak nodded at the dog. "It doesn't make that dog tick."

We all looked at the dog. "It's hard to tell what makes it tick."

Lin Musharraf was a short guy with black hair and a hooked nose that dominated his face. He had carved his skin with swirling patterns of glow implants, so he stood out as cobalt spirals in the darkness as he jumped down from his chartered HEV.

The centaurs went wild about the unauthorized visitor and corralled him right up against his ship. They were all over him and his DNA kit, sniffing him, running their scanners over his case, pointing their 101s into his glowing face and snarling at him.

I let him sweat for a minute before calling them away. The centaurs backed off, swearing and circling, but didn't slag him. Musharraf looked shaken. I couldn't blame him. They're scary monsters: bigger and faster than a man. Their behavior patches make them vicious, their sentience upgrades give them the intelligence to operate military equipment, and their basic fight/flight response is so impaired that they only know how to attack when they're threatened. I've seen a half-slagged centaur tear a man to pieces barehanded and then join an assault on enemy ridge fortifications, dragging its whole melted carcass forward with just its arms. They're great critters to have at your back when the slag starts flying.

I guided Musharraf out of the scrum. He had a whole pack of memory addendums blinking off the back of his skull: a fat pipe of data retrieval, channeled direct to the brain, and no smash protection. The centaurs could have shut him down with one hard tap to the back of the head. His cortex might have grown back, but he wouldn't have been the same. Looking at those blinking triple fins of intelligence draping down the back of his head, you could tell he was a typical lab rat. All brains, no survival instincts. I wouldn't have stuck mem-adds into my head even for a triple bonus.

"You've got a dog?" Musharraf asked when we were out of reach of the centaurs.

"We think so." I led him down into the bunker, past our weapons racks and weight rooms to the common room where we'd stored the dog. The dog looked up at us as we came in, the most movement it had made since Jaak put it in the cage.

Musharraf stopped short and stared. "Remarkable."

He knelt in front of the animal's cage and unlocked the door. He held out a handful of pellets. The dog dragged itself upright. Musharraf backed away, giving it room, and the dog followed stiff and wary, snuffling after the pellets. It buried its muzzle in his brown hand, snorting and gobbling at the pellets.

Musharraf looked up. "And you found it in your tailings pits?"

"That's right."

"Remarkable."

The dog finished the pellets and snuffled his palm for more. Musharraf laughed and stood. "No more for you. Not right now." He opened his DNA kit, pulled out a sampler needle and stuck the dog. The sampler's chamber filled with blood.

Lisa watched. "You talk to it?"

Musharraf shrugged. "It's a habit."

"But it's not sentient."

"Well, no, but it likes to hear voices." The chamber finished filling. He withdrew the needle, disconnected the collection chamber and fitted it into the kit. The analysis software blinked alive and the blood disappeared into the heart of the kit with a soft vacuum hiss.

"How do you know?"

Musharraf shrugged. "It's a dog. Dogs are that way."

We all frowned. Musharraf started running tests on the blood, humming tunelessly to himself as he worked. His DNA kit peeped and squawked. Lisa watched him run his tests, clearly pissed off that SesCo had sent out a lab rat to retest what she had already done. It was easy to understand her irritation. A centaur could have run those DNA tests.

"I'm astounded that you found a dog in your pits," Musharraf muttered.

Lisa said, "We were going to slag it, but Bunbaum wouldn't let us."

Musharraf eyed her. "How restrained of you."

Lisa shrugged. "Orders."

"Still, I'm sure your thermal surge weapon presented a powerful temptation. How good of you not to slag a starving animal."

Lisa frowned suspiciously. I started to worry that she might take Musharraf apart. She was crazy enough without people talking down to her. The memory addendums on the back of his head were an awfully tempting target: one slap, down goes the lab rat. I wondered if we sank him in a catchment lake if anyone would notice him missing. A biologist, for Christ's sake.

Musharraf turned back to his DNA kit, apparently unaware of his hazard. "Did you know that in the past, people believed that we should have compassion for all things on Earth? Not just for ourselves, but for all living things?"

"So?"

"I would hope you will have compassion for one foolish scientist and not dismember me today."

Lisa laughed. I relaxed. Encouraged, Musharraf said, "It truly is remarkable that you found such a specimen amongst your mining operations. I haven't heard of a living specimen in ten or fifteen years."

"I saw one in a zoo, once," Jaak said.

"Yes, well, a zoo is the only place for them. And laboratories, of course. They still provide useful genetic data." He was studying the results of the tests, nodding to himself as information scrolled across the kit's screen.

Jaak grinned. "Who needs animals if you can eat stone?"

Musharraf began packing up his DNA kit. "Weeviltech. Precisely. We transcended the animal kingdom." He latched his kit closed and nodded to us all. "Well, it's been quite enlightening. Thank you for letting me see your specimen."

"You're not going to take it with you?"

Musharraf paused, surprised. "Oh no. I don't think so."

"It's not a dog, then?"

"Oh no, it's quite certainly a real dog. But what on Earth would I do with it?" He held up a vial of blood. "We have the DNA. A live one is hardly worth keeping around. Very expensive to maintain, you know. Manufacturing a basic organism's food is quite complex. Clean rooms, air filters, special lights. Re-creating the web of life isn't easy. Far more simple to release oneself from it completely than to attempt to re-create it." He glanced at the dog. "Unfortunately, our furry friend over there would never survive weeviltech. The worms would eat him as quickly as they eat everything else. No, you would have to manufacture the animal from scratch. And really, what would be the point of that? A bio-job without hands?" He laughed and headed for his HEV.

We all looked at each other. I jogged after the doctor and caught up with him at the hatch to the tarmac. He had paused on the verge of opening it. "Your centaurs know me now?" he asked.

"Yeah, you're fine."

"Good." He dilated the hatch and strode out into the cold.

I trailed after him. "Wait! What are we supposed to do with it?"

"The dog?" The doctor climbed into the HEV and began strapping in. Wind whipped around us, carrying stinging grit from the tailings piles. "Turn it back to your pits. Or you could eat it, I suppose. I understand that it was a real delicacy. There are recipes for cooking animals. They take time, but they can give quite extraordinary results."

Musharraf's pilot started cycling up his turbofans.

"Are you kidding?"

Musharraf shrugged and shouted over the increasing scream of the engines. "You should try it! Just another part of our heritage that's atrophied since weeviltech!"

He yanked down the flight cocoon's door, sealing himself inside. The turbofans cycled higher and the pilot motioned me back from their wash as the HEV slowly lifted into the air.

Lisa and Jaak couldn't agree on what we should do with the dog. We had protocols for working out conflict. As a tribe of killers, we needed them. Normally, consensus worked for us, but every once in a while, we just got tangled up and stuck to our positions, and after that, not much could get done without someone getting slaughtered. Lisa and Jaak dug in, and after a couple days of wrangling, with Lisa threatening to cook the thing in the middle of the night while Jaak wasn't watching, and Jaak threatening to cook her if she did, we finally went with a majority vote. I got to be the tie-breaker.

"I say we eat it," Lisa said.

We were sitting in the monitoring room, watching satellite shots of the tailings mountains and the infrared blobs of the mining bots while they ripped around in the earth. In one corner, the object of our discussion lay in its cage, dragged there by Jaak in an attempt to sway the result. He spun his observation chair, turning his attention away from the theater maps. "I think we should keep it. It's cool. Old-timey, you know? I mean, who the hell do you know who has a real dog?"

"Who the hell wants the hassle?" Lisa responded. "I say we try real meat." She cut a line in her forearm with her razors. She ran her finger along the resulting blood beads and tasted them as the wound sealed.

They both looked at me. I looked at the ceiling. "Are you sure you can't decide this without me?"

Lisa grinned. "Come on, Chen, you decide. It was a group find. Jaak won't pout, will you?"

Jaak gave her a dirty look.

I looked at Jaak. "I don't want its food costs to come out of group bonuses.

We agreed we'd use part of it for the new Immersive Response. I'm sick of the old one."

Jaak shrugged. "Fine with me. I can pay for it out of my own. I just won't get any more tats."

I leaned back in my chair, surprised, then looked at Lisa. "Well, if Jaak wants to pay for it, I think we should keep it."

Lisa stared at me, incredulous. "But we could cook it!"

I glanced at the dog where it lay panting in its cage. "It's like having a zoo of our own. I kind of like it."

Musharraf and the Pau Foundation hooked us up with a supply of food pellets for the dog and Jaak looked up an old database on how to splint its busted bones. He bought water filtration so that it could drink.

I thought I'd made a good decision, putting the costs on Jaak, but I didn't really foresee the complications that came with having an unmodified organism in the bunker. The thing shit all over the floor, and sometimes it wouldn't eat, and it would get sick for no reason, and it was slow to heal so we all ended up playing nursemaid to the thing while it lay in its cage. I kept expecting Lisa to break its neck in the middle of the night, but even though she grumbled, she didn't assassinate it.

Jaak tried to act like Musharraf. He talked to the dog. He logged onto the libraries and read all about old-time dogs. How they ran in packs. How people used to breed them.

We tried to figure out what kind of dog it was, but we couldn't narrow it down much, and then Jaak discovered that all the dogs could interbreed, so all you could do was guess that it was some kind of big sheep dog, with maybe a head from a rottweiler, along with maybe some other kind of dog, like a wolf or coyote or something.

Jaak thought it had coyote in it because they were supposed to have been big adapters, and whatever our dog was, it must have been a big adapter to hang out in the tailings pits. It didn't have the boosters we had, and it had still lived in the rock acids. Even Lisa was impressed by that.

I was carpet bombing Antarctic Recessionists, swooping low, driving the suckers further and further along the ice floe. If I got lucky, I'd drive the whole village out onto a vestigial shelf and sink them all before they knew what was happening. I dove again, strafing and then spinning away from their return slag.

It was fun, but mostly just a way to kill time between real bombing runs. The new IR was supposed to be as good as the arcades, full immersion and feedback, and portable to boot. People got so lost they had to take intravenous feedings or they withered away while they were inside.

I was about to sink a whole load of refugees when Jaak shouted. "Get out here! You've got to see this!"

I stripped off my goggles and ran for the monitoring room, adrenaline amping up. When I got there, Jaak was just standing in the center of the room with the dog, grinning.

Lisa came tearing in a second later. "What? What is it?" Her eyes scanned the theater maps, ready for bloodshed.

Jaak grinned. "Look at this." He turned to the dog and held out his hand. "Shake."

The dog sat back on its haunches and gravely offered him its paw. Jaak grinned and shook the paw, then tossed it a food pellet. He turned to us and bowed.

Lisa frowned. "Do it again."

Jaak shrugged and went through the performance a second time.

"It thinks?" she asked.

Jaak shrugged. "Got me. You can get it to do things. The libraries are full of stuff on them. They're trainable. Not like a centaur or anything, but you can make them do little tricks, and if they're certain breeds, they can learn special stuff, too."

"Like what?"

"Some of them were trained to attack. Or to find explosives."

Lisa looked impressed. "Like nukes and stuff?"

Jaak shrugged. "I guess."

"Can I try?" I asked.

Jaak nodded. "Go for it."

I went over to the dog and stuck out my hand. "Shake."

It stuck out its paw. My hackles went up. It was like sending signals to aliens. I mean, you expect a bio-job or a robot to do what you want it to. Centaur, go get blown up. Find the op-force. Call reinforcements. The HEV was like that, too. It would do anything. But it was designed.

"Feed it," Jaak said, handing me a food pellet. "You have to feed it when it does it right."

I held out the food pellet. The dog's long pink tongue swabbed my palm.

I held out my hand again. "Shake." I said. It held out its paw. We shook hands. Its amber eyes stared up at me, solemn.

"That's some weird shit," Lisa said. I shivered, nodding and backed away. The dog watched me go.

That night in my bunk, I lay awake, reading. I'd turned out the lights and only the book's surface glowed, illuminating the bunkroom in a soft green aura. Some of Lisa's art buys glimmered dimly from the walls: a bronze hanging of a phoenix breaking into flight, stylized flames glowing around it; a Japanese woodblock print of Mount Fuji and another of a village weighed down under thick snows; a photo of the three of us in Siberia after the Peninsula campaign, grinning and alive amongst the slag.

Lisa came into the room. Her razors glinted in my book's dim light, flashes of green sparks that outlined her limbs as she moved.

"What are you reading?" She stripped and squeezed into bed with me.

I held up the book and read out loud.

Cut me I won't bleed. Gas me I won't breathe.

Stab me, shoot me, slash me, smash me

I have swallowed science

I am God.

Alone.

I closed the book and its glow died. In the darkness, Lisa rustled under the covers.

My eyes adjusted. She was staring at me. "'Dead Man,' right?"

"Because of the dog," I said.

"Dark reading." She touched my shoulder, her hand warm, the blades embedded, biting lightly into my skin.

"We used to be like that dog," I said.

"Pathetic."

"Scary."

We were quiet for a little while. Finally I asked, "Do you ever wonder what would happen to us if we didn't have our science? If we didn't have our big brains and our weeviltech and our cellstims and—"

"And everything that makes our life good?" She laughed. "No." She rubbed my stomach. "I like all those little worms that live in your belly." She started to tickle me.

Wormy, squirmy in your belly,
wormy squirmy feeds you Nelly.
Microweevils eat the bad,
and give you something good instead.

I fought her off, laughing. "That's no Yearly."

"Third grade. Basic bio-logic. Mrs. Alvarez. She was really big on weeviltech."

She tried to tickle me again but I fought her off. "Yeah, well Yearly only wrote about immortality. He wouldn't take it."

Lisa gave up on the tickling and flopped down beside me again. "Blah, blah, blah. He wouldn't take any gene modifications. No c-cell inhibitors. He was dying of cancer and he wouldn't take the drugs that would have saved him. Our last mortal poet. Cry me a river. So what?"

"You ever think about why he wouldn't?"

"Yeah. He wanted to be famous. Suicide's good for attention."

"Seriously, though. He thought being human meant having animals. The whole web of life thing. I've been reading about him. It's weird shit. He didn't want to live without them."

"Mrs. Alvarez hated him. She had some rhymes about him, too. Anyway, what were we supposed to do? Work out weeviltech and DNA patches for every stupid species? Do you know what that would have cost?" She nuzzled close to me. "If you want animals around you, go to a zoo. Or get some building blocks and make something, if it makes you happy. Something with hands, for god's sake, not like that dog." She stared at the underside of the bunk above. "I'd cook that dog in a second."

I shook my head. "I don't know. That dog's different from a bio-job. It looks at us, and there's something there, and it's not us. I mean, take any bio-job out there, and it's basically us, poured into another shape, but not that dog...." I trailed off, thinking.

Lisa laughed. "It shook hands with you, Chen. You don't worry about a centaur when it salutes." She climbed on top of me. "Forget the dog. Concentrate on something that matters." Her smile and her razor blades glinted in the dimness.

I woke up to something licking my face. At first I thought it was Lisa, but she'd climbed into her own bunk. I opened my eyes and found the dog.

It was a funny thing to have this animal licking me, like it wanted to talk, or say hello or something. It licked me again, and I thought that it had come a long way from when it had tried to take off Jaak's arm. It put its paws up on my bed, and then in a single heavy movement, it was up on the bunk with me, its bulk curled against me.

It slept there all night. It was weird having something other than Lisa lying next to me, but it was warm and there was something friendly about it. I couldn't help smiling as I drifted back to sleep.

We flew to Hawaii for a swimming vacation and we brought the dog with us. It was good to get out of the northern cold and into the gentle Pacific. Good to stand on the beach, and look out to a limitless horizon. Good to walk along the beach holding hands while black waves crashed on the sand.

Lisa was a good swimmer. She flashed through the ocean's metallic sheen like an eel out of history and when she surfaced, her naked body glistened with hundreds of iridescent petroleum jewels.

When the sun started to set, Jaak lit the ocean on fire with his 101. We all sat and watched as the sun's great red ball sank through veils of smoke, its light shading deeper crimson with every minute. Waves rushed flaming onto the beach. Jaak got out his harmonica and played while Lisa and I made love on the sand.

We'd intended to amputate her for the weekend, to let her try what she had done to me the vacation before. It was a new thing in L.A., an experiment in vulnerability.

She was beautiful, lying there on the beach, slick and excited with all of our play in the water. I licked oil opals off her skin as I sliced off her limbs, leaving her more dependent than a baby. Jaak played his harmonica and watched the sun set, and watched as I rendered Lisa down to her core.

After our sex, we lay on the sand. The last of the sun was dropping below the water. Its rays glinted redly across the smoldering waves. The sky, thick with particulates and smoke, shaded darker.

Lisa sighed contentedly. "We should vacation here more often."

I tugged on a length of barbed-wire buried in the sand. It tore free and I wrapped it around my upper arm, a tight band that bit into my skin. I showed it to Lisa. "I used to do this all the time when I was a kid." I smiled. "I thought I was so bad-ass."

Lisa smiled. "You are."

"Thanks to science." I glanced over at the dog. It was lying on the sand a short distance away. It seemed sullen and unsure in its new environment, torn away from the safety of the acid pits and tailings mountains of its homeland. Jaak sat beside the dog and played. Its ears twitched to the music. He was a good player. The mournful sound of the harmonica carried easily over the beach to where we lay.

Lisa turned her head, trying to see the dog. "Roll me."

I did what she asked. Already, her limbs were regrowing. Small stumps, which would build into larger limbs. By morning, she would be whole, and ravenous. She studied the dog. "This is as close as I'll ever get to it," she said.

"Sorry?"

"It's vulnerable to everything. It can't swim in the ocean. It can't eat anything. We have to fly its food to it. We have to scrub its water. Dead end of an evolutionary chain. Without science, we'd be as vulnerable as it." She looked up at me. "As vulnerable as I am now." She grinned. "This is as close to death as I've ever been. At least, not in combat."

"Wild, isn't it?"

"For a day. I liked it better when I did it to you. I'm already starving."

I fed her a handful of oily sand and watched the dog, standing uncertainly on the beach, sniffing suspiciously at some rusting scrap iron that stuck out of the beach like a giant memory fin. It pawed up a chunk of red plastic rubbed shiny by the ocean and chewed on it briefly, before dropping it. It started licking around its mouth. I wondered if it had poisoned itself again.

"It sure can make you think," I muttered. I fed Lisa another handful of sand. "If someone came from the past, to meet us here and now, what do you think they'd say about us? Would they even call us human?"

Lisa looked at me seriously. "No, they'd call us gods."

Jaak got up and wandered into the surf, standing knee-deep in the black smoldering waters. The dog, driven by some unknown instinct, followed him, gingerly picking its way across the sand and rubble.

The dog got tangled in a cluster of wire our last day on the beach. Really ripped the hell out of it: slashes through its fur, broken legs, practically strangled. It had gnawed one of its own paws half off trying to get free. By the time we found it, it was a bloody mess of ragged fur and exposed meat.

Lisa stared down at the dog. "Christ, Jaak, you were supposed to be watching it."

"I went swimming. You can't keep an eye on the thing all the time."

"It's going to take forever to fix this," she fumed.

"We should warm up the hunter," I said. "It'll be easier to work on it back home." Lisa and I knelt down to start cutting the dog free. It whimpered and its tail wagged feebly as we started to work.

Jaak was silent.

Lisa slapped him on his leg. "Come on, Jaak, get down here. It'll bleed out if you don't hurry up. You know how fragile it is."

Jaak said, "I think we should eat it."

Lisa glanced up, surprised. "You do?"

He shrugged. "Sure."

I looked up from where I was tearing away tangled wires from around the dog's torso. "I thought you wanted it to be your pet. Like in the zoo."

Jaak shook his head. "Those food pellets are expensive. I'm spending half my salary on food and water filtration, and now this bullshit." He waved his hand at the tangled dog. "You have to watch the sucker all the time. It's not worth it."

"But still, it's your friend. It shook hands with you."

Jaak laughed. "You're my friend." He looked down at the dog, his face wrinkled with thought. "It's, it's…an animal."

Even though we had all idly discussed what it would be like to eat the dog, it was a surprise to hear him so determined to kill it. "Maybe you should sleep on it." I said. "We can get it back to the bunker, fix it up, and then you can decide when you aren't so pissed off about it."

"No." He pulled out his harmonica and played a few notes, a quick jazzy scale. He took the harmonica out of his mouth. "If you want to put up the money for his feed, I'll keep it, I guess, but otherwise…." He shrugged.

"I don't think you should cook it."

"You don't?" Lisa glanced at me. "We could roast it, right here, on the beach."

I looked down at the dog, a mass of panting, trusting animal. "I still don't think we should do it."

Jaak looked at me seriously. "You want to pay for the feed?"

I sighed. "I'm saving for the new Immersive Response."

"Yeah, well, I've got things I want to buy too, you know." He flexed his muscles, showing off his tattoos. "I mean, what the fuck good does it do?"

"It makes you smile."

"Immersive Response makes you smile. And you don't have to clean up after its crap. Come on, Chen. Admit it. You don't want to take care of it either. It's a pain in the ass."

We all looked at each other, then down at the dog.

Lisa roasted the dog on a spit, over burning plastics and petroleum skimmed from the ocean. It tasted okay, but in the end it was hard to understand the big deal. I've eaten slagged centaur that tasted better.

Afterward, we walked along the shoreline. Opalescent waves crashed and roared up the sand, leaving jewel slicks as they receded and the sun sank red in the distance.

Without the dog, we could really enjoy the beach. We didn't have to worry about whether it was going to step in acid, or tangle in barb-wire half-buried in the sand, or eat something that would keep it up vomiting half the night.

Still, I remember when the dog licked my face and hauled its shaggy bulk onto my bed, and I remember its warm breathing beside me, and sometimes, I miss it.

Echo (2005)

ELIZABETH HAND

ELIZABETH HAND (b. 1957) is the author of *Mortal Love*, *Glimmering*, *Generation Loss*, and several other novels. She began publishing short fiction in the late 1980s and has produced about three dozen stories, including *Illyria*, "Chip Crockett's Christmas Carol," and "Last Summer at Mars Hill."

Mythic and lyrical, "Echo" is a sad and affecting tale.

T HIS IS NOT the first time this has happened. I've been here every time it has. Always I learn about it the same way, a message from someone five hundred miles away, a thousand, comes flickering across my screen. There's no TV here on the island, and the radio reception is spotty: the signal comes across Penobscot Bay from a tower atop Mars Hill, and any kind of weather—thunderstorms, high winds, blizzards—brings the tower down. Sometimes I'm listening to the radio when it happens, music playing, Nick Drake, a promo for the Common Ground Country Fair; then a sudden soft explosive hiss like damp hay falling onto a bonfire. Then silence.

Sometimes I hear about it from you. Or, well, I don't actually hear anything: I read your messages, imagine your voice, for a moment neither sardonic nor world-weary, just exhausted, too fraught to be expressive. Words like feathers falling from the sky, black specks on blue.

The Space Needle. Sears Tower. LaGuardia Airport. Golden Gate Bridge. The Millennium Eye. The Bahrain Hilton. Sydney, Singapore, Jerusalem.

Years apart at first; then months; now years again. How long has it been since the first tower fell? When did I last hear from you?

I can't remember.

This morning I took the dog for a walk across the island. We often go in search of birds, me for my work, the wolfhound to chase for joy. He ran across the ridge, rushing at a partridge that burst into the air in a roar of copper feathers and beech leaves. The dog dashed after her fruitlessly, long jaw open to show red gums, white teeth, a panting unfurled tongue.

"Finn!" I called and he circled round the fern brake, snapping at bracken and crickets, black splinters that leapt wildly from his jaws. "Finn, get back here."

He came. Mine is the only voice he knows now.

There was a while when I worried about things like food and water, whether I might need to get to a doctor. But the dug well is good. I'd put up enough dried beans and canned goods to last for years, and the garden does well these days. The warming means longer summers here on the island, more sun; I can grow tomatoes now, and basil, scotch bonnet peppers, plants that I never could grow when I first arrived. The root cellar under the cottage is dry enough and cool enough that I keep all my medications there, things I stockpiled back when I could get over to Ellsworth and the mainland—albuterol inhalers, alprazolam, amoxicillin, Tylenol and codeine, ibuprofen, aspirin; cases of food for the wolfhound. When I first put the solar cells up, visitors shook their heads: not enough sunny days this far north, not enough light. But that changed too as the days got warmer.

Now it's the wireless signal that's difficult to capture, not sunlight. There will be months on end of silence and then it will flare up again, for days or even weeks, I never know when. If I'm lucky, I patch into it, then sit there, waiting, holding my breath until the messages begin to scroll across the screen, looking for your name. I go downstairs to my office every day, like an angler going to shore, casting my line though I know the weather's wrong, the currents too strong, not enough wind or too much, the power grid like the Grand Banks scraped barren by decades of trawlers dragging the bottom. Sometimes my line would latch onto you: sometimes, in the middle of the night, it would be the middle of the night where you were, too, and we'd write back and forth. I used to joke about these letters going out like messages in bottles, not knowing if they would reach you, or where you'd be when they did.

London, Paris, Petra, Oahu, Moscow. You were always too far away. Now you're like everyone else, unimaginably distant. Who would ever have thought it could all be gone, just like that? The last time I saw you was in the hotel in

Toronto, we looked out and saw the spire of the CN Tower like Cupid's arrow aimed at us. You stood by the window and the sun was behind you and you looked like a cornstalk I'd seen once, burning, your gray hair turned to gold and your face smoke.

I can't see you again, you said. *Deirdre is sick and I need to be with her.*

I didn't believe you. We made plans to meet in Montreal, in Halifax, Seattle. Gray places; after Deirdre's treatment ended. After she got better.

But that didn't happen. Nobody got better. Everything got worse.

In the first days I would climb to the highest point on the island, a granite dome ringed by tamaracks and hemlock, the gray stone covered with lichen, celadon, bone-white, brilliant orange: as though armfuls of dried flowers had been tossed from an airplane high overhead. When evening came the aurora borealis would streak the sky, crimson, emerald, amber; as though the sun were rising in the west, in the middle of the night, rising for hours on end. I lay on my back wrapped in an old Pendleton blanket and watched, the dog Finn stretched out alongside me. One night the spectral display continued into dawn, falling arrows of green and scarlet, silver threads like rain or sheet lightning racing through them. The air hummed, I pulled up the sleeve of my flannel shirt and watched as the hairs on my arm rose and remained erect; looked down at the dog, awake now, growling steadily as it stared at the trees edging the granite, its hair on end like a cat's. There was nothing in the woods, nothing in the sky above us. After perhaps thirty minutes I heard a muffled sound to the west, like a far-off sonic boom; nothing more.

After Toronto we spoke only once a year; you would make your annual pilgrimage to mutual friends in Paris and call me from there. It was a joke, that we could only speak like this.

I'm never closer to you than when I'm in the seventh arrondissement at the Bowlses', you said.

But even before then we'd seldom talked on the phone. You said it would destroy the purity of our correspondence, and refused to give me your number in Seattle. We had never seen that much of each other anyway, a handful of times over the decades. Glasgow once, San Francisco, a long weekend in Liverpool, another in New York. Everything was in the letters; only of course they weren't actual letters but bits of information, code, electrical sparks; like neurotransmitters leaping the chasm between synapses. When I dreamed of you, I dreamed of your name shining in the middle of a computer screen like a ripple in still water. Even in dreams I couldn't touch you: my fingers would hover above your face and you'd fragment into jots of gray and black and silver. When you were in Basra I didn't hear from you for months. Afterward you said you were glad; that my silence had been like a gift.

For a while, the first four or five years, I would go down to where I kept the dinghy moored on the shingle at Amonsic Cove. It had a little two-horsepower engine that I kept filled with gasoline, in case I ever needed to get to the mainland.

But the tides are tricky here, they race high and treacherously fast in the Reach; the *Ellsworth American* used to run stories every year about lobstermen who went out after a snagged line and never came up, or people from away who misjudged the time to come back from their picnic on Egg Island, and never made it back. Then one day I went down to check on the dinghy and found the engine gone. I walked the length of the beach two days running at low tide, searching for it, went out as far as I could on foot, hopping between rocks and tidal pools and startling the cormorants where they sat on high boulders, wings held out to dry like black angels in the thin sunlight. I never found the motor. A year after that the dinghy came loose in a storm and was lost as well, though for months I recognized bits of its weathered red planking when they washed up onshore.

The book I was working on last time was a translation of Ovid's *Metamorphoses*. The manuscript remains on my desk beside my computer, with my notes on the nymph "whose tongue did not still when others spoke," the girl cursed by Hera to fall in love with beautiful, brutal Narkissos. He hears her pleading voice in the woods and calls to her, mistaking her for his friends.

But it is the nymph who emerges from the forest. And when he sees her Narkissos strikes her, repulsed; then flees. *Emoriar quam sit tibi copia nostri!* he cries; and with those words condemns himself.

Better to die than be possessed by you.

And see, here is Narkissos dead beside the woodland pool, his hand trailing in the water as he gazes at his own reflection. Of the nymph,

She is vanished, save for these:
her bones and a voice that calls out
amongst the trees.
Her bones are scattered in the rocks.

She moves now in the laurels and beeches, she moves unseen
across the mountaintops.
You will hear her in the mountains and wild places,
but nothing of her remains save her voice,
her voice alone, alone upon the mountaintop.

Several months ago, midsummer, I began to print out your letters. I was afraid something would happen to the computer and I would lose them forever. It took a week, working off and on. The printer uses a lot of power and the island had become locked in by fog; the rows of solar cells, for the first time, failed to give me enough light to read by during the endless gray days, let alone run the computer and printer for more than fifteen minutes at a stretch. Still, I managed, and at the end of a week held a sheaf of pages. Hundreds of them, maybe more; they made a larger stack than the piles of notes for Ovid.

I love the purity of our relationship, you wrote from Singapore. *Trust me, it's better this way. You'll have me forever!*

There were poems, quotes from Cavafy, Sappho, Robert Lowell, W. S. Merwin. *It's hard for me to admit this, but the sad truth is that the more intimate we become here, the less likely it is we'll ever meet again in real life.* Some of the letters had my responses copied at the beginning or end, imploring, fractious; lines from other poems, songs.

Swept with confused alarms of
I long and seek after
You can't put your arms around a memory.

The first time, air traffic stopped. That was the eeriest thing, eerier than the absence of lights when I stood upon the granite dome and looked westward to the mainland. I was used to the slow constant flow overhead, planes taking the Great Circle Route between New York, Boston, London, Stockholm, passing above the islands, Labrador, Greenland, gray space, white. Now, day after day after day the sky was empty. The tower on Mars Hill fell silent. The dog and I would crisscross the island, me throwing sticks for him to chase across the rocky shingle, the wolfhound racing after them and returning tirelessly, over and over.

After a week the planes returned. The sound of the first one was like an explosion after that silence, but others followed, and soon enough I grew accustomed to them again. Until once more they stopped.

I wonder sometimes, How do I know this is all truly happening? Your letters come to me, blue sparks channeled through sunlight; you and your words are more real to me than anything else. Yet how real is that? How real is all of this? When I lie upon the granite I can feel stone pressing down against my skull, the trajectory of satellites across the sky above me a slow steady pulse in time with the firing of chemical signals in my head. It's the only thing I hear, now: it has been a year at least since the tower at Mars Hill went dead, seemingly for good.

One afternoon, a long time ago now, the wolfhound began barking frantically and I looked out to see a skiff making its way across the water. I went down to meet it: Rick Osgood, the part-time constable and volunteer fire chief from Mars Hill.

"We hadn't seen you for a while," he called. He drew the skiff up to the dock but didn't get out. "Wanted to make sure you were okay."

I told him I was, asked him up for coffee but he said no. "Just checking, that's all. Making a round of the islands to make sure everyone's okay."

He asked after the children. I told him they'd gone to stay with their father. I stood waving, as he turned the skiff around and it churned back out across the dark water, a spume of black smoke trailing it. I have seen no one since.

Three weeks ago I turned on the computer and, for the first time in months, was able to patch into a signal and search for you. The news from outside was scattered and all bad. Pictures, mostly; they seem to have lost the urge for language, or perhaps it is just easier this way, with so many people so far apart. *Some things take us to a place where words have no meaning.* I was readying myself for bed when suddenly there was a spurt of sound from the monitor. I turned and saw the screen filled with strings of words. Your name: they were all messages from you. I sat down elated and trembling, waiting as for a quarter-hour they cascaded from the sky and moved beneath my fingertips, silver and black and gray and blue. I thought that at last you had found me; that these were years of words and yearning, that you would be back. Then, as abruptly as it had begun, the stream ceased; and I began to read.

They were not new letters; they were all your old ones, decades old, some of them. 2009, 2007, 2004, 2001, 1999, 1998, 1997, 1996. I scrolled backward in time, a skein of years, words; your name popping up again and again like a bright bead upon a string. I read them all, I read them until my eyes ached and the floor was pooled with candle wax and broken light bulbs. When morning came I tried to tap into the signal again but it was gone. I go outside each night and stare at the sky, straining my eyes as I look for some sign that something moves up there, that there is something between myself and the stars. But the satellites too are gone now, and it has been years upon years since I have heard an airplane.

In fall and winter I watch those birds that do not migrate. Chickadees, nuthatches, ravens, kinglets. This last autumn I took Finn down to the deep place where in another century they quarried granite to build the Cathedral of Saint John the Divine. The quarry is filled with water, still and black and bone-cold. We saw a flock of wild turkeys, young ones; but the dog is so old now he can no longer chase them, only watch as I set my snares. I walked to the water's edge and gazed into the dark pool, saw my reflected face but there is no change upon it, nothing to show how many years have passed for me here, alone. I have burned all the old crates and cartons from the root cellar, though it is not empty yet. I burn for kindling the leavings from my wood bench, the hoops that did not curve properly after soaking in willow-water, the broken dowels and circlets. Only the wolfhound's grizzled muzzle tells me how long it's been since I've seen a human face. When I dream of you now I see a smooth stretch of water with only a few red leaves upon its surface.

We returned from the cottage, and the old dog fell asleep in the late afternoon sun. I sat outside and watched as a downy woodpecker, *Picus pubescens,* crept up one of the red oaks, poking beneath its soft bark for insects. They are friendly birds, easy to entice, sociable; unlike the solitary wrynecks they somewhat resemble. The wrynecks do not climb trees but scratch upon the ground for the ants they love to eat. "Its body is almost bent backward," Thomas Bewick wrote over two hundred years ago in his *History of British Birds,* whilst it writhes its head and neck by a slow and almost involuntary motion, not unlike the waving wreaths of a serpent. It is a very solitary bird, never being seen with any other society but that of its female, and this is only transitory, for as soon as the domestic union is dissolved, which is in the month of September, they retire and migrate separately.

It was this strange involuntary motion, perhaps, that so fascinated the ancient Greeks. In Pindar's fourth Pythian Ode, Aphrodite gives the wryneck to Jason as the magical means to seduce Medea, and with it he binds the princess to him through her obsessive love. Aphrodite of many arrows: she bears the brown-and-white bird to him, "the bird of madness," its wings and legs nailed to a four-spoked wheel.

And she shared with Jason
the means by which a spell might blaze
and burn Medea, burning away all love she had for her family
a fire that would ignite her mind, already aflame
so that all her passion turned to him alone.

The same bird was used by the nymph Simaitha, abandoned by her lover in Theocritus's *Idyll*: pinned to the wooden wheel, the feathered spokes spin above a fire as the nymph invokes Hecate. The isle is full of voices: they are all mine.

Yesterday the wolfhound died, collapsing as he followed me to the top of the granite dome. He did not get up again, and I sat beside him, stroking his long gray muzzle as his dark eyes stared into mine and, at last, closed. I wept then as I didn't weep all those times when terrible news came, and held his great body until it grew cold and stiff between my arms. It was a struggle to lift and carry him, but I did, stumbling across the lichen-rough floor to the shadow of the thin birches and tamaracks overlooking the Reach. I buried him there with the others, and afterward lit a fire.

This is not the first time this has happened. There is an endless history of forgotten empires, men gifted by a goddess who bears arrows, things in flight that fall in flames. Always, somewhere, a woman waits alone for news. At night I climb to the highest point of the island. There I make a little fire and burn things that I find on the beach and in the woods. Leaves, bark, small bones, clumps of feathers, a book. Sometimes I think of you and stand upon the rock and shout as the wind comes at me, cold and smelling of snow. A name, over and over and over again.

Farewell, Narkissos said, and again Echo sighed and whispered
Farewell.
Good-bye, good-bye.
Can you still hear me?

The New York Times
at Special Bargain Rates (2008)

STEPHEN KING

STEPHEN KING (b. 1947) is the author of *Carrie, It, 'Salem's Lot, Cujo, Under the Dome,* and many other novels and stories. But, seeing as how he has been one of the world's most popular writers through the past four decades, you probably knew that already.

In 2007, he edited a volume of *The Best American Short Stories*. The experience inspired him to try his hand at writing a short story again, just to see if he still had it. Sure seems like he does, no?

S HE'S FRESH OUT of the shower when the phone begins to ring, but although the house is still full of relatives—she can hear them downstairs, it seems they will never go away, it seems she never had so many—no one picks up. Nor does the answering machine, as James programmed it to do after the fifth ring.

Anne goes to the extension on the bed-table, wrapping a towel around herself, her wet hair thwacking unpleasantly on the back of her neck and bare shoulders. She picks it up, she says hello, and then he says her name. It's James. They had thirty years together, and one word is all she needs. He says *Annie* like no one else, always did.

For a moment she can't speak or even breathe. He has caught her on the exhale and her lungs feel as flat as sheets of paper. Then, as he says her name again (sounding uncharacteristically hesitant and unsure of himself), the strength slips from her legs. They turn to sand and she sits on the bed, the towel falling off her, her wet bottom dampening the sheet beneath her. If the bed hadn't been there, she would have gone to the floor.

Her teeth click together and that starts her breathing again.

"James? Where *are* you? *What happened?*" In her normal voice, this might have come out sounding shrewish—a mother scolding her wayward eleven-year-old who's come late to the supper-table yet again—but now it emerges in a kind of horrified growl. The murmuring relatives below her are, after all, planning his funeral.

James chuckles. It is a bewildered sound. "Well, I tell you what," he says. "I don't exactly know where I am."

Her first confused thought is that he must have missed the plane in London, even though he called her from Heathrow not long before it took off. Then a clearer idea comes: although both the *Times* and the TV news say there were no survivors, there was at least one. Her husband crawled from the wreckage of the burning plane (and the burning apartment building the plane hit, don't forget that, twenty-four more dead on the ground and the number apt to rise before the world moved on to the next tragedy) and has been wandering around Brooklyn ever since, in a state of shock.

"Jimmy, are you all right? Are you…are you burned?" The truth of what that would mean occurs after the question, thumping down with the heavy weight of a dropped book on a bare foot, and she begins to cry. "Are you in the hospital?"

"Hush," he says, and at his old kindness—and at that old word, just one small piece of their marriage's furniture—she begins to cry harder. "Honey, hush."

"But I don't *understand!*"

"I'm all right," he says. "Most of us are."

"Most—? There are *others?*"

"Not the pilot," he says. "He's not so good. Or maybe it's the co-pilot. He keeps screaming, 'We're going down, there's no power, oh my God.' Also 'This isn't my fault, don't let them blame it on me.' He says that, too."

She's cold all over. "Who is this really? Why are you being so horrible? I just lost my husband, you asshole!"

"Honey—"

"Don't call me that!" There's a clear strand of mucus hanging from one of her nostrils. She wipes it away with the back of her hand and then flings it into the wherever, a thing she hasn't done since she was a child. "Listen, mister—I'm going to star-sixty-nine this call and the police will come and slam your ass…your ignorant, unfeeling *ass.…*"

But she can go no further. It's his voice. There's no denying it. The way the call rang right through—no pick-up downstairs, no answering machine—suggests this call was just for her. And...*honey, hush*. Like in the old Carl Perkins song.

He has remained quiet, as if letting her work these things through for herself. But before she can speak again, there's a beep on the line.

"James? *Jimmy?* Are you still there?"

"Yeah, but I can't talk long. I was trying to call you when we went down, and I guess that's the only reason I was able to get through at all. Lots of others have been trying, we're lousy with cell phones, but no luck." That beep again. "Only now my phone's almost out of juice."

"Jimmy, did you know?" This idea has been the hardest and most terrible part for her—that he might have known, if only for an endless minute or two. Others might picture burned bodies or dismembered heads with grinning teeth; even light-fingered first responders filching wedding rings and diamond ear-clips, but what has robbed Annie Driscoll's sleep is the image of Jimmy looking out his window as the streets and cars and the brown apartment buildings of Brooklyn swell closer. The useless masks flopping down like the corpses of small yellow animals. The overhead bins popping open, carry-ons starting to fly, someone's Norelco razor rolling up the tilted aisle.

"Did you know you were going down?"

"Not really," he says. "Everything seemed all right until the very end—maybe the last thirty seconds. Although it's hard to keep track of time in situations like that, I always think."

Situations like that. And even more telling: *I always think.* As if he has been aboard half a dozen crashing 767s instead of just the one.

"In any case," he goes on, "I was just calling to say we'd be early, so be sure to get the FedEx man out of bed before I got there."

Her absurd attraction for the FedEx man has been a joke between them for years. She begins to cry again. His cell utters another of those beeps, as if scolding her for it.

"I think I died just a second or two before it rang the first time. I think that's why I was able to get through to you. But this thing's gonna give up the ghost pretty soon."

He chuckles as if this is funny. She supposes that in a way it is. She may see the humor in it herself, eventually. *Give me ten years or so*, she thinks.

Then, in that just-talking-to-myself voice she knows so well: "Why didn't I put the tiresome motherfucker on charge last night? Just forgot, that's all. Just forgot."

"James...honey...the plane crashed two days ago."

A pause. Mercifully with no beep to fill it. Then: "Really? Mrs. Corey *said* time was funny here. Some of us agreed, some of us disagreed. I was a disagreer, but looks like she was right."

"Hearts?" Annie asks. She feels now as if she is floating outside and slightly above her plump damp middle-aged body, but she hasn't forgotten Jimmy's old habits. On a long flight he was always looking for a game. Cribbage or canasta would do, but hearts was his true love.

"Hearts," he agrees. The phone beeps, as if seconding that.

"Jimmy...." She hesitates long enough to ask herself if this is information she really wants, then plunges with that question still unanswered. "Where *are* you, exactly?"

"Looks like Grand Central Station," he says. "Only bigger. And emptier. As if it wasn't really Grand Central at all but only...mmm...a movie set of Grand Central. Do you know what I'm trying to say?"

"I...I think so...."

"There certainly aren't any trains...and we can't hear any in the distance... but there are doors going everywhere. Oh, and there's an escalator, but it's broken. All dusty, and some of the treads are gone." He pauses, and when he speaks again he does so in a lower voice, as if afraid of being overheard. "People are leaving. Some climbed the escalator—I saw them—but most are using the doors. I guess I'll have to leave, too. For one thing, there's nothing to eat. There's a candy machine, but that's broken, too."

"Are you...honey, are you hungry?"

"A little. Mostly what I'd like is some water. I'd *kill* for a cold bottle of Dasani."

Annie looks guiltily down at her own legs, still beaded with water. She imagines him licking off those beads and is horrified to feel a sexual stirring.

"I'm all right, though," he adds hastily. "For now, anyway. But there's no sense staying here. Only..."

"What? What, Jimmy?"

"I don't know which door to use."

Another beep.

"I wish I knew which one Mrs. Corey took. She's got my damn cards."

"Are you…" She wipes her face with the towel she wore out of the shower; then she was fresh, now she's all tears and snot. "Are you scared?"

"Scared?" he asks thoughtfully. "No. A little worried, that's all. Mostly about which door to use."

Find your way home, she almost says. *Find the right door and find your way home.* But if he did, would she want to see him? A ghost might be all right, but what if she opened the door on a smoking cinder with red eyes and the remains of jeans (he always traveled in jeans) melted into his legs? And what if Mrs. Corey was with him, his baked deck of cards in one twisted hand?

Beep.

"I don't need to tell you to be careful about the FedEx man anymore," he says. "If you really want him, he's all yours."

She shocks herself by laughing.

"But I did want to say I love you—"

"Oh honey I love you t—"

"—and not to let the McCormack kid do the gutters this fall, he works hard but he's a risk-taker, last year he almost broke his fucking neck. And don't go to the bakery anymore on Sundays. Something's going to happen there, and I know it's going to be on a Sunday, but I don't know which Sunday. Time really *is* funny here."

The McCormack kid he's talking about must be the son of the guy who used to be their caretaker in Vermont…only they sold that place ten years ago, and the kid must be in his mid-twenties by now. And the bakery? She supposes he's talking about Zoltan's, but what on *Earth*—

Beep.

"Some of the people here were on the ground, I guess. That's very tough, because they don't have a clue how they got here. And the pilot keeps screaming. Or maybe it's the co-pilot. I think he's going to be here for quite a while. He just wanders around. He's very confused."

The beeps are coming closer together now.

"I have to go, Annie. I can't stay here, and the phone's going to shit the bed any second now, anyway." Once more in that I'm-scolding-myself voice (impossible to believe she will never hear it again after today; impossible *not* to believe), he mutters, "It would have been so simple just to…well, never mind. I love you, sweetheart."

"Wait! Don't go!"

"I c—"

"I love you, too! Don't go!"

But he already has. In her ear there is only black silence.

She sits there with the dead phone to her ear for a minute or more, then breaks the connection. The non-connection. When she opens the line again and gets a perfectly normal dial-tone, she touches star-sixty-nine after all. According to the robot who answers her page, the last incoming call was at nine o'clock that morning. She knows who that one was: her sister Nell, calling from New Mexico. Nell called to tell Annie that her plane had been delayed and she wouldn't be in until tonight. Nell told her to be strong.

All the relatives who live at a distance—James's, Annie's—flew in. Apparently they feel that James used up all the family's Destruction Points, at least for the time being.

There is no record of an incoming call at—she glances at the bedside clock and sees it's now 3:17 PM—at about ten past three, on the third afternoon of her widowhood.

Someone raps briefly on the door and her brother calls, "Anne? Annie?"

"Dressing!" she calls back. Her voice sounds like she's been crying, but unfortunately, no one in this house would find that strange. "Privacy, please!"

"You okay?" he calls through the door. "We thought we heard you talking. And Ellie thought she heard you call out."

"Fine!" she calls, then wipes her face again with the towel. "Down in a few!"

"Okay. Take your time." Pause. "We're here for you." Then he clumps away.

"Beep," she whispers, then covers her mouth to hold in laughter that is some emotion even more complicated than grief trying to find the only way out it has. "Beep, beep. Beep, beep, beep." She lies back on the bed, laughing, and above her cupped hands her eyes are large and awash with tears that overspill down her cheeks and run all the way to her ears. "Beep-fucking-beepity-beep."

She laughs for quite a while, then dresses and goes downstairs to be with her relatives, who have come to mingle their grief with hers. Only they feel apart from her, because he didn't call any of them. He called her. For better or worse, he called her.

During the autumn of that year, with the blackened remains of the apartment building the jet crashed into still closed off from the rest of the world by yellow police tape (although the taggers have been inside, one leaving a spray-painted message reading CRISPY CRITTERS LAND HERE), Annie receives the sort of e-blast computer-addicts like to send to a wide circle of acquaintances. This one comes from Gert Fisher, the town librarian in Tilton, Vermont. When Annie and James summered there, Annie used to volunteer at the library, and although the two women never got on especially well, Gert has included Annie in her quarterly updates ever since. They are usually not very interesting, but halfway through the weddings, funerals, and 4-H winners in this one, Annie comes across a bit of news that makes her catch her breath. Jason McCormack, the son of old Hughie McCormack, was killed in an accident on Labor Day. He fell from the roof of a summer cottage while cleaning the gutters and broke his neck.

"He was only doing a favor for his dad, who as you may remember had a stroke the year before last," Gert wrote before going on to how it rained on the library's end-of-summer lawn sale, and how disappointed they all were.

Gert doesn't say in her three-page compendium of breaking news, but Annie is quite sure Jason fell from the roof of what used to be their cottage. In fact, she is positive.

Five years after the death of her husband (and the death of Jason McCormack not long after), Annie remarries. And although they relocate to Boca Raton, she gets back to the old neighborhood often. Craig, the new husband, is only semi-retired, and his business takes him to New York every three or four months. Annie almost always goes with him, because she still has family in Brooklyn and on Long Island. More than she knows what to do with, it sometimes seems. But she loves them with that exasperated affection that seems to belong, she thinks, only to people in their fifties and sixties. She never forgets how they drew together for her after James's plane went down, and made the best cushion for her that they could. So she wouldn't crash, too.

When she and Craig go back to New York, they fly. About this she never has a qualm, but she stops going to Zoltan's Family Bakery on Sundays when she's home, even though their raisin bagels are, she is sure, served in heaven's waiting room. She goes to Froger's instead. She is actually there, buying doughnuts (the doughnuts are at least passable), when she hears the blast. She hears it clearly even though Zoltan's is eleven blocks away. LP gas explosion. Four killed, including the woman who always passed Annie her bagels with the top of the bag rolled down, saying, "Keep it that way until you get home or you lose the freshness."

People stand on the sidewalks, looking east toward the sound of the explosion and the rising smoke, shading their eyes with their hands. Annie hurries past them, not looking. She doesn't want to see a plume of rising smoke after a big bang; she thinks of James enough as it is, especially on the nights when she can't sleep. When she gets home she can hear the phone ringing inside. Either everyone has gone down the block to where the local school is having a sidewalk art sale, or no one can hear that ringing phone. Except for her, that is. And by the time she gets her key turned in the lock, the ringing has stopped.

Sarah, the only one of her sisters who never married, *is* there, it turns out, but there is no need to ask her why she didn't answer the phone; Sarah Bernicke, the one-time disco queen, is in the kitchen with the Village People turned up, dancing around with the O-Cedar in one hand, looking like a chick in a TV ad. She missed the bakery explosion, too, although their building is even closer to Zoltan's than Froger's.

Annie checks the answering machine, but there's a big red zero in the MESSAGES WAITING window. That means nothing in itself, lots of people call without leaving a message, but—

Star-sixty-nine reports the last call at eight-forty last night. Annie dials it anyway, hoping against hope that somewhere outside the big room that looks like a Grand Central Station movie set he found a place to re-charge his phone. To him it might seem he last spoke to her yesterday. Or only minutes ago. *Time is funny here*, he said. She has dreamed of that call so many times it now almost seems like a dream itself, but she has never told anyone about it. Not Craig, not even her own mother, now almost ninety but alert and with a firmly held belief in the afterlife.

In the kitchen, the Village People advise that there is no need to feel down. There isn't, and she doesn't. She nevertheless holds the phone very tightly as the number she has star-sixty-nined rings once, then twice. Annie stands in the living room with the phone to her ear and her free hand touching the brooch above her left breast, as if touching the brooch could still the pounding heart beneath it. Then the ringing stops and a recorded voice offers to sell her *The New York Times* at special bargain rates that will not be repeated.

The Paper Menagerie (2011)

KEN LIU

KEN LIU (b. 1976) was born in Lanzhou, China, and moved to the United States with his family when he was eleven years old. After college, he spent several years working in the technology industry before attending law school. He now works as an IP litigation consultant in the Boston area, where he lives with his wife and daughters. He began publishing fiction early in the twenty-first century, and in the past five years he has published several dozen stories, establishing himself as one of the leading new writers in the field. His debut novel, *The Grace of Kings*, is scheduled to be published in 2015.

"The Paper Menagerie," like many of Liu's stories, draws on his Asian heritage. It was the first story ever to win the Hugo, Nebula, and World Fantasy awards.

O NE OF MY earliest memories starts with me sobbing. I refused to be soothed no matter what Mom and Dad tried.

Dad gave up and left the bedroom, but Mom took me into the kitchen and sat me down at the breakfast table.

"Kan, kan," she said, as she pulled a sheet of wrapping paper from on top of the fridge. For years, Mom carefully sliced open the wrappings around Christmas gifts and saved them on top of the fridge in a thick stack.

She set the paper down, plain side facing up, and began to fold it. I stopped crying and watched her, curious.

She turned the paper over and folded it again. She pleated, packed, tucked, rolled, and twisted until the paper disappeared between her cupped hands. Then she lifted the folded-up paper packet to her mouth and blew into it, like a balloon.

"Kan," she said. *"Laohu."* She put her hands down on the table and let go.

A little paper tiger stood on the table, the size of two fists placed together. The skin of the tiger was the pattern on the wrapping paper, white background with red candy canes and green Christmas trees.

I reached out to Mom's creation. Its tail twitched, and it pounced playfully at my finger. *"Rawrr-sa,"* it growled, the sound somewhere between a cat and rustling newspapers.

I laughed, startled, and stroked its back with an index finger. The paper tiger vibrated under my finger, purring.

"Zhe jiao zhèzhi," Mom said. *This is called origami.*

I didn't know this at the time, but Mom's kind was special. She breathed into them so that they shared her breath, and thus moved with her life. This was her magic.

Dad had picked Mom out of a catalog.

One time, when I was in high school, I asked Dad about the details. He was trying to get me to speak to Mom again.

He had signed up for the introduction service back in the spring of 1973. Flipping through the pages steadily, he had spent no more than a few seconds on each page until he saw the picture of Mom.

I've never seen this picture. Dad described it: Mom was sitting in a chair, her side to the camera, wearing a tight green silk cheongsam. Her head was turned to the camera so that her long black hair was draped artfully over her chest and shoulder. She looked out at him with the eyes of a calm child.

"That was the last page of the catalog I saw," he said.

The catalog said she was eighteen, loved to dance, and spoke good English because she was from Hong Kong. None of these facts turned out to be true.

He wrote to her, and the company passed their messages back and forth. Finally, he flew to Hong Kong to meet her.

"The people at the company had been writing her responses. She didn't know any English other than 'hello' and 'good-bye.'"

What kind of woman puts herself into a catalog so that she can be bought? The high school me thought I knew so much about everything. Contempt felt good, like wine.

Instead of storming into the office to demand his money back, he paid a waitress at the hotel restaurant to translate for them.

"She would look at me, her eyes halfway between scared and hopeful, while I spoke. And when the girl began translating what I said, she'd start to smile slowly."

He flew back to Connecticut and began to apply for the papers for her to come to him. I was born a year later, in the Year of the Tiger.

At my request, Mom also made a goat, a deer, and a water buffalo out of wrapping paper. They would run around the living room while Laohu chased after them, growling. When he caught them he would press down until the air went out of them and they became just flat, folded-up pieces of paper. I would then have to blow into them to re-inflate them so they could run around some more.

Sometimes, the animals got into trouble. Once, the water buffalo jumped into a dish of soy sauce on the table at dinner. (He wanted to wallow, like a real water buffalo.) I picked him out quickly but the capillary action had already pulled the dark liquid high up into his legs. The sauce-softened legs would not hold him up, and he collapsed onto the table. I dried him out in the sun, but his legs became crooked after that, and he ran around with a limp. Mom eventually wrapped his legs in Saran Wrap so that he could wallow to his heart's content (just not in soy sauce).

Also, Laohu liked to pounce at sparrows when he and I played in the backyard. But one time, a cornered bird struck back in desperation and tore his ear. He whimpered and winced as I held him and Mom patched his ear together with tape. He avoided birds after that.

And then one day, I saw a TV documentary about sharks and asked Mom for one of my own. She made the shark, but he flapped about on the table unhappily. I filled the sink with water, and put him in. He swam around and around happily. However, after a while he became soggy and translucent, and slowly sank to the bottom, the folds coming undone. I reached in to rescue him, and all I ended up with was a wet piece of paper.

Laohu put his front paws together at the edge of the sink and rested his head on them. Ears drooping, he made a low growl in his throat that made me feel guilty.

Mom made a new shark for me, this time out of tinfoil. The shark lived happily in a large goldfish bowl. Laohu and I liked to sit next to the bowl to watch the tinfoil shark chasing the goldfish, Laohu sticking his face up against the bowl on the other side so that I saw his eyes, magnified to the size of coffee cups, staring at me from across the bowl.

When I was ten, we moved to a new house across town. Two of the women neighbors came by to welcome us. Dad served them drinks and then apologized for having to run off to the utility company to straighten out the prior owner's bills. "Make yourselves at home. My wife doesn't speak much English, so don't think she's being rude for not talking to you."

While I read in the dining room, Mom unpacked in the kitchen. The neighbors conversed in the living room, not trying to be particularly quiet.

"He seems like a normal enough man. Why did he do that?"

"Something about the mixing never seems right. The child looks unfinished. Slanty eyes, white face. A little monster."

"Do you think *he* can speak English?"

The women hushed. After a while they came into the dining room.

"Hello there! What's your name?"

"Jack," I said.

"That doesn't sound very Chinesey."

Mom came into the dining room then. She smiled at the women. The three of them stood in a triangle around me, smiling and nodding at each other, with nothing to say, until Dad came back.

Mark, one of the neighborhood boys, came over with his *Star Wars* action figures. Obi-Wan Kenobi's lightsaber lit up and he could swing his arms and say, in a tinny voice, "Use the Force!" I didn't think the figure looked much like the real Obi-Wan at all.

Together, we watched him repeat this performance five times on the coffee table. "Can he do anything else?" I asked.

Mark was annoyed by my question. "Look at all the details," he said.

I looked at the details. I wasn't sure what I was supposed to say.

Mark was disappointed by my response. "Show me your toys."

I didn't have any toys except my paper menagerie. I brought Laohu out from my bedroom. By then he was very worn, patched all over with tape and glue, evidence of the years of repairs Mom and I had done on him. He was no longer as nimble and sure-footed as before. I sat him down on the coffee table. I could hear the skittering steps of the other animals behind in the hallway, timidly peeking into the living room.

"*Xiao laohu,*" I said, and stopped. I switched to English. "This is Tiger." Cautiously, Laohu strode up and purred at Mark, sniffing his hands.

Mark examined the Christmas-wrap pattern of Laohu's skin. "That doesn't look like a tiger at all. Your Mom makes toys for you from trash?"

I had never thought of Laohu as *trash*. But looking at him now, he was really just a piece of wrapping paper.

Mark pushed Obi-Wan's head again. The lightsaber flashed; he moved his arms up and down. "Use the Force!"

Laohu turned and pounced, knocking the plastic figure off the table. It hit the floor and broke, and Obi-Wan's head rolled under the couch. *"Rawwww,"* Laohu laughed. I joined him.

Mark punched me, hard. "This was very expensive! You can't even find it in the stores now. It probably cost more than what your Dad paid for your Mom!"

I stumbled and fell to the floor. Laohu growled and leapt at Mark's face.

Mark screamed, more out of fear and surprise than pain. Laohu was only made of paper, after all.

Mark grabbed Laohu and his snarl was choked off as Mark crumpled him in his hand and tore him in half. He balled up the two pieces of paper and threw them at me. "Here's your stupid cheap Chinese garbage."

After Mark left, I spent a long time trying, without success, to tape together the pieces, smooth out the paper, and follow the creases to refold Laohu. Slowly, the other animals came into the living room and gathered around us, me and the torn wrapping paper that used to be Laohu.

My fight with Mark didn't end there. Mark was popular at school. I never want to think again about the two weeks that followed.

I came home that Friday at the end of the two weeks. *"Xuexiao hao ma?"* Mom asked. I said nothing and went to the bathroom. I looked into the mirror. *I look nothing like her, nothing.*

At dinner I asked Dad, "Do I have a chink face?"

Dad put down his chopsticks. Even though I had never told him what happened in school, he seemed to understand. He closed his eyes and rubbed the bridge of his nose. "No, you don't."

Mom looked at Dad, not understanding. She looked back at me. *"Sha jiao* chink?"

"English," I said. "Speak English."

She tried. "What happen?"

I pushed the chopsticks and the bowl before me away: stir-fried green peppers with five-spice beef. "We should eat American food."

Dad tried to reason. "A lot of families cook Chinese sometimes."

"We are not other families." I looked at him. *Other families don't have moms who don't belong.*

He looked away. And then he put a hand on Mom's shoulder. "I'll get you a cookbook."

Mom turned to me. *"Bu haochi?"*

"English," I said, raising my voice. "Speak English."

Mom reached out to touch my forehead, feeling for my temperature. *"Fashao la?"*

I brushed her hand away. "I'm fine. Speak English!" I was shouting.

"Speak English to him," Dad said to Mom. "You knew this was going to happen someday. What did you expect?"

Mom dropped her hands to her sides. She sat, looking from Dad to me, and back to Dad again. She tried to speak, stopped, and tried again, and stopped again.

"You have to," Dad said. "I've been too easy on you. Jack needs to fit in."

Mom looked at him. "If I say 'love,' I feel here." She pointed to her lips. "If I say *'ai,'* I feel here." She put her hand over her heart.

Dad shook his head. "You are in America."

Mom hunched down in her seat, looking like the water buffalo when Laohu used to pounce on him and squeeze the air of life out of him.

"And I want some real toys."

Dad bought me a full set of *Star Wars* action figures. I gave the Obi-Wan Kenobi to Mark.

I packed the paper menagerie in a large shoebox and put it under the bed.

The next morning, the animals had escaped and taken over their old favorite spots in my room. I caught them all and put them back into the shoebox, taping the lid shut. But the animals made so much noise in the box that I finally shoved it into the corner of the attic as far away from my room as possible.

If Mom spoke to me in Chinese, I refused to answer her. After a while, she tried to use more English. But her accent and broken sentences embarrassed me. I tried to correct her. Eventually, she stopped speaking altogether if I was around.

Mom began to mime things if she needed to let me know something. She tried to hug me the way she saw American mothers do on TV. I thought her movements exaggerated, uncertain, ridiculous, graceless. She saw that I was annoyed, and stopped.

"You shouldn't treat your mother that way," Dad said. But he couldn't look me in the eyes as he said it. Deep in his heart, he must have realized that it was a mistake to have tried to take a Chinese peasant girl and expect her to fit in the suburbs of Connecticut.

Mom learned to cook American style. I played video games and studied French.

Every once in a while, I would see her at the kitchen table studying the plain side of a sheet of wrapping paper. Later a new paper animal would appear on my nightstand and try to cuddle up to me. I caught them, squeezed them until the air went out of them, and then stuffed them away in the box in the attic.

Mom finally stopped making the animals when I was in high school. By then her English was much better, but I was already at that age when I wasn't interested in what she had to say whatever language she used.

Sometimes, when I came home and saw her tiny body busily moving about in the kitchen, singing a song in Chinese to herself, it was hard for me to believe that she gave birth to me. We had nothing in common. She might as well be from the Moon. I would hurry on to my room, where I could continue my all-American pursuit of happiness.

Dad and I stood, one on each side of Mom, lying on the hospital bed. She was not yet even forty, but she looked much older.

For years she had refused to go to the doctor for the pain inside her that she said was no big deal. By the time an ambulance finally carried her in, the cancer had spread far beyond the limits of surgery.

My mind was not in the room. It was the middle of the on-campus recruiting season, and I was focused on resumes, transcripts, and strategically constructed interview schedules. I schemed about how to lie to the corporate recruiters most effectively so that they'd offer to buy me. I understood intellectually that it was terrible to think about this while your mother lay dying. But that understanding didn't mean I could change how I felt.

She was conscious. Dad held her left hand with both of his own. He leaned down to kiss her forehead. He seemed weak and old in a way that startled me. I realized that I knew almost as little about Dad as I did about Mom.

Mom smiled at him. "I'm fine."

She turned to me, still smiling. "I know you have to go back to school." Her voice was very weak and it was difficult to hear her over the hum of the machines hooked up to her. "Go. Don't worry about me. This is not a big deal. Just do well in school."

I reached out to touch her hand, because I thought that was what I was supposed to do. I was relieved. I was already thinking about the flight back, and the bright California sunshine.

She whispered something to Dad. He nodded and left the room.

"Jack, if—" she was caught up in a fit of coughing, and could not speak for some time. "If I…don't make it, don't be too sad and hurt your health. Focus on your life. Just keep that box you have in the attic with you, and every year, at *Qingming*, just take it out and think about me. I'll be with you always."

Qingming was the Chinese Festival for the Dead. When I was very young, Mom used to write a letter on *Qingming* to her dead parents back in China, telling them the good news about the past year of her life in America. She would read the letter out loud to me, and if I made a comment about something, she would write it down in the letter too. Then she would fold the letter into a paper crane, and release it, facing west. We would then watch, as the crane flapped its crisp wings on its long journey west, toward the Pacific, toward China, toward the graves of Mom's family.

It had been many years since I last did that with her.

"I don't know anything about the Chinese calendar," I said. "Just rest, Mom."

"Just keep the box with you and open it once in a while. Just open—" She began to cough again.

"It's okay, Mom." I stroked her arm awkwardly.

"*Haizi, mama ai ni—*" Her cough took over again. An image from years ago flashed into my memory: Mom saying *ai* and then putting her hand over her heart.

"All right, Mom. Stop talking."

Dad came back, and I said that I needed to get to the airport early because I didn't want to miss my flight.

She died when my plane was somewhere over Nevada.

Dad aged rapidly after Mom died. The house was too big for him and had to be sold. My girlfriend Susan and I went to help him pack and clean the place.

Susan found the shoebox in the attic. The paper menagerie, hidden in the uninsulated darkness of the attic for so long, had become brittle, and the bright wrapping paper patterns had faded.

"I've never seen origami like this," Susan said. "Your Mom was an amazing artist."

The paper animals did not move. Perhaps whatever magic had animated them stopped when Mom died. Or perhaps I had only imagined that these paper constructions were once alive. The memory of children could not be trusted.

It was the first weekend in April, two years after Mom's death. Susan was out of town on one of her endless trips as a management consultant and I was home, lazily flipping through the TV channels.

I paused at a documentary about sharks. Suddenly I saw, in my mind, Mom's hands as they folded and refolded tinfoil to make a shark for me, while Laohu and I watched.

A rustle. I looked up and saw that a ball of wrapping paper and torn tape was on the floor next to the bookshelf. I walked over to pick it up for the trash.

The ball of paper shifted, unfurled itself, and I saw that it was Laohu, who I hadn't thought about in a very long time. *"Rawrr-sa."* Mom must have put him back together after I had given up.

He was smaller than I remembered. Or maybe it was just that back then my fists were smaller.

Susan had put the paper animals around our apartment as decoration. She probably left Laohu in a pretty hidden corner because he looked so shabby.

I sat down on the floor, and reached out a finger. Laohu's tail twitched, and he pounced playfully. I laughed, stroking his back. Laohu purred under my hand.

"How've you been, old buddy?"

Laohu stopped playing. He got up, jumped with feline grace into my lap, and proceeded to unfold himself.

In my lap was a square of creased wrapping paper, the plain side up. It was filled with dense Chinese characters. I had never learned to read Chinese, but I knew the characters for *son*, and they were at the top, where you'd expect them in a letter addressed to you, written in Mom's awkward, childish handwriting.

I went to the computer to check the Internet. Today was *Qingming*.

I took the letter with me downtown, where I knew the Chinese tour buses stopped. I stopped every tourist, asking, *"Nin hui du zhongwen ma?" Can you read Chinese?* I hadn't spoken Chinese in so long that I wasn't sure if they understood.

A young woman agreed to help. We sat down on a bench together, and she read the letter to me aloud. The language that I had tried to forget for years came back, and I felt the words sinking into me, through my skin, through my bones, until they squeezed tight around my heart.

Son,

We haven't talked in a long time. You are so angry when I try to touch you that I'm afraid. And I think maybe this pain I feel all the time now is something serious.

So I decided to write to you. I'm going to write in the paper animals I made for you that you used to like so much.

The animals will stop moving when I stop breathing. But if I write to you with all my heart, I'll leave a little of myself behind on this paper, in these words. Then, if you think of me on Qingming, when the spirits of the departed are allowed to visit their families, you'll make the parts of myself I leave behind come alive too. The creatures I made for you will again leap and run and pounce, and maybe you'll get to see these words then.

Because I have to write with all my heart, I need to write to you in Chinese.

All this time I still haven't told you the story of my life. When you were little, I always thought I'd tell you the story when you were older, so you could understand. But somehow that chance never came up.

I was born in 1957, in Sigulu Village, Hebei Province. Your grandparents were both from very poor peasant families with few relatives. Only a few years after I was born, the Great Famines struck China, during which thirty million people died. The first memory I have was waking up to see my mother eating dirt so that she could fill her belly and leave the last bit of flour for me.

Things got better after that. Sigulu is famous for its zhezhi papercraft, and my mother taught me how to make paper animals and give them life. This was practical magic in the life of the village. We made paper birds to chase grasshoppers away from the fields, and paper tigers to keep away the mice. *For Chinese New Year my friends and I made red paper dragons. I'll never forget the sight of all those little dragons zooming across the sky overhead, holding up strings of exploding firecrackers to scare away all the bad memories of the past year. You would have loved it.*

Then came the Cultural Revolution in 1966. Neighbor turned on neighbor, and brother against brother. Someone remembered that my mother's brother, my uncle, had left for Hong Kong back in 1946, and became a merchant there. Having a relative in Hong Kong meant we were spies and enemies of the people, and we had to be struggled against in every way. Your poor grandmother—she couldn't take the abuse and threw herself down a well. Then some boys with hunting muskets dragged your grandfather away one day into the woods, and he never came back.

There I was, a ten-year-old orphan. The only relative I had in the world was my uncle in Hong Kong. I snuck away one night and climbed onto a freight train going south.

Down in Guangdong Province a few days later, some men caught me stealing food from a field. When they heard that I was trying to get to Hong Kong, they laughed. "It's your lucky day. Our trade is to bring girls to Hong Kong."

They hid me in the bottom of a truck along with other girls, and smuggled us across the border.

We were taken to a basement and told to stand up and look healthy and intelligent for the buyers. Families paid the warehouse a fee and came by to look us over and select one of us to "adopt."

The Chin family picked me to take care of their two boys. I got up every morning at four to prepare breakfast. I fed and bathed the boys. I shopped for food. I did the laundry and swept the floors. I followed the boys around and did their bidding. At night I was locked into a cupboard in the kitchen to sleep. If I was slow or did anything wrong I was beaten. If the boys did anything wrong I was beaten. If I was caught trying to learn English I was beaten.

"Why do you want to learn English?" Mr. Chin asked. "You want to go to the police? We'll tell the police that you are a mainlander illegally in Hong Kong. They'd love to have you in their prison."

Six years I lived like this. One day, an old woman who sold fish to me in the morning market pulled me aside.

"I know girls like you. How old are you now, sixteen? One day, the man who owns you will get drunk, and he'll look at you and pull you to him and you can't stop him. The wife will find out, and then you will think you really have gone to hell. You have to get out of this life. I know someone who can help."

She told me about American men who wanted Asian wives. If I can cook, clean, and take care of my American husband, he'll give me a good life. It was the only hope I had. And that was how I got into the catalog with all those lies and met your father. It is not a very romantic story, but it is my story.

In the suburbs of Connecticut, I was lonely. Your father was kind and gentle with me, and I was very grateful to him. But no one understood me, and I understood nothing.

But then you were born! I was so happy when I looked into your face and saw shades of my mother, my father, and myself. I had lost my entire family, all of Sigulu, everything I ever knew and loved. But there you were, and your face was proof that they were real. I hadn't made them up.

Now I had someone to talk to. I would teach you my language, and we could together remake a small piece of everything that I loved and lost. When you said your first words to me, in Chinese that had the same accent as my mother and me, I cried for hours. When I made the first zhezhi animals for you, and you laughed, I felt there were no worries in the world.

You grew up a little, and now you could even help your father and me talk to each other. I was really at home now. I finally found a good life. I wished my parents could be here, so that I could cook for them, and give them a good life too. But my parents were no longer around. You know what the Chinese think is the saddest feeling in the world? It's for a child to finally grow the desire to take care of his parents, only to realize that they were long gone.

Son, I know that you do not like your Chinese eyes, which are my eyes. I know that you do not like your Chinese hair, which is my hair. But can you understand how much joy your very existence brought to me? And can you understand how it felt when you stopped talking to me and won't let me talk to you in Chinese? I felt I was losing everything all over again.

Why won't you talk to me, son? The pain makes it hard to write.

The young woman handed the paper back to me. I could not bear to look into her face.

Without looking up, I asked for her help in tracing out the character for *ai* on the paper below Mom's letter. I wrote the character again and again on the paper, intertwining my pen strokes with her words.

The young woman reached out and put a hand on my shoulder. Then she got up and left, leaving me alone with my mother.

Following the creases, I refolded the paper back into Laohu. I cradled him in the crook of my arm, and as he purred, we began the walk home.

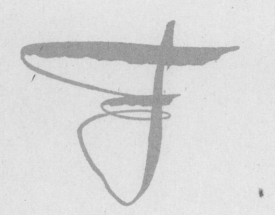